A Pullein-Thompson Treasury of Horse and Pony Stories

A Pullein-Thompson Treasury of Horse and Pony Stories

by Josephine, Christine and Diana
Pullein-Thompson

Illustrated by
Eric Rowe

AWARD PUBLICATIONS LIMITED

To Jennifer Luithlen

ISBN 0-86163-750-X

This edition first published 1995
Shandy, Lost on the Moors and *Tarragona* first published 1976
in T*rue Horse & Pony Stories*
Lettie Lonsdale is taken from *A Pony for Sale* first published 1951
The Runaway Boy is taken from *Ride to the Rescue* first published 1979
Ebony Joins the Circus is taken from *Black Ebony, Black Beauty's Clan*
first published 1975
The Race is taken from *Save the Ponies* first published 1983
The Storm is taken from *The No-Good Pony* first published 1981

First Published 1995
Fifth impression 2005

Published by Award Publications Limited,
The Old Riding School, Welbeck Estate,
Nr Worksop, Nottinghamshire S80 3LR

Printed in Singapore

CONTENTS

Hoofprints in the Sand

Christine Pullein-Thompson

I didn't want to go on holiday, nor did Daniel. The best show of the year was only a week away; the ponies were fit and entered. Our first inkling of such a disaster was when we found Mum cleaning out the caravan, then stocking it up with food and fizzy drinks.

"Yes, we are going away for a few days," she told us. "And don't pull long faces, you'll enjoy it when we get there."

"But..." began Daniel, who is eighteen months younger than me.

"No buts," answered Mum.

"We are entered for the Stilton Show, so actually we can't go," I said, putting on a posh voice.

"Oh we are, are we?" replied Mum, imitating me. "Well, Dad needs a break and so do I; we've been waiting for weather like this all the summer, and we're not going to miss it now it's come. Okay?" she asked.

"When do we leave?" demanded Daniel, angrily kicking a stone across the drive.

"Tomorrow at 4 a.m.," she said.

"And who looks after the ponies?" I asked.

"Susie, okay?"

Susie is Mum's best friend, a trained vet and one hundred per cent reliable, so we could find nothing wrong with that arrangement.

I imagined an early morning; the sun rising, the towns empty, then a long straight road to the sea.

"How long are we going for?" asked Daniel.

"It depends on the weather, probably about ten days." Mum is young for her age and looks about twenty-five though actually she's ten years older. Dad is a self-employed builder. He built our loose boxes and the tack room; also the rail fence around our paddock.

We took our ponies apples and tried to explain about going away. I own Cloud who is dapple-grey and thirteen hands, two and three-quarter inches. Daniel has Crumble who is dun and fourteen hands. They both win family pony classes and sometimes working hunter events as well. They nuzzled our pockets, while we thought of the Stilton Show and of what we were going to miss by being away.

"I don't even like swimming," complained Daniel.

"And we're too big for sandcastles," I added.

Later Dad came home and we started packing, and then it was bedtime and in no time at all half past three in the morning. Mum shook us awake, and even at that hour you could feel the heat in the air promising a scorching day.

We drank tea and ate bowls of cereal while Mum wrote out a message for the milkman and Dad put our night things in the caravan. Colonel Blimp, Blimpie for short, was coming too. He is half Border terrier, half poodle, and very courageous. He tore round us yapping with excitement as we ran down to the paddock fence. Cloud and Crumble were lying down asleep, their backs towards us and, as Daniel said, it seemed a shame to wake them. Five minutes later we were on our way, Mum map-reading, Dad humming happily and Daniel and I still wishing we could stay behind with our ponies.

Five hours later we were driving on to a caravan site, our behinds sticking to the car seats in the heat, sweat running off our faces like rain. Beyond the sand-dunes we could see the sea, stretching away until it met the sky. People were running about like ants in the distance, and a solitary sail was moving gently over the waves.

"It's nice. Well done, Brian," said Mum, patting Dad's knee.

We threw ourselves out of the car on to parched seaside grass. Children were playing ball, an elderly man lay outside a caravan with a newspaper over his face. From another caravan came the sound of pop music. I wanted to be at home. It was an ache inside me which no sea, however beautiful, could drive away or make up for Cloud standing unridden under the trees in the paddock. And nothing could be as wonderful as the Stilton Show.

"You can't expect anything better at this time of the year; everywhere's crowded," said Dad.

A van was selling ice cream. Dad bought us expensive cornets. Mum changed into shorts and a bikini top.

"Not a horse in sight," I muttered sadly.

"Get changed," shouted Mum. "What are you waiting for? Don't you want to get into the sea?"

"You're wrong, Dawn," said my brother. "There are

white horses. Waves make them, didn't you know?"

"Very funny," I replied.

We had to step over bodies to reach the sea. The sand was burning hot, the sea full of people screaming and splashing each other. I yearned for home as one yearns for water when one is thirsty.

There was a camp shop full of frozen food, sweets, balls, surfboards, everything you needed at the seaside.

We went to bed early. Blimpie was happy, Dad said that everything was fine, Mum was making the best of it and Daniel and I were quiet. "Too quiet," Mum said.

We spent the next day on the beach. The sun shone relentlessly from a cloudless blue sky. The caravan site was full to bursting. Milk and newspapers were delivered while the ice cream van went ceaselessly round and round the site playing a hideous tune.

"If we were at home we would be practising now," I told Daniel.

"Or swimming in the Osmans' pool, which is much better than the sea," he replied.

"Or seeing friends," I added.

"I'm missing Stephen," Daniel said.

"And I'm missing Maureen," I replied. "And nothing ever happens on holidays. They're as dull as a wet Sunday."

"You're dead right," shouted Daniel.

"Shut up, you two, you're spoiling everything," cried Mum, lying in her bikini beside Dad on the sand.

"Spoiling what?" asked Daniel.

"Our first holiday in years. Why don't you sunbathe and get a tan, Dawn?" she asked me.

"I hate sunbathing. It's boring," I answered.

And then on the next day something *did* happen.

It was evening. The camp smelt of fish and chips. Everyone seemed to be eating or drinking except us.

"We're just going to the pub," said Dad. "You'll be all right won't you? Stay by the caravan until we're back."

"And how long will that be?" asked Daniel, sounding old and experienced, as though he had seen it all before.

"Not more than half an hour," replied Dad. But we knew Dad's half-hours, which turned into hours and hours.

Mum was combing her hair. "We'll hang around," I promised. "We may just pop down to the sea, but no further."

"Don't talk to strange men," Mum answered nervously. "And don't accept sweets. Shout 'Help' if anyone stares at you."

"And don't swim," added Dad.

The minute they had gone, we called Blimpie and made for the sea. It was coming in and the sand was almost empty, just one old dear was walking a Labrador. And then three boys appeared running towards us, laughing.

"I never knew you could throw like that, Charlie," cried one.

"You should take it up, learn to throw the javelin," shouted another.

"And what a result!" cried the third.

And Charlie laughed, his big mouth open, showing a row of rotting teeth to the whole world.

Then Daniel said, "Look, Dawn, look straight

ahead." There were two horses coming towards us, or rather a horse and a pony. They were trotting with trailing headcollar ropes. They looked anxious and surprised to be free, like children just let out of school.

"We had better catch them," said Daniel.

We held out our hands. They stopped and looked at us, summing us up, deciding whether we were friend or foe. We didn't move but just waited for their decision.

"We're all right, we're horsey," Daniel said.

"Whoa, steady, where are you going then?" I asked.

Another minute and we were holding them. One was skewbald, solid, kind and about fifteen two with a touch of Shire in his head. The other was a pony, cream coloured with large and trusting eyes.

"What are we going to do?" asked Daniel.

"I don't know."

"There's a field next to the camp. It looks fenced," suggested Daniel.

We led them there; they seemed pleased to be with us. But when we let them go they set off at a trot, heads up, exploring the field.

"What next?" asked Daniel.

"The skewbald was being ridden," I answered.

"How do you know?" Daniel asked.

"He had the imprint of a rider on his back. That's how," I said.

"We can follow the hoofprints then," answered Daniel.

"If we hurry – remember the tide's coming in," I said.

We started to run and Blimpie ran ahead of us, yapping. The hoofprints continued and led across wet sand,

then round a corner to another cove where red rock met chalk, topped by grass, and a notice read BEWARE OF FALLING ROCK. The hoofprints petered out here but we could see a path winding up the side of the cliffs. I thought of Mum and Dad drinking, then returning and looking for us. "We'd better hurry," I said anxiously.

"We should have brought the horses with us; it would have been more sensible," said Daniel.

There were more hoofprints on the path, and the sand was now pale and dry – sand-dune sand.

"They can't have escaped from a field because they're wearing headcollars and ropes," I reasoned. "And you don't turn horses out with ropes on."

"Look at Blimpie!" shouted Daniel. He was running ahead of us now, yapping excitedly, while across the sea the setting sun was turning the clouds into golden islands.

"I see an arm," said Daniel.

"And I see a leg," I added.

"Supposing it's dead?" Daniel asked nervously, stopping in his tracks.

"It's a she," I answered.

We bent over the woman. She was quite old and dressed in baggy cords, an anorak, old shoes and yellow socks.

"She's not dead," said Daniel.

"No, I am *not,* I am glad to say," replied the woman. "But I can't move. I think I've smashed my pelvis." She had blue-grey eyes and tangled greying hair.

"Have you lost two horses?" asked my brother.

"Yes, that's me," she said.

"We've put them in a field," I told her.

"Thank you very much." Her face was pale and she looked ill.

Daniel bent over her. "Are you in pain? Can you walk?" he asked.

"No. I'm done for," she answered. "Finished. Ready for the knacker's yard."

"No, you're not. We'll get an ambulance," I said. "And don't worry. We'll look after the horses."

"There's a key in my pocket. Hang on," she said. "Just follow the path. My cottage is at the top. There's three little dogs inside but they won't worry you. Dial 999. Tell them to come to Drover's End and follow the path to the sea. They'll know what you mean." She handed us an enormous old-fashioned key. "Thank you. You're marvellous," she said. "Thank God you came. Some boy stoned us. Groucho came down on top of me. It wasn't his fault."

"The boys on the beach," I cried. "We met them."

"I think they must be insane," she said.

"What about a name?" asked Daniel. "Shouldn't we tell the ambulance people who you are?"

"Jan Williams from Drover's End. They'll know," she said.

We started to run. "I think she's in great pain. And she's very brave," said Daniel.

"I would like to murder that monster called Charlie," I cried.

The cottage was small with thatch to the windows. Daniel unlocked the door beneath the porch and three little dogs ran round Blimpie, yapping.

"Bags I telephone," I said.

There were horse brasses festooning the walls, a

saddle on the arm of a chair, and bits of hay in the hall. We found the telephone in the kitchen. I dialled 999 and a voice asked me which service I required and I said "Ambulance". Then I gave the name and address and added, "It's urgent. It's a serious accident, please don't be long."

I replaced the receiver and we started back towards the sea, but we could not shake off the dogs so finally Daniel stayed behind while I continued alone. "I'll come with the ambulance men. I'll guide them to the spot," he called after me. Blimpie stayed with him so I was suddenly alone, running down the sandy path between the dunes, imagining Groucho jumping, stumbling on the hillocks, falling on poor Jan Williams. The boys should go to prison, I thought, but I expect they will get off or be put on probation.

Jan Williams raised herself on one elbow when she saw me returning. "You will look after the horses, won't you?" she asked. "And the dogs."

I nodded.

"Then when I'm gone, go to the pub and the landlord will ring my daughter. She lives nearly a hundred miles away but she'll come," she said. She had been crying, and I'm not used to grown-ups crying. I didn't know how to comfort her.

"We'll see to everything," I promised. "Don't worry. Worry never changed anything." It sounded like my mother speaking, not me at all.

"Animals are such a responsibility. You realise it on occasions like this. Have you any?" she asked next.

"Yes, two ponies and our little dog."

"That's why you're so sensible," she said.

She was shivering violently now, though the sand was still warm and everything was still, without a trace of wind anywhere. I thought of our ponies and the show we were missing and it didn't matter any more. Rosettes are just cream on the cake, I thought. One can do without them. This is far more important.

At last I could hear voices approaching, then Blimpie appeared and hurled himself at my feet, panting like a mad thing. I could hear Daniel saying, "She thinks she's broken her pelvis." He sounded important, like someone in charge.

"You won't forget will you? You're my only hope," said Jan Williams.

"We'll bring back the horses, feed the dogs, and ask the publican to ring your daughter. We'll look after everything until she comes, okay?" I said.

"You'll go to heaven," Jan Williams answered.

The ambulance men knelt down beside her. They had brought a stretcher. "We'll do our best, but we could do with a doctor," one said.

Suddenly I was thinking of our parents, imagining them returning from the pub and looking for us, then calling, "Daniel, Dawn. Where are you?"

"We must go now," I said. "We'll see to the horses first, don't worry. Good luck."

"Our parents will be furious, you know that, don't you?" I cried, running ahead of Daniel towards the cove below. "We can see them and smooth things over and then bring the horses back here. Okay?" I continued.

"Okay," he answered.

I could hear Jan Williams calling something and I shouted back, "Sorry, can't stop. We'll come and visit you in hospital." Then we were at the end of the path and there wasn't a cove any more, just the sea lashing the rocks, no sand, no way back.

"We'll have to find another way. Let's go back to Drover's End," cried Daniel, after a moment's stupified silence.

"Where then?" I asked.

"We don't know, do we? Perhaps we can ring the caravan site from the cottage."

"Some hope," I said. "Do you know its name? Is it Drover's End?" I asked.

Daniel didn't answer.

We were running again and soon we reached the place where we had left Jan Williams; we could see the dent where she had lain. Blimpie ran ahead of us. Then we could see the cottage and shadows lay on it now – the shadows of evening. "We should have remembered the tide," I said, breaking into a walk, trying to think, trying to make a plan.

"It's really rather exciting," announced Daniel, looking suddenly younger than his years. "I never imagined anything like this could happen to us."

"Nor did I. Let's stop and think. If we follow the road round, it must come to the caravan site in the end. It's common sense," I said, starting to run again.

"Do you think we could ride the horses back? Because if that old woman can ride Groucho bareback and lead the other, they must be quiet," cried Daniel.

"We'll have to see," I said.

As we were passing the house, we decided to stop there and feed the dogs. We found tins of dog food in a cupboard in the kitchen, but it was ages before we found a tin-opener.

"They will have rung the police by now; they'll be frantic," said Daniel, alluding to our parents.

We put water in a fruit bowl for the three dogs because we couldn't find anything else suitable. All the time Blimpie was growling and snarling at the other dogs, jealous and uneasy, wondering when he would be getting his dinner.

"What about the key?" I asked when we had locked the front door again.

"We'll just have to leave it with the landlord at the

pub," replied Daniel, after a moment's thought.

"Supposing we don't find the pub?"

"We must find it," he said.

Dusk had come now. The sky and the sea were almost one. The pub was suitably called The Ancient Mariner. It was quaint and pink, with deep thatch and small lattice windows. We rushed straight into a crowded bar. Heads turned to look at us.

"Can we see the landlord?" asked Daniel. "There's been an accident."

Everyone was staring at us by now.

"He's over there." A woman perched on a stool pointed to the man behind the bar. He beckoned us to the yard outside. "Can't hear a thing in there," he said. "Now, what is it?"

We explained briefly. "And here's the key," finished Daniel. "You'll give it to Jan Williams's daughter, won't you – please?"

"She *would* ride them bareback. I told her time and time again it wasn't safe. But I might just as well have spoken to that there wall," said the landlord. "Bareback and in halters. I ask you! Do you ride?"

"Yes, we do," I answered.

"We have to go now," said Daniel. "We're late already, very late."

"I'll ring her daughter Samantha right away; she's a lovely kid, she'll come," promised the publican, and then we were running again with a cool wind in our faces smelling of the sea.

"Dad will kill us," Daniel shouted. "Run. Can't you run any faster? We can cut across the sand-dunes. Look over there, there's the site," cried Daniel, pointing towards an ocean of caravans below. We ran on, stumbling over hillocks.

The site was orderly when we reached it. Rows and rows of caravans stood on concrete; there was a bingo hall, a restaurant, even a nightclub; but it was not *our* camp. We stood and looked at one another and Daniel started to cry, silently like someone who is disappointed beyond words. Then he wiped his eyes with the back of his hand.

"We'll ask," I said, looking round for help.

"I don't want to speak to a murderer," replied Daniel. "Or a kidnapper. We don't know anyone here."

"There's a car coming," I cried, dazzled by headlights.

We stood to one side while a voice yelled, "Where have you been? Your mother's nearly out of her mind with anxiety."

Blimpie ran to the voice, wagging his tail, and Daniel cried, "It wasn't our fault, please don't be angry, Dad, please."

"Get in," shouted Dad. "Don't say another thing, get in. We were about to call the coastguards out. We've rung the police already. Where have you been?" he yelled, revving up the engine; then we were leaving the camp with Dad as stiff and hard as iron at the steering wheel.

"We found someone hurt, her pelvis was broken," I said, trying to sound calm, cool and collected. "We couldn't get away."

"You could have telephoned us," he answered, as though we were at home with a telephone in the hall.

"Where to? Don't be silly, Dad," I replied.

Mum threw her arms round us when she saw us. "We were afraid you were drowned, murdered, such terrible things happen," she cried. "We searched the whole beach; the tide was in, we thought you had been washed away. We'll never leave you again – never!"

A few minutes later we were telling our parents what had really happened, taking it in turns to speak. When we had finished Dad said, "I owe you an apology, don't I? You were right to do what you did and I'm proud of you."

"What about the horses?" I asked. "We were supposed to take them back and it's dark now."

"I'll see the site owner. We'll try to leave them here until tomorrow," Dad answered.

"We ought to see them now," said Daniel. "There may be glass about, or wire. We didn't look."

"Or a broken gate, or weedkiller," I cried, suddenly

alarmed to think that we had turned them out without following any of the elementary rules of pony management.

We found a torch and Mum came with us, while Dad walked across to the caravan site office. Groucho and the pony were standing under a tree. They looked very fat, as though they had been eating without stopping for hours. After a search we found a trough full of water and two gates, both shut, and the fences were all standing up.

"Okay, now we can sleep soundly," Mum said.

Dad was waiting by the caravan when we returned. "It's all right. I've telephoned the chap who owns the field and they can stay until the morning."

It was too late to cook, so Dad bought fish and chips and we ate them in the caravan.

The next day we took the horses back. We led them along the beach and up the windy path and they dragged us with them, eager to be going home. Samantha, Jan Williams's daughter, had just arrived. She was one of those country-spun people with her hair in a plait, wearing sandals and a long skirt and peasant blouse.

"How can I ever thank you both? You saved my mother's life," she said. "The tide could have come up and washed her away. I might never have seen her again but for you."

"The horses saved her, not us," I answered. "We found them loose on the beach."

"How is she?" asked Daniel.

"Comfortable, you know what hospitals are like." Samantha shrugged her shoulders as we led Groucho and his friend through a five-barred gate and turned them loose. Now there was sunlight everywhere and the smell of the sea.

"I should give you a reward," said Samantha. "But I don't know what."

"Don't be silly," replied Daniel. "You can save us one day."

"Here come Mum and Dad."

"Coffee. You must all come in for coffee," cried Samantha, while the three little dogs barked and jumped higher and higher, trying to lick our faces.

Later we went to visit Jan Williams in hospital. She looked like everyone else now, washed clean and in a hospital nightie, but she had one leg suspended from a pulley. She was still drowsy from the anaesthetic so we did not stay long, but she invited us to visit her and now every year we stay with her, in our caravan. Last year we took our ponies with us and rode them along the beach and into the sea. Next year we are competing in the annual Bank Holiday Show there. Jan Williams has asked me to jump Groucho and Daniel is riding the cream coloured pony in the handy hunter competition; so in a funny way everything seems to have come full circle. We may have missed Stilton Show but we have gained another, even better, one.

Mum puts it in a different way, she says that the good you put into life is always repaid in some other way; either way that particular holiday turned out much better than we expected.

Hamstrung

Christine Pullein-Thompson

"Jo Jo wants to ride. Go for her sake, Jamie, please," my mother said.

"But have you seen their father? He wears a deer-stalker. He's like something out of *The Forty-Nine Steps* or Sherlock Holmes," I cried.

"I want to go," shrieked my beastly little sister, whose name is Josephine though everyone calls her Jo Jo. "They breed Highland ponies and Flora is about my age."

"And their mother Morag keeps asking you over," added my mother. "They" lived in a large old house with turrets at each end.

I won't tell you their name, nor mine either, for fear of reprisals. I'll just say that their name was Scottish and ours isn't, though my mother was raised in the Highlands. We were there for the summer holidays and I was perfectly happy walking Binkie, our Jack Russell terrier, along the side of the lake, which in Scotland is called a loch. But of course my sister is different. At home our house bulges with her friends; they stay all day. They bring packed lunches and erect portable

Wendy houses in the garden. In other words they are a pain with a capital P. At home Jo Jo is forever organising parties. A week without a party is a catastrophe for her.

"You can go this afternoon. Get your riding-hats. I'll run you over," said my mother, so firmly that I knew it was prearranged.

We found our riding-hats, put on riding-boots. Jo Jo was laughing and smiling; she always does when she gets her own way.

"I *would* go with her, but I haven't been invited," said my mother apologetically.

I made no reply. I felt too angry to speak. I hate meeting new people. I hate being pushed into things. I hate playing the elder brother.

"Look after Jo Jo, do you hear me? Don't let her do anything silly," my mother said.

The driveway to the house where they lived was long, with fields fenced by wire on each side. Hugh, Duncan and Flora were waiting for us by a modern stable block.

"We've tacked up the ponies ready for you," cried Flora, who was small with tousled, dark hair, and rosy cheeks.

Duncan was sturdy; while Hugh resembled his father, being tall with an arrogant tilt to his head.

"You want to ride, don't you?" Hugh asked as Mother left.

"Yes, of course. Aren't they lovely. Are they all Highland?" cried my sister, running from pony to pony in a most unhorsemanlike way. "They're such fantastic colours," she went on. "And look at their dorsal stripes,

Jamie." But I was not interested in dorsal stripes. I disliked the family instantly. Even their mother Morag, smiling sweetly and saying nothing, seemed to me to be unpleasant.

"Right, let's go," said Hugh.

We rode for what seemed hours. My pony was called Bullrush and was a strange dun colour. He was steady and sure-footed and about as exciting to ride as an overworked riding-school nag.

"I suppose you're used to Arabs and thoroughbreds?" asked Duncan after a while.

I nodded. "I do a lot of dressage and a spot of show-jumping," I said, in a voice so lordly that even I was surprised by it.

"I thought so. You have that sort of seat," Hugh replied scornfully.

Flora and Jo Jo, having hit it off straight away, were chattering and laughing together. Every few moments Jo Jo lent down to pat her pony, which was called Curlew. "He's so lovely," she enthused. "He's the nicest pony I've ever ridden."

Beastly little liar, I thought sourly, recalling the ponies she rode at the superior riding-school we attended at home.

After an hour we turned homewards. Evening was nigh and midges charged out of the bracken to attack us like invading armies. Duncan had stopped trying to talk to me. I wasn't surprised. I just couldn't relate to him however hard I tried, but worse than that I was filled with such loathing for them all that it frightened me.

We turned the ponies out into a field before eating scones in a large, airy kitchen. Then Flora took Jo Jo off to look at some foals, while I kicked the gravel impatiently with my heels and thought of our house in Wimbledon which is now worth half a million, or would be if we turned it into flats.

"How much is this place worth?" I asked Hugh after a long silence.

"About five hundred thousand if you count the land as well," he replied, sounding surprised.

"Same as our house then. We are only here while Dad does his study of the habitat," I said, "though I've no idea what's so special here."

Hugh nodded. "By the sound of it you don't like being here," he said.

"Yes and no," I replied. "But to be quite honest, it's a bit far from the bright lights for me."

"I thought so."

And the funny thing was, as I behaved in this negative uncouth fashion, I was hating myself.

I looked around. "Why don't you use the stables over there; the stone ones?" I asked, pointing. "They've

even got the remains of a room at the end, which would be ideal for a tack room. Wouldn't they be cooler in summer and warmer in winter than your new timber ones?"

"Yes, they would be, but we can't use them. No horse will go inside. They're haunted," replied Hugh.

"Oh, tell me another! You don't mean to say you actually believe in ghosts?" I cried, delighted to discover a crack in his armour of superiority.

"They are out of bounds. It's as simple as that. And I advise you to keep away from them," Duncan said firmly.

When the time came to go home Flora said, "Don't come over tomorrow, Jo Jo, because we're going to be out all day and we'll be back very late. The one after would be fine. Bring lunch and stay all day. I'll look after you. We can school in the paddock and jump the cross-country course – if you want to."

"Of course I want to," cried Jo Jo, beaming.

I turned to look at the old stables before I left. I could see that once there had been a cobbled yard there and two doors; but now the roof was falling in and the cobbles were overgrown with weeds.

Duncan was watching me. "Keep away from it, Jamie. Do you hear me?" he said.

And unexpectedly I replied, "Aye, I hear you all right." I had always said "yes" until this moment, never "aye".

As we walked home the sun was setting over the loch. The hills were bathed in the light of its rays. The water in the loch did not move. Heaven knows what secrets it hid in its deep, dark waters.

"I'm glad I'm not going with you again, Jamie. You were really horrible. I was ashamed to call you my brother," Jo Jo said. "And they were so kind, that's what made it so much worse. And isn't Duncan handsome? Much more handsome than disagreeable old you," she teased.

I didn't answer. I felt drawn now to the old stable as wasps to jam. I saw myself there tomorrow. When the family I can't name returned from their day out, I would be sitting on a bucket, chewing a blade of grass, and I would say, "Now who's afraid of big bad ghosts?" I would laugh. I would show them that I had more courage than the three of them put together. I felt light-headed with hate and a little mad as we reached our rented house.

Jo Jo reported my uncouth behaviour; she always does.

"Oh, Jamie, how could you behave like that?" Mother asked. "They won't ask you again."

"They haven't. And I don't care. I'm going for a hike tomorrow with Binkie. I'm not looking after Jo Jo again," I replied angrily.

"But why are you so angry, Jamie? It's not like you, darling," Mother said. "What's happened?"

"I don't like being called Jamie. I'm James. And I'm not darling," I said, going to my bedroom and slamming the door after me. Next day I rose late. Mother packed me sandwiches and a flask of coffee.

"Expect me when you see me," I said.

She did not answer. I think she was glad to be rid of me. I called to Binkie, "Come on – walkies. Hurry, I haven't got all day."

I heard mother say, “What’s come over him?” and Jo Jo’s reply:

“I don’t know. He was foul yesterday. It was so embarrassing.”

“Perhaps the walk will do him good,” replied Mother.

“He was even rude about the ponies, and they are so lovely. A thoroughbred could never have managed the hills and the rocks,” Jo Jo continued.

But I didn’t care. I walked away from them with Binkie at my heels, full of aggression and spite, bent on showing up the family I can’t name as a pack of wimps.

I walked a long way round to the house where they lived. Binkie was very hot by the time we reached it and the midges were everywhere. The Highland ponies were standing head to tail in the field. In the loose boxes the straw was stacked up round the sides. Everything was quiet and empty. Because I had slept so late it was already evening and a mist was coming down as I stood looking at the empty stable, the old one, which drew me to it like a magnet.

A pony neighed in the field. An aeroplane droned in the sky above. Suddenly I was afraid. I sat on the grass near the old stable and ate the sandwiches and drank the coffee Mother had prepared. Binkie was restless. He did not like the stable either. He looked into my eyes and whined. He wanted to go home, now, straight away. He, too, was afraid. At last I stood up, returned the remains of my picnic to my backpack and said sternly to myself, “James, you are not a wimp. Go forth and conquer.”

I left my backpack on the grass and called to

Binkie, "Come on you old fool, hurry," before walking towards the stable, my heart lurching, my limbs shaking. Dusk was descending. Soon the family would return. Time was running out. I told myself this, but still my legs refused to move any faster and my hands felt clammy with fear. At the same time I felt dragged forwards by some unexplained force, while Binkie held back, whining pathetically, his tongue hanging out, his hackles up, his tail down. Nothing would make him enter the stable, neither kind words nor anger. So I went in alone.

It was dark and musty inside. Cobwebs brushed my face, brambles scratched my hands, creepers wrapped themselves round my arms, impeding my progress. The windows were no more than slits in the walls and let in no light. The earth floor was pitted with holes. The stalls were rough and ready, their partitions broken. The mangers were crumbling into dust, the hayracks collapsed. A rat scurried across my feet. The whole place smelt of dust and decay. But now I felt triumphant, for I had braved the building and there was no ghost. I was about to leave when a bat flew past soundlessly; then another and another, more and more of them until suddenly I wanted to scream. I thought I understood then that the old stable was a sanctuary for bats, an endangered species.

So that's it, I thought. They lied to me because they didn't want the bats disturbed. Well, I've done it now. And who cares? The bats will return soon enough. But though my thoughts were brave, I was actually scared by the bats; imagining them in my hair, in my clothes, sucking my blood; my body trembled with fear, my face grew hot. They're really vampires, I thought, moving through a cloud of them towards the faint light which came through the open doorway. In a minute they'll overwhelm me, knock me down, go for my jugular vein.

Now there were other sounds; the neighing of terrified horses followed by the voice of an old man screaming in a tongue I did not understand. Chains clanked. Dogs barked. Doors swung shut. I think I prayed then, though what I said I can't remember. Another second and a man stood in front of me, waving an enormous broadsword which in Scotland is called a claymore. He was long haired, wild-eyed, unshaven,

almost naked, and without shoes. There was only one word I understood in his whole vocabulary and that was my name, James. And the fact that he knew my name only added to my terror. Another second and he had thrown down his claymore and was clawing at my face with his hands. Bending low I went for his stomach – only it wasn't there. I put my hands round him and they met without anything between. I threw my weight against him and almost fell down on the far side. Yet his presence was everywhere. And there was the dreadful smell of a man who has not washed for years mixed with the smell of sweating horses and the excrement of bats.

Then without warning fear possessed me. My body went limp with it. My eyes stopped focusing. I was overcome by an indescribable feeling of terror. The man had picked up his weapon again and I knew he was about to launch his final blow. I tried to protect my head with my hands. Then my feet began slipping on the earth floor. Next there was a dreadful cracking noise, a splintering of wood. Everything appeared to be spinning until something fell with a rush of dust and dirt and old birds' nests, hitting me full on. Then I lay in the dust and the dirt, unable to move, while the man laughed a cackling, unearthly, triumphant laugh before everything fell silent again, as silent as the grave.

I cannot tell you how long I lay there. When I came round, faithful Binkie was licking my face and whining. The sky had cleared. Moonlight cast gruesome shadows. My mouth was full of dust and dirt, my shirt sticky with blood, my right shoulder hurt and my head ached unbearably. There was no sign of the man now. I was alone, lying in an empty stable with Binkie urging me to get up, yapping hoarsely and urgently.

Then I heard voices shouting, "There he is. Look, over there!" The voices were high with excitement.

I struggled from beneath the rafter which lay across me.

"I said he would be there, the idiot, didn't I?" called Duncan.

"He deserves to be hung," shouted Hugh like a judge passing sentence.

"He's hurt, he's covered with blood," cried soft-hearted Flora. "But he's moving. Oh, thank heavens, he's moving."

"I had better ring up his parents. They must be beside themselves with worry," cried Morag, hurrying towards the house.

I was escorted inside, my shoulder examined, a doctor called.

"He's related to our enemies. I discovered that this afternoon," said their father (or the head of the house, whichever you prefer). "His mother's family stole our sheep. She's a — ," and he named a name I even now do not wish to reveal for fear that someone will say it isn't true.

"There was a feud. They came at night and they hamstrung our horses in that very stable." And this man, whose forebears had been our enemies, looked at me with the coldest, greyest eyes I've ever seen.

"The ghost, if it was a ghost, talked in a strange language," I said.

"Gaelic, of course," Duncan replied scornfully.

"We told you not to go in there," insisted Hugh.

"So why did you?" demanded Flora, looking at me with wonderful green eyes.

But of course I couldn't tell them the truth. I tried to wash my face and rinsed my mouth out in their bathroom, dried myself with a towel. I could not do much because now it hurt to move my right arm in any direction.

My parents arrived at the same time as the doctor. They carted me off to hospital to have my broken collar bone put back in place. Otherwise, miraculously, I was unhurt. But inside it was a different story. I felt devastated by what had happened and my head ached unceasingly.

When we reached the hospital, Mother said, "How could you go where you were forbidden to go, Jamie?"

"I don't know."

"It was a compulsion. I think I understand him. His whole personality was taken over. You saw a change, so did Jo Jo," replied Father.

"But why?"

"It's to do with your side of the family," Father replied glumly. "They lived not far from here. Is that correct? That's what your friends say anyway."

Mother nodded, while I sat on a chair in a long corridor waiting to see a doctor, sick of the whole beastly business.

"What was his name? You know, that ghastly great-great-grandfather of yours," continued Father.

"James. James Hamish."

"And he was one of the worst rustlers in the whole of the Highlands. He stole another clan's sheep and burnt their houses to the ground. It's all in an old book of yours," Father continued. "You know, the one with the pages stuck together; the one you never open."

Mother sat saying nothing. I looked up and down the long corridor, hoping a doctor would appear. Jo Jo had been left with a neighbour called Mrs McDonald who makes the most wonderful scones I've ever eaten.

"James Hamish had rather a nasty habit, Jamie," continued Father, looking at me. "When he had stolen the sheep and burnt the other clan's houses, he would cut the hamstrings on their horses before he left."

"So they couldn't give chase?" I asked. "And they never could, could they? They were finished."

Father nodded.

And then, suddenly, the tears came. I was almost fourteen and still I cried. My parents looked away. Then Mother said, "Oh, Jamie, stop, please stop. You're not responsible for the sins of your forefathers."

"The man who attacked you was only protecting his horses. I don't think he will come back," Father said.

"I didn't think you believed in ghosts. I thought only fools and old people believed in ghosts," I said, holding my aching head.

"There are many strange things in the world we don't understand," replied Father. "Think about an ant, Jamie, so tiny, but everything is still there, brain, genes, reproductive organs – it works. Anything is possible," he said as a doctor appeared at last, followed by a nurse.

"So you were attacked by a ghost," said the doctor, smiling at me. "I haven't had such a case before. It should be interesting."

Because I had passed out in the old stable, I was kept in hospital that night. I couldn't sleep. I relived the last few hours over and over again. I kept hearing the horses struggling, their anguished neighs, the cries of the man in Gaelic. When I slept I woke with bats in my hair, screaming, but of course there were no bats. A nurse gave me a sedative. When I woke again the sun was streaming through the windows in the ward where I lay.

"He cut their hamstrings, all of them," I said to a new nurse who appeared, shaking a thermometer.

"What are you talking about?" she asked.

"The ghost."

She looked at me as though I was crazy. "Open your mouth, I want to take your temperature," she said. "And stop your silly talk," she added.

"You don't believe in ghosts then?"

"No, I don't."

"The hamstrings are the tendons above the hocks on horses' hind legs," I explained, unable to get the awful truth out of my mind.

"Keep your mouth closed," she replied, hurrying off to deal with another patient, an old man who might have been the ghost if he had not been washed, shaven and smooth-faced.

I went home later that day. Everyone was very kind. I went straight to bed. Jo Jo brought me a cup of tea on a tray. Morag had flowers delivered. Binkie slept on my feet, unable to tear himself away from me. I stayed in bed the whole day. My mind wandered. Several times I cried uncontrollably, burying my face in the pillow so no one would hear. Mother said that I was suffering from delayed shock.

In the evening a get-well card was delivered by

hand. Inside was written: "The feud is over. The ghost has gone. Dad has bulldozed the building and erected safe homes for the bats." It was signed: Hugh, Duncan and Flora. Flora had added some kisses after her name. At the bottom a PS had been added. This is what it said:

"Our forefathers were awful too. We have a dungeon underneath our house where prisoners were chained to the rings still there in the walls. There is also a barrel with spikes inside, in which prisoners were rolled down a nearby hill, to an agonising death, of course. So you see our forebears were savages just like yours!"

I wrote back saying I wanted us to be friends. I apologised for my behaviour and for that of my forebears. As for the ghost, he never did return. In killing me he had no doubt revenged the death of his horses, for they must have been destroyed later by someone unable to bear their agony. I try not to think about the incident any more. But I still sometimes wake screaming in the night. And I know it really did happen for I have the proof – a scar which has never faded on my right shoulder, a scar in the shape of a claymore.

A Little Grey Foal

Christine Pullein-Thompson

From the moment Littlecote Riding-School closed down, I had wanted a pony. For two years I had helped there at weekends and in the holidays. I had saved every penny for riding lessons and second-hand riding-clothes. Then suddenly, without warning, the whole establishment was sold to a developer for a million pounds. I was eleven then and whenever another advertisement appeared offering desirable homes for thousands and thousands of pounds on the Littlecote estate, I felt like tearing it down. But the worst part was not knowing where the ponies went, because we were never told.

I lived with my parents and two brothers at number nine Derby Road, in a terraced house with a garden twenty-five metres long and three bedrooms and a lounge-diner. Both my parents went out to work, so did my brothers. I was the baby of the family and hated it.

Without the riding-school I had nowhere to go and nothing to do at weekends, apart from delivering the Sunday papers for Mr Crossman at the corner shop, and baby-sitting for the Lamberts, who lived in a modern house and owned a paddock which lay between them and the other houses on the estate.

The Lamberts' baby was teething one evening and they were grateful because I'd managed to soothe him to sleep, so grateful that Mr Lambert said, "I've just thought of something, Sharon. I know you want a pony. You can keep him in our paddock if you like. We won't charge you anything. You can have it for nothing."

"You don't mean it, not really?" I gasped. "Oh, thank you!" So I started saving again, every penny I earned went in a tin with PONY written on its lid. Mum put spare change in it from time to time and once, when she was feeling rich, a five-pound note. But Dad was against the whole idea.

"You haven't got the time and you'll never have the money," he told me. "Horses are for the rich, Sharon, not for us."

"Oh, yeah? You wait and see, Dad," I replied.

Everybody seemed to want me for baby-sitting that long hot summer, so that by October I had over one hundred pounds in my tin. I knew that it wouldn't buy much, but I decided to go to the monthly horse sale in the cattle market just the once because that would give me an idea of how much money I needed. It was held on a Friday and luckily it was half-term. I borrowed a money belt from one of my brothers and put my money in it. I was too excited to eat any breakfast. I had persuaded Richard, my best friend, to accompany me. He's tall and fair-haired and good at passing exams. We caught a bus together.

"I think you're crazy, Sharon. What are you going to do with a horse?" he asked, paying both our fares.

"Ride it, of course," I said.

The market was crowded with people and there were horses everywhere – thin, broken down, overweight, neighing wildly, looking round for lost friends. Frightened, anxious, resigned, and a few, which I supposed had never been ill-treated or sold before, were looking interested and alert. I wiped my eyes with a tissue.

"You're not crying, are you?" demanded Richard.

"Yeah. What does it look like?" I retorted.

We watched them being sold in the big building beyond the pens. They went for hundreds of pounds, or most of them did.

"It's hopeless, they're too expensive. We might as well go home, Sharon," Richard said, pulling at my arm.

"Not yet. Let's wait a little longer."

The sale was nearly over when a foal appeared, looking anxiously around for its mother. It brought a lump to my throat. It was mousey grey with a well-bred head and small, neat, grey hoofs, and a tail the shape of a fox's brush.

People were drifting away. Richard was still pulling at my arm when I raised my hand and called out "Fifty".

And heard the auctioneer reply, "Fifty I'm bid, fifty."

"He'll be much too small for you, Sharon," Richard whispered.

"I don't care, I've got to save him," I whispered back.

At first a tall, thin woman with a worn face was bidding against me, but at sixty pounds she dropped out and a fat man took over. And I kept marvelling that I was being taken seriously, that no one had demanded to see my money first, or asked whether I was eighteen.

"One hundred," I shouted raising my hand, my stomach churning.

"One hundred I'm bid, one hundred. For the last time, one hundred," shouted the auctioneer as his hammer fell.

"He's yours," said Richard, as though I hadn't noticed!

He was put in a pen with another foal. He had baby teeth and wouldn't eat the bread I offered him. Richard went with me to the auctioneer's office where I handed over one hundred pounds, some of it in fifty-pence pieces.

Then I said to the clerk, "I don't know how to get him home, that's the problem," while Richard sighed beside me.

"Ask the bloke over there," said the clerk, pointing at an enormous man with a hat on the back of his head, smoking a cigar. "He's Mr Collins. He'll help you."

"Will do," Mr Collins said when I explained my predicament. "I'll deliver him, but it won't be till late afternoon. What's your address?"

Richard told him.

"Let's say four o'clock then. It'll cost you a fiver. And that's a lot less than I usually charge," Mr Collins said, smiling at us both.

Richard produced a fiver and gave it to him.

"You didn't have to," I said as we walked away. "But thanks all the same. I'll pay you back, I promise."

I said goodbye to Richard when we got off the bus. Then I rushed home and took the plastic bucket from under the sink, filled it with water and carried it to the Lamberts' field. After that I knocked on their back door, but they weren't at home and nor were Mum and Dad, and suddenly I felt alone and rather scared. What if I can't manage the foal? I thought. What if the Lamberts are angry? Supposing he leans over the wire and eats their roses? But a huge cattle truck was just drawing up outside our house. A minute later Mr Collins was letting down the ramp and asking, "Where do you want him then?"

We took the foal to the field together, me pulling, Mr Collins pushing. "Bit small for you, isn't he?" he asked as I slammed the gate shut.

"Yes. I'm not going to ride him, I'm going to look after him," I said.

"Well, I'll be off then," said Mr Collins, handing me a tatty hemp halter. "Best of luck."

I called the foal Prince because I wanted him to feel he was someone special. He spent that first evening walking round and round the small field, looking lost and frightened, and I knew he wanted his mother. Later, while it was still light, Mum and Dad and the Lamberts looked at him. Mum said he was a sweetie, Dad said that he would be a lot of trouble. Prince kept his distance, trusting no one.

"Don't look so worried. He'll be all right with time," said Mr Lambert, rumpling my hair.

"You can teach our kiddies to ride on him, dear," suggested Mrs Lambert, smiling.

"He's too young. He's just a little grey foal," I said.

I visited Prince every day. I brought him oats and bran from the pet shop and soon he stopped looking for his mother, and looked for me instead. He would stand with his little head over the fence and his nostrils would tremble as he saw me approaching along the road with his food. He knew the times of my visits exactly. The Lamberts fed him too, on apple peelings and bits of carrot, and slowly October became November and the weather grew cold. I longed to buy Prince a rug then but I hadn't enough money. I started to buy him bales of hay, pushing them home from the pet shop in a wheelbarrow. Soon rain fell in bucketfuls and I wished I could afford a shelter, but of course I hadn't enough money for that either. There were muddy patches in the field now, and busy moles threw up great mounds of dark earth. I always seemed to be in a mackintosh and muddy boots. Mum said that the house was beginning to look like a farmyard. The kitchen floor kept getting muddy and my bedroom had bits of hay scattered everywhere.

I boiled up potato peelings for Prince and begged carrot peelings and cabbage leaves from my friends. I spent ages just talking to him, telling him that next year he would have a shelter and a brand-new waterproof rug. For my birthday I asked for money, nothing else. There wasn't much baby-sitting available now and I needed every penny I could earn for hay.

I stopped seeing Richard when he told me I was beginning to look like a horse. I didn't miss him because Prince was taking up my spare time.

Soon Prince grew a thick coat. Frosts arrived and ice formed on the two water buckets I had bought. Prince was always hungry. There was almost nothing left for him to eat in the field now, not a nettle and hardly a blade of grass. As the days grew shorter I had less and less time to spend with Prince. On weekdays it was still dark in the mornings when I fed him, and dark when I returned from school in the evenings. In the end my torch battery ran out and I hadn't the money to buy another one. Then Richard dropped in one evening.

"Diane's having a disco at her place on Saturday night. How about coming? It doesn't start till seven, so it won't affect your pony watching," he said with a laugh.

"Go on, go. You haven't been anywhere for ages," Mum said.

"But I haven't anything to wear and look at my hair!" I wailed.

"It doesn't matter. Jeans will do," Richard said. "You must go out sometimes."

I fed Prince quickly that evening. Then I washed my hair and had a bath. Mum lent me a blouse and I put on my best jeans and some high-heeled boots which were too small and pinched my toes. Dad took me to the disco in the car. "Don't be late, do you hear, Sharon. Be back by ten, love. Ring up when you're ready to leave."

"Ten! Don't be daft, Dad. Midnight's more likely," I cried.

It was lovely to be with my friends again. The music was deafening. And straight away Richard seized me by the arm crying, "Come on, you pony girl, have a drink."

Everybody seemed pleased to see me. I felt as though I had been away for a long time; Diane had changed her hairstyle. Bobby was laughing. They were all there, all my friends. There were wonderful eats, and drinks which were different colours – blue lagoons and green lagoons, Diane called them. "They're cocktails, but nearly all lemonade. So don't worry, Sharon, they won't make you drunk," she cried, handing me another and another.

"I must be home by midnight. Dad will kill me if I'm not," I said.

"You will be. Don't look so worried, Sharon," said Richard, laughing.

After a time everyone seemed to be a long way off, rather as though I was looking through binoculars the wrong way round. Then I started to feel giddy.

"She had better lie down for a bit," Diane said, and she sounded hazy and miles away, and everything was going round and round. I lay on a divan and someone put a blanket over me. I kept thinking of Prince, waiting for me. Several times Diane leaned over me to ask, "Are you all right? Are you sure?" And all I could do was smile in return. Then everyone was gone. Someone had left a side light on, and there was a faint glow from the streetlamp outside.

Diane appeared again. "Are you all right? We've spoken to your dad. My mum will run you home first thing, all right?"

I nodded. My head was still spinning and I felt very tired. When I woke again it was morning. My mouth was dry and my head felt on fire. I sat up and started shouting straight away, "What about Prince? I haven't fed Prince. He'll be starving."

"Stop yelling, you'll wake everyone up," said Diane, appearing in a dressing-gown. "Calm down. Why did you buy him anyway?"

"Because he needed a home. I've got to go home at once," I cried, looking for my boots. "What's the time anyway?"

"Eleven o'clock."

Eleven o'clock! And outside the rain was cascading down.

"Mum will take you," Diane said. "Mum, where are you, Mum?" Her mother was young and beautiful.

"Don't you want any breakfast?" she asked.

I shook my head. "I've got to feed Prince," I said.

"Prince is her pony," explained Diane, sounding exasperated.

A few minutes later I was on my way home, the windscreen wipers working full-speed. "Why can't your parents feed the pony?" Diane's mother asked.

"They don't know anything about ponies," I said. "Anyway, Mum and Dad are not like that, they're not that sort of parents; if you know what I mean. They're always working. And anyway, I didn't ask them. I told

Dad I would be home by midnight."

There was a horse box parked by the field gate and a small crowd of people. My stomach knotted as I leapt out of the car shouting, "Thanks awfully." Then I was running towards the field, my heart hammering. Next I saw a police car and slowed to a walk. Mum and Dad were there too.

"There she is, there's Sharon," Mum shouted.

"We're taking your foal to the horse sanctuary," said a tall, thin woman with a worn face. "He needs a vet and a warm stable and nursing."

"He got caught in the wire. Some girls on horses went by and he got caught up," Mum explained. "The girls rang the police."

But I knew what had happened. Prince had waited and waited for me to feed him and I hadn't shown up. I had let him down and now he was hurt, and it was my fault.

"It's the best thing, love," the policeman said. "We were going to call the RSPCA, but it's better if he goes to the sanctuary."

"They would have sent him to us anyway," the thin lady said.

"But he's mine," I said in a small voice.

Prince was in the horse box, one foreleg scarlet with blood. He looked very small and alone.

"It's for the best, Sharon," insisted Mum.

"I want him back, when can I have him back?" I asked, shivering in the rain.

"You can come and visit him whenever you like. He's still yours. You can come and help us. We're only a bus ride away. We always need people like you," said the lady from the sanctuary, who told me she was called Melanie Jones. She lifted up the horse box ramp. "It was no life for him here, was it? All alone. He's only a baby. He needs friends and he needs his hoofs trimmed and he needs worming. But he's still yours," she insisted, handing me a tissue. "We aren't stealing him."

"Can I see him tomorrow?" I asked.

"Of course, whenever you like. I saw you at the sale. We were bidding against each other for a time. I'll buy him from you if you like," she continued. "You saved him from the meat-man, Sharon, and that's something important."

I watched the horse box leave. "You could have fed Prince," I said, turning to my parents. "Just once."

"Once, twice, all the time, that's the way it goes. You couldn't cope, you know you couldn't. And the Lamberts are selling up; they're selling the field for building. I didn't tell you, because I knew you'd be upset, but now I can." Mum had her arm round my shoulder now, we were both wet to the skin. The police and the horse box had gone. I looked at the field and saw it as a muddy little prison where a small foal had stood all alone waiting for me, because there was no one else. I saw heaps of dung which had grown and grown. The two plastic buckets which never seemed to hold enough water. Prince would have friends now. His hoofs would be trimmed. He wouldn't stand alone in the rain ever again, waiting by the gate for me to return from school. And soon the field wouldn't be there either, because dozens of new houses would rise up where Prince had once stood.

"It's all for the best, love," Mum said, opening our back door. "You just sit down and have a cuppa. You look terrible. Did you drink alcohol at the party?"

"I don't know. I passed out and when I woke up it was morning," I said. "I shouldn't have gone. I should have stayed and looked after Prince. I thought I would be home by midnight, I thought . . . " but really I didn't know what I thought any more. "But I want him to stay mine," I said slowly, blowing my nose.

"You heard what the lady said. We'll all go there tomorrow. Dad will take us to the sanctuary, won't you, Dad?" asked Mum.

Dad was checking the football results. He looked up and nodded. "It's all right with me," he said.

So next day the three of us went. Prince was with

another foal in a loose box bedded deep in straw. His leg was bandaged. He looked at me and nickered softly and that seemed the nicest thing that had happened to me for a long time. Soon Melanie Jones appeared. “He’s fine. I’m so glad you saved him, Sharon. I was desperate when we couldn’t have him. Sadly, we have limited funds,” she said.

I knelt in the straw and Prince put his head on my shoulder and blew down my neck. And I knew that now he had all the things I could never have given him, which I had wanted him to have so much. “I’ll come every weekend and help, if that’s all right,” I offered.

“That’ll be lovely,” replied Melanie Jones, smiling.

“And I’ll have one of your collecting-boxes too,” I added.

We had arrived late and now it was time to leave. “See you next Saturday then,” I said, getting into the car. “Goodbye.”

A great weight seemed lifted from my shoulders. The struggle for money and spare time for Prince had gone. He wouldn’t be waiting in the muddy field for me any more but I could still see him every weekend and in the holidays. And he would be all right now, whatever happened to me.

“Thank goodness that’s over,” Mum said. “What you would have done without a field I don’t know. Don’t go buying another pony till you’ve got a good job and somewhere decent for him, please, Sharon.”

“I shall make my fortune or marry a farmer,” I answered, and imagined an old farmhouse, acres and acres of land and Prince grazing in the midst of friends, mine again, and safe for ever.

Isobel's Pony

Christine Pullein-Thompson

"You do remember the children, don't you?" asked Mum on our way out to the station. "We all met at the British Museum when you were quite small. Clara bought you a packet of fudge."

I nodded. Clara was Mum's cousin.

"Shall I call her Aunt Clara?" I asked. There was a knot in my stomach. I hated leaving home, but most of all I hated leaving my dun pony, Crispin.

"Yes, and call George Uncle George. It sounds more polite. I expect Clara will meet you at Meadowhill and – *remember* – don't talk to strange men on the train."

We had reached the station. Mum had made me wear a skirt which I had topped with my favourite sweater, orange with a polo neck.

My train was waiting. "Have a good time," said Mum, kissing me goodbye. "And don't worry. Uncle George and Aunt Clara are very kind."

"Say goodbye to Crispin for me," I answered, though I had said goodbye to him three times already. "I hope he will be all right. I hope Mr Chambers will remember to check his water. I hope he doesn't get laminitis. I hope . . . "

But the train was pulling out of the station and Mum was getting smaller and smaller, until at last I could see her no longer.

I shut the window and tried to read a book, but I couldn't concentrate. I had never been away on my own before, and I kept wondering what would happen if Aunt Clara and I failed to recognise each other. Or if I alighted at the wrong station. Or if I hated her children. Or, worse still, they hated me.

Meadowhill station was small, and bathed in evening sunlight when I reached it. I could not see Aunt Clara anywhere. I stood on the platform, trying to keep calm, holding my small suitcase. The ticket-collector eyed me anxiously. A puppy in a wicker transport basket whined. Outside, birds sang.

"There she is!" shouted a voice, and two boys dashed into the station, while behind them a girl called, "Wait, don't we need tickets?"

They had long hair and wore jeans and tee shirts.

"Isobel Browne?" said the eldest. "Here, let me take your case."

The girl was dressed in the same way, but her hair was longer still and she wore no shoes.

"I was looking for Aunt Clara," I said.

"Well, we'd better introduce ourselves," said the largest boy. "I'm Larry. This is Paul, and this odd-looking female is called Patricia."

"Shut up, beast," replied Patricia, aiming a kick at him.

I remembered them as small in neat coats, and with

short, brushed hair. In those days they had a nanny. They had been meek and polite, wearing shiny leather shoes and ankle socks.

"Sorry about the old bus," said Larry, opening the door of a battered car. "The old man won't subscribe to anything better."

"Larry gets through a car a month," said Paul.

"Did you have a good journey?" asked Patricia.

"Yes, thank you." I felt small and out of place and idiotic in my skirt.

Their house looked across a small, tumbling river to wooded hills. Beside it stood the remains of a castle.

I looked hopefully in the fields for ponies, but there were none. Larry parked the car in front of the house and kicked off his shoes.

"Patricia will show you your room," he said, thrusting my case at his sister.

She took it and, saying "Beast!" again, led me barefoot up a wide flight of stairs. "He's mad," she said. "It's very sad. Where have your parents gone?"

"Romania and Hungary. Dad's selling agricultural machinery. It's the first time Mum's gone with him," I replied.

"Lucky them."

My bedroom window looked across the remains of the castle to the tree-shadowed river. Once the castle must have dominated that particular stretch of the river completely; now only some of its outer walls remained, while inside, thistles grew. I imagined knights stepping out of boats, the peaceful splash of oars. Patricia put my case on a chair.

"Did anyone tell you anything about this place?"

she asked, looking at me anxiously. "I mean, are you nervous? Do you get upset easily?"

"I don't know. I don't think so. It depends. I would be upset if Crispin died, or Mum or Dad."

"Of course," replied Patricia impatiently. "Well, I suppose there's no point in beating about the bush, but I wish Daddy had told you before you came."

"What?" I was beginning to feel alarmed. "About what?"

"About our ghost."

"What sort of ghost?"

I could feel the hair standing up on my neck, but when Patricia said, "It's a pony," all my alarm vanished. "Or it may be a horse. I don't know. It's grey, anyway," she continued.

"Well, I don't mind a horse. I love them. I've got a pony of my own."

"That's all right then," said Patricia, sounding relieved. "The poor animal is looking for something. It only comes at this time of the year, and is utterly harmless. See you at dinner; it's in ten minutes. Owly still beats a gong." She ran out of the room, slamming the door after her.

I sat on my bed, suddenly homesick. Patricia and her brothers have dreamed up this ghost to frighten me, I thought. What wonderful hospitality! But I'm not going to be frightened, I decided, washing my hands. I'm going to sleep like a top. Wishing that I was as tall and arrogant as my cousins, I put on my oldest pair of jeans. Then a gong boomed and someone called, "Isobel, it's dinner."

Aunt Clara and Uncle George were sitting at each

end of the large dining-room table. They stood up to shake hands with me. It was all horribly formal. I was made to sit on Uncle George's right, because I was a guest. Owly waited at table, as she apparently had for the last forty years. She wore large spectacles – which only partially hid large owl-like eyes – a black dress and a plain white apron. She called me "Miss Isobel". I used my dessert spoon for my soup and mixed up my knives. Aunt Clara and Uncle George talked to me about agricultural machinery – of which I knew nothing. If they had talked about Crispin and the Pony Club, everything would have been all right; as it was, dinner for me was a complete disaster.

Afterwards Patricia suggested a game of Monopoly, and we played until bedtime, sitting at a table in the hall, while Paul sat on the stairs, playing his transistor at full volume.

When I went to bed, I found the curtains drawn and my pyjamas waiting for me on my pillow. The rest of my clothes had been unpacked and put away. I was suddenly tired. The morning seemed to belong to another life.

Patricia came in to say goodnight. "Don't worry about footsteps in the night," she said. "The boys stay up for hours."

"I won't," I answered, getting into bed.

"Is everything all right?" she asked next, glancing round the room. "Has Owly given you enough towels, soap, everything?"

I nodded. I felt very far from home, and much preferred my own more humble bedroom with pictures of horses pinned to the walls, and my few rosettes above my bed.

"And remember, if you hear a neigh or two in the night, it's just our ghost. Nothing to worry about. A few more weeks and he will be gone until next summer."

"I shall certainly look out if I hear a neigh," I answered. "I've always wanted to see a ghost. But if it's one of your awful brothers pretending, I shall be absolutely furious. In fact, I shall probably throw something at him."

"They're not that mad," replied Patricia, laughing, before she left the room.

I lay in my luxurious bed and, being too tired to read, switched off my elegant bedside light. Moonlight filtered in through the curtains, a light wind stirred the trees outside. I could hear Paul's transistor still playing in the distance; otherwise everything was quiet. I wondered whether Crispin had missed my usual evening visit, and whether my parents had landed in Bucharest yet. Somewhere in the house a clock chimed ten times. I thought I heard Uncle George saying goodnight to someone. Then a door slammed and there was silence. After that I must have slept, though I cannot remember falling asleep. I know I dreamed that Crispin had escaped from the orchard and that he was neighing. He walked up and down below my window, and then he neighed again, and this time it was like a call for help. He seemed to be crying "Come, please come".

And then I was sitting up in bed, sweating, knowing that it wasn't a dream any more, that there really was a pony outside, calling to me in the moonlight. My heart started to beat in an idiotic manner. It's the ghost, I thought. Patricia wasn't joking after all. There really is one!

I stepped out of bed on to shaky feet, and a minute must have passed before I found the courage to draw back the curtain and look out.

The moon was partly covered by a cloud, but I could see the pony clearly, standing alone in the long grass by the castle. He was looking up, his eyes searching for something or someone. He wore the sort of tack ponies wore long ago, including a saddle which was stained with something that looked like blood. His head was small, set on a fine arched neck, and he shook a long, blood-soaked mane before he trotted away like a dancer, without looking back.

My teeth were chattering now. I was suddenly certain that I had seen the pony somewhere before. But where? And when? It was obvious he had existed years and years ago; so how could I know him? But the feeling remained, and I had difficulty in stopping myself from going down to him. I wanted to put my arms round his poor neck, to comfort him, to say – to say what? The words were there, some pet words in the back of my brain which belonged to him. I'm going mad, I thought. I don't know the pony. I can't. Tears were streaming down my face. I opened the window, but the pony had vanished. And now the first of the birds was singing, and dawn was breaking above the river.

I returned to my bed. So Patricia *wasn't* joking, I decided, putting on the light. There is a ghost. And I know him! Somehow, somewhere, we have met. But you know that is impossible, Isobel, you fool, I told myself. He belongs to the days of knights. He's a palfrey. How could you, for pity's sake? Where's your sanity?

But sanity and reason had nothing to do with it. It was beyond and above such things. I was attracted to him by something far stronger than either, and my brain seemed to be going round and round in a mad circle, saying, "I want to go to him, I want to go." I felt as though I was floating across the room and out of the window, as though some great force was dragging me, something I had no hope of understanding, and I was crying, "I don't want to go, I don't want to . . . "

Then Patricia was shaking me and saying, "It's me, Isobel. Wake up." And I didn't know where the hours had gone, for morning had come, and the room was full of sunlight.

"Are you all right?" Patricia asked anxiously, peering into my face. "You look awful."

"As though I've seen a ghost, no doubt," I said, trying to laugh.

"Did you?"

"Yes."

"It's ten o'clock. We couldn't wake you. I've been up here five times."

"He neighed twice," I explained. "I saw him. He's grey."

"That's what he always does. I ignore him now, I think he's a bore really. But, then, I'm not crazy about horses," said Patricia, who was looking very healthy this morning. "You weren't frightened, were you?"

"Of course not," I lied bravely, trying to ignore the horrors of the night. "I shall be able to tell everyone at school about it. None of them has ever seen a ghost."

"Well, get up then, lazy-bones," cried Patricia. "We're going sightseeing today."

Breakfast was still waiting for me in the dining-room. Aunt Clara was reading a newspaper. She looked up at my approach. "I hear our ghost came again last night. I hope he didn't worry you. He's quite a friendly ghost really," she said.

"He's super," I answered breezily, helping myself to cornflakes. "What happened to him? Why does he come?"

"It's a long story and rather a sad one," replied Aunt Clara. "I think it might upset you."

"I don't mind," I replied, though I could feel a lump rising in my throat already.

"I'll tell you one day, but not this morning," answered Aunt Clara, returning to her newspaper. "It's too sad for such a lovely day."

We looked round the local museum in the morning, and after a cold lunch Patricia taught me to row on the river. It was one of those golden summer days which, looking back, seemed to have no beginning and no end.

I was not very successful at rowing. My restless night had left its mark. My arms felt weak and lifeless, and sometimes I felt as though I was a spectator looking at us both from a long way off. It was an eerie sensation. We were too late for tea when we returned to the house, and dinner was formal again, with Owly waiting on us. Aunt Clara stared at me with some consternation as I sat down.

"Are you all right, Isobel?" she asked. "You don't look very well to me. Did our ghost upset you last night? Would you like to have Patricia's room? It's on the other side of the house."

"No, thank you, I'm quite all right," I replied quickly, though now Uncle George and Aunt Clara both seemed to be fading into the distance.

"Oh dear, I do hope you're not going to be ill," exclaimed Aunt Clara, growing smaller and smaller every minute.

"Get her a glass of water," said Uncle George. "Hurry."

"I'm quite all right," I said, as they came into focus again. "I don't need water. It's just that I keep hearing hoof beats and someone crying . . . "

"Oh dear," said Aunt Clara. "What are we going to do?"

"Nothing. They've gone. I'm quite all right," I answered, spooning soup into my mouth.

The boys had gone out to a party. After dinner Patricia and I watched television in the small sitting-room by the kitchen, which had once been the servants' hall. Aunt Clara popped her head round the door from time to time to ask, "Are you all right, Isobel dear? Quite all right? Are you sure?"

"Yes, thank you," I answered each time. "I'm fine."

When we went to bed, she gave us each a cup of Ovaltine. Mine had two sugar-lumps on the saucer and I put them in my dressing-gown pocket.

"Are they for the ghost?" asked Patricia, watching me. "Because he won't eat them. He fades away at the least sound. The boys tried to make friends with him years ago, but he just faded away into the shrubbery with one last desperate neigh. If you're scared, come into my room. Wake me up. I shan't mind. Promise."

"All right, I promise." I wanted to be alone now, for I felt as though I had an important appointment which I must keep at all costs. "Goodnight," I said. "Sleep well. See you tomorrow."

I opened my window and leaned out. Everything was still and beautiful – almost too beautiful for the heart to bear. There was hardly a ripple on the river, and the sky was darkening into night. It was easy to imagine the castle as it had been – full of people, with knights coming and going, and a great fire in the hall, horses being led away to stables, the clank of armour. I left the curtains undrawn and climbed into bed, and I must have fallen asleep immediately for right away I started to dream. I was riding a grey pony. I sat sideways in a long skirt with a groom following on a big horse. Everything was extremely vivid, not blurred nor muddled as dreams so often are. The trees were green with leaves and there were flowers everywhere. I had a feeling of intense happiness, as though suddenly all my dreams were coming true.

I was humming a tune when the neigh rang out,

and I sat up in bed instantly, because I had known all along that it would come, that my appointment was with the grey pony outside – whether I wanted it or not. I still wore my dressing-gown, and my legs carried me unasked out of the room and down the wide stairs. My hands knew how to draw back the bolts on the door into the garden. The grass was wet with dew and there was a smell of roses which I had not noticed before.

The grey pony stood just where he had the night before, his ears pricked, his eyes searching for me, and then I was running, tripping over the lawn, wrenching open the iron gate. I no longer wore my pyjamas and dressing-gown, but a long skirt which reached to my ankles, a cloak and a hat with a feather in it.

"Silver!" I cried. "Silver!" The pony whinnied, recognising me at once, and all the misery left his eyes. He came towards me as a friend, his nostrils nickering. I held out my hand with the sugar in it.

I felt his whiskers brush against my fingers, his breath on my hand. Then he gave a loud sigh, a sigh of pure contentment. The sort of sigh one might give when one had reached home after a long and arduous journey. And then, without warning, everything was changed; Silver was gone, and I was fighting for my life with a cloak over my head. I tried to scream, but no words would come, and I knew now without doubt that I was dying, falling into space, into nothingness, and I didn't want to die. And then there was darkness, silent and absolute, and I knew this was the end . . .

"He knew me," I said.

I felt as though I had been away for a long time and come back. Mum was sitting at the end of my bed,

wearing her navy-blue suit. "She's coming round!" she exclaimed.

Aunt Clara was sitting in a chair. Sunshine streamed through the cracks in the drawn curtains.

"How did you get here?" I asked, sitting up. "What's the time? Is it Sunday or Monday?"

"It's Wednesday, darling," cried Mum, bending forwards to kiss me.

"Give her some water," said Aunt Clara. "Here, take the glass."

"He knew me," I announced again, without really meaning to, rather as a record keeps saying the same thing when the needle is stuck. I drank some water. It had ice in it.

"There was blood on his neck. It wasn't a dream, was it?" I asked. "It did really happen, didn't it?"

"Of course, darling," replied Mum in a soothing voice, the sort of voice one might use to a very small child.

"We found you lying by the castle," added Aunt Clara. "Patricia was anxious, so she went outside to look."

"He was alive, because he took the sugar. Is it the same day?" I asked. "The morning after?"

"No, you've been delirious for two days," replied Mum. "I came to be with you. Don't talk too much."

"I'm so sorry," I answered.

"It wasn't your fault, darling."

"He hasn't been back. I don't think he will ever come back again," said Aunt Clara.

"He knew me. How did he know me?" I asked slowly. "He whinnied to me. He took the sugar."

Everything was suddenly crystal clear. "He took the sugar," I repeated. "I know he did. I felt his whiskers."

"Don't get excited," said Mum.

"We know he took the sugar," Aunt Clara told me. "Patricia searched for it. She looked in your pockets, too."

"Rest, darling," said Mum. "Lie back. Dr Perkins will be here again soon."

"I will get you something to eat," said Aunt Clara, tiptoeing from the room.

I felt weak, but happy too in a strange, exhausted way. I felt as though I had accomplished something of great importance. Silver's all right, I thought. He's found peace at last. And I'm going to be all right, too. I'm not even mad, and I can move all my limbs and open and shut my eyes and everything works!

Dr Perkins was tall and dark. He took my pulse and temperature. He looked into my ears and eyes with a torch. He asked me to look in different directions and knocked my knees with a little hammer.

"We could X-ray her skull," he said, sounding a bit perplexed.

"She seems quite well now – quite her usual self, in fact," replied Mum.

"A spontaneous recovery," said Dr Perkins. "But keep her quiet for the next twenty-four hours. I will call again tomorrow, unless you're worried."

Aunt Clara showed him out.

"I'm all right," I said. "Why can't I get up? I'm sick of bed. I want to go outside."

"Well, you can't," said Mum. "Anyway, don't you want to hear the story?"

"What story?"

"Silver's, of course."

"How do you know it?" I was sitting up again now, tense with excitement.

"It belongs to Isobel, too," answered Mum. "Aunt Clara told me it yesterday when you were delirious. I think the two Isobels were fighting over your body, but thank goodness my Isobel won."

Aunt Clara had returned with a tray covered with cups and saucers and plates, bread and butter, jam, three kinds of cake and a pot of tea.

"You tell her about Silver, Clara. You will tell it better than me," said Mum, pouring tea.

"Is she well enough?"

Mum nodded. "The colour is back in her cheeks. You are feeling all right now, aren't you, Isobel?"

"Yes." I took a piece of cake and waited, while downstairs in the hall a clock chimed four times. Patricia came into the room and sat down on a chair.

"It all happened a long time ago," began Aunt Clara, as though she was reading from a book, and I could see it all in my mind – the ruined castle, standing tall and brave, with turrets at each end, a landing-stage on the river, a flag flying.

"The house wasn't here, of course. Our ancestors lived in the castle – yours as well as ours, Isobel. The castle was big, with dungeons –"

"And turrets at each end," I interrupted.

"Yes, I will show you a drawing of it later."

"And Isobel came on her grey pony, followed by a groom. And there were a great many trees. She came through a forest."

"How do you know?" asked Aunt Clara.

"I just do," I replied.

"She had reared Silver from a foal. They were inseparable," continued Aunt Clara. "She was expecting a baby, and her husband had inherited the castle. He was dead, but no one had told her."

"This is the awful part," said Patricia.

"He had died fighting in France. But she was expecting, and if the baby was a son, he would inherit the castle."

"So she was killed," I cried. "She was happy because she thought she was going to live in the castle with her husband. She thought his relations would welcome her."

"But her uncle-in-law wasn't like that," said Aunt Clara. "He had her brutally murdered when she arrived on a dark September night, and they buried her and her servant where this house now stands."

"He was one of our ancestors," said Patricia, biting her nails.

"What about Silver?" I asked.

"They drove him away, into the forest, but he kept coming back, so, in a fit of anger, they killed him. But he still came back each September, looking for Isobel."

"Until three nights ago," said Mum.

"What no one at the castle knew was that Isobel already had a baby girl, your great-great-great-grandmother," said Aunt Clara.

"You haven't said nearly enough greats," exclaimed Patricia.

"And because of your relationship to her, you look like the first Isobel," said Mum.

"I don't just look," I answered, "I *was* her. I knew I had met Silver before, the moment I saw him. I've just been back through time. But he's all right now. He'll never come back."

Soon after that I fell asleep again, and a day later Mum and I left to join Dad in Romania. I have never returned to the house, but I write to Patricia from time to time, especially around September, and she assures me that Silver has never been back.

Green With Envy

Christine Pullein-Thompson

Our horses were not good enough for the Highbury Horse Trials, so we went as spectators. The first thing my brother said on arrival was, "Oh look, trust Fiona Tompkinson to be here."

We all disliked Fiona because she had everything we hadn't – two expensive horses, perfect clothes, marvellous rugs and a trailer with two ramps. Sometimes, when her father wasn't around, she had a groom as well. It was the same at Pony Club Camp: she had a fantastic fold-up bed, the best sleeping bag in the world, the very latest in grooming tools and perfect tack. She was good-looking too, with a straight nose and blue eyes, and her purse was always awash with money. In spite of this she was far from generous and not popular with other pony clubbers.

"She's brought Jackpot, so she'll probably win the junior event," I said.

Jackpot was a fifteen-two, half thoroughbred, bay gelding, and had cost five thousand pounds. As we walked the course together I think we were all green with envy. I know I was. When we returned to the main ring Fiona was lying second in the dressage section. Her father was fussing around her, looking incredibly rich in designer clothes, his grey hair perfectly arranged.

"You never see her mother," observed Paul.

"She looks rather worn, not at all like her dad," said Sharon, who is my best friend.

Paul, who was eighteen, soon found a friend called Thomas, and they stood together discussing Fiona, sounding unkind and rather patronising.

"I wish they would shut up. She always pats her horses and I've seen her crying at Pony Club Camp," I said.

"Oh sure. Great. She's the most stuck-up person I've ever met. She never talks to anyone. We're down there as far as she's concerned," replied Sharon, pointing at the ground.

We watched Mr Tompkinson pull up Jackpot's girth, then hold the offside stirrup as she mounted. Then he started to give her advice. Sharon and I hurried to the water jump.

"Maybe she'll fall in it," said Sharon hopefully.

But Fiona and Jackpot cleared the water jump like champions.

"They're going to win again. They'll be jumping for England next year," said Sharon.

As we went in search of Paul, I imagined jumping the course on my grey pony, Capricorn, though I knew we would never have reached the water, being in a different league altogether. Fiona had dismounted near a row of trailers, and steam like mist was rising off Jackpot. She was staring at the trailer with her mouth

half open. I stared too and for a moment I couldn't take in what I saw – two police cars, four policemen and Mr Tompkinson, still without a hair out of place, being taken away in handcuffs. As she watched, Fiona's face seemed to crumple like a half-baked cake going down. She didn't move, didn't speak, just stood with tears streaming down her face.

"Oh my goodness!" exclaimed Sharon.

"What are we going to do?" I asked. "She's in our Pony Club, even if she isn't exactly a friend. We must do something to help."

"She'll hate us for it. She's always ignored us, treated us like dirt, had everything she wanted. She's never been generous to anyone, not once," replied Sharon.

Fiona was walking towards the trailer now, leading Jackpot, while the loudspeaker announced that she had jumped a clear round. I ran after her. “Can we help?” I asked, catching up.

“I knew it would happen one day. I told him to stay away today. They knew he would be here, they knew he wouldn’t miss me jumping cross-country, not for anything,” she said, not looking at me. “And now I can’t get home because I haven’t got a driver.”

“My brother can drive. He’ll take you home. We all will,” I heard myself say.

The two police cars were leaving. “I always knew it would happen,” Fiona repeated. “Mum kept saying it would, but he wouldn’t listen. He wanted me to have the best, and I didn’t want it. I wanted to be like you in old clothes, riding cheap ponies which I had schooled myself; that’s what I wanted,” she continued, taking off Jackpot’s tack. “I don’t care about winning. I just want to be happy, that’s all, with friends like everyone else.”

I waved to Paul. “You’ll have to take Fiona home, she hasn’t got a driver,” I called.

“No hassle,” he answered a moment later. “ I saw what happened and I’m sorry.”

“There’s still the showjumping,” I said.

“I don’t care about it. I just want to go home,” Fiona said in a voice muffled by tears, rugging up Jackpot automatically. “We’re finished, can’t you understand, finished,” she said, bandaging his tail. “I knew it would end like this.”

We threw up the ramp. Paul started the Range Rover’s engine and we all got into the car. None of us felt like talking as we travelled to the sumptuous house where Fiona lived, which had an indoor swimming-pool and gold-plated taps everywhere. We turned Jackpot out while Fiona found her mother. And we didn't feel envious any more. Mrs Tompkinson appeared from the house to thank us. Her face was etched with lines and her eyes looked tired from crying.

"It was nothing, we were glad to help," said Paul, holding out his hand.

"If we can do anything else to help, please let us know," I added.

"We've got some surplus land, if you want to turn your horses out somewhere," Paul said.

"They won't let him out on bail, not this time," said Mrs Tompkinson. "We'll have to sell everything, of course. But he wasn't stealing, only using other peoples' money." She made Mr Tompkinson's dishonesty sound like a disease.

We didn't talk much as we walked home together. I think we were all sorry that we hadn't got to know Fiona better. We parted from Sharon when we reached her house.

"I always thought Fiona was hiding something," said Paul, as we turned up our familiar drive. "Now I know what it was."

"It must have been hell," I answered, thinking of Dad working from dawn to dusk in old jeans and a darned sweater, comparing him to Mr Tompkinson and suddenly knowing that we were the lucky ones after all.

Just a Bit Different

Christine Pullein-Thompson

"It's that Sophy girl again. She thinks Pixie may have laminitis," said Mum, holding out the telephone receiver.

"Why doesn't she have the vet?" asked my brother Andrew, without moving a centimetre from his bowl of breakfast cereal.

"Because they can't afford him; it's the same old story," I answered.

"It's your turn anyway, Ginny," my brother said.

We were all tired of Sophy Stevens and her strange parents who were forever borrowing things, who could not afford a vet or find time to cut the nettles in their garden.

I took the receiver reluctantly. "It's Ginny here. What is it this time?" I asked, sounding bored.

"It's Pixie. He's standing oddly. Will you come and look? He's been lying down. I'm sure it's laminitis. I've looked it up in my *Veterinary Notes from A-Z*," she told me in a worried, childish voice.

"All right. I'll be with you in five minutes," I said, banging down the receiver.

"Finish your breakfast first," said Mum as I hunted

for and eventually found, my shoes.

"I want to get it over with. Can I borrow your bike, Andrew?"

My brother nodded, his mouth full of cornflakes. The kitchen sparkled with sunlight. Mum started to fill the washing-machine with dirty clothes. The day was warming up. It's going to be another scorcher, I thought, mounting Andrew's racing bike. Trying to work out whether it really was my turn to help Sophy Stevens, I pedalled through the village which was buzzing with tourists taking pictures of the old almshouses or staring into the small rushing river as though all the secrets of the world were there.

The Stevens live in a stone cottage. The outside buildings have been turned into a workshop where Mrs Stevens restores pictures. Mr Stevens teaches art at our local College of Further Education and has a beard. I parked Andrew's bike against the stone wall by the yard gate.

"It is so good of you to come," said Mrs Stevens, emerging from her workshop, her hair dangling down her back in a long, loose plait. "Sophy is so worried about Pixie, poor darling, and we daren't call the vet because we haven't paid the last bill."

And that was another strange thing about the Stevens, they told you everything – did what Mum called "Washing your dirty linen in public".

"It does seem to happen rather often doesn't it? I mean she's always worried about something; if it isn't his shoes, it's a snuffle in his little nose," I said. "And we are actually trying to get ready for the show the day after tomorrow."

"Oh yes, the show! Sophy's going too. I'm going with her on my bike. That's why she's so worried, poor kid, she's been looking forward to it for so long."

"Mum says disappointments are good for the character," I replied firmly, going in search of Sophy, thinking of all the things I should be doing at home, like schooling Seagull before it became too hot, or putting a double bridle together for the working hunter class.

Sophy was sitting in the pony shelter in the small paddock behind the cottage, where the grass was so thin you could see the earth showing through. Pixie was lying on a heap of clean straw, relaxed like someone on a beach in summer. Sophy's small, square face was puckered with worry. Leaping to her feet she said, "He's lying down, Ginny, and his hoofs feel hot. I'm so glad you could come. I'm sure it's laminitis, but I don't want to call the vet unless I have to. Shall I hose his hoofs with cold water? What do you think?" She was wearing

an ancient sports shirt, old-fashioned trousers and strap shoes.

I knelt down to feel Pixie's hoofs. "They're quite normal for a hot day," I said, standing up again to look at the tubby bay pony whose head was set on wrong.

"I found him here this morning, stretched out with his eyes shut. For a moment I thought he was dead. I did really," related Sophy, staring at me with large, soft, amber eyes. "And you know so much about ponies. I mean I don't know anything really; but you and your brother are experts," she continued while I was half flattered, half annoyed by the compliment.

"No one knows everything and even vets make mistakes," I said, feeling Pixie's short, thick legs, running my hand along his stomach, watching for any sign of pain in his rather small piggy eyes. "But honestly, Sophy, you are an idiot," I exclaimed, straightening up. "It's a hot day. Obviously Pixie has been sleeping, then having a nice rest away from the flies, and you think he's ill. If you ask me, it's you who's ill, a real nutcase. Can't you see how bare your paddock is? Why, it wouldn't give a Shetland laminitis; let alone a twelve-two pony."

As I spoke I could feel anger growing inside me. I thought of the hot bike ride back and of the time I had wasted, time which I would never have again; all because of a silly, neurotic girl called Sophy, whom I did not even like.

"Look, he eats all right," I said, giving Pixie crumbs from my pocket before pulling him to his feet. "And he looks all right and walks all right," I said, leading the fat pony across the paddock. "So how can he have laminitis?" I finished.

"I am sorry. I am truly. Please forgive me," whined Sophy.

And that was another thing I hated about Sophy – she grovelled and had no pride and was always ready to apologise.

"You like inventing illnesses because you're bored. Why don't you cut nettles instead? Your whole place is full of them. Soon they will be growing in your kitchen," I said, looking at the overgrown garden which stretched to the road, a jungle of nettles.

"Mummy keeps them for conservation; she says it's for the butterflies and ladybirds. She won't let anyone touch the nettles," explained Sophy in a small, defeated voice.

"Well, some of us are busy. So think twice before you ask us over to look at a sick pony next time," I snapped, mounting Andrew's bike, sweat trickling down my face. "Just count to a thousand. Or is that too much to ask?"

Mrs Stevens called from the doorway of her workshop as I rode past. "Coffee, Ginny? The kettle's on."

I shook my head and rode away to find Andrew, large, brown-eyed and efficient, in our stable yard at home. "Well, what is it this time?" he demanded, taking his bike from me.

"Nothing, absolutely nothing," I said.

"I would have murdered her. Why don't her parents sort her out?" asked Andrew.

"Because they are daft too."

"We won't go again. Next time we'll say no."

"And then it will be something really serious – raging colic, or acute laminitis, or a brain tumour, and we will be haunted by remorse for the rest of our lives," I said.

Hearing my voice, Seagull whinnied. Andrew had caught up our horses and he was looking over his stable door, with his head which tears at your heart-strings and a mane which is dark grey and casts a shadow on the whiteness of his neck.

"Pixie is so ugly. I don't know why Sophy loves him so," I said, starting to groom Seagull. "He's put together all wrong, so there's absolutely no hope of turning him into anything. And his quarters are higher than his withers and his head is set on wrong, so he will never flex properly."

"You are preaching to the converted, Ginny," said Andrew.

"But they paid five hundred and fifty pounds for him. Apparently someone told them he was a show pony," I said.

"The previous owner, of course, who then went laughing all the way to the bank," replied Andrew.

"Why didn't they take someone to advise them?" I asked.

"Because they are the sort of people who don't need advice," Andrew answered.

"Except from us," I said.

"They're arty-crafty, that's what they are," Andrew announced with a laugh.

"With nettles for butterflies and ladybirds," I said.

"They would preserve dry-rot for posterity. In other words they are nuts," said Andrew, putting my saddle on Seagull's door.

I thought about our parents as I tacked up Seagull.

Dad runs a successful do-it-yourself shop. Mum is a trained accountant. They are both down-to-earth and successful and our garden is perfect – half an acre of mown grass, beautiful shrubs, a patio where we hold barbecues, a swimming-pool. The stables are new, wooden loose boxes which Dad erected himself and there's a tack room and a feed and hay store. Our Land-Rover is also used to deliver goods from the shop, as is our new double trailer. The house is perfect, too, with fitted carpets throughout and all the latest gadgets in the kitchen . . . But now Andrew was leading out Earnest, his plain dark-brown hunter, tacked up in a double bridle and general-purpose saddle.

"I'm going to school him for the working hunter class," he said.

It was not necessary. We both knew that Earnest would win the class with or without schooling, because he had won it for the last three years.

Seagull is fourteen hands. He often wins family pony classes and is always placed in working pony competitions. He is an Arab–Welsh cross and a wonderful all-rounder. I know I shall never have another pony like him. He is one in a thousand. Now I mounted silently, cursing Sophy for wasting my valuable time, forcing me to ride during the hottest part of the day.

Sophy telephoned again on the evening before the show. "I was wondering whether you could tell me what one does in a family pony class. I am such an ignoramus," she said.

I had just finished cleaning my tack and was about to start on my boots. "You have to show the judge that

Pixie is quiet and well-behaved. You may be given a set test, or you might need to be able to make up your own," I said, trying to keep a feeling of impatience from my voice.

"Do I have to plait?" she asked next.

I recalled Pixie's thick neck. Nothing would change it; a few fat flabby plaits would only make it look worse.

"It's up to you. You don't have to. I wouldn't. Anyway he's a bit small to win a family pony class," I told her.

"I don't expect to win. I only get specials or consolation rosettes, but I don't care. We can't all be brilliant like you," Sophy said.

"I'm not brilliant. Will that be all?" I asked coldly, like someone serving behind a counter in a shop.

"Not quite. How long will it take me to get to Rushbrooke?"

"An hour and a half, if you want to rest him when you arrive, and don't forget a headcollar and a feed," I answered after a moment's thought.

"Mummy's bringing the feed and headcollar on her bike. Please can I tie Pixie to your lovely trailer?" Sophy asked next.

"I suppose so," I answered ungraciously, thinking that Andrew would be furious when he saw Pixie tied with our horses, as though we owned him.

"Shall I go by the road then?" she asked next.

"Yes," I yelled, not telling her about the bridle-way, which would not be suitable for her mother's bike, which I thought she would never find anyway because she's so incompetent.

"Thanks a million," she said.

"Not Sophy again?" asked Mum as I put down the receiver. "That child is becoming a menace."

The morning of the show was overcast. We rose early, groomed and plaited. Everything else we had done the night before, except for the rugging and bandaging which only took a few minutes. Dad had a business appointment so could not go with us.

"Bring back plenty of rosettes," he said, wolfing down bacon and eggs. "If I can get away I will be there by eleven to cheer you on."

He was wearing a suit, a pale grey tie, black shoes; he looked prosperous and successful. Mum was wearing a track suit. She loaded the Land-Rover with bottles of wine, sandwiches, Thermos, and a host of other things including mackintoshes, umbrellas and canvas chairs. It started to drizzle and I thought of Sophy setting off in the rain, poor inadequate Sophy with her mother peddalling beside her, sitting upright and peculiar on her old-fashioned bike, with oats and a brush in a knapsack on her back and a headcollar wound round her waist. Suddenly I wished I had told them about the bridle-way, because it would have saved them nearly a mile.

"I should have told them about Dog Lane," I said, struggling into my best jodhpurs.

"Who are you talking about?" exclaimed Mum. "Not Sophy and her mother? For goodness sake, they seem to think we're some sort of charity, the way they keep ringing up for things."

"Exactly," agreed Andrew, tying his Pony Club tie in front of the mirror by the back door.

It was still raining when we set off. Dad had just left in the BMW.

"Which way? Main road or lanes?" asked Mum.

"Main road. It's quicker and I need half an hour to warm up Earnest," replied Andrew.

The main road was full of holiday traffic and most of it was travelling very fast.

"I should have gone the other way," Mum said presently.

"How was I to know it would be like this?" asked Andrew.

"It's August, people go on holiday in August," I said.

"They're in a hurry to get to the sea. Let them hoot. I'm not driving any faster," said Mum, who doesn't like driving the Land-Rover. Blinding rain was hitting the windscreen now, while the wipers worked overtime. Suddenly, crammed together on the front seat, we seemed shut in our own small world. Andrew looked at his watch and sighed. Cars raced past us, their drivers hunched over their steering wheels, children and grannies in the back, wives in the front, caravans lurching, tents on roof racks.

"There's plenty of time, Andrew," said Mum, flashing her lights at a driver who missed us by centimetres.

Then without warning the wipers stopped working, and suddenly our world was blanketed in driving rain with our visibility down to a few metres.

"Blast, it was only serviced last week," exclaimed Mum, her hands small and white-knuckled on the steering wheel, her body as tense as a horse's before a race.

Suddenly I was overcome by a feeling of impending doom, while my brother asked, "Shall I get out and see what I can do?"

"Not in this traffic. I daren't stop now. Later, perhaps," replied Mum. Mum's quite short and she looked overhorsed, like someone on an eighteen hand horse when they should be riding a pony.

"Everything is going to be all right," Andrew said, as though talking to a nervous animal. "Don't worry."

"Famous last words! Touch wood!" I yelled back.

What happened next was, I suppose, inevitable. A barrage of lights came towards us through the pouring rain. There was the blaring sound of a car horn and the muffled noise of tyres screeching on wet road. Then the terrifying moment, which seemed so long and yet was only the fraction of a minute, while we waited for the impact of the crash and Andrew screamed, "Put your heads down." There was a thundering, shattering noise which shook us to the marrow of our bones and then the sound of splintering wood and, at the same moment, the crackly sound of shattering glass. There followed an awful second when we pitched forward and were held with a sharp jerk of pain by our seat belts, followed by a feeling of terror as we turned over – the whole of us, trailer and Land-Rover, and then the unbelievable sound of hoofs tearing into wood, which shook my inside and twisted it.

"Everyone all right?" shouted Andrew.

"The horses," I screamed. "The horses are hurt."

We were in a heap, but alive, as we struggled to undo our seat belts, panic gnawing at us, making our hands clumsy and our heads feel on fire. A moment later we knew we were wedged against a bank. But soon faces were peering at us, wet-faced and anxious. "Are you all right? We've sent for an ambulance," said a man who, in the circumstances, seemed grotesquely calm.

"The horses! Where are the horses?" I cried, wedged between Andrew and the bank, like someone in a strait-jacket.

Later, I was to discover that my knees were bruised and one hand was bleeding, but now I felt no pain; only a terrible anguish, as I shrieked, "Get us out. Please get us out."

"Steady there, steady, don't get excited. You are going to be all right." The man's voice was calming and his calm seemed like an insult. Then someone was helping Mum out, and I could see Earnest held by a man, his rug askew. Andrew got out next, then it was my turn, and someone kept saying, "Steady, take it easy. Easy now," as though I were a horse.

In the road a Mini lay upside down. For a terrifying moment I thought I was going to collapse. Then I was shouting, "Where's Seagull?"

There are some moments you never forget, moments which haunt you for ever. This was to be one of them. A plump woman with a shiny handbag hanging over one arm was leaning over Mum, who had fainted. Andrew was holding Earnest who was staring into the distance, his eyes wild and panic-stricken. Several people were talking loudly, at the tops of their voices. All this I took in automatically, without any of it really registering. Then a police car drew in behind me and, at the same time, I noticed that the Land-Rover's wipers were working again as it lay in the ditch, started no doubt by the crash, and this seemed the maddest thing of all. Then I was running, past the ACCIDENT sign just erected by the police and on past a line of angry, fuming drivers, with

the rain splashing against my legs and hammers going in my head, my eyes hardly focusing, imagining only Seagull injured, Seagull dying, Seagull dead.

Soon cars were swerving to avoid me. A driver hooted, another put down his window to shout at me, "Fool!" Let them hoot, let them yell, I thought insanely. Let me be killed if need be, but please God let Seagull be alive, not lumps of meat on the road. And as I ran, I remembered Seagull arriving at our place on my birthday, with a card tied with ribbon round his neck, reading HAPPY BIRTHDAY VIRGINIA. From that moment he had been everything to me – friend, confidante, my greatest joy. Tears were running down my cheeks now, unasked. My stomach was tied in knots, my legs as flabby and weak as jelly, yet still I ran. And then, suddenly, I stopped and I seemed to be waking from a dream as I stood looking at the traffic, knowing that if Seagull was still alive he could have gone the other way anyway. Then someone leaned out of a car to call "Are you all right, dear?" and I saw for the first time that I was spattered with blood. I didn't answer but stood like an idiot in the rain, with tears pouring down my face, tortured by indecision, not knowing whether to go back or carry on, lost in a deluge of grief and uncertainty.

A couple approached me now and gently led me to the side of the road. "You look shocked. Where are your parents?" the woman asked.

"I'm looking for my horse. We've been in an accident," I said and my voice was shaky and seemed to be coming from a long way off.

They started to talk to one another then as though I was not there. They appeared to be discussing hospitals, so I told them, "I'm not going anywhere. I am perfectly all right. My brother and mother are just down the road. I was just looking for my horse." My voice was steady but sounded unusually belligerent.

"You've been thrown, haven't you?" demanded the woman, who was dressed in a polyester dress which showed her rather large knees.

I shook my head, which made the hammers start again, *bang, bang,* each blow hurting more than the one before. "I tell you I am all right," I shouted, unnecessarily loudly. "I am simply looking for my horse."

Another car had drawn up now and a voice called, "Can I help?" I imagined myself being taken to hospital and kept under observation. And I hadn't found Seagull.

Then, like something in a dream, I saw him threading his way through the traffic, his grey head high and his eyes nervous. He was dancing rather than walking and for a terrible moment I thought, It isn't true. I'm seeing things and in a moment he won't be there.

A voice called "Ginny, are you all right?" and I saw that leading Seagull was Sophy, dressed in an old school mackintosh and wellington boots, her riding-cap on her head. She was soaked to the skin and her pudgy, red cheeks were glistening with rain. Her mother followed, pushing her old-fashioned upright bike.

"He stopped when he saw Pixie. He's all right. There's nothing but a few scratches," called Sophy.

They had straightened his rug, but part of his head-collar was broken and his bandages were twisted. I threw my arms round his neck and at the same moment Dad drew up behind us in the BMW.

"For God's sake, Ginny, you're covered with blood," he shouted as he got out. "Get off the road at once."

"Are you all right? I thought Seagull was dead but he isn't," I cried, burying my face in his mane. "Why are you here? Why aren't you at work, and where's Mum and Andrew?"

"My customer failed to show up. I was on my way to watch you win your class," Dad said. "Hop in, you need to see a doctor." I saw that Mum was lying in the back of the car.

"I can't. I can't leave Seagull," I answered, my eyes suddenly full of silly, wild, happy tears.

"We will take him home for you, don't worry," said Sophy, sounding quite grown up.

"Where's Pixie and what about the show? You can't

miss that," I cried. "Not after you've got ready and entered."

We had drifted into a lay-by to talk and it felt strangely peaceful after the road.

"Pixie is tied to a GIVE WAY sign. Sophy will fetch him, then we'll lead Seagull home for you – no problem," replied Mrs Stevens, leaning her bicycle against a convenient bank before taking hold of Seagull's headcollar rope.

"But you can't miss the show and it's three miles to our place," I cried.

"We don't care about the show. I wouldn't have won anything anyway, you know that," insisted Sophy, looking at me with her pale amber eyes. "And it is the least we can do considering how you've helped us time and time again."

"Exactly. A friend in need is a friend indeed," agreed her mother.

"And Earnest? What about Earnest and Andrew?" I asked.

"Andrew wasn't hurt at all; he's leading Earnest home already. Now hop in and stop making a fool of yourself," said Dad, holding the car door open.

Hesitating, I shouted to Sophy who had already set off to collect Pixie, "But will you be all right?"

And Sophy answered, "Yes, of course." And I knew they would too, because they were not such fools after all – just a bit different.

Skeleton Rider

Christine Pullein-Thompson

"My, you *have* done well! Just look at your rosettes!" exclaimed a tweedy lady holding a bull-terrier on the end of a lead.

The Melletts were accustomed to compliments. Derek, the eldest, raised his crash-cap and said, "Thank you, madam."

Felicity patted her grey pony and smiled. Lucy, who was only seven, pushed the cup she had won into her coat pocket. Simon leaned forward to count the rosettes on Hercules' bridle.

The show was over and the judges were standing together, drinking whisky. Ponies were being loaded into trailers. A weary steward was taking down the ring ropes.

"We always win a lot but today we really swept the board," said Derek, to no one in particular.

They had come to the moors for the holidays, bringing their ponies to the old farmhouse which Mr Mellett had recently bought as an investment. It stood in a valley, completely alone.

"If you're going back to Hellsbottom Farm," a man

shouted to them, "you had better get going because it will be dark soon."

"We're just off," replied Derek. "Anyway, we like the dark. We've got cats' eyes."

"You'll need them, mate," shouted the man. "And keep off Devil's Pike. It's no place for kids at night."

"Silly old fool," muttered Derek rudely. "We'll go where we like."

"He's drunk," said Felicity.

"We'll take the short cut," said Derek firmly, taking a map from his pocket. "It will save at least five miles." The ponies were in a hurry. Derek led the way on his skewbald, which was called Mousetrap and had pale hoofs and a wall eye. Felicity followed on the grey, Socrates. He was kind and wise, and had just won the under-fourteen jumping with three clear rounds. Simon's Hercules was quick-tempered and excitable. He wore a pelham with a running martingale on the bottom rein. Lucy's little brown Flyaway had a white star and made a noise when he galloped. They were all in a hurry to be home. They jogged and tossed their heads, while dusk came slowly over the wild countryside.

After a time the Melletts decided to sing. They began with "Ten Green Bottles," Lucy shouting louder than anyone. Then they sang "She'll be Coming Round the Mountain", "John Brown's Body" and "This Old Man". And then, because they were out of breath, they started to discuss the show again.

"I've won the most. I've got seven rosettes, one for each class I entered," boasted Simon.

"Well, I've got six firsts," cried Felicity. "And the Jumping Championship rosette; so I must be better. And what about Derek? He won the Gymkhana Championship."

"And I've won a cup, and it's going to have my name on it," cried Lucy, bouncing up and down in the saddle.

"We really showed the locals. They won't forget us in a hurry," said Derek, his voice full of pride, as he halted Mousetrap and took the map from his pocket.

"We should be on the front page of the local paper," suggested Simon.

"We turn off here," said Derek, stuffing the map back into his pocket. "We go over Devil's Pike."

"What a name!" replied Felicity, shuddering slightly.

"I don't like devils. I hope there are none around," Lucy said with a giggle.

They cantered along a track, Felicity looking back to see that Lucy was all right, while the boys raced ahead, yelling and whooping.

Flyaway puffed and shied at rocks. Lucy kept one hand on the cup in her pocket. She was beginning to feel afraid. The night was almost upon them and it made the scattered bushes look like monsters, and ahead lay Devil's Pike, a long dark ridge with nothing on it save two twisted trees, looking grotesque in the gathering darkness. But she did not say anything, because the Melletts never admitted to being afraid. One had to appear brave, however frightened one felt. It was a matter of pride, and the Melletts were a proud family.

Felicity was feeling nervous too. The boys were still ahead. She was glad to be riding Socrates, who did not mind waiting for Flyaway. In the distance, Devil's Pike appeared unwelcoming and hostile. She thought the trees along the top looked like tortured people, begging for mercy, and she wished that the moon would rise so that she could see what lay on each side of them.

But now the boys were coming back. "There's someone else riding. We heard hoofs and a neigh," explained Simon. "It wasn't an ordinary neigh." His voice was shaking.

"You're not afraid? Oh, Simon!" exclaimed Felicity.

"Of course not. Don't be ridiculous. I just thought you might like to know."

"I hope it's not the Devil," said Lucy, giggling.

"Do hurry up," Derek shouted impatiently. "It's getting later and later. Do you have to dawdle?"

He sounded on edge and suddenly they all felt uneasy, and the ponies sensed it and jibbed, refusing to go on. They ran backwards into each other. Stirrup banged against stirrup. Derek swore. Lucy started to cry. And now the night seemed darker than ever, and twisted trees looked weird and blighted, and a bird hovered overhead, calling like a voice of doom.

"For goodness sake, can no one ride?" cried Derek, beating Mousetrap with his whip. And then, at last, they were riding forwards again towards the pike, while the first glimmer of moonlight made a pool of yellow in the sky.

"I wish we had gone the longer way," said Felicity.

"So do I. Those trees look like devils, real devils," said Lucy.

"What's the matter – scared?" asked Derek in a mocking voice.

"No, but I don't like it here. Can you hear the wind moaning? It's saying something. Listen!" cried Felicity.

"Belt up," replied Simon, shivering. "People picnic here. I bet there's litter bins on the top."

Lucy was trying to think about the show. She remembered winning the cup. She patted Flyaway, then kissed him on the neck, and thought, God will keep the Devil away.

Then Derek spoke, and his voice was quite different from usual. His words seemed to dribble out in bits and pieces, and all of his arrogance was gone.

"Look, there's someone riding behind Lucy," he said.

They turned their heads and at the same moment their ponies started to gallop in a mad frenzy towards the pike. Felicity screamed. It was a scream which came from the depths of her being. It went on and on, echoing and re-echoing across the empty landscape. Lucy was frozen with fear. She was like a rabbit mesmerised by a stoat. She wanted to scream, but no scream came. Her hands were limp on the reins; she was incapable of doing anything; she seemed to have no strength left.

Derek simply dug his heels into Mousetrap. It was automatic. He didn't think. He simply fled.

Simon screamed. "It isn't real. It's an apparition." But the words never left his throat. He could feel his heart thudding against his ribs like an engine revving up, and sweat, cold as ice, running down his face.

What they saw was the skeleton of a boy, his teeth protruding, a faded crash-cap pushed down against his eyeless sockets.

His bones were ivory white in the pale moonlight. He wore an old coat which hung shapelessly on his fleshless bones, reaching to his knees which were encased in tattered breeches. His skeleton hands clutched reins, which led to a skeleton mouth full of ancient teeth – for the horse he rode had no flesh either, though he reached into his bridle as though he had once been a racer, and what was left of his cheek was wide, and his empty eye sockets were large and generous.

Lucy only looked once. She had no hope of outpacing the skeleton pair. Her sister and brothers had

drawn away from her now. Flyaway was roaring, his sides going in and out like bellows. The race was lost before it was begun. She was alone with the apparition, with no hope of escape, no chance, nothing.

From the skeleton's mouth came the words, "Beware, beware. Pride comes before a fall."

And then Lucy forced herself to look again at the mouth grinning down at her, and suddenly she could bear it no longer. She let go of her reins, her feet left the stirrups and, screaming silently, her small face contorted with fear, she fell into what seemed like nothingness and rolled over and lay still. And the skeleton laughed, a long hollow laugh, while Flyaway trotted on after the others towards the pike.

Socrates could not outpace the skeleton pair either. Felicity stared at the skull beneath the hat. "Go away," she whispered. "Please, please go away."

She started to pray. "I will never be nasty again if he goes. Please God, make him go. I'll go to church every Sunday. I'll be a nurse. I will devote my life to doing good – if only he will go away."

His hands were reaching out for her now, skeleton hands at the end of skeleton arms. "No!" she screamed. "No!" Then somehow she swung Socrates away, dear brave Socrates who never lost his head, and she was galloping away from the pike towards she knew not what, still praying.

Simon gripped his whip. Hercules could gallop no further. His breath came in gasps, his sides were lathered in sweat. The skull grinned at Simon, his mouth opened to speak. Simon lunged forward and hit the grinning mouth, but he seemed to be hitting nothing, and the mouth only grinned more hideously. Then Simon found his voice.

"Who are you?" he yelled. "Go away. I'll fetch the police. Help, help!"

He felt a bony arm round his neck, pulling him off. It smelt of nothing; it was light, lighter than plastic. It had no real substance. His knees clutched vainly at Hercules' expensive saddle, his hands tried to wrestle with the skeleton hands; then he was down, lying across a boulder, listening to the skeleton's laugh and his words which belonged with the wind, "You didn't win that time." And Hercules was gone, everything was black and without hope and he thought, We're all dead.

But Derek was still galloping and Mousetrap was fast and agile. He turned the skewbald this way and that, hoping to outwit his pursuers, but still the skeleton pair were gaining. The moonlight was brighter and the trees on the pike were pale gold, and somewhere far away a train could be heard rushing through the night, showing that sanity lived on, that trains still ran, that somewhere people were still eating and drinking, while Derek lived through this horror alone with his gallant Mousetrap.

"You won't get me!" yelled Derek into the face of the skeleton, if you could call it a face. "This isn't musical chairs. This is life and death, and I'm not afraid. I'm a Mellett, my father is a director of fourteen companies. My mother is the film star Marlene Carson. We're used to winning. We are on the up and up. We belong to the ruling class."

But his voice was carried away by the moaning wind and the skeleton went on grinning unperturbed. Derek's confidence started to ebb then, it was as though all his strength was going, all his beliefs, all his pride.

"Go away," he hissed. "I'm a prefect. Next year I'll be head boy. My grandmother was related to the Queen. My grandfather won the VC in 1918. You can't touch me. You wouldn't dare."

But he knew it wasn't true. The skeleton was not interested in his relations. He was out to get him. Derek could stand waiting no longer.

"I'll get you!" he screamed. "I'll teach you a lesson, you swine, I'll beat the daylights out of you. I'll break your arms, I'll kick your guts out." And then he leapt, his arms outstretched, his hands reaching for the grinning skull; but his arms met nothing, and the hoofs went on across the moors, and he heard a laugh which echoed and re-echoed. Then there was nothing but the dry grass, the pale moonlight, the moaning wind, and he was drifting away and could not fight any more.

He tried to say, "I'm a Mellett. My father is a director of fourteen companies, my mother . . . " but the words wouldn't come. Instead the wind moaned, "Pride comes before a fall." And the hills echoed it, and without another word, Derek passed out.

Felicity was still galloping. She could see a light now, which meant safety, but she was still too frightened to think properly and over everything else lay the fearsome catastrophe of Lucy. What had happened to her? Where was she? Felicity blamed herself. If only I had stayed with her. If only, if only . . . The words went on ringing in her head as she drew rein by a small farmhouse. Her tears were coming unasked in an unstoppable flood.

She tied Socrates to a gate. His head hung low, his

sides were drenched in sweat. He suddenly looked old and too tired to take any interest in anything any more.

She ran to the house and knocked on a low wooden door, crying at the same time, "Is anyone at home? Please open up. Be quick, please be quick."

"What is it?" asked an old woman, opening the door a crack and peering out as though she expected the Devil himself.

"I need help – the police, anyone," cried Felicity.

"You've been up on them hills, haven't you?" asked the old lady after a short, agonising pause. "Didn't anyone tell you that's not a place to go of a night on account of the old squire's son?"

Felicity shook her head. She felt like screaming. Everything was taking far too long.

"I've lost my two brothers and my little sister, Lucy, and she's only seven. Can I telephone? Please, I must be quick." She could feel panic running through her in sharp stabs of pain, and her teeth started to chatter as though they didn't belong to her any more, and that made her remember the skeleton's teeth.

But the old lady was opening the door now, calling over her shoulder at the same time. "George, George! Here's a young lady who's lost her brothers and little sister up on the pike." Felicity could see the telephone on a table in a small, low-ceilinged room, and it was like a miracle.

She rushed inside and picked it up. Another three seconds and she was saying, "Daddy, is that you?" thanking God that she had remembered the number.

"We've met a ghost," she shrieked through her chattering teeth. "I got away, but I lost the others. I don't

know where they are. They may be dead or something. I don't know, I don't know."

It was like someone else talking, and all the time her tears were falling like rain on a pad of paper which said "Messages" in red at the top.

"What *are* you talking about?" Mr Mellett shouted down the line. "I thought you were at a show. Who is lost?"

"Them. The others," whispered Felicity as the room spun round and round. "I'm in a farmhouse. We met a ghost."

"There's no such thing," answered Mr Mellett. "Speak up. Where's Derek?"

But Felicity had fainted.

George was putting rugs and a Thermos of tea into a

Land-Rover. He was old and slow. "He caused enough trouble when he was alive, but he's fifty times worse dead," he said.

"The girl's fainted. I've given her father directions," replied his wife. "Hurry, George. The little girl is only seven. They can die of fright at that age."

"I don't know what parents are coming to, letting little girls ride on the moors at night," grumbled George.

"Here they are now!" exclaimed his wife, as a car pulled up and Mr and Mrs Mellett stepped out of their Mercedes.

"Where is Felicity? Has she come to?" cried Mrs Mellett, smelling of perfume and wearing a suede coat.

"In there. I will take you inside. You must excuse the state of the house," replied the old woman, wiping her hands on her apron.

"I shall come with you," Mr Mellett told George, climbing into the Land-Rover. "I expect they are all right. We're a tough lot, tough as old leather."

He was wearing suede shoes and a suit.

"I've known little girls die of fright, like baby rabbits," George replied gloomily, starting the engine.

They found Lucy first, small and huddled like a hurt animal in the beam of the headlights. She was screaming. She had been screaming for a long time and her voice was hoarse and her eyes were not focusing properly. She stopped screaming when she saw them and started to shout "I want Mummy, I want Mummy" over and over again.

"It's all right, darling," said George, wrapping her in a rug. "We're taking you to Mummy."

He propped her up on the seat at the back of the Land-Rover where she sat staring at the canvas sides of the vehicle without seeing them, and drove on.

Simon was walking in a circle, concussed. He seemed to be concentrating very hard. He shook George by the hand and said, "I expect to win the jumping," in an aggressive voice; then he started to clap loudly and to shout, "Well done, Derek, well done . . . "

They sat him opposite Lucy, whom he ignored, and drove on.

Derek was lying like someone dead, his face was ashen in the moonlight, and for one second Mr Mellett's heart gave an uncomfortable leap and he thought, He's dead. But George knew better. "He's in a coma, or unconscious," he said. "Let's lift him into the Land-Rover – gently does it."

"Well, that's the lot," said Mr Mellett, grim-faced. "Now tell me about the maniac who is responsible and I'll have the police after him. I'll have him arrested and put inside, if it's the last thing I do. I know the local magistrate here, and the chief constable. I'll leave no stone unturned. I've got influence, you understand."

"There's some influence won't influence," said George, darkly. "And one of them is ghosts."

Later, sitting in front of a turf fire, George told Mr and Mrs Mellett and Felicity, who had recovered enough to listen, about the squire's son. All the ponies had been found by this time, Lucy, Simon and Derek were in bed in various parts of the house, and the doctor had been called.

Mr and Mrs Mellett sipped ginger wine, and the fire cast strange shadows on the old walls.

"It's the old squire's son, and it's a sad tale," said George, lighting his pipe. "As sad as any you read in the newspapers these days. He lived where you live now, what's called Hillsbottom Farm nowadays, though most people round here call it Hellsbottom. It was a big place in the old days and old squire Brownly lived there with his slip of a wife and their six sons, but it was the eldest, young Rufus, who ruled the roost. There wasn't anyone that wasn't afraid of him, except, some said, the squire. He was a terrible lad by all accounts. He beat and kicked the farm lads, and twice he galloped a horse to death. Not for any need, you understand, just for the fun of it. He set fire to the barn one year after a tiff with his father and burnt all the hay put by for the winter."

"That was in my mother's time," interrupted the old lady. "She was kitchen-maid at the house, and scared to death of young Rufus."

"But the squire was decent enough," continued George, "and, with time, he came to hate Rufus. He used to shout at him, 'It's your arrogance I can't stand. Pride comes before a fall. Why won't you learn that, you fool?' 'What fall?' Rufus would shout. 'I'm not going to fall.'

"Anyway, it ended in a quarrel. Some say the old squire had had too much to drink and didn't know what he was saying," continued George. "But I think he was sensible enough, though they say he was as mad as an old bull and had a gun in his hand."

"He turned him out," said the old lady, her voice cracking.

"He told him to get out and never come back," continued George, "and young Rufus took the best horse in the stable, his father's pride and joy. He rode out on yon pike and the snow was coming down in barrowloads, and the wind was howling like a pack of wolves."

"And he never came back," said Felicity.

"They thought he would but he never did. The squire rode up to look for him, and to this day no one knows what happened. Some say there was a shot, some say the squire shot him, but no one knows for sure," continued George, as though Felicity had never spoken.

"And they never found a body, nothing to point to where he went," said the old lady, "but they say he still rides up there on his father's horse."

"The house was burnt down, some said it was done out of spite, some said Rufus did it," said George, prodding the glowing turf.

Pride comes before a fall, thought Felicity. He was proud, and so were we. But we are still alive . . .

"I shall sell the farm," said Mr Mellett. "I only bought it as an investment. We'll go back to Berkshire in the morning."

Felicity thought, Dear, safe, beautiful Berkshire. Poor Rufus, perhaps he meant to go back, to repent and say he was sorry. Instead he died there up on the pike.

"We saw him, he was there this evening," she said slowly, and she remembered her prayers and how they were answered. We've got a second chance, she thought. We can try to be nicer.

The old lady had risen and was opening the door for the doctor.

Felicity looked at her father. He seemed much smaller, crouched over the turf fire. "You will have to believe in ghosts now," she said.

Downright Cruelty

Christine Pullein-Thompson

"He's tethered out there on the common, all weathers," said Mrs Beazley, enormous in flowered pinny and white sandals. "And he's stretching his poor neck for every bite. He's not a young pony either, you can see that. Mr Smith's talking about reporting them to the RSPCA."

"Them" were the Colchesters, a new family who had come to live in the village.

It was late breakfast time and nearly the whole of the Leadbetter family were in the beamed farmhouse kitchen, leaning against the Aga with mugs in their hands.

"We'll have to see them, won't we?" asked Sally, who was ten with blue eyes. "We'll have to tell them they're cruel."

"But nicely," said Mummy.

"I don't see how we can be nice, because cruelty isn't nice," said Eddie. "So why should we be nice? I vote we go and give them hell."

"I suggest you leave them alone; it's their business, not ours, and their pony has nothing to do with us," said Dad.

"A crowd of us can go," continued Eddie, as though Dad had never spoken. "I'll get some of my friends for back-up support."

"And it *is* our business, Dad," said Sally. "Because we love horses, that's why."

"It's downright cruelty, that's what it is," said Mrs Beazley firmly, picking up a dustpan and brush. "All weathers with nothing but mud to stand on, it shouldn't be allowed."

"Leave them alone," said Dad, putting on his wellington boots. "That's my advice. Don't interfere."

"You mean turn a blind eye," answered Eddie. "It's like saying nothing when your neighbour is battering his children to death. We all have a duty, Dad. And if that poor old pony is being ill-treated, we must do something. After all, we *do* know about ponies."

Sally thought that was like Eddie; everything was cut and dried with him, black and white, as though grey did not exist. "I think we should investigate," she said.

They checked their own ponies, who were still out, before Eddie went to the telephone and rang his friends. Sally could hear him talking, sounding important. "There's this pony tethered on the common standing on bare mud, never moved," he said. "I want us to go and see his owners, will you come and back me up? . . . Yes, well I suppose Sally will have to come too. You know how she is . . . okay, seven o'clock then . . . "

He put down the receiver. "We're going this evening; then we'll be able to talk to Mr Colchester," he said.

"Why not Mrs?" asked Sally.

"Better to talk to the man," Eddie replied grandly.

Evening seemed a long time coming. It was September and the leaves were changing colour on the trees, the ponies shedding their summer coats, the loft stacked high with hay.

Eddie's friends wore leather jackets and smelt of motor-bike oil. "Well, let's get this little business settled then," the largest said.

The Colchester children were talking to the pony when they reached the common; he was dark brown with a small star and about twelve hands high.

"What's he called then?" asked Eddie.

"Star," said the girl, who looked about eight.

"We want to see your dad," Eddie said next.

"He's not in yet," said the boy. "Can I take a message?"

"We'll wait... but it's about Star actually," Eddie said. "There have been some complaints."

"Yes, we know. He got loose yesterday but he won't get loose again," the girl said. "He slipped his strap. Ben didn't do it up tight enough."

"It's not that," said Eddie.

"What is it, then?" asked the boy.

"We'll wait for your dad," said Eddie.

"Yes, we will," agreed one of Eddie's friends.

"I'll just get Star some water," said the girl nervously. "I won't be a minute."

As though we need her around, thought Eddie, while Sally thought of her own pony, alone in five acres, rolling when he liked, standing under the big sycamore or in the shelter when it was hot.

She started to pat Star, saying, "He's quite fat, actually."

"We know he needs shoeing," said the boy, apologetically. "Being new we had a job to find a blacksmith, but he's coming next week; it's all fixed up."

And suddenly Sally felt doubtful for the first time.

"It's nothing to do with his shoes, son," said Eddie, sounding like Dad. "We all have blacksmith problems."

"Have you got many horses then?" asked Ben.

"Twelve. We breed Welsh cobs," said Eddie.

"How lovely," said the girl, holding a bucket of water up to Star. "So you must have acres of land. I wish we had."

"Here's Dad," said the boy as a car approached, which they followed into an untidy yard full of upturned wheelbarrows and old plastic bags.

Mr Colchester was a big man in a suit, with a striped shirt underneath.

"They've come to see us about Star, Dad," Ben said.

"What now? I'm in a hurry. And he isn't free, you can't ride him," he said, looking at Sally. "Sorry."

"We've got twelve horses of our own," Eddie replied icily. "So we don't need to borrow yours."

"That's all right then." Mr Colchester was going towards the house now.

"It's about the way you look after your pony, sir," called Eddie. "The village doesn't like it; they don't think he should stand on mud, chained in all weathers, straining for every mouthful of grass. Everybody's fed up with it, actually. Why don't you move him regularly, or buy him a longer chain if you're too lazy to move him to a new patch? It's bad enough being tethered, without being starved as well."

Sally thought, He's going too far, there's no need to be rude.

Mr Colchester seemed to be growing bigger and for an awful moment Sally thought he was about to pick up Eddie by the collar and fling him into the road. Then he seemed to explode.

"My wife is an AI; she's trained. She has probably forgotten more about horses than you'll ever learn. Star is tethered out here because he gets laminitis; and if he has hay or is in the stable he gets asthma. He has problems, that's why we have him, because no one else will. Have you ever seen a pony with laminitis? Do you know how painful it is? Would you like to talk to my wife? We're building him a shelter in the yard, only it isn't ready yet. Do you want to know anything else . . . ?"

"No," said Eddie suddenly scarlet. "Nothing, you've made your point."

"Clear off then," shouted Mr Colchester. "Before I do something I may regret later, and next time you go accusing someone of cruelty get your facts right first."

"Yes," said Eddie.

"You weren't to know," said the boy.

"It isn't their fault, Dad. There's no need to shout," cried the girl after his retreating figure.

And turning for home Sally thought, They're so nice. We should have talked to them first; now they will hate us for ever. We should never have believed Mrs Beazley.

The Old Dun Pony

Christine Pullein-Thompson

"I want that one, or that one. Not the old dun pony," I cried, standing in the dealer's yard, appealing to my parents.

"We'll have the dun," Mum said, unrelenting. "We want something safe and reliable."

"After all, it is your first pony," added Dad.

The dealer was unrelenting too. "You can come back and buy one of the others next year," she said pleasantly. "When you are experienced. I always have one or two sound blood ponies in my yard."

The dun was fourteen hands with an enormous eye and strong back and legs. "A real family pony," the dealer said. "And she knows everything – gymkhana-ing, hunter trials, hunting, even Pony Club polo. You name it and she's done it."

"And she won't show the dirt," said Mum.

She was called Sasha and arrived the next day done up in bandages with bits of foam under them. We turned her out in our paddock and watched her roll. I was still longing for something beautiful with an Arab head and long flowing mane. I wanted a pony which would impress my friends, which would prance a little and have slender legs and a coat as fine as silk. And she looked just like the ponies at the riding-school down the road.

Later Gareth telephoned to ask, "Have you got a pony yet?"

"Yes, and she's dun and plain," I answered.

"Oh. Did you say dun?" he asked despairingly.

And I thought of his chestnut with flashy socks.

"Yes, dun," I shouted.

"Let's ride together tomorrow. I'll call after school about five and show you the bridle-ways," he suggested.

"I'm riding with Gareth tomorrow," I told Mum later. "I only wish I had a better pony; Flashlight is half Arab and he doesn't half move."

Gareth is one of those people who never stops talking. He appeared in our driveway dead on time the next evening and said, "Oh, she's not too bad; she looks a real good sort."

"Don't be late, remember it's dark at six," Mum called nervously. "Are you wearing your hat?"

I felt disheartened as we set off together because Mum was treating me like a child and Sasha was merely "a good sort".

"I thought we'd go through the woods and then through Valley Farm," said Gareth. And then he started to talk and because he talked so much, we hardly trotted, so that when we reached the woods they were already dark and silent.

"We had better hurry," I said, pushing Sasha into a trot.

"The woods are always dark; don't worry," said Gareth, still talking. "It'll be light outside. Are you coming to the Pony Club rally next week?"

"Mum doesn't like me being out after dark," I said. "And it's getting darker all the time."

When we came out of the wood it was really dusk; cars had their lights on, and several drivers hooted and yelled out of their windows at us.

"Mum will be doing her nut," I said. "She'll be furious. She won't let me ride with you again, Gareth."

"Not to worry – I know a short cut. We can nip across the railway line," cried Gareth, pushing Flashlight into a trot.

"What does that mean?" I shouted.

"I know a crossing. It's all right, it's nearly always manned. Anyway, you can see the signal. It's quite safe," said Gareth.

We tore along a road past council houses. Flashlight shied at every dustbin but Sasha kept going, her ears pricked, enjoying it. And then we saw the crossing gates. Gareth halted in front of them. "Anyone about?" he called. There was a little hut on the far side, locked and silent. "It doesn't matter," said Gareth. "We can still get across. I'll just have a look at the signal."

Suddenly I felt fear gnawing at my insides. "Are you sure it's safe?" I asked nervously.

"Yes. We just have to be quick; no problem," answered Gareth, dismounting to open the narrow gate for pedestrians because the larger ones were padlocked. "You had better get off or you'll knock your knees. It's all right, the signal is down," he said.

I led Sasha through the gate.

"I'll hold her while you shut it. Hurry!" Gareth cried.

I slammed the gate and latched it. At the same moment Flashlight kicked Sasha and then she was trotting away along the railway lines towards goodness knows where, and Gareth was calling, "Whoa, little pony, whoa!"

I was screaming, "She'll be killed." And then we heard the signal change . . . "We'll all be killed in a minute," I shouted.

"Don't run after her," said Gareth. "Don't chase her."

"I'm not," I said, holding out my hand and calling to her softly, my heart beating against my side like a piston.

"I'm sorry," shouted Gareth. "I'll tie up Flashlight and help."

"He'll break his reins. You know he doesn't tie up. And you know you can't catch him. Don't be an idiot," I shouted, not daring to look ahead and wondering how many minutes we had left before the train came racing down the track and killed us both.

"But it's all my fault," cried Gareth, unable to keep quiet even now.

Sasha was grazing at the side of the track. I thought, If only I had owned her a few days longer she would have come to me now. But I'm really a stranger; and then, far away, the train was hooting as though it knew that somewhere ahead there was a fool like me on the line.

Sasha stared at me, trying to make up her mind, her ears pricked and her eyes calm. Some moments are with you for ever and this was one of them. How long will it take her to decide whether to trot off up the line

to certain death or wait for me? I wondered wildly. Please, God, help me . . .

And then she turned towards me. Running forwards I grabbed the reins and ran, dragging her after me towards Gareth and the gates, and all the time I knew that the train was bearing down on us like a devil out of hell, hooting wildly. Then I was by the gates with Gareth and Flashlight and the train was thundering past, full of travellers sitting at little tables, and then was gone into the night like a snake weaving its way through the dark.

"Well done," cried Gareth. "What a pony. I would never have caught Flashlight, not in a thousand years."

"I know. She's all right," I answered. "And I don't want a Flashlight. I don't even want a show pony any more. Sasha's perfect. And I'm going to order stirrup lights and a fluorescent waistcoat before I ride with you again, Gareth Westlake." And I imagined what another pony might have done and it made me shake in my boots.

Mum was waiting in the road outside our house. "Are you all right?" she called. "You're late. I've been so worried."

"Only just; it's a long story, but you were right about Sasha," I said. "And I don't want another pony, not as long as I live."

Burnt Rosettes

Christine Pullein-Thompson

I had been looking forward to Eastcote Gymkhana for a long time. It was quite near and reserved for novices so I had the chance of winning a rosette. My small grey pony, Dizzy, is super at gymkhanas, much better than I am, but somehow recently we had lacked co-ordination. Dad was away selling components in Saudi Arabia. Mum doesn't know much about ponies.

"You can go and see Mrs West. I rang her yesterday," Mum told me, seeing the despair on my face. "She says she'll help you and she's trained teams for the Pony Club so she must know what she's doing."

"But I don't know her," I said.

"Oh, go on Patrick, don't be so wet, she's expecting you," Mum replied.

As I tacked up Dizzy, he put down his head and coughed twice. "Don't start that again," I said, riding into the road.

Mrs West lives quite near and was waiting for me in a small paddock. "Nice to see you, Patrick," she called, waving a work-worn hand.

Dizzy stopped to cough again. It was a dry, hacking

cough. "I don't like the sound of that. Let's loosen his drop noseband, it's far too tight," said Mrs West, sounding worried.

When she had loosened the noseband, she told me to drop my stirrup leathers a couple of holes. "You are riding so short that you're sitting right on the back of the saddle," she continued, staring at me with piercing blue eyes. "Okay, now walk round on a loose rein."

"Aren't we going to practise gymkhana events?" I asked impatiently.

"Later, when your seat's right and your pony's relaxed," replied Mrs West, before Dizzy put his head down and coughed again.

I tried trotting, but he only coughed worse than ever.

"Come over here," called Mrs West. "Now listen to me, Patrick. Your pony isn't fit to go to a gymkhana. If you take him, you'll break his wind and he'll be ruined, Patrick, and I mean ruined for life."

"Not go to the gymkhana?" I repeated, my mouth falling open.

"Yes, that's right. Put your pony before yourself, Patrick. There will be other gymkhanas, but there will only ever be one Dizzy. Call a vet. Go on, get off and lead him home. I'll ring your mother and explain," she finished.

I dismounted, fighting back tears of disappointment. "Could he die then?" I asked miserably.

"Yes, he could," she said.

I led Dizzy home. Mum was waiting in the road. "Mrs West rang me just now," she said.

"I'm going. She's not stopping me. I don't care what

she says. It's only a little cough," I shouted.

"Well, he looks all right now. His ears are up," Mum said, staring at my miserable face. "And it does seem hard after all the work you've put in. Let's pretend we called the vet, if she says anything. He may be better in the morning. Everyone knows that Mrs West is an old battle-axe. She's always on at people over their animals."

We smiled at each other, united in our dislike of Mrs West.

Later I groomed Dizzy and turned him out with a feed and a wedge of last year's hay. Then I cleaned my tack in the kitchen, while Mum polished my jodhpur boots.

After that I ran up and down the lawn in a sack, because I was determined to win the sack race.

At nine o'clock next morning I was on my way to the gymkhana and Dizzy was still coughing. I kept praying that he would stop, but every time I trotted he started again – the same dry barking sound, which now sent a shudder down my spine.

The gymkhana was in full swing when I arrived. I entered for the clear round jumping and it took me three rounds to win the coveted red rosette, my first ever. Dizzy was still coughing and several times I had to stop to let him catch his breath.

I heard people muttering about him, things like "That pony shouldn't be here" and "Why doesn't the judge disqualify him?" But by now I had the hide of a hippopotamus, and no one was going to stop me winning more rosettes.

I won the sack race easily and came third in the musical poles. They were my first real rosettes and Mum was proud. "If only your father were here," she said.

But now a girl of about eighteen approached us. "Don't you think you had better go home?" she asked. "Your pony is spreading germs whenever he coughs, and I don't want my ponies to catch flu."

"Who's talking about flu?" asked Mum.

"I am. You're killing your pony. You should be prosecuted," shouted the girl, her face red with fury.

"You had better go. She's crazy," Mum said, but her voice was so shaky that suddenly my hands were trembling as I tied my rosettes to Dizzy's bridle.

"You're killing your pony," echoed in my ears as I rode away from the gymkhana – still in full swing. I saw Dizzy dead, his beloved head still, and eyes vacant. But it won't happen, she's just another scaremonger like Mrs West, I told myself, dismounting to lead Dizzy the last bit home.

Mum had bedded Dizzy's box deep in straw.

"The forecast says rain. And I don't want him to get worse. If he's still coughing in the morning, we'll get a vet. You were marvellous, Patrick. Did you hear me cheering you on?" she asked.

I nodded, but suddenly my feeling of triumph had died on the way home.

We gave Dizzy chilled water and lots of hay and a warm mash. I meant to look at him later, but was so tired I went to bed at eight o'clock and when I woke it was another day. Pulling on clothes I dashed downstairs. Mum was on the telephone. Outside it was raining cats and dogs. There was no welcoming head looking over the stable door, just empty space, for Dizzy was lying down with his sides going in and out like bellows, his

breathing punctuated by bouts of coughing and, as I stood staring at him, all the warnings I had been given came back to me. Why hadn't I listened?

Then I was tearing indoors shouting, "Mum, get a vet. Dizzy's dying. Hurry, please hurry."

"Don't panic," she cried, picking up the telephone.

"His wind's broken and he's dying," I sobbed as she started to dial. "He's ruined and it's all my fault."

"She'll be here as soon as she can," Mum said, putting down the telephone.

I went back to Dizzy. He wouldn't eat anything, not even an apple. I put my arms round his neck and told him that he mustn't die. "I'll never forgive myself if you do," I said. I looked down the road for the vet. It was empty. I rushed back indoors shouting, "Where is she? Why doesn't she hurry? Did you tell her it was urgent?"

"She's coming as soon as she can," Mum said.

I went upstairs to my room and looked at my rosettes. I had wanted them so much, more than anything else on earth, but now I hated them because Dizzy was dying and all because of them. For what were they compared to Dizzy? Nothing! Just bits of ribbon stitched together. In a fit of rage and despair I tried to tear them apart but they were too well-made; so I took them downstairs and burnt them in the open grate in the sitting-room. It took ages, but at least I was doing something to expiate my guilt.

Then the vet arrived. She was brisk, matter-of-fact and quiet at the same time. She knelt in the straw, listening to Dizzy's breathing, and waiting for her verdict was like waiting for a death sentence.

Dizzy liked her. I could see that. I think he was probably saying to himself, "Here's someone sensible at last!" Then she stood up and, looking at us with hazel eyes, said, "He's got a very bad attack of asthma. He shouldn't be bedded on straw and I think your hay affects him too."

"Is it fatal?" I asked, my legs as weak as water.

"Not unless you ride him, which could break his wind or, worse still, give him a heart attack. And you wouldn't do that, would you?" she asked, going to her car.

"I reckon it's been building up, and the straw was the final thing," she continued, slipping a needle into Dizzy's chest.

Afterwards she had a mug of coffee and wrote out a list of instructions, and told us where we could get shavings, and specially treated hay called horsehage, which wouldn't give Dizzy asthma.

"I'll drop in tomorrow, just a routine visit, that's all, because I know you'll look after him, Patrick, because you love him, and he's got a lovely home."

I wanted to cry, "You are wrong! I nearly killed him yesterday." But I knew it would never happen again, because from now on I would always put Dizzy first whatever happened, because compared to him rosettes were nothing, just great to win and great to hang up, but not worth a single pony.

The sky had cleared and the sun was shining. Dizzy stood up and, looking over his door, nickered softly.

"He's got to go out. Fetch his halter, Patrick. Don't just stand there gawping," Mum said.

But I wasn't gawping, I was thanking God for the second chance I had been given.

Firkin's Ghost

Christine Pullein-Thompson

The field was empty without Firkin. The grass was long and luscious. The branches of the oak-tree dipped low above it – everywhere was yellow with daisies. I missed his small mealy nose nuzzling my pockets, his bright eyes.

It had all happened while we were abroad basking on sundrenched beaches, but now I missed him beyond words. Mum had said it was for the best. "He will only suffer while we are away, become worse and worse. You know what the vet said, he said he had chronic laminitis," she told me.

Mum had grown up abroad where animals count for less, where they are not kept as pets, friends of a family. She has eaten turtles and lizards and snails. She does not understand.

But Dad had called the young vet, who arrived with a red-haired girl in his car, and the young vet had said, "He's had a good innings, after all. He's eighteen, that's not such a bad age . . . "

I could see that he was in a hurry, that he wanted to get back to his red-haired girlfriend, that he did not really care for poor Firkin, a round, middle-aged pony who ate too much.

"Can you do it while we are away?" Dad had asked. "Without us?"

"No trouble at all. Just leave his halter on the gate. We will arrange everything. We won't even charge you," the young vet said, and I saw that he had a pimple by his nose.

"Next Tuesday, then?" asked Dad.

"Will do," replied our vet, as though it was of no importance – just one more pony down the drain.

"What about the carcass – the remains?" asked Dad, avoiding my eye and looking all wrong in a striped town shirt with gold cuff-links.

"We'll see to everything, Mr Moore – no problem," called the young vet, hurrying back to his four-wheel drive car. "Tuesday it will be." And so the time had been decided like a death sentence, and we had gone to Spain.

Now I stood in the field in the evening light, missing Firkin. My heart ached for him, and his tack hanging by the back door was a living reproach.

"Still mooning about Firkin?" asked Mum when I returned indoors. "Listen, we'll buy you another pony, a better one." As though he was a piece of clothing, a coat, a skirt, or furniture – as though he could be replaced just like that.

"I don't want another pony, I want Firkin," I replied. "I want his mealy nose and his little ways. I don't want a better one; anyway, he was the best pony in the whole world."

"Laminitis and all," laughed Mum.

I took to haunting his field. It was flat, and lay under a wood where birds sang cheerily. And it was here one evening I first saw Firkin come back to life. He was staring into the field, his mealy nose like a beacon in the dusk, his small hoofs shiny with rain.

"Firkin," I yelled. "Firkin." But when I reached the wood he had vanished.

I returned indoors. "I've just seen a ghost," I announced. "Firkin's ghost."

"Don't be absurd, there's no such thing as ghosts," replied Mum, dishing up fish-fingers. "You're imagining things, and I don't like you out in the field so late. Anything could happen."

"He's returned to haunt us because we murdered him," I cried, and burst into tears.

I had supper in bed that night. Mum sat beside me, explaining that ghosts don't exist, that such things are just part of one's imagination. "When you wake up in the morning, everything will be different," she said.

But it wasn't. I was still missing Firkin. It was a wet day, and in the evening I returned to the field and found hoofprints in the wood, leading along a narrow track. But the ghost of Firkin did not come – there was no sound but the sighing of the wind in the trees, and the scuttling of rabbits in the undergrowth, and the falling rain.

When I returned to the house Mum said, "I don't want you loafing about the field any more. You'll be kid-napped. Stay in and watch television, and what about preparing for school?"

"There were hoofprints," I said, "small ones. How does a vet kill a pony?"

"Don't be morbid," replied Mum.

"I want to know."

"With a humane killer. It is all over in a moment," said Mum, buttering toast.

I imagined the young vet with the pimple by his nose killing Firkin. Perhaps the red-haired girl had assisted, and a truck with a winch, which called itself a horse ambulance, had taken him away to be turned into dogs'-meat.

I hated myself for not fighting harder to save poor Firkin. I looked at his tack and thought, He'll never wear it again, never, never, never. And all because I was too feeble to fight for him. His bit was small and worn, his browband large, because he had had a broad fore-head.

"Here, let me hide it. I'll put it somewhere else," cried Mum, seeing the tears rolling down my cheeks.

"And don't go to the field any more – okay?" And she put the tack in the cupboard under the stairs.

"We'll buy you a puppy, a lovely, lovely, cuddly puppy," she said.

"Laminitis is curable, isn't it?" I asked.

"No, not if it's chronic. Here, I'll look up the word 'chronic' in the dictionary," said Mum, going through into the sitting-room. "But he was just a pony; you musn't turn him into a human – they *are* different."

"Yes, nicer, ponies are much nicer," I answered. "They don't start wars, or drop bombs, or murder one another . . . "

"Here it is – 'Chronic – confirmed, permanent, bad, intense, severe, etc.'," read Mum. "'Established, abiding.' It doesn't say incurable, but it means it."

"We could have had a second opinion," I argued, staring through the window into the dark outside. "If he had been human, we would have had a second opinion. You don't put humans down, do you? And his death must have been violent, or he wouldn't be haunting us now."

I slept very badly that night. I dreamed that Firkin was back in our field. I heard him whinny. He came to the gate and called to me, and it was so real that I woke up crying. It was five o'clock, and dawn was breaking. I suddenly felt that Firkin was very near, that I had to find him. I dressed in jeans and a sweater, put on wellington boots because the grass would be wet with dew, and silently let myself out of the house without even the creak of a board.

Outside the world was new and damp and empty. It was all mine, except for a cat padding softly along our rather suburban road, and birds perched on telegraph wires, surveying the scene.

The road looked beautiful – the houses slept, their curtained windows like closed eyes, the cars outside still and lifeless. I slipped under the rail fence, waded through dew-wet grass. A mist lay on the woods, cobwebs more fragile than spun glass festooned the brambles. Why don't I do this every morning? I thought, while above me the sky turned rosy pink. I had reached the woods now. I thought I heard a whinny and there were fresh hoofprints on the soft earth.

Then I saw something moving in the distance, misty in the morning light, and my heart began to race – Firkin! I started to run, stumbling over roots, brambles, tearing my jeans, fear mixed with suspense. He will fade away in a minute, I thought, become part of the mist, because ghosts fade with the dawn. I am only just in time.

I rounded a corner. Beech trees stood as tall and straight as guardsmen on parade, but Firkin had gone. Cocks crowed in the distance, birds sang, while tears ran down my cheeks like rain. I waited for my heart to stop beating, for reason to come back. I told myself it was useless. I told myself that Firkin was dead and that everything was in my imagination, that I was going mad. I looked at the trees, so tall and silent, and cried, "Help me, please, someone help me," but nothing moved nor spoke, and then I saw the hoofprints again, clear and definite in the damp earth, and decided to go on. The path wound between the trees and I imagined my parents getting up, seeing my open door, looking for me. I imagined them going down to the field and calling my name. "Olivia, Olivia, where are you? It's breakfast, Olivia. It's schooltime. Hurry!"

But I felt drawn to the hoofprints like a hound to a scent. I had to go on. I turned another corner and the sun was sparkling on the cobwebs and the dew was drying. The track led downhill and there was the smell of cow in the air; it was wide and clear, and I started to run, imagining the school bus leaving without me.

I reached a clearing where rabbits clustered like people at a bus stop. I turned left, following the hoof-prints, and heard a donkey braying, "Hee-haw, hee-haw."

Next I saw rooftops and then a farm snuggling at the end of the track, and still the hoofmarks led on. I stopped there and thought, Suppose I really have imagined the whole thing... What can I say? My boots were wet and shiny, my hair full of brambles, my sweater stuck with burrs, while I stood wavering, wondering what I could say if anyone asked me why I had come. I could see chickens scratching round a barn door, and a Jersey cow standing by a gate. Should I say I'd seen a ghost? No, that would make me well and truly mad. I would pretend I had lost a dog, a puppy called Maisie. It would be a lie, but only a white one, I reasoned, walking on slowly towards the farm.

Everything needed painting; it was about as far as you could get from our neat suburban home, where chosen shrubs filled the garden and the lawn is mown every other day throughout the summer.

Nettles grew in clumps about the yard. A donkey was tethered on what once had been a lawn. Then I heard someone calling, "Hurry, for heaven's sake, or we'll be late for school again."

And another voice replying, "Blast school."

Then something which made my blood run cold.

"Have you put Firkin in?"

"Not yet."

And Firkin was *my* pony.

"Well, he's waiting."

"He always is."

I walked into the yard then and looked around. A tall boy came out of a shed and asked, "Who are you?"

He had blue eyes which looked straight at you, a scornful mouth, long hands. He was wearing dungarees.

I was struck dumb.

"We've got a visitor," he yelled. "I think it's the little girl who used to own Firkin." And three more children appeared and stared at me.

"So?" asked a girl with a long plait down her back, the largest of the three. "What do you want? As far as you are concerned Firkin is dead. You wanted it that way. You wanted your beastly holiday in Spain. You wanted him turned into dogs'-meat. You didn't want to nurse him. Well, we've nursed him back to health."

"But the vet said – " I began.

"Why do you listen to vets? Especially Patrick. Everyone knows he's useless," the girl said.

"We thought it was for the best," I said, and suddenly I felt very small and feeble. "I wouldn't have come all this way if I hadn't cared. I loved him. I didn't want him put down."

"Why did you let it happen then?" asked the girl. "Surely you can manage your parents."

"Shut up," the boy said. "Can't you see she's crying?"

"You can have him. I don't mind. I just want to see him sometimes, that's all," I said. "I thought it was his ghost. I never thought he could be alive. I'm so happy. I just want him to be alive. If I can't have him, it doesn't matter. I don't deserve him anyway."

"He's over there," said the boy, taking my arm, and there was Firkin waiting outside the barn door. "We starved him, then kept him on shavings and fed him only on straw. He was all right in a week. Of course you must have him back, he's yours. We'll help you look after him. You can have Matthew for company. He's the donkey; but you must ride Firkin every day and keep him in while you are at school. All right?"

Firkin whinnied when he saw me. He looked slim and lovely and his little hoofs were neat and newly

trimmed. "He's such a lovely pony," the girl said. "He deserves a good home."

"How did you know he was going to be – put down?" I asked, my arms round Firkin's neck.

"We wanted Patrick to look at the cow's udder and he offered to fit it in with a visit to put down your little pony," related the boy. "We couldn't believe it."

"So we kidnapped Firkin, halter and all, and left a message saying 'We've changed our minds. We're keeping the pony.' It took some nerve, didn't it, Phil?" said the girl.

Phil nodded. "Keep him in all day. We'll bring him over this evening with Matthew," he told me.

"But I haven't got a stable," I answered.

"Use the garage, turn the cars out. Don't be dim," Phil said. "We'll help you. We understand laminitis, don't we, Briony?"

"Sure."

"We must get on or we'll be late for school, you too," said Phil. "See you about five."

"Why was he in the wood?" I asked.

"There was nowhere else to put him," said Briony, opening the barn door. "We have hardly any grass."

"Do you know the way back?" asked Phil.

"I think so."

"Don't get lost."

The wood was warm and friendly now, even the trees seemed to be singing in the breeze. I ran and everything looked greener and more beautiful because Firkin was alive after all. Mum was just up when I burst into the kitchen.

"Good Lord!" she cried. "Where have you come

from? I was just going to get you up. I thought you were in bed."

"I'm hungry, terribly hungry," I cried, seizing a cereal bowl. "You were right about ghosts, they don't exist, or only in one's imagination." And I started to laugh and couldn't stop for ages. When I did, I said, "Guess what? Firkin is alive; he's coming back this evening. Isn't it wonderful?"

"Now I know you really are mad!" exclaimed Mum.

"Just wait and see, wait until five o'clock. He's coming with a donkey and he's got to live in the garage in the daytime. He's cured," I cried, gobbling cornflakes. "I can ride again, every day. He must be exercised. The vet was wrong; it wasn't chronic. Oh, I'm so happy."

"I'll believe it when I see it," cried Mum. Then she mouthed at Dad, who had just come into the kitchen, smelling of aftershave, "She thinks Firkin's coming back. She had better see a doctor."

School dragged by, and by the time it was over I had decided it was all a dream. But punctually at five there was the pad of unshod hoofs on the road outside and Phil's voice calling, "We're here." And the three of them were by our gate, Firkin, Matthew and Phil, and it was the happiest moment of my life, and even Mum couldn't say it wasn't true.

Please Tame Him

Diana Pullein-Thompson

At the animal sanctuary Jason Cook and Jane Wright were known as the two Jays. They looked like brother and sister, both being fair with blue eyes, but were actually friends and neighbours. Jason loved the birds and Jane their enemies the cats, and both adored the dogs who often arrived in a desperate state. The sanctuary was run by Pete and Debbie Brown, assisted by volunteers, and, of course, the two Jays, who petted the dogs and cats, helped with cleaning runs and cages, and went for sponsored walks in aid of the place. Naturally they longed and longed to take all the animals home, but, since their parents had dogs, Pete thought this might be unwise.

"They'd frighten the birds, quarrel with the cats and be jealous if you imported one of their own kind into their homes," he said.

But one wet day, when Jason and Jane dropped in on their way back from school, all that changed.

"Come and see our new arrival," said Debbie, looking harassed as she pushed a strand of dark hair out of her peat-brown eyes. "We can't keep him." She took the children to a small dark shed, opened the door a crack and pointed at a terrified blue roan pony cowering in a corner.

"Of course, we don't usually take ponies, as you know, but we had to break our rules for this one – I mean, look at those scars. He's obviously been beaten. But he can hardly turn round in here and he needs daylight."

"Can we look after him, please?" chorused the Jays.

And they knew that thought had already crossed Debbie's mind when she said, "You've got outbuildings, haven't you, Jason?"

"Not a stable," he replied doubtfully. "Sheds."

"But a garage you don't use," cut in Jane.

"Full of junk and it only has broken double doors."

"We could leave them open and I could buy six brackets and put bars across," Debbie said. "We would supply bedding and food." She glanced at Jane too. "Please tame him for us?"

"Yes, yes, oh please yes," cried Jane.

"I'll have to check with Mum and Dad," said Jason.

"Fair enough," agreed Debbie. "He's called Smoky, by the way, and he's not dangerous and, anyway, he has no shoes, so if he did kick it wouldn't be fatal. But he needs oceans of loving care, and Pete and I . . . well you know how busy we are. I mean there's fund-raising as well as the caring and the assessing."

"We'll make friends with him. Show him we care," declared Jane.

"You've hit the nail on the head," said Debbie. "I knew you would understand."

"Our holidays start tomorrow," said Jason. "Come

on, Jane, let's find Mum and Dad." He ran to his bike and the next moment the two Jays were cycling down the track that led to the lane that ran beside their houses.

Of course, it wasn't easy. Mr Cook was afraid Smoky might interfere with Jason's work when term started again and Mr Wright wondered whether the responsibility was too great, and both mothers were afraid their children might be bitten or kicked. "Wild animals are not to be trusted," Mrs Cook said. "And supposing he escapes and rampages all over the garden."

"Listen," Jason said, "if we don't win Smoky round he could be destroyed. This is a matter of life or death."

"Please," pleaded Jane. "If we all worried about what might happen we would never move at all."

"She's right," exclaimed Mrs Wright. "And if the pony needs help . . . "

"Oh, go ahead," said Mr Cook. "That garage could do with a clear-out, anyhow."

"As long as they keep him off my borders," murmured his wife.

"We promise," said Jason.

The next morning the Jays moved the junk and Pete and Debbie brought the brackets and rails, and bales of hay and straw, and turned the garage into a sort of stable.

"And here's a worm dose for him, too," Debbie said. "And some insecticide to kill his lice when you can get near enough to spray him."

In the afternoon a friendly cattle truck driver backed his vehicle to the Browns' shed, from which Debbie gently shooed Smoky up the ramp. Then it took less than ten minutes to cover the mile to Jason's small, well-kept home. The children were waiting, a Labrador, Olivio, at their side with Mrs Cook, who cried, "Oh no! My turf, my turf. Oh, not the pansies, please not the pansies," as the truck thundered up the grass track to Smoky's new stable.

"The grass will soon grow again, madam, and look, the flowers are all right," the driver said, before reversing to the entrance of the building and putting down the ramp. Debbie then crawled in through a small hatch at the side of the truck and the terrified Smoky plunged down into the stable.

"Super," said Debbie, fixing the rails.

"Brilliant," said Jane.

"Great," said Jason.

"That was a piece of cake," said the driver, lifting the ramp. "I never expected it to be quite so easy."

When the truck and the Browns had left, the Jays filled a net with hay and hung it in the stable on a peg which had once held a worn-out vacuum cleaner, and put a bucket of water close to the rails. Then they sat down in the straw.

"Isn't he lovely!" Jane said. "But we won't try to touch him. We'll wait for him to touch us."

"I read in a book once – I think it was called *The Children of the New Forest* –" said Jason, "that when people in the old days wanted to tame ponies they kept them short of food, so in the end they welcomed the owners, because they knew their arrival meant the end of hunger."

"Smoky's not wild, though. He's just terrified because he's been bashed about," Jane said, looking at the pony as he stood trembling, as far away from the children as possible.

After an hour Smoky, driven by hunger, moved closer to the haynet which hung quite close to where the children were sitting.

"You see . . . " began Jane, and then stopped as the sound of her voice sent the pony back to the far end of the stable again.

"Idiot, " said Jason.

"Shut up," said Jane. "I'm getting tired of sitting here."

"Why don't you go home and get a book?" suggested Jason. "Then, while you sit and read, I'll get one for myself."

At six o'clock Mrs Wright arrived. "You've got to come back for tea," she said.

"All right," agreed Jane. "Jason?"

"I'll stay," he said. "And then you do the same for me."

So Smoky had someone sitting with him from three in the afternoon until nine at night, when the children had to go to bed. And in that time he came near enough to them to pull a few mouthfuls from the net.

The next day Jason and Jane refilled his haynet, gave him fresh water and sat down again in the straw and played dominoes. And Smoky watched them with wide dark eyes in a blue roan face which sported a middling sized blaze, and they ignored him. After a bit he edged nearer to the haynet, but leapt back when they started an argument about the game.

"We shouldn't have shouted," Jane said.

"He's got to get used to our voices," insisted Jason.

"Yesterday you called me an idiot," Jane said.

"Yesterday was yesterday and today is today," Jason countered.

"That's gobbledygook," said Jane, stretching out in the straw. "I suppose we'll have to try and muck him out tomorrow."

"I don't know," mused Jason. "Didn't Pete say one of those scars was caused by a pitchfork?"

"Look," whispered Jane, "he's surprised to see me lying down. Why don't you lie down, too?"

"Oh, all right."

"See," hissed Jane, raising her head. "He's not trembling any more."

"We're less threatening flat out," Jason said. "He's got a very delicate head."

"Sensitive," murmured Jane. "When he gets fatter he'll be brilliant."

Now Smoky moved from his corner and very cautiously approached the haynet. As the Jays froze, he started to eat within touching distance, but when Jane said "Brilliant", he bolted back to the rear of the stable. Then they kept talking and after a bit, accustomed to their voices, he returned and started to eat again. They went to lunch at different times, so he was not alone, and in the afternoon they sat very still in the straw, holding out hands full of pony nuts, and by four o'clock he had fed from both their hands.

"We're winning," said Jason and almost threw his arms in the air in triumph.

"Why was he beaten?"

Jason shook his head. "Who knows?"

Jane repeated the question when Debbie turned up to see how the Jays were managing, and Debbie said Smoky had been bought by a violent man for his daughter. "A beastly spoiled brat called Tracey, a rotten rider, who thought she knew everything. I don't know the whole story, but I'm told she held Smoky on such a tight rein that he couldn't jump properly and when he knocked the jumps down she hit him. Then, because he was so frightened of his mouth being hurt, his head went up; he started star-gazing and Tracey put him in a tight running martingale and a long-cheeked pelham and he felt trapped. Then Tracey's father bought an old stockman's whip, so that he could hit Smoky on take-off to make him jump higher, but the bit and the running martingale coupled with Tracey's tight rein were too much, Smoky panicked, refused to approach the jumps at all, and finally plunged in all directions, and reared until he chucked Tracey off and she broke an arm. After that Smoky wouldn't leave the stable at all, unless Tracey's father got behind him with the whip or hit him with a pitchfork. When Tracey's arm mended she announced she wasn't going to ride any more, and then her parents' marriage broke up, and after that Smoky was simply left in the stable with next to no food and water."

"What a horrid man. Why did he buy a pony?" asked Jane.

"He wanted to please Tracey and he wanted to keep up with one of his mates, whose little girl was winning all the prizes for miles around."

"And how did you hear about him?" asked Jason.

"From Mrs Gutteridge, who runs the local branch of the RSPCA," replied Debbie. "She asked me to help, as she's looking after nineteen abandoned dogs single-handed and hasn't space for a pony, and there isn't much chance of bringing a case for cruelty, because Tracey's father's gone abroad. However, she threatened his ex-wife with a charge, and the horrid woman, who didn't care a button, said, 'Take the pony. We don't want it.' End of story so far."

"How could they have been so foul?" asked Jason.

"When violent men are unhappy they take it out on someone. His wife got the better of him, so he beat the pony. Simple," said Debbie.

After Debbie left, the Jays took Olivio and the Wrights' Border terrier, Biscuit, for a walk, and when they returned Smoky whinnied a welcome so they rushed and put their hands through the bars and fed him handfuls of pony nuts. Then, after refilling his net and bucket, they sat in the stable and after a bit he sniffed Jane's back, touching her spine with his grey lips.

"He knows we're his friends," Jane said.

"He has no one else," observed Jason. "Ponies are herd animals, aren't they? Which means they are lonely without company. He *needs* us."

"And we need him. Think how bored we might have

been," reflected Jane. "Mum would have dragged me out shopping, and you . . . ?"

"Dad was thinking I might join a junior sports club."

"Mum says riding lessons are too expensive – ten pounds an hour."

"Wouldn't it be great if we could go on another pony-trekking holiday?" said Jason, harking back to two idyllic weeks on a Welsh farm, where they had looked after the ponies as well as riding them.

"Not enough money," said Jane.

"Same here," agreed Jason.

When Pete called that evening, he handed the Jays a canvas headcollar. "Try to get it on him, then you'll have some control," he said. And to their surprise Smoky stood quietly while they did just that.

"Well done, you're winning," said Pete. And Jane put her face against the pony's neck and rubbed her cheek along his coat.

"He knows we love him," she said.

"Yes, but see . . . " Pete put out an arm and Smoky jumped back, ". . . he doesn't trust me yet."

"You've done wonders," Mrs Wright said, looking over the bars later that evening. "But he won't be able to stay in this garage for ever."

"Tomorrow we'll give him his worm dose," Jane told her, "and then he may get fatter. Look at his ribs, terrible – and the next day, and the day after," she giggled, "perhaps we can ride him."

"Don't count your chickens before they're hatched," warned Mrs Wright. And she was right, for next morning when the Jays went to the stable before breakfast, the

top bar was down and there was no sign of Smoky.

"Stolen," shrieked Jane.

"Why?"

"For meat. I want to kill them."

"He might have got out," Jason said. "Come on." They fetched their bikes and searched all the lanes and looked in all the nearby fields and returned weak with hunger to find Mrs Cook in her gateway, furiously waving her arms.

"My herbaceous border," she wailed. "And you promised – hoofmarks everywhere and two peonies broken and the golden rod . . . !"

"Sorry," cried Jason. "He must have nudged the bar out of its bracket. Listen, Mum, we'll clean out his stable and give you all the manure for your roses."

"Big deal!" cried Mrs Cook, "Manure won't replace the peonies. It's odd," she continued, calming down a little, "Olivio didn't bark."

"I think a thief tried to steal Smoky and he escaped," said Jane, "which means he's still loose somewhere. I am terribly sorry about your flowers."

"Of course he's loose," said Mrs Cook. "I saw him with my own eyes, didn't I?"

"But where?" shrieked Jane. "You didn't tell us and we've been looking everywhere."

"You've only just got back," pointed out Mrs Cook. "He's behind the garage, stripping the leaves off my beech hedge."

"Behind the stable?"

"Steady," said Jane, as Jason rushed down the path. "We mustn't frighten him. Let's get some pony nuts first." But to their amazement Smoky walked up to the children as if they were old friends.

"He knows we're not like Tracey," Jason said, with a thread of triumph in his voice.

"I expect ponies can smell aggression, like dogs," remarked Jane, stroking the pony's neck. "Let's tie him to that post and muck out the stable and give your mum the manure you promised, and then spray him. And tie the rails to the brackets."

"Breakfast first," said Jason.

The children were busy all morning mucking out the stable and grooming Smoky with their dogs' brushes. They saw lice at the roots of his mane, but, finding he was terrified of the spray, they left them there.

" He's so good, I think he's reverting to an earlier self, in the days before Tracey," Jane said.

"Just in time," said Jason. "I don't think I could have spent another day sitting in the straw."

"Nor me," agreed Jane.

When Pete came to see how they were getting on he said, "Great stuff. Keep it up." When they told him they couldn't use the spray, he showed them how to pick out the lice and crush them.

"Ugh!" cried Jane.

"You can't be squeamish if you're looking after abandoned animals," Pete said. "It can be horrific cleaning them up. Think of yourself as a nurse, Jane."

"I'll do it," said Jason.

"Can we try riding him?" asked Jane.

"Oh, I don't know about that. We don't want any broken bones, do we? I think we must leave that to the experts." Pete laughed kindly as though trying to lessen the blow, before driving off in the sanctuary's van.

Fixing Smoky's haynet later that evening, Jane said, "We are his friends, look how he nuzzles my pockets. Why should a pony mind his friends on his back?"

"I suppose Pete knows," said Jason.

"He's not a riding expert," replied Jane. "We must try where there's long grass, so we won't break anything if Smoky bucks us off."

"There's no long grass here," said Jason, filling the water bucket.

"In our garden, then," Jane said, "You know my mum calls weeds wild flowers. And Dad's too engrossed in his computers to care."

The next morning, which was Monday, the Jays were relieved to find the rails in place. They gave Smoky his worm dose in a feed and took him for a long walk after breakfast, with the dogs, letting him stop here and there in the lanes to graze on the banks. Their parents were at work, but Mrs Wright had arranged to pop back from the shop she ran, selling second-hand clothes for children, to see how they were getting on. Last holidays she had known they were both safe helping at the sanctuary. Jason's mother had told him to phone her at lunch-time at the building society where she worked, to confirm that they were all right.

"Anyone would think we were nine-year-olds," complained Jason, who, like Jane, was thirteen.

The children put Smoky back in the stable while they raided the Cooks' refrigerator for food, before leading him to a neglected patch in the Wrights' garden, where willow herb, ragged robin and grass all fought for space and trumpets of convolvulus ran riot on a broken-down fence.

"It's a pity we haven't got any tack," said Jason.

"And lucky that we learned to ride bareback taking the ponies back to their fields last summer."

"They weren't like Smoky," Jason reminded her. "They were quiet because they were trekking on the hills all day." Jane picked two strands of grass so that they could draw lots, and Jason drew the shortest so she had first go. Jason held Smoky with one hand and gave Jane a leg-up with the other, and then he led Smoky round and round the disused patch of garden.

"He feels lovely, but his back bone – it digs in a bit," said Jane.

"He's clever enough to know that we would tack him up if we were going to try driving him over jumps," said Jason. "My turn."

The Jays rode Smoky at the walk, making him stop when they pulled at the headcollar and said "Whoa!" and continue walking when they squeezed with their calves and said "Walk on". Now and then they gave him a handful of cake from their pockets. And because he had no bit he wasn't frightened of his mouth. After an hour they took him back to his stable. And later in the afternoon they were upset to find him lying down in the straw.

"We've worked him too hard," cried Jane. "He's still weak."

"He feels safe," said Jason. "We've won the first battle."

Then Smoky got up and stretched and they felt a rush of pride coupled with the inner warmth people experience when they achieve something they care about very much.

When Pete came in the evening with more hay and straw, Jason could not contain his enthusiasm.

"We rode him bareback and he was wonderful," he cried.

"I told you not to!" exploded Pete. "Supposing he bucked you off and broke your arms. Your parents could sue me."

"We'll get their permission," Jane promised. And that evening she badgered her parents until they said:

"All right, if you're very, very careful and wear your crash-helmets."

But during the night when she was in bed, Jane heard her mother say to her father, "They are getting too attached to that pony, when Debbie finds him a permanent home they'll be heartbroken."

"There's no way we can keep him here," Mr Wright said, "and with both of us out at work . . . " Jane felt her blood turn cold.

"He'd need a field," her mother said. "I don't think they understand that a pony is a great responsibility. I mean, they'd give their lives for him now, but in a year or two when they've got exams . . . "

". . . And want a social life," added Mr Wright.

"Exactly," agreed his wife. "And then who's left holding the baby?"

At this point, aware that she was eavesdropping by mistake, and not wanting to hear any more, Jane blocked her ears.

On Tuesday the Jays put on their crash-helmets and led Smoky down the lanes, taking it in turns to ride him. It was a wild day with strong winds and light rain. The scudding leaves, the weekend picnickers' paper and plastic wrappings rustled and fluttered as though they had a life of their own, but Smoky was too interested in the grass on the banks to bother, and the children let him graze for an hour.

"I wish we had a bridle, then we might trot him," Jason said. "As it is, with everyone so afraid we might break our arms, perhaps it's too risky in a headcollar."

"Anyway, we shouldn't ask him to trot when he's still so thin," said Jane.

Then the next weekend they struck lucky when Jason's father, a builder and decorator, insisted he went with him to a car boot sale. "Come on, son, don't let me down," he said, for until Smoky's arrival Jason had gladly gone with him.

Jason returned triumphant with a bitless bridle in

his hand. "Three pounds fifty pence. Dad paid. They call it a hackamore," he said. And astonishingly, for such coincidences don't often occur in life, it fitted.

"God meant you to find it," Mrs Cook said.

So that day the Jays trotted Smoky along a track which ran between two lanes. And then they rode him to the sanctuary, very carefully because the road was busy. Pete was trying to clean oil off a white duck and Debbie was in the kennels, sitting with a small brown dog which had been found tied to a post on the edge of a motorway. But they both paused in their work to look briefly at Smoky.

"You've done wonders," said Debbie.

"A bit more weight and he'll be smashing," said Pete.

"We got this hackamore, because we thought he would be frightened of a bit," said Jason.

"Good for you," said Pete, returning to his duck.

"And soon, Mum says, you'll want to find him a permanent home?" hazarded Jane, with a heart like lead.

"Afraid so," said Debbie, "unless your parents want you to have him, but he needs to have a field and other ponies. He can't spend his life in a converted garage, once he gets fit."

"We'll talk to them," Jason said, sticking out his jaw. "Make them see sense."

"I'm not sure it is sense," admitted Jane on the way home. "Debbie is right. He should be out in a field with other ponies."

" And if he gets another bad home? We understand him, that's what matters."

But the parents, who knew each other well because of the Jays' friendship, were united in their opposition. Times were bad, they argued. There wasn't a lot of building work for Mr Cook and Mrs Cook was afraid she might lose her job in the next cutback. Mrs Wright's shop only made a small profit and Mr Wright was putting money by for their old age.

"You can have all our pocket-money," offered Jane, "and we won't need to be taken on holiday."

"And we won't go on school trips," added Jason.

"And we'll earn money, too."

"Doing what?" asked Mr Wright.

"Washing cars," replied Jason.

"It's not on," said Mr Cook. "That's final."

"But," said Mr Wright kindly, "you can both have a pony-trekking holiday next spring. Right, Geoff?"

"Agreed," said Mr Cook, "on condition, Jason, that you join the sports club, so you won't be too one-sided."

That night Jason and Jane slept badly and Biscuit, who shared Jane's bed, snuggled up against her as though understanding her misery. Jane remembered that, although there were a few permanent residents, a wounded owl, a one-eyed cat and a peacock with one leg, for example, it was the sanctuary's policy to get its patients back into the wild or into homes as soon as they were fit.

"Otherwise we've no room for new cases," Pete said.

As days passed by, Smoky grew fatter and calmer, and never failed to welcome the children with a whinny. They rode him down the lanes and round and round the wild patch in the Wrights' garden, and without jumps, whips or bits to frighten him, he behaved beautifully.

Watching them with Smoky one afternoon, Debbie said, "You've done so well. I can't thank you enough, but now it's time we looked for an expert to reschool him properly."

Jason turned on his heel and walked away. Jane led Smoky back to his stable and put her arms round his neck.

"I know you're going to miss him," Debbie said, "but we have to put our animals' interests first."

Jane went home, prepared tea for her mother and herself and then ran next door again and found Jason moodily slumped in front of the television set. "I've got an idea," she said.

"What?"

"We ask the riding-school for advice tomorrow."

"We can't take Smoky down the main road," snapped Jason without looking round. "And he needs shoes."

"We can bike there with the snaps Mum took of him."

"So?"

"See if they can help."

"He's not ours to sell."

"Who said sell? He's ours if we want him, if our parents agree."

"Oh, all right," agreed Jason, who wanted to watch his television programme in peace. "A mad idea, but I'll come."

It was a five-mile bike ride and when they arrived the yard was so smart they hardly dared enter. At last a pupil saw them at the gate and asked what they wanted.

"To see Christina Philby-Jones," said Jane, who had got the owner's name from a school-friend who rode there.

"Come in," said the pupil. "My name's Ottoline."

"We're Jason and Jane."

At the tack room door, Ottoline offered them a can of Coke to drink and rang a bell. Then Christina Philby-Jones sauntered across the yard. Tall, in tight fitting cream breeches and black rubber boots, her fair hair bobbed, her eyes green-grey like the sea, she was everything Jane wanted to be.

"What can I do for you?" she asked. "Do you want to book lessons? – The appointment book, please, Ottoline."

"No, no, look!" Jane pushed the snapshots into her hands.

"A half starved pony." Christina said, screwing her eyes up against the sun. "Not yours?"

"No. You tell her, Jane," said Jason.

"Well," began Jane, and then suddenly the whole story poured out.

"Hang on," Christina said, when Jane had finished. "Let's look at those photos again. What do you think?" she said, passing them to Ottoline.

"Could be Bilberry," Ottoline said. "Poor pony, he was such a super four-year-old! I heard he had changed homes."

"Could be super again," said Christina. She looked hard at Jane and Jason. "He came here to be backed and broken. He's New Forest with just a touch of Arab . . . You look surprised. It's not such a coincidence because we are the only people breaking-in ponies for miles around. And we don't charge the earth because it gives our working pupils experience."

"We don't want to lose him," Jane said.

"He trusts us," Jason added. "We're riding him in a hackamore because he's frightened of a bit."

"That's fine," Christina said, "so long as it's a temporary measure. Hackamores press on the nose and can interfere with the breathing in fast work – cross-country, that sort of thing. Listen, we could make use of a pony like that in the school."

"We don't want to lose him," repeated Jane, her mind running on a single track.

"I thought we might come to some sort of arrangement," continued Christina. "Supposing we give you both lessons, an hour each a week in term-time, more during the holidays, in exchange for the use of Smoky? And we'll reschool him for you. I've got a brilliant girl called Patience starting here soon – a wonderful name, isn't it? – and Smoky would be just the job for her. You see, I like my pupils to learn to ride and train all sorts and, from what you say, Bilberry – sorry, Smoky – is an interesting case. I shall put him in an unjointed rubber snaffle. Can you bring him over?"

"We're not allowed to ride on the main road," said Jason.

"Quite right," said Christina. "Shall I pop over to see him then?" The Jays said yes, of course, and they must talk to Debbie and Pete, and Christina said the sanctuary people were wonderful but not exactly equitation experts. Then she took Jason's address and shook the children's hands as though they were grown-up. "I'll phone tonight," she finished. "Take great care biking back."

And heading homewards the children suddenly realised at the same moment that a dream was coming true.

"Lessons," shrieked Jane. "We shall learn properly, at such a posh place, too."

"It's unbelievable," Jason shouted against the wind and the sound of the cars racing past them. "But something's sure to go wrong."

But it didn't because Christina wanted to help the children, who reminded her of own struggles to learn to ride, and Smoky because she remembered him as a very sweet pony with great potential, and she hated to see a good pony ruined.

The next evening at a meeting between Christina, Debbie, Pete, the Wrights, the Cooks and the Jays, Christina's offer was accepted. Three days later the kind cattle truck driver returned and this time Smoky was led up the ramp by Jason.

"To go to school with us," Jane said.

Patience, who had freckles and nut-brown hair in a single plait down her back, lunged Smoky in the covered school, then rode him, first in the hackamore, later in the rubber snaffle, and whenever he put his head too high or started plunging, she circled him or rode serpentines. Watching from the gallery the children could see he was relaxing more each day, partly, they thought, because he had returned to a place where he had been well-treated and was going back over lessons he had already learned there. Soon they rode him in the school, too, and Patience took him over poles on the ground and then cavaletti, always on a loose rein, and gradually he began to enjoy jumping again.

So they all learned together, and a year later Jane and Jason each won third prize on their reschooled Smoky, at a local show, one in a jumping class and the other in a handy pony competition.

When he was fifteen Jason shot up to 170 centimetres and grew out of Smoky, but Jane never grew taller than 165 centimetres. Jason stopped riding and later became an airline pilot. Jane trained as a landscape gardener and married a fruit farmer called Crispin. And when Smoky was a little old for riding-school work he came to live with Jane and Crispin and Crispin's horse, George, and when he was twenty he helped teach their daughter, Josie, to ride. And so he ended his days happily in a paddock near their house, cherished by Jane, and, if he wanted extra attention, he would hang his head over the timber fence to be petted by Crispin's pick-your-own customers.

Too Much Trouble

Christine Pullein-Thompson

We all cried when we sold Gypsy to the Strongs, Fiona most of all. They seemed such a nice family, three children and a rich dad and they had promised to give her a good home.

"When you sell her we want first refusal. We don't want her to go anywhere else," said Fiona seriously. "We want her back."

"That's all right, dear, you'll have her back, not to worry, darling," said Mr Strong, large and affable.

"You'll buy her a friend, won't you?" insisted Fiona. "Because ponies are herd animals and shouldn't be kept alone."

And I remember I thought, Fiona's got one hell of a cheek!

"We'll buy another pony and a hunter for me, that's a promise," said Mr Strong.

When Gypsy finally went we felt bereaved. Fiona cried for hours. It was no good telling her that her feet were nearly on the ground when she rode Gypsy. It was no good explaining that Gypsy would have hated hanging about doing nothing. Fiona had won dozens and dozens of rosettes on Gypsy and she wasn't winning any on her new pony, Holly.

It was nearly a year later that we decided to visit Gypsy. We were going that way to see Aunt Betty and it was Mum's idea. We filled our pockets with bits of carrot and bread and Fiona said that we must stop to buy Gypsy some Polos, because she loved them more than anything else.

The Strongs' house was called The Chestnuts and was new pretending to be old. It had a three-car garage and a swimming-pool, and a paddock of five acres and three new loose boxes. We made straight for the paddock. Fiona was leading and already calling, "Gypsy, Gypsy. Come up, Gypsy."

Everything was immaculate, without a weed to be seen. The paddock was immaculate, too, with decorative trees planted and newly-mown grass, but there was no Gypsy in it.

"She's not there. She's gone," shrieked Fiona, with tears streaming down her face.

"There must be an explanation," said Mum, sounding worried. We hurried to the house and Mum pushed a bell which went *ding-dong* and in seconds Mrs Strong appeared, looking like a model.

"We dropped in, because we thought we might see Gypsy," Mum said.

"Oh yes, Gypsy. Well, she isn't here any more. She was too much trouble. She had trouble with her feet, we had to have the vet. We didn't know ponies were so much trouble. Then she got out on to the lawn and ruined it."

"She was lonely. I told you she needed a friend,"

cried Fiona. "Would you like to live in solitary confinement, Mrs Strong?"

"She was dangerous. She threw the children off. And you are a very rude little girl," replied Mrs Strong, starting to close the door.

"Dangerous?" cried Fiona in disbelief.

"Where did she go?" I asked.

"I can't tell you. My husband dealt with it," replied Mrs Strong before shutting the door with a bang.

I don't think Aunt Betty enjoyed our visit. None of us felt like eating and Fiona was crying all the time.

When we reached home Mum rang Mr Strong. "He says Gypsy threw off the kids and was a load of trouble. He says she made the whole place smell of horse and there was hay everywhere. They sent her to a sale three months ago," said Mum when she had put down the receiver.

"What are we going to do?" I asked.

"Ring everyone we know," cried Fiona, and did all evening.

"I think she's gone for dog's-meat," Fiona said later.

"I think she's tethered somewhere with nothing to eat, with no water and flies everywhere, which is probably worse," I said.

"I'll try to get catalogues of all the sales held recently. We may be able to trace her. Don't give up hope," Mum said.

Later Dad suggested that we advertised for Gypsy. So we wrote out an advertisement which went like this: WANTED: NEWS OF SMALL BAY PONY CALLED GYPSY SOLD IN JANUARY. REWARD OFFERED and we put our telephone number and address underneath. We sent it to three local papers and a riding magazine and waited – and waited – Fiona by the telephone for hours on end, while I waited in the road for the post morning and afternoon. Mum said we were going mad. Dad said that we had everything out of proportion. "There are people starving to death in Africa and you fuss like this over a pony," he complained.

"But we know her. We've never met the people starving in Africa," replied Fiona. "There is a difference, Dad."

Then at last, after a week had passed, the telephone did ring. Fiona was upstairs so I got to it first and a childish voice said: "I think I know where Gypsy is. I ride her every Saturday. She's at a riding-school. She's lovely."

"A riding-school? Which one?" I cried.

She told me the address of the Littlebrook Riding-School. "And it's all right. I don't want any reward," she added before putting down her receiver.

We were all overjoyed until we started to imagine the riding-school.

"I bet she works all day long and is half starved," Fiona said.

"With a saddle pressing on her withers," I added.

"She's probably like a toast rack. Oh, I do hate people," cried Fiona.

The riding-school was fifty miles away, but we went there the very next day. We filled our pockets with oats and carrots and bits of bread again, and Mum drove because Dad was working.

"If it's a terrible place we'll have to bring her home straight away. We couldn't leave her there. Have you got your cheque book with you, Mum?" Fiona asked.

"Bring her home fifty miles?" asked Mum.

"Yes, I can ride her," said Fiona defiantly.

"But you are too big."

"I'll lead her then," said Fiona.

As we drew near the riding-school, we all felt on edge. I was biting my nails to pieces and Fiona had screwed herself up into a tight ball of nerves.

"I have got my cheque book, but they may not want to sell her to us and we can't make them," Mum said, as though preparing us for a catastrophe.

"We'll steal her then, or have them prosecuted," replied Fiona.

"Now you're being silly," snapped Mum.

The riding-school had a magnificent yard with loose boxes on three sides. Mum led the way to a door with OFFICE on it.

"We are looking for a small pony called Gypsy. She used to be ours," she said to the proprietor, who was slim and dark-haired.

"Oh, she's here all right. Was she stolen or something? We bought her at a sale in January in good faith," she said.

"She taught us to ride," said Fiona, suddenly meek and awed, I thought, by the size and poshness of our surroundings.

"We just want to see her, that's all," I said.

"Well, she's over here. Follow me," said the proprietor, whom we later learned was called Sally Timpson. "She's a lovely little pony, isn't she? I knew as soon as I saw her that she was all right . . . And she's a real character. She had been mismanaged, that's all. She'd had

laminitis and was far too fat even though it was January."

And then we saw Gypsy being led out of a loose box, her eyes shining, her bay coat glistening with good health.

"She's a great favourite here," said Sally Timpson. "You don't want to buy her back, do you? I would hate to lose her, I really would."

"No, we just wanted to see that she was all right, and she is, isn't she?" asked Mum, smiling at Fiona and me.

"Even better than when she was with us," I said.

"But how did you know she was here?" asked Sally Timpson.

I told her about the advertisement and then about the girl who had telephoned.

"Oh, that would be Emily Lester. She brings Gypsy Polos every Saturday," said Sally Timpson, laughing.

"Oh yes, she loves Polos," cried Fiona.

"We are going to give Emily a reward, though she said she didn't want one. What would she like?" asked Mum.

Sally Timpson said that Emily would like a big book on riding, full of coloured illustrations. "She's only seven and mad about horses. A real sweetie," she said.

"So you see there are happy endings sometimes," Mum said as we left. "Life isn't all bad homes and lonely ponies."

"I would like to meet Emily. I would like to thank her myself," Fiona said. "And I would like to pay her back for all the Polos she's bought Gypsy."

"I hate the Strongs, because if Sally Timpson hadn't been at the sale and hadn't bought Gypsy, anything could have happened," I said. "She could have been dead by now or ruined for life. And they did make some promises, didn't they?"

"I know one thing, if we ever have to sell a pony again, I'll be much more careful. I'll get references and written assurances. I'll never trust anyone again," said Mum, driving towards home.

The Ponies Must Go

Diana Pullein-Thompson

Megan Jones's dad had worked in the mines since his teens, like his father before him who had trained the pit's ponies. As long as Megan could remember, he had grumbled about the dirt, the back-breaking labour and the dust which might damage his lungs. But when the pit closed and Mr Jones was out of a job he became like an angry dog, snarling at everyone. Now that he had all the time in the world, he simply didn't know what to do with himself, and, although he had been paid a large sum of money to compensate him for his dismissal, he was afraid to spend it. Other retired miners took their wives, and maybe children, for a holiday in Spain or the Greek islands or even to the United States of America, but not Dylan Jones.

When he was a miner he had spent many of his spare hours helping Megan with Snowman and Romilly, plaiting their manes before shows, using the horse trailer he hired to pull behind his car so that Megan, who was an only child, should not ride along busy roads. And he had never tired of telling her the stories his father had told him about the gallant little ponies which had worked so hard pulling trucks of coal along the underground railway.

Megan's mother said the closing of the mine had been too sudden. Everyone had thought the government would save it and when it didn't the shock had been too much for her husband. "Give him time and he'll be his old self again."

But Mr Jones, afraid he might never find another job, could only see poverty ahead and one evening, after he had spent a useless hour at the Job Centre, he told Megan the ponies must go. "We've all got to tighten our belts," he said, "and I can't go on paying for their shoes, their vet's bills and their winter fodder."

"Both?" she asked in a small, stricken voice.

"Yes, both, before the autumn."

Megan didn't cry. At thirteen and a half, she thought she was too old for tears. Instead she went up over the hill to the rough fields, which the Jones's had rented from the Coal Board. She sat on an upturned bucket and looked sadly across to the area her dad had fenced off and rolled for a schooling ring and at the jumps he had made for her, and at the shelter and shed he had built for the ponies and their tack and fodder. Although these things had meant a great deal to Megan, she now felt her father had wasted his time. Poor Dad. Would anyone else want them now? Or would the weeds grow rank and tall, and the wood rot, and the place become tumbledown. But, most of all, her heart cried out for the ponies. She imagined the emptiness of her life when they had gone and the anxiety she would feel about their new homes.

Megan had come a long way since the day, sunlit

and glorious, when she had set out with her dad to buy Snowman, a dappled grey Welsh pony of twelve-two. It was hard at first because there wasn't a local Pony Club, and she had learned much of her riding from books, but one year when Mr Jones was working a lot of overtime he had paid for her to go on a course where she had been taught elementary dressage. Then, by chance, she had met Mrs Fairweather, an ex-riding-instructress who lived in the next village, who had driven over once a week to teach her.

"I love coming and you keep me in practice. It's such a pity my own kids don't like riding," she said. But, because Mrs Fairweather was married to a pit manager who sided with the government, Mr Jones put a stop to the lessons.

"We don't need her charity," he said.

Now, as Megan sat on the bucket, her mind ran back over all these and other events, dwelling longest on the show where she had won first prize as the best rider. Was all this really coming to an end?

With a heavy heart she went across to the shelter where Snowman and Romilly were sheltering from the sun and the flies, and they whinnied to her. She stroked their necks and then examined them as her father had taught her, to check that they had suffered no cuts or bruises during the day. Snowman ruffled her thick dark hair with his lips and Romilly nuzzled her pockets for tit-bits. She stood between them, feeling for a moment that special peace which came when she was with her ponies, before anger and resentment made her shake her thick hair and vow that she would not stand by and let the ponies go. She would fight, find a way to pay for their keep. Calamity did not have to follow calamity. Dad would be glad because he loved the ponies, too, although the fight had gone out of him. And Mum? Well, even Mum, who was allergic to animals because of her asthma, didn't really want them to go. How many times had she said to Megan, "I want you to be happy."

Now Megan ran her hands over Romilly's coat, remembering how Dad had admired his colour when they bought him. "Duns," Dad had said, "are hardy. They keep going all day. They're more reliable than chestnuts and tougher than greys."

"I'm going to keep you," Megan said. "We belong to each other." And she felt determination crushing her sadness. Then, after checking the ponies' water, she walked down the hill into the valley.

The next day was Saturday, so the new strong Megan caught a bus into the nearest town and scanned a newsagent's notice board where usually some people advertised for jobs and others for workers. But this time there wasn't a single notice offering employment. So Megan went to a café and asked to see the manageress, who was plump and blonde with very high heels.

"Do you need anyone to wash up?" Megan asked.

"You must be joking. With five hundred adults unemployed in this town, do you think we would take on a child?"

"I'm not a child, I'm a teenager," Megan said.

"Oh, you are, are you? Well, to me you don't look a day older than eleven. Please don't waste my time." The manageress turned on her heel and went back to the kitchen.

Next Megan visited a pet shop. "I was just wondering whether you need anyone to mind your animals?" she asked the doggy-looking owner, while inspecting the guinea-pigs.

"You want to be paid?" the owner asked, blinking through her large spectacles.

"Yes," stammered Megan. "I need money."

"Don't we all," said the owner. "If I need a paid minder I'll give my own daughters the job. Sorry, dear."

Then Megan caught the bus home, spending the last of her pocket-money. She walked to the field and tacked up Romilly and went for a ride across the rough land by the disused pit and along the road and tracks which had once been busy with lorries moving coal. She saw the great slag heaps and the huge piles of fuel no one wanted and the chimneys through which no smoke would pass again. And she thought of all the little ponies who had spent the best part of their lives toiling down in the pit without ever seeing the light of day.

She wished she wasn't the only girl at her school who rode and Romilly and Snowman were not the only ponies on the hill. If they sold just one, she thought miserably, the other would be lonely. Autumn, Dad had said, because that was when they would start to need hay and their bin of pony nuts would be finished. It was now mid-September. When did autumn begin? October? November?

If only, Megan reflected, I could play the violin like Rhiannon Hughes or the clarinet like Darren Lloyd, I might try busking, or, if I had a voice like Margaret Morgan I might sing at parties or join a church choir. As it was, with so little money around, Dad would accept the first offer which came along, for since the pit closed he had lost all interest in the ponies.

As Megan rode down the terraced street passers-by stared at Romilly, who was very handsome with his black mane and tail, his black points and list and noble head. She saw him reflected in the one shop's window, ears pricked, tail well carried, for as usual he was walking with an air as though the world belonged to him. But duns were out of fashion these days. Everybody seemed to want palominos. Snowman would be easier to sell, because, although he had lost some of his dapples with age, he still looked like a very expensive Victorian rocking-horse. Dad, she remembered, had already decided they should preface the Snowman advertisement with *Suitable for beginners.*

It was odd, Megan thought; for months and years everything went on the same and you never expected it to change and then suddenly something happened and your life fell apart. What would she do when she returned from school and had no ponies to care for? Most of the young people in her street were much older than she was and her few school friends lived several miles away. Dad said she would have to buckle down and study hard. There was no future, he said, for those like himself, who had never been to college.

So deeply was Megan immersed in her thoughts that it was several moments before she became aware of a whimpering down in the ditch on her left. Then she brought Romilly to a halt, dismounted, and found a black sack half covered with earth. At first she drew back, thinking it might be rotting rubbish, but then the whimpering started again and she saw a tiny black paw sticking out of a hole.

Holding Romilly's reins over one arm, Megan knelt down, pushed her fingers in the hole and ripped open the sack, and out fell a thin, half-dead puppy.

"Oh! Oh, you poor little thing!"

Romilly might have pulled back, jerking the reins from her arm, but, being very sensible, he stood stock-still, while Megan held the puppy close and it weakly licked her hand with a tiny pale tongue and tried to wriggle its body by way of thanks. Megan's instinct was to take the puppy home, but, remembering her mother's asthma and her father's depression, she rode instead, with the puppy under her arm, to the police station.

The officer on duty said he had no record of a lost dog. "We've got a kennel at the back, but you know he'd be lonely there, so small he is. And the dogs' home van won't call before Monday. Could you not be keeping him yourself while we make inquiries?"

"Mum's allergic to fur," Megan said. "I think he's thirsty."

"Right you are, to be sure," the officer said. "Here I am talking while he's wanting water. Terrible the way people treat animals now, a scandal if you ask me."

"I could keep him with the ponies," Megan said, as the puppy drank, "while we search for his owner, but Dad's lost his job and I've no money for food."

The officer fetched her a tin of meat and the packet of biscuits the station kept to feed lost dogs before they went to the dogs' home.

Soon Romilly, tired of standing tied to an iron fence, pawed the ground and Megan, after the officer had taken down her name and address, rode home with the puppy snoozing under her coat.

Luckily the tin didn't need an opener and, although Megan was afraid the meat wasn't suitable for a puppy, the little dog wolfed it down and the biscuits, too, after she had softened them in water. She made the puppy a nest of hay in the box she used for grooming tools and, when he had fallen asleep, she shut the fodder room door and ran home.

"A girl rang asking for you," Megan's mum said. "And can you guess what's happened? I've got a job, part-time at the shop, bring us in fifty pounds a week it will, and there were ten women after it – ten, but they took me!"

"Oh, Mum, I'm so pleased," cried Megan. "And Dad?"

"A little bit jealous. You know, typical man. I've written that number down for you."

When Megan rang, the child's voice at the other end said, "You've got my Jack Russell, Snippet. Can we come and fetch him?"

Then another voice said, "Say thank you."

Megan said, "Who are you?"

"Melanie Paxton. And thank you."

Then a grown-up took the phone and said, "Megan Jones? I'm Mrs Paxton. The police tell me you've rescued my daughter's little puppy, which disappeared early yesterday morning. We can't thank you enough. Melanie has been totally heartbroken. May we come and collect him this evening?" And Megan, of course, said yes.

So at six o'clock the Paxtons arrived at the field and Megan handed seven-year-old Melanie the little puppy, who didn't look so thin now that he had been fed. Mrs Paxton explained that he had been snatched out of their garden.

"By terrible boys," added Melanie.

"They haven't been caught and we don't know why they took him," Mrs Paxton said, "It may have been a prank that went wrong, but I think they wanted to hurt us and the puppy because they were unhappy. Or perhaps they wanted Snippet for themselves and then changed their minds, and being callous and evil just left him to die."

"Eight miles away!" Megan said, raising her eyebrows.

"Or perhaps they stole him for somebody who turned him down," continued Mrs Paxton. "Some mysteries are never solved. And the important thing is we've got him back, thanks to you." She smiled at Megan, "Lovely ponies," she said, looking across the field.

"I've got to sell them – Dad's out of work."

"Oh, but that's terrible!"exclaimed Mrs Paxton.

"Can I ride the little grey?" asked Melanie.

"Darling, don't be cheeky!" cried her mother.

"Of course, you're welcome," said Megan. "I'll get the tack and stuff my riding-hat with paper so it fits you, just this once. Dad gave up so much for the ponies," Megan continued, as she groomed and saddled Snowman. "He hardly drank, didn't smoke, never went on holiday. He seemed to live for the horse shows. You know, he was up here every evening and now he won't come at all. Isn't that odd?" She paused. Why was she confiding in Mrs Paxton? Was it because she didn't belong to the village and was a stranger?

"He probably can't bear to come because he loves the ponies so much," Mrs Paxton said. "To look at them is to tear his heart apart."

"You may be right," agreed Megan. "But he never says so."

"Some people can't voice their deepest feelings,"

Mrs Paxton explained. "They run away from life instead or shut themselves up."

"That's Dad," Megan said, then inwardly cursed herself for being disloyal.

Melanie handed her mother Snippet and put a foot in the stirrup. "It's all right, I've had loads of lessons," she said.

"She's been riding for a year, but what she really wants, of course, is a pony of her own, but we've no fields around, and I work, and what with one thing and another . . . " Mrs Paxton helped her daughter adjust her stirrups.

"And I have two. It isn't fair, is it? Dad couldn't resist buying Romilly – his father was pony-mad, you see, and he considers Snowman to be the best Welsh pony that ever walked."

Melanie rode Snowman round the school. She sat well, but sometimes her toes went down.

"She needs someone to ride with," Mrs Paxton said.

"She could ride with me."

"I suppose she needs more lessons. You're not old enough to teach, are you?"

"Definitely not. But I know a qualified teacher."

"But what are we talking about? You're selling the ponies."

Melanie started to canter Snowman in circles.

"She rides very well," Megan said. "Snowman likes her. He won a prize once as best family pony. Of course I'm a bit big for him now."

"They sort of fit," Mrs Paxton said. "I suppose . . . "

"What did you say?"

"Just a thought."

"He's lovely," cried Melanie, cantering up to them. "The best pony I've ever ridden." She dismounted. "Thanks a million, Megan. Can we come again?"

"Whenever you like until he's sold."

"You don't really mean to sell him? You can't." shrieked Melanie.

"Yes, it's awful," agreed Megan.

"Can we buy him, Mummy? Oh, please can we?" wailed Melanie, undoing the girth.

"We would have to talk to Daddy."

"I'll make him agree," said Melanie. "We could keep him here. Pay Megan to look after him. And if that's too expensive I could share him with Anna . . . that's my best friend," she said, turning to Megan. "It would be cheaper than having lessons, and the school's so far away."

"I'll talk to Daddy," repeated Mrs Paxton.

"You said you got a rise last week," Melanie reminded her.

They turned Snowman loose, patted Romilly, and Melanie took Snippet.

"Thanks to a wet summer, I shan't have to start feeding hay for a few more weeks," observed Megan.

"You rent this field?"

"Yes, on a long lease, for peanuts. There's not much demand for grass round here."

"If you promise to ride with Melissa when she wants to hack around, I could pay you a bit over the odds and then you could keep both ponies," said Mrs Paxton. "I want her to be safe. How much are you asking for Snowman?"

"I shall have to consult Dad," Megan said, thinking, This isn't true. "He's a registered Welsh pony."

"So we both want to get agreement from the male members of the family," exclaimed Mrs Paxton. "Great! I'll phone you tonight. And thank you again for rescuing Snippet. You're a marvellous girl. Come on Melanie. Home."

When Mrs Paxton telephoned she asked for two

weeks' trial. "Just to see everything's okay."

Dylan Jones, still down-in-the-mouth, said, "I leave it to you, Megan. You'll be fourteen soon and that's the age my old father started work down the pits and gave a few shillings every week to his mother."

So Megan asked fifty pounds more than her father had paid for Snowman and forty pounds for the tack and Mrs Paxton agreed. They fixed a livery fee too, which included a little extra for the use of the jumps, for Mrs Paxton was a fair woman. Adding it all up Megan realised that if Romilly kept well the monthly payment would cover all his keep, too. When the fortnight was over and the cheque for Snowman and the tack came, Mr Jones gave Megan the money in case she needed to pay vets' bills.

"But it's yours," objected Megan. "You bought Snowman."

"It's pony money, so it goes back to the ponies," declared Mr Jones.

"But you need it."

"Listen, girl," Mr Jones said, "I'm getting a bit of carpentry work coming along, and when this recession's over there'll be more of that, so we're not on the bread-line yet, see. And maybe you'll need a bit of extra money when you get to college, so go along with your mother and put the cheque in a building society, quick."

Thanks to Mrs Paxton the ponies stayed, and Melissa loved Snowman as much as Megan did. Now and then Mrs Paxton hired a trailer to take both ponies to shows for, she said, Melissa needed Megan there, and, after a bit, Mr Jones came to watch them, enjoying every moment as he had in the old days.

A Ghost in the Family

Christine Pullein Thompson

I didn't want to be forever riding with the Nelsons because I like riding alone, composing poetry in my head and singing my favourite songs with no one to laugh at my monotonous, tuneless voice. But they kept ringing up.

We were new to the district. Dad is a doctor and had become Registrar at the local hospital, and Mum had found herself a job at the library. At fifteen, I was a gangling, brown-haired beanpole. Dad said the Nelsons must think I was lonely, and Mum, who has a romantic mind, said they probably wanted an escort for their three daughters.

I had two ponies then – grey Nimrod and black Jack Daw. Jack Daw was my favourite, though he had appalling manners. I think I preferred him because he was a challenge to ride and he was black. I have always loved black horses, and because of this I hope to join the Household Cavalry when I leave school.

The Nelsons were a strange family. There were five children, three girls and two boys, and they lived in a house called Dark Dingle. They rode quite differently from me, galloping over stones, along verges, leaping stiles, their ponies' manes unbrushed, their crash-caps pushed low over their eyes. But one couldn't help liking them, for they were always full of ideas and for ever running things – from jumble sales and fêtes to gymkhanas. Locally they were known as "them young devils from the Dingle", and they had a reputation for supreme recklessness.

I liked Carl and Melanie best. Carl had a wild face which made you think of gipsies, and he was immensely generous and would lend you the last penny he had. Melanie was musical in a disorderly way. She was always singing and could play the guitar. George and the twins, Jenny and Debby, were more ordinary. They wore less peculiar clothes and talked about books.

The Nelsons had only three ponies between them, and were always hinting that Nimrod needed exercising, but I explained that Jack Daw's legs were dicey and I needed a second horse. In this way I kept them at bay.

We had ridden several times together when Carl suggested that we hacked up to Hangman's Cross one night and looked for ghosts. I was in their kitchen at the time, drinking coffee, while Jack Daw stood tied up in the yard.

"Ghosts! You must be mad," I said. "Or do they swing from a gibbet in the dark?"

Melanie smiled. "But they do exist, don't they, Carl? Though they don't exactly swing . . . " she said.

It was nearly the end of November. The trees were almost bare of leaves now, and there was an uneasy wind which seemed to tell of storms to come.

"We're serious," said Carl. "Will you come with us

tonight, Francis? Or are you chicken?"

"Dad isn't keen on me riding in the dark," I answered.

"We can lend you a stirrup light – tell him that," said Melanie.

"I don't see the point – why ride in the dark at all?" I said.

"To see the ghosts," said Melanie.

"Have you seen them?" I asked.

"Yes, of course. Lots of people have."

"Actually it's our great-great-great-grandfather being murdered. That's what makes it so interesting for us," said Melanie.

"Oh yeah, tell me another," I said scornfully.

"It's true," replied Carl. "Now are you coming? Or are you scared? We go every year and we don't ask just *anyone* to come with us. It really *is* a compliment."

"I'll come, but I don't believe in ghosts and I think you're both mad," I answered.

"It's an awful experience," said Carl. "And if I could get my hands on the murderer I would tear him to bits . . . "

"Very funny," I said.

"It sends my blood pressure up to bursting-point – and your father's a doctor, so you know what that means," said Carl.

"You're talking drivel, but I'll come anyway," I said.

When I reached home Dad was hanging pictures. I had seen them all before. They were what you call family portraits: aunts and great-aunts, great-uncles and great-great-uncles, grandfathers and great-grandfathers. Some were on horses, but mostly they sat on sofas with their hands folded neatly in their laps, or stood, with strange-looking dogs lying at their feet.

Fortunately my parents had been invited to a party, so I didn't have to tell them I would be going out in the dark. Presently they left, dressed in clothes suitable for cocktails. I cooked myself sausages and baked beans in our rather stately kitchen, which belongs to an earlier age when there were cooks and scullery maids and a butler in the pantry. The house is far too large for us, but it was much cheaper than more convenient homes, which was why Dad bought it.

I decided to take Nimrod, because, being grey, he would show up better in the dark than Jack Daw. He bit me as I tightened his girth and obviously thought it outside pony rules to be taken out so late at night.

It was a particularly dreary November evening, with drizzle falling like dew. I like riding in the dark; it has no fears for me. I imagine I am a Cavalier, fleeing from the Roundheads, or a doctor riding to see a dying patient. But Nimrod was not too keen and left our old-fashioned stable yard reluctantly.

The road to the Nelsons' was straight and empty. They were waiting for me at the end of their drive, Carl riding Cobby Choirboy, who looked more like an old man than a horse. Melanie was on the roan, Roman-Nosed Stepmother, and George rode his big bay, High Court Judge, known simply as Judge. I have never understood why they always chose such long-winded names for their horses.

"So you've come," observed Carl.

"Of course I've come," I said.

"Fantastic!" cried Melanie.

We had no lights between us, not even a torch. I wondered what my father would say if he saw us. He deals with road accidents at the hospital and is always lecturing on road safety and how carelessness costs lives. So, as we rode towards Hangman's Cross, I prayed that he wouldn't find out.

There is a long hill up to Hangman's Cross.

"Don't you want to know a little more about the ghosts?" asked Melanie, as a car hooted and dipped its lights at us.

"No, we'll be ghosts ourselves soon enough," I replied. "And I thought you were bringing stirrup lights."

"Don't be such a fuss-pot," said Carl. "How can man die better than on the back of a horse?"

"Not at fifteen," I answered.

"We must hurry," said Melanie, looking at her watch. "It's due at eight."

"What is?" I asked.

"The stagecoach. He stops it at the top of the hill, the swine. They always did that, because the horses were out of breath and incapable of galloping away."

"What horses?"

"The ones pulling the stagecoach, of course."

"It's the night coach," added Carl. "So they've put the lame and the blind to pull it. They will have left the Coaching Inn at Hellborough half an hour ago."

"And our great-great-great-grandfather is on the box," said Melanie.

"The stagecoach men were like pop stars then," explained Carl. "Some of them accepted bribes from highwaymen, but our great-great-great-grandfather never did, and that's why he was shot. He was only forty, but then they didn't live long in those days. They drank too much. They had to, or they would have frozen to death on the box. They were a special breed of men," continued Carl.

"You seem to have made quite a study of them," I observed.

"Wouldn't you if your great-great-great-grandfather had been murdered by a criminal, just three miles from where you lived?" asked Carl.

"And can't rest in peace even a hundred and forty years later," added Melanie.

"Who was the highwayman?"

"History doesn't tell. I think he was caught and hanged. I hope so, but no one is sure. We don't know his name, but he had a cultured voice, the stinking rat," said Carl.

We were nearly at the top of the hill. Nimrod was sweating. There was a thick mist. "Not so many cars come this way now," said George. "Not since they built the motorway."

George was thickset. He rode with his legs forward and seat well back in the saddle. His riding set my teeth on edge, if you know what I mean. I wanted to say: "Why don't you consider poor old Judge? You wouldn't want to carry a great lump on your back; you would want it near your shoulders like a knapsack. It's much easier there." But I didn't.

There was nothing at Hangman's Cross except a signpost and a few trees. The wind whispered in our ears, and far below we could see lights from cottages and smaller, moving lights, flickering like glow-worms along hedge-fenced roads.

"It's fantastic up here at night, isn't it? Don't you agree, Francis?" asked Melanie.

"Eerie," I answered. "Like the top of the world. Listen, I can hear sheep. What's the time? The cocktail party ends at eight-thirty. If Dad discovers that I've been out, there will be one heck of a row."

"Three minutes to," said Melanie. "We had better get off the road. Not that side. The highwayman hides between those trees."

"Of course, they may not come, but it's the right day and the right time," said Carl. "Eight o'clock was quite late then."

The horses stood very still, close together, their ears pricked. The wind continued whispering. The drizzle had stopped.

"Gosh, it's quiet," said George.

"Listen, I hear hooves," Melanie said quietly. "They're down in the valley. Listen."

"It's coming then," said Carl.

There seemed to be something moving on the far side of the road, behind a clump of trees. There was a muffled neigh and the click of a gun. Nimrod broke into a sweat, none of us spoke. We could hear hooves distinctly now, coming steadily, *clip-clop, clip-clop* . . .

There was a rattle of iron-rimmed wheels. My heart was thumping against my ribs, and the atmosphere was extraordinary – everything seemed to be waiting, waiting . . .

All at once four horses came into sight, their heads down, their nostrils sending up clouds of steam, their breathing laboured.

"Stop!" shouted a voice. "Everyone get out."

A man sat astride a black mare, easily, alone. And the driver on the box, swathed to his ears in a great cape, shouted, "No, not this time, you devil! I would rather die!" He reached inside his cape for a gun, and then there was a single shot and he fell from the box and lay quite still on the road, while the horses stood panting, their coats wet with sweat . . .

And I stared at the highwayman and I knew him.

"That's the end," said Melanie in a small voice, as though we were in the cinema and had come to the end of a film. "There's never any more."

"I wish I knew what happened next," said Carl.

As I looked at the road again, I saw that it was empty, just as it had been before.

"Well?" asked George. "Do you believe us now, Francis?"

"Yes, of course," I answered, trying to place a face, a long straight nose beneath a mask, a high forehead under a hat. In a minute I would know. I would fix the two pieces together – the face I had seen, and the other face.

"He shot him at point blank range; he didn't give him a chance," said Melanie.

"There were rich pickings on board, jewels galore," said George.

"Cowboys were the same – the survivor was the one who was quickest on the draw," I answered.

"You're not sticking up for the highwayman, are you?" said Melanie. "He's a robber – a robber and a killer."

"I wonder why," I said. The faces were coming together now, my memory was piecing them together,

and I knew then that the face was that of my great-great-great-grandfather in the hall, the one who, they said, loved black horses – just like me. I didn't know what to say, I had heard so much about him; he had been a very rich man when he died, and we still benefitted from his wealth. He had owned a pack of hounds and had built a fine house. And yet there was no mistaking him, for in the picture in our hall he sat astride the same horse – the highwayman's black horse.

"You're very silent," said Melanie, after we had been riding homewards for some time. "What's the matter?"

"I'm thinking," I answered. "It's all very difficult really because – well, that man on the black horse – I believe he was my great-great-great-grandfather!"

"He can't be," replied Carl after a short, shocked silence. "I told you, no one knows who he was . . . "

"His picture hangs in our hall. Come and see it tomorrow," I suggested. "It's the truth. I wish it wasn't."

After a pause Melanie said, in a voice tight with emotion, "We can't know you now. We can't ever speak to you again. Our great-great-great-grandfather was a wonderful man, he could drive a team of four anywhere. He was the most famous stagecoach driver of his time."

"No wonder you are so well off," said George with a short laugh. "Have you still got any of the jewels he stole?"

"I think we have. Goodnight," I answered.

I trotted away from them, suddenly wishing that I had never spoken. Nimrod was glad to be going home. Cars hooted at me. One driver wound his window down to shout, "Where's your lights, you idiot?"

My father was waiting for me, grim-faced in our big

hall. "What the devil have you been doing?" he shouted.

Mum said, "We've been scared. We were about to ring the police. What's the matter? You look as though you've seen a ghost."

"I have – several," I told them. It all seemed impossible, and yet I knew it was true. I turned to stare at the portrait of the man who had been my great-great-great-grandfather on my father's side, and it was the same man on the same horse, only now he was dressed like a rich gentleman. I wanted to laugh, but couldn't.

"He was a highwayman," I said, pointing at the portrait. "I saw him tonight, holding up a coach driver at the top of Hangman's Hill. Ask the Nelsons. He was murdering their great-great-great-grandfather. Funny, isn't it. He was just a common robber." I was half crying, half laughing.

"You had better go to bed," said Dad. "You look all in."

"Everything will seem different in the morning," added Mum, as though I were a small, overtired child.

But as I climbed our wide, as yet uncarpeted stairs, I knew it wouldn't. I lay in bed, dreading what the Nelsons might do. Supposing they told the whole neighbourhood? I tossed and turned, and since everything always grows worse at night in bed, I imagined Dad losing his job, Mum sacked by the library, and all because I had told the Nelsons the truth.

In the morning, Melanie telephoned. Her voice was small and determined. "We don't want to see the portrait. We believe you," she said. "But since blood is thicker than water, we have decided that we can never speak to you again. I hope you understand." And with that passing shot she put down the receiver.

"That's that," I said.

Dad was behind me. I relayed what Melanie had just told me.

"But he wasn't your great-great-great-grandfather," Dad said. "Tell them to come over here. I can explain everything. You needn't be enemies."

"But you can't explain. He's there!" I cried, pointing. "Even the horse is the same."

"Do as you're told. I've got an hour to spare. Tell them to come at once." Dad picked up the telephone receiver. "Number?" he asked. "What's their number?"

"Two six seven two."

I could hear Melanie answering, then Dad was saying:

"Will you come over at once? I want to put the record straight about your great-great-great-grandfather and the highwayman."

Melanie sounded surprised. There was a short silence before she replied, "Okay, we'll come."

Mum began to clean the hall in a demented manner. "Why do you always ask people when the house is in a mess?" she asked.

"The Nelsons don't notice mess. You should see their house," I said.

Dad unlocked a drawer in his desk and took out an ancient envelope with red sealing-wax on it. "Skeletons in the family cupboard," he said. "I never thought I would have to do this. And why did we name you Francis, for heaven's sake? Why not James?"

Rain was falling outside now, washing the last of the leaves from the trees. I ate a bowl of cornflakes in the kitchen without noticing what I was doing, and buttered some bread automatically, like a robot.

Five minutes later, Carl, Melanie and George arrived on an odd assortment of bicyles.

"That was quick. Come in," Dad said to them as he opened the door.

"We are eaten up with curiosity," Melanie told him.

"And there he is!" cried Carl, looking at the portrait. "It's unmistakable. Even the horse is the same!"

"Yes," murmured Melanie, standing behind her brother, while George said:

"I don't know why we are here. This place makes me sick."

"Steady there, not so fast," replied Dad in his best bedside manner. "You mustn't judge without hearing the evidence."

"We've seen that on Hangman's Hill," declared George.

"I'd better tell you our side of the story, then," said Dad. "And in this envelope, I have the proof. The man you're looking at on the wall is my great-great-grandfather, Sir James Welberry Sincock; the highwayman you saw was his twin brother, Francis Welberry Sincock, twenty minutes younger and never to have the title, or much money, because of that."

"But the horse?"

"He's the same. James acquired him after his brother was hanged. He was particularly fond of black horses. I have all the documents here." Dad waved the ancient envelope. "There's even a cutting from a newspaper describing the public hanging. It was a great scandal in its day and never mentioned again in our family. Poor Francis, he never fitted in; he needed money and never had enough. He grew up in a stately home, and became a gambler. The women he loved refused to marry him, his family disowned him; the more his brother prospered, the lower he sank. It was as though one was born with all the virtues and the other with all the vices. But he was a superb horseman, by far the better of the two."

"So he *was* hanged then," said Carl, looking at me.

"Penniless and disowned. News travelled slowly, if at all in those days," said Dad. "And your great-great-great-grandfather wasn't the only coachman he killed. The news of his shameful death may never have reached your family."

Carl held out his hand and shook mine. It was a firm, steady handshake. "Our great-great-great-grandfather was a bit of a rogue too," he admitted. "They say he beat his wife and drove sick, lame and blind horses. You can't sink much lower than that, can you?"

"It was a different world," said Dad.

"I hope you will come and ride with us again soon, Francis," Melanie said, with an apologetic smile.

"And let bygones be bygones," added Carl.

The rain had stopped. When we opened the door everything outside looked washed clean.

"I *do* believe in ghosts now," I said.

"I think we are nicer than our ancestors – much, much nicer," said Melanie to Dad. "I mean, a doctor is a far better person than a highwayman, isn't he?"

"Why *did* you call me Francis, rather than James?" I asked after the Nelsons had left.

"I think because James was awful too, but in a different way. He had everything, but he cheated and seduced young girls and rode horses to death in the hunting field. He was a hypocrite. He looked all right on the outside, but really his behaviour was appalling. At least Francis never pretended to be good," explained Dad. "But perhaps we should have played safe and called you John," he added, laughing.

"I thought it was nice to have a ghost. Now I'm not so sure," I said.

"Your mother's family was okay. They were the salt of the earth. Now – I must be off. I'm late," said Dad. "And while I remember, don't ever go riding at night without a light again – or there'll be another ghost in the family!"

What a Turnabout!

Christine Pullein-Thompson

Neither of us liked Claire. Only a year or two older than us, she seemed to know everything there was to know about horses, and she always appeared as though by magic when anything went wrong. When my pony Mascot fell on the road and spoilt his knees, there she was asking whether he'd had his anti-tet and who our vet was. When we couldn't catch our ponies one rainy day, she appeared to tell us to hide our headcollars behind our backs and to advance slowly. And she was always proved right, that was the annoying part of it.

Jonathan, my brother, disliked her more than I did. He disliked her for other things as well – for the rosettes she won in every class she entered, for her horse's perfect appearance, for her fantastic clothes and, most of all perhaps, for the lush horse box which took her everywhere while we travelled by ancient trailer, pulled by Dad's old Volvo. Jonathan has dark hair and blue eyes. Mum calls him a real Celt – whatever that means. I have mousey hair and hazel eyes, and I'm small for my age, which means I can school naughty ponies for other people, but it makes me feel inferior whenever I meet

Claire who, at fourteen, is already 165 centimetres tall. Jonathan is older than I am. He hates cleaning tack and his room is chaotic. He's quite tall for his age so can look Claire straight in the eye, but however hard he looks she never flinches.

Claire lives in a big house with a long drive. Her father is a director of a large company that makes zip-fasteners. Her mother stays at home and arranges the flowers, at least that's what Jonathan says. We live in a small ranch-type house, which usually has a scattering of oats on the kitchen floor and saddles in the kitchen. Occasionally saddle soap gets into the cooking and then everyone's cross.

Dad is an electrical engineer and Mum works in our local library part-time. Jonathan and I go to a nearby school, while Claire goes to St. Audrey's, a private school in the nearby town. She has wonderful blonde hair and steady, unflinching blue eyes. Her nose is a little long, and her chin a little forceful. She is slim with long legs. She is everything I would like to be; instead I'm small, dumpy, with tangled hair and a turned-up nose.

Claire is an important part of the local Pony Club. She is in several teams and sometimes helps out instructing the younger members. We all know that she is destined to be head girl at St Audrey's, which is a girls-only school, for she is a born prefect, a born organiser of games and probably a future district commissioner of some poor Pony Club. Her horses are equally grand; they live in sumptuous loose boxes and are called Hope, Faith and Charity. Hope is a working hunter, Faith is a showjumper, and Charity goes like a dream across country. I love my pony, Mascot, who is grey and cuddly and fourteen hands. But I must admit to an occasional twinge of envy. Jonathan's half Dale, Black Magic, is tireless, large-hoofed and tough. He will outstay all others on a long-distance ride. He'll jump almost anything, but is slow against the clock in a jump-off. We have four cups between us. Claire has a cabinet full. She has two pedigree dogs and a bedroom especially designed for her. She lives next door to us and sometimes seems to be observing everything we do – each bale of hay wheeled out into our muddy paddock, each lunging session, each jump refused or knocked down.

Mum says that all comparisons are odious, and that we have things she hasn't; but sometimes I look for these things and I can't see them anywhere.

And of course Claire has someone to look after her horses. She is in her thirties and is called Emma. Claire also has her own instructor. He's called Hans. Everyone expects that one day Claire will represent Britain, either in showjumping or across country.

Dad says it's on the cards. Mum says it's a dead cert. And, worse than that, they both admire Claire, seeing in her virtues that we lack, insisting she has guts, drive and dedication. In other words, in Dad's own words, 'She is destined to go far.'

This story really begins in August on a fantastic evening with the air just beginning to cool and the faintest breeze stirring the leaves on the trees in our garden. We were in the stable yard about to ride, having waited all day for the heat to subside. We had sprayed the ponies with insect repellent and Mascot had stood on

Jonathan's toe and he was holding it up in agony and blaming me, when Charity hurtled into the yard, her stirrups swinging, her reins broken and no Claire on board.

"Steady there, steady, whoa," I addressed Charity while a thousand dreadful possibilities flashed through my mind at the speed of a jet fighter.

"Where on earth is Claire?" asked Jonathan, rather unnecessarily.

"Lying hurt or hobbling home. How do I know?" I yelled, angry that I didn't know, while I grabbed hold of

Charity and scanned her for injury and found none.

"Let's take her home. I can't think why she came here; it's crazy," my brother said.

We led her next door and, though I didn't like Claire, my heart was hammering with suspense while my head spun with worry.

There was no one in Claire's stable yard besides Faith and Hope. Faith was weaving (which is a nervous complaint causing a horse to sway from side to side, shifting from one hoof to another). Hope neighed frantically with eyes agog and lower lip trembling.

Claire's pedigree golden Labradors barked in their posh pen fifty metres away while I untacked Charity, checking that she had water in her immaculate box. Jonathan rang the front door bell on the Georgian house where Claire lived. There was no one at home, no one anywhere. Just a mind-boggling emptiness. Our parents were not at home either. They were both working.

"We had better look for her," Jonathan said.

"On our horses," I added.

The sun was sinking red and gold as we tacked up.

"Which way?" Jonathan asked.

"To the park. She always rides through there," I replied.

"I looked into the hall through the letterbox. I couldn't see a message," Jonathan told me and we looked at each other, both recalling that we are never allowed to ride anywhere without leaving a note saying where we've gone. So she isn't perfect after all, I thought.

"And if she's not in the park?" Jonathan asked a moment later.

"We'll search the other ride, the one through the farmyard," I answered.

By this time we were going at a spanking trot, Black Magic's hoofs slapping down on the road like someone playing the clappers. Mascot's head was up, his ears were pricked, his eyes shining, for they both knew by some sixth sense that this ride was different from usual.

As soon as we reached a grass verge we galloped, then hurtled into the park, ignoring the sign which says NO RIDING AFTER SUNSET. From behind electric fencing, cattle raised their heads and stared.

"What are we going to do if we do find her?" I asked. "Suppose she's dying."

"Don't be stupid. She may be quite all right," my brother answered. "She's probably looking for Charity."

But we both knew that was unlikely, because if Claire was all right she would be halfway home by now and we'd have seen her.

Then looking at my worried face, Jonathan added, "Let's play it by ear," which is something Dad says. "We'll be helping her, just for a change, can't you see?" continued my brother.

Then we saw her in the distance, lying by one of the cross-country fences, which have notices all round them saying NOT TO BE JUMPED WITHOUT PERMISSION. She looked very still and rather small. We crossed the park towards her, faster than either of us had ever ridden before.

As we drew near my brother threw himself off, then threw his reins to me. I dismounted more slowly. Claire looked up at us both. "Is Charity all right? I think I've bust my leg," she said.

"Charity's fine. She's in her box." I replied, my eyes unexpectedly smarting with tears.

"You'll have to get an ambulance," said Claire, looking very pale and very beautiful lying on the dry summer grass.

"What about your parents?" I asked. "Shouldn't we get them?"

"They're in the south of France," she replied.

Claire then told us both to go for help, so that while one telephoned, the other could hold the horses.

She appeared quite sensible in spite of her broken leg. So we galloped to the big house in the park, which is called Bramley's Hall, and the owner came out and said that he would drive over in his Land-Rover and pick her up, and what did she think she was doing jumping his fences?

Jonathan said, "I think she needs an ambulance."

And I added, "She shouldn't be moved. Can we use your phone, please?"

"What about her parents?" asked the man, who was called Lord Markham. We explained that they were not at home and then he went indoors to telephone for an ambulance.

We rode back to Claire and my brother said, "Thank goodness she's alive."

I said, "She looks much smaller lying there, and quite different."

"She shouldn't be on her own in that huge house," my brother replied.

"Our parents wouldn't leave us," I agreed. "But perhaps they're just spending the day in the south of France," I suggested.

"It didn't sound like it to me," Jonathan replied. "And it's an awfully long way to go for a day."

Soon Lord Markham appeared with a blanket and put it over Claire. "The ambulance is on its way. I would like to bring you a drink, but I daren't because you might need an anaesthetic," he said.

Claire's teeth were chattering by this time, but she managed to smile as she said, "I know I was wrong to be jumping your fences, but I couldn't resist them, and now I'm being punished, aren't I?"

Lord Markham replied, "No, it was just bad luck. But don't do it again. You set a bad example to the young ones."

Suddenly the thought of Claire being a head girl went right out of the window.

"Everyone will know, won't they? I can't enter for the horse trials now, can I?" she asked.

"You won't be well enough, anyway. But it was cheating, wasn't it? There's really no other name for it, is there?" asked Lord Markham coldly.

Fortunately, just at that moment the ambulance appeared and the man and woman inside took over. As Claire was removed on a stretcher she cried, "Ring Emma. She'll know what to do. Please don't forget," and the ambulance drove away.

We mounted and I saw that my brother was crying.

"Another illusion shattered?" I suggested.

"But I like her. I actually like her much more now; even if she is a cheat," my brother cried. "And why is she on her own? She's only fourteen. No one should be left alone day and night at her age."

Our ponies were hyped up now and wouldn't walk.

They tossed their heads and pulled and our arms were soon aching. But we made them walk and when we reached home Mum was there. We told her what had happened and she rang Emma. Afterwards, when she had heard our story, she said, "Poor pet, being left alone like that. I told you not to envy her, didn't I? You see, no one has everything. Life is swings and roundabouts; what you lose on the swings you make on the roundabouts."

Later Emma appeared and sat in the kitchen drinking tea. "I knew she shouldn't be left on her own. Her parents! Honestly, they're terrible, they never let up; her mother's the worst, though her father spoils her rotten – but not in the right way of course. He just gives her everything she wants, like those two dogs. How can she look after them when she's at school all day? It's ridiculous. And I can't do it all. I'm only there for a few hours, morning and evening." Then she told us she had rung Claire's parents and they were returning. "Actually, they were furious," Emma related. "Her mother said 'There's my suntan gone for a Burton', and her dad said 'We'd better sell that wretched horse'."

"She was cheating, jumping the fences in the park. Charity must have stopped, or maybe she fell on her," I suggested.

"They all cheat, the whole family. He fiddles the books. And they never pay me on time," Emma said, getting up to leave. "And as for her horses, they'll all be weaving before long unless she turns them out somewhere. They can't stay cooped up while her leg mends. It just isn't fair."

Next day we went to see Claire in hospital. She was

in a general ward, and when she saw us she sat up and cried, "Thank goodness you're here. Please ask Emma to bring my night things. I can't stand this hospital nightie a minute longer."

She was going to have her leg set later that day. She told us what had happened, how Charity had hit the top rail and turned over. "And I went with her. And now I shan't be able to enter the horse trials. Hans will be furious. He wanted me to prove how good he is; that's why I was practising; I wanted to win to please him, not for myself... I don't care really, or not like he does. He wants more pupils and more money, that's the problem," she said, smiling at Jonathan.

I said, "How awful."

"Winning does grow on you, though. I suppose it's rather like being an alcoholic – the more you have the more you need," she said. And then, surprise, surprise, she added, "But you can ride Charity if you like,

Jonathan. Hans will coach you. Daddy will pay. You can ride him at all the trials and make a name for yourself."

Half of me was hoping that my brother wouldn't agree. But Jonathan was smiling and his eyes were shining as he said, "That would be fabulous. Do you really mean it?"

"Of course I do. The other horses can be turned out. But you can have Charity for the next two months." I saw a spasm of pain cross Claire's face as she spoke. She was trying to be brave; and she was brave, I saw that now, braver than I would ever be.

Then we saw her parents approaching. Her mother wore dark glasses and an expensive dress. Her father wore a white shirt, white trousers, and a yachting cap. "Oh my poor darling," cried her mother. "You quite spoilt my sunbathing."

"And my drinking," added her father, laughing.

"But we had to come at once, my poor darling," her mother continued.

"We'll have you moved into a private room straight away," said her father, looking for a nurse.

"This is where we go," Jonathan told me. "Come on, move."

"Come again soon, please. And I meant what I said, Jonathan," cried Claire in a desperate voice. "I really did. Come tomorrow. Promise."

"Yes," cried Jonathan. "I promise."

"You really like her now, don't you?" I asked Jonathan as we walked outside into the hot morning air.

"Yes I do, and I'm going to reorganise her horses. I'm going to see that they are turned out for at least three hours a day, starting at once," Jonathan told me.

"What about Hans?" I asked.

"I don't know yet. I'm keeping an open mind." Jonathan wasn't really walking now, he was dancing along the pavement towards the bus stop while I trailed behind, wondering how anyone can be so wrong about anyone, as we had been about Claire. I was thinking that Jonathan would spend much of his time next door now, and that he was falling in love with Claire. And, though I didn't envy her any more, I felt a twinge of jealousy for someone who could enslave my brother so easily.

Then we looked at each other and laughed and Jonathan said, "Goodness, what a turnabout, and we really hated her, didn't we?"

"I rather liked hating her," I answered. "I think she's what Dad would call an opportunist. I shall never really trust her whatever she says. Think of cheating like that, it was a dreadful thing to do."

But, looking at my brother, I knew that he had already forgiven her. He felt he was her equal now. She would never look down on him again, or preach or tell him what to do, and if he won the trials on Charity he would move up into a different realm of horsemanship, a realm we had only dreamed about before.

Waiting for the bus, it seemed impossible that life could change so quickly in less than twenty-four hours. It made anything seem possible; even me accomplishing all the things I wanted to do, like starting a clinic for naughty ponies and becoming a top instructor.

So, leaping on to the bus, I said, "You never know what's going to happen next, do you?"

"Exactly. That's what makes life so exciting," replied my brother.

Life and Death

Diana Pullein-Thompson

The gypsies were back, but only one family this time with a horse rather than a lorry or car, which was rare these days. They had a foal, too, pretty and skewbald, plump as a well-stuffed toy.

I loved the gypsies' ponies with their long, thick tails and their feathered legs. But my mother distrusts gypsies; she claims they are dishonest and leave litter.

She is restless when they camp on the moor at the end of our field, hanging out their washing, lighting fires and tethering their animals all over the place.

"But they're old-fashioned gypsies this time," I told her. "They have a gorgeous old caravan and just one little boy."

"Horse thieves you mean. Keep the gates padlocked," my mother said.

We have two ponies, Woodpecker, who belongs to Mum, and Mistletoe, who is mine. And, I tell you, they are the sweetest, kindest animals on earth, except occasionally on wild, windy days when they buck and shy.

The night after the gypsies arrived a storm blew across the moors, howling like lonely dogs around our isolated house, thrashing the two pines which stand like sentinels at the gate and bringing down the telephone lines.

We locked and bolted all the doors and checked the windows before going to bed. And I was glad that our ponies had a shed in which to shelter. But I thought of the pretty caravan shaken by the storm and the foal with his dish face and large eyes. Would he mind being soaked by the rain?

I slept very lightly, my sub-conscious sensitive to the dangers of the night, and wakened suddenly, instinctively aware that something was wrong; voices had penetrated a muddled dream, real voices.

I leaped from bed, flung back the curtains. The storm had abated. For a moment the moors lay brown and green, below a moon that shone between clouds grey like charcoal.

The voices had gone, but there were hoofbeats on the lane as a grey pony cantered into the distance – Mistletoe – and on her back, crouched forward like a jockey, rode the gypsy boy. For a moment I couldn't believe my eyes. My mind went blank, then cleared. Mother, who had gone to bed early with a headache, was right; her fear had become a reality. The boy was a thief. But I wouldn't wake her because she wasn't well and I was fourteen. He was small and I could deal with him. I dragged on jeans and a sweater, ran to the field, bridle in hand, and called Woodpecker, who trotted up to me. The locked gate had been lifted off its hinges then dragged back into place. A fact, I decided, to point out to the police when I had captured the boy. I vaulted on to Woodpecker, jumped him over the hedge which separated our field from the moor, and set his head against the wind. The night was fresh, the sky a sea of whirling clouds, the air scented with a myriad wild moorland smells.

"Stop! Hey, stop!"

My voice was caught and lost by the wind. Now, where the lane became a track, the boy took to the wilder stretches of the moor, confident of Mistletoe's sure-footedness. He rode so well, so naturally, bareback, it was hard to imagine him in a saddle. Ten or eleven years old, he seemed as agile as an Indian in a well-cast cowboy film. Soon the boulder-strewn ground became hard and soft in turn, treacherous to those who did not know the terrain. Keeping the boy in view, I guided Woodpecker along the sheep paths winding drunkenly round the hillsides. Far away in the valley a single light shone from a house in the village.

Suddenly I was frightened by the fury which welled up in me. I wanted to drag the boy off Mistletoe, shouting, "She's mine, mine!" And this hatred drove me on.

Woodpecker, longing to catch up with Mistletoe, began to gain ground, his hoofs throwing up sparks when steel met flints and sending stones flying down the hillsides. My legs were tired as they pressed his sides and my hands cold as they lay either side of his solid neck. Then I saw the silver phantom which was Mistletoe take off and clear a chasm. Woodpecker followed and, hanging on to his mane, I only just stayed on.

Then the moon slipped behind clouds, leaving us in semi-darkness with the village light our beacon. Woodpecker was sweating. And Mistletoe? Supposing the wretched little thief broke her wind or lamed her? I

hate gypsies, I thought, I hate, hate, hate them!

"Whoa!" I shouted. "Stop! You'll ruin her legs on the stones. Stop now and I promise not to call the police."

But still the boy rode as though his life depended on reaching the village in record time. And now I could just see his face, wind-weathered brown with black hair and sloe-eyes, for we were gaining on him, and then at last we were beside him.

"My pony," I screamed. "Give me back my pony." Putting out a hand I tried to grab the halter rope.

"The doctor," the gypsy boy gasped. "The doctor!"

"Who's ill then?" I shouted back.

"Gran," he said. "I've got to reach the village. Our old horse is done-in, no good on the moors."

"You could have asked," I said, like a prim child in a school classroom, as the ponies, glad to be together again, slowed down to a trot. "You mustn't take things which don't belong to you."

"She's dying," he said. "My gran's dying. Big storm. Wires down. Me and your little grey are friends." He patted Mistletoe. "We talk over the fence. She doesn't mind, she trusts me."

"You've stolen her."

"Borrowed," he shouted back.

We crossed a stream, cantered through a line of trees and came to a dark road running like black treacle down the hill.

"Which house?" He turned his flat face to me.

"The one with the light, I think." We dismounted outside together and I pulled the old-fashioned bell.

"Come, come quickly," the boy said, clasping his

hands together, Mistletoe's halter rope tucked under one arm. Then a light came on in the hall; there were footsteps, the pulling back of a bolt, and an elderly man in a dressing-gown looking at us with bleary eyes.

"Yes?"

"Gran," the boy said.

"One of the travellers, are you? And you?" He strained his eyes. "The Macdonald girl?"

"The caravan's by our house. The old lady's very ill." My voice sounded too cool for the awful news it brought and the conflict raging inside myself.

"Good heavens! You're not out alone? Your mother? Couldn't she bring you by car?"

"Please come quickly," I said. "Mum's asleep."

"But what if she wakes and finds you gone . . . ? Dangerously ill, did you say?"

"Very bad," the boy replied. "Doesn't move any more."

"I'll be there," the doctor said. "Just let me get some trousers on."

We rode back together, as the dawn spread islands of pink and grey across a sky which had lost its anger. Cocks started to crow and we heard a cow bellowing for a bull and, in the distance, dogs barking. We didn't speak much because we found it hard to understand each other, for, now that the emergency was over, the boy mumbled. When we got back the doctor's car was parked by the caravan. The boy handed me Mistletoe and ran off without a word and I thought he should at least have thanked me. I tied the ponies to a post and fetched the key, unlocked the padlock, dragged the gate open and put them back in the field, where they rolled, caking their sweaty bodies with mud. Mum was still asleep.

Crawling back into bed, I could not believe the ride had actually happened. Would Mum believe me? Reliving the chase, I heard the ambulance arrive at the caravan and the gypsies' grey lurcher barking. So, I thought, it is real and his gran is going to hospital. And the boy? Is he asleep or lying awake like me?

"Have they gone?" my mother shouted against the nine o'clock news, as she poured out her cornflakes at breakfast time.

"Who?"

"The gypsies."

"No, no. I'm sure they haven't gone."

Then we heard the garden gate click open, slow footsteps on the path and a whinny. "It's the man," my mother said. "And he's brought the foal with him. I expect he wants us to buy it from him. Gypsies are always selling something. They would sell their own grandmothers if they got the chance."

I went to the door.

"Take care. Put the chain up," my mother warned. The boy's father stood there with the skewbald foal. His eyes were dark, too, and his brown face weathered like the rocks on the moor.

"We don't buy at the door." My mother hovered behind me.

"It's for you," the man said, pushing the foal forwards.

"Me?"

"You let us have the grey pony," he said. "The doctor was just in time, and the ambulance men with the oxygen. I am a Romany. Romany people do not forget."

"But, but . . . " I meant to say, "But I can't." Then I saw that the man's pride demanded that he should present me with this foal and that I should accept. "Are you sure? Your son . . . ? He rides beautifully."

"Please take her," the man said quietly. "We leave now to be nearer the hospital, at the roadside."

He thrust the halter rope into my hand, which looked ridiculously white next to his. He turned away as I called out my thanks.

I remembered how fiercely possessive I had been of Mistletoe, how I had hated seeing the boy on her back, and felt ashamed.

"What is it? Doesn't he want money?" my mother asked.

"It's a long story and you're never going to believe me," I said. "But you had a headache and . . . "

I wanted to ask the boy to come and ride with me, but his father was striding purposely away, so, instead, I called, "Thank you, thank you very much," again. And I put my arm round the neck of the foal, who must have been about six months old, and tried to comfort him as his mother pulled the caravan away up the lane towards the city nine miles away.

Only Five Days Left

Christine Pullein-Thompson

Everyone knew Astronaut. He had won literally hundreds of prizes. I had sold my junior jumper to buy him, my father finding the extra money, and now he was stopping and I knew it was my fault. He was a rangy sixteen-two liver-chestnut and his previous owner had said, "You will go straight to the top on him, there's no doubt about that."

Then I had ridden him over an enormous course which he had jumped flawlessly. And now he was stopping. I lay in bed imagining the remarks which would pass when he stopped with me in public. "He can't ride that horse and he hasn't got a clue. What a shame."

Next day my father and I sat in the kitchen trying to work out what was wrong. Years ago my father had jumped for England. "He always stops at the third in a combination," he said after some time spent lighting his pipe. "So we'll concentrate on that."

"There's only five days left until our first show," I reminded him. "What about a short term solution, a change of bit or a martingale?"

"No, you stick to your snaffle. Come on, out into

the paddock and we'll get started."

I tacked up Astronaut. He was a kind horse, the sort which puts his head down to be bridled and will gallop till he drops dead.

I loosened Astronaut up while Father made a combination of fences, a gate, an upright fence and then a small rail fence with a ground line.

"We must rebuild his confidence," he said.

"What, in five days?"

"We can try."

"If I stop at the show I shall look the biggest fool in all England," I said.

"You are not going to stop," replied my father.

"But it must be me. I must be doing something wrong," I argued.

I rode over the combination half a dozen times; then Father raised the last fence as high as the others and he jumped that too. We rewarded him handsomely with horse cubes.

"We'll send him down the lane tomorrow, loose. We'll have a pile of carrots at the end, that should whet his appetite," my father said.

I hacked him during the afternoon and he felt great. I dreamed that night that all my friends were laughing at me, sitting like sparrows on a stable door. And I knew why they were laughing; Astronaut had stopped three times in the young riders open class.

The next day we sent Astronaut down the lane; he was a bit apprehensive at first, then he started to enjoy it. By the time we had finished, he was jumping a four-foot six combination without putting a hoof wrong.

"You'll jump for England yet," Father said.

"He may, but I won't," I replied gloomily.

I jumped Astronaut once more before the show; I got a few strides wrong, otherwise everything went like clockwork.

A crowd of Astronaut admirers appeared as soon as I arrived at the show. My legs felt like jelly. I was wishing I had bought an unknown horse which I could have produced like a rabbit out of a hat.

Mark, a friend of mine, called, "He won't get round. He'll stop somewhere, you'll see."

"You mean I can't ride him. Is that what you mean?" I asked.

"I leave that for you to decide," Mark said, riding away on a large grey.

"I'm surprised that they let you have him; I am honestly," said one of my female friends. "And I'm surprised your father bought him for you."

At last I was waiting to go into the ring.

"Don't listen to what anyone says," advised Father. "Just ride the best you can. And don't worry about the combination, because if you do Astronaut will too."

The fences looked enormous. It is a big leap from novice to open classes; even the atmosphere is different, with grooms instead of parents, bigger horses. Did I imagine it? Or did a hush fall as I entered the arena? The commentator announced me as Darren Shore riding that well-known jumper Astronaut for the first time. Somewhere in the stands Astronaut's previous owner was watching, waiting to see how I performed. But now the bell had gone.

Astronaut reached into his bit and I turned for the

first fence, he lengthened his stride. I tried to keep him balanced as fence followed fence. I checked him a little for the combination. One, two, three, the last fence was a spread. After that it was plain sailing; then a burst of applause as we rode out. Father was waiting, his face creased in smiles.

"It was all right wasn't it?" I cried, throwing myself to the ground. "I didn't let him down, did I? I rode all right after all."

"You were terrific," Father said. "You bought a stopper and he didn't stop."

"That's right," cried Mark. "He's been stopping for weeks; no one expected you to get round. That's why he was sold, didn't you know?"

I looked at my father. "I didn't tell you, because if you had known, you would have expected it, and then he would have gone on stopping. He needed a change of bit and a change of rider and a bit more kindness. He'll be all right now," he said.

"But he jumped all right when I bought him," I said.

"Think back; was there a combination?" my father asked.

I thought. "No, there wasn't, was there?" I said at last. "He had lost his nerve, hadn't he?"

"That's right, and we've cured him. But don't get too big for your boots, there's still the jump off," Father said. "Take it fairly steady today; next week you can speed up a bit. You are on the road to being a champion but we must take it steady. You've got plenty of time now."

Shandy

Diana Pullein-Thompson

We once owned a pony called Shandy Gaff. We bought him as a sucker at a sale of New Forest ponies at Reading Market. He had just jumped out of his pen and bloodied his nose falling on hard concrete the other side. He was the colour of lemon shandy with a little white star and trickle down his face, and he was very cheap!

Jumping, we soon saw, was Shandy's speciality. We took him for walks with us like a dog and, although he was then only just over eleven hands, he jumped all the stiles with gusto. He also jumped from field to field at home for sheer enjoyment.

One day Shandy overdid his jumping and slipped his stifle. The vet said he must rest, so we tethered him in the paddock on a rope tied to a stake with a swivel. The stake was driven deep into the ground so that there was no chance that the rope could wind round it. All went well at first, then one afternoon we took Shandy into the kitchen and fed him handfuls of coarse oatmeal from the bin in which it was kept for making porridge. Shandy liked the kitchen. It was warm, with an Aga and red flagstoned floor.

It was autumn, with rain in the air, so that night he was tethered again in the shelter of a tree. We slept soundly, unaware that the sky was stormy and tempestuous, and in the morning we came down to find the kitchen in chaos. Broken eggs lay on the wet floor, the oatmeal bin was tipped over and empty, a box of cutlery lay upside down amongst the eggs. The door was wide open, for our father had come in late from a meeting and not latched it securely. Who could have caused the chaos? There were little hoofmarks here and there on the floor and our first thought was Shandy! But, on looking out of the window, we saw that he was standing docilely beside his tethering stake, back to the wind. The rain had stopped. Yet he was the only pony who knew about the oatmeal bin, although there were others who had come for brief moments into the kitchen.

For a while we were mystified, until the time came to take Shandy a drink and an armful of hay. He wasn't thirsty, the night's rain had wetted him enough, but as he stretched his neck to pull at the hay, we saw that his rope was severed. In a flash we knew what had happened. He had broken free, jumped the palings into the garden, crossed the rosebed and made his way to the kitchen, then, after satisfying his curiosity, filling his belly with oatmeal and having a warm-up by the Aga, he had returned to his allotted place.

But why the deceit? Had he a sense of right and wrong? Or did he simply return to be in the right place for his food and drink? We shall never know.

Status Symbol

Christine Pullein-Thompson

The pony was lying in his bare, wire-fenced field. It was February, the wind was blowing like a tempest and no one had broken the ice on the water trough.

"We can't just walk past," David said, and I knew it was true. We had to do something.

"Let's see if the Bullocks are in," I cried, throwing down my bike and running towards the door of their modern bungalow. David banged the knocker, I rang the bell. A small tabby cat was miaowing by the front door.

"Let's go home and ask Mum what to do," suggested David, who is younger than me. We pedalled madly. Our own pony, Dreamy, was still in the stable munching hay. Mum was reading in the kitchen.

"The Bullocks' pony is lying down, she looks ill; and there's no one in," I said.

"I think she's dying," added David emphatically.

"There's no hay or anything," I said.

David looks like Mum, broad shouldered, dark haired, and he's sensible. I am more like Dad, with long legs, long hands, high cheekbones, and hair the colour of beech nuts.

"You're a nurse, you'll know what to do," I said. "Please help, Mum. It's urgent . . ."

"Okay, just let me get my boots . . ."

This time we took the car, and oats, and a headcollar, plus paper and a pen because Mum is efficient and thinks of everything.

Presently she was kneeling beside the pony, listening to her breathing; "I think she's got pneumonia," she said, standing up. "See if she's got a rug in the stable . . ."

"She hasn't got a stable," said David.

"Try the house again. Make sure there isn't a message pinned on the back door," said Mum.

David disappeared while I sat by the pony. She was liver-chestnut with a small white star and her breathing sounded like an engine gone wrong. "She's going to die, isn't she?" I asked.

"We'll have to get her home," replied Mum as David returned with his thumbs down.

"Do you think she can walk that far?" I asked.

"She'll have to. I'll just write a message for the

Bullocks to tell them what we're doing," Mum said, putting Dreamy's headcollar on the sick pony.

We pulled the pony to her feet. "What's her name?" I asked.

"Cocoa, they call her Cocoa," replied David, who goes to school with the Bullock children.

She was very thin and her sides were soaked in sweat. David fetched a tartan rug from the car and put it over her, while Mum put a note through the letterbox.

"You lead. I'll follow in the car," she said.

We had to stop every few minutes to let Cocoa rest. The trees were frosted and the grass crisp and white. Dreamy whinnied when we reached the yard. Mum had bedded down the shed next to his box.

"I've rung the vet. She'll be over at once," she told us, filling a bucket with water.

We put one of Dreamy's rugs on Cocoa and made a bran-mash; then our vet Mrs Chivers arrived and after listening to Cocoa's breathing she said, "They ought to be prosecuted. She's got pneumonia and she's had it for some time."

"Will you put it down in writing? We don't want to be accused of theft," asked Mum.

"Yes. Certainly I will," answered Mrs Chivers.

Later that day the Bullocks came storming round to our place. Dad was home by then.

"Where's our pony? What have you done to her?" demanded Mr Bullock, a massive man with hardly any hair on his head and bulging grey eyes.

The three children, two girls and one boy were snivelling. "We want Cocoa back. We want to ride. You've stolen our pony."

"She isn't fit to ride; she's dying!" I shouted, my voice shrill with anger.

"You took her without asking. How dare you?" snapped Mrs Bullock, in high heels and mauve suit.

Our parents took them aside. When they left they walked straight past us without a word.

"What did you tell them?" I asked.

"We had to threaten them with the RSPCA. It was most unpleasant, but it worked," replied Mum.

We gave Cocoa the best of everything, so that when spring arrived she was looking marvellous. We loved her second only to Dreamy. On the third day of the Easter holidays all the Bullocks appeared in our backyard, the children dressed for riding.

"We want our pony back – now," said Mr Bullock bluntly. "She isn't yours and you are not having the use of her a minute longer."

"Actually we haven't ridden her once," I replied, seething.

"She still needs looking after; she was lousy, starving and nearly dead when we fetched her," Mum said as we walked across the orchard, with David following in floods of tears.

They pulled a tatty halter over Cocoa's neat, chestnut ears and dragged her away.

"They didn't even say thank you," wept David.

"They are clever; the first fine day and they take her back," said Mum.

"And don't offer to pay a penny," I added.

None of us could bear to see Cocoa alone in her horrible paddock, so we avoided going that way; and when at last David and I went past with Dreamy and a bike, she wasn't there. The Bullocks were playing in the garden so, summoning all my courage, I called, "Where's Cocoa?"

And the boy shouted, "It's none of your business."

"She's gone to the sale," called the smallest Bullock. "She went after we had our breakfast, in a big lorry. She will probably go for meat and then we can all have new bikes. You made her naughty. She was all right until you had her. Daddy said you ruined her. We hate you."

"She was quiet because she was dying," I shouted.

"Which sale?" yelled David, turning Dreamy round.

"The sale."

"They mean Wickham, it's today," I wailed.

I leapt on the bike while David, ignoring the hardness of the ground, kicked Dreamy into a gallop. Mum was at home and I rushed indoors yelling, "Cocoa's gone to Wickham market. The Bullocks have sent her and she's going for meat. We made her all fat and lovely and all for nothing."

I heard the orchard gate slam, and a minute later David was flinging his arms round Mum's neck, crying, "We must do something! We must buy her, please, please, please. Don't say no. Please don't say no. She can't go for meat."

"Keep calm. We may be too late and I don't know what your father will say," Mum cried, searching for her handbag.

"I need a pony. Dreamy's too strong for me, please Mum," continued David. "Dreamy's too big for me. I can't mount him."

"Come on, we're off," cried Mum.

We leapt in the car. It took us forty minutes to

reach Wickham market. All the lights were against us and there was a traffic jam in the centre of the town. We parked the car and rushed to the market. There were horses everywhere but we couldn't see Cocoa.

"Perhaps it's the wrong market."

"She's probably gone already. We took too long getting here; if only we could have flown," said David, looking desolate.

We walked up and down the rows of horses, old sad ones, bright hopefuls; a large anxious horse, his knees scarred; ponies straight off the fens, thin as toastracks; two-year-olds shod and advertised as quiet to ride. Mum

bought a catalogue and there she was, *Number 28, Cocoa, 12.2hh, eight-year-old mare* – nothing else. We knew it was as good as a death warrant.

"They are selling Number 53. We're too late," said Mum, leading the way into the sunlit street outside.

"But where is she?" wailed David.

"Sold. Gone," snapped Mum. "We were too late. We did our best, our very best, but we were too late."

"I'd like to kill the Bullocks," cried David, climbing into the car. "She was so sweet, so perfect, so good and now . . ."

"Don't go on, David," Mum said and we saw she was crying too.

We were nearly home when we saw the cattle truck parked in a lay-by. Mum slowed down and we could see ears through the slats, pony ears.

"It just could be taking them to the abbatoir," said Mum, stopping.

We rushed across the road. The driver was reading a newspaper. David and I clambered up the side of the truck and we could hear him talking to Mum, "My mate's gone to get a cup of tea. Then we'll be off again . . .

"You're right, horses shouldn't go for meat; but there's nothing I can do. No one wants them for riding."

"We do," shrieked David.

Mum gave the driver the hundred and fifty pounds that Cocoa had fetched at the auction and we led her home. We couldn't do anything about the others and they haunt me still; they'll always haunt me. Why do people breed horses if there aren't enough good homes? That's what I keep asking myself.

Lost on the Moors

Diana Pullein-Thompson

The road that runs from Elvanfoot to Moffatt in the lowlands of Scotland, not far from the English border, was no place for a rider, even in the fifties, when, with a girl called Ailsa Ravencroft, I rode from John O'Groats to Land's End, so that we should know our own country from top to bottom. It wasn't very long since I had lain in bed for almost a year with tuberculosis, when it was a much-feared disease for which rest was part of the cure, and I think I also wanted to prove to myself and my relations that I was now completely fit and well.

On that particular day when I was lost on the moors, Ailsa's horse, aptly named None The Wiser (for although pleasant-looking he never seemed to learn any sense), had lost his nerve, hating the foul-smelling lorries which pounded their way through the Scottish landscape, and I had gone on alone after arrangements had sadly been made for him to follow by horsebox. I didn't *feel* alone because I had the company of Favorita, and if I spoke to her she always put back one elegant flea-bitten grey ear to catch my words.

It wasn't agreeable for either of us as we made our

way along the shining tarmac, regretting the absence of a verge and flinching at the noise and the smell of the traffic. The drivers cared nothing for a solitary rider – many came so close that damp dust spattered us, and the motorbikes irritated us almost beyond endurance. And all the time to our left lay the great, tempting moors of Moffatt, desolate, empty and quiet but for the call of the curlews and the distant baaing of sheep.

My map showed a Roman road, a track that ran almost all the way, it seemed, to Moffatt, which was a mile from the place where I had arranged to meet Ailsa at half past six. No one had been able to tell me whether the way was still open, for no one but the shepherds walked the moors and none of them were to be found. But at Elvanfoot there had been people who were optimistic.

"Och, as likely as not it'll be open," they told me. "It's a grand ride when the weather's all right." But I knew from experience that there were Scotsmen who, when in doubt, said what they thought you wanted to hear.

It wasn't long, however, before the contrast between the busy, exasperating road and the brown sweep of moorland was too much.

"Nothing venture, nothing win," I told myself, turning up a track that led through a farmstead right to the Roman road.

As I went, my heart lifted and a new spring came into Favorita's long, swinging stride. It was lovely to escape the traffic at last, to canter across the damp green fields with the cool heather-scented breeze in my face and the wide clear sky above, streaked with soaring birds, touched by pale sunshine.

Soon I left the pasture and came to the bleaker moors that seemed to stretch for miles and miles, undulating like corrugated cardboard. Large trees gave way to stunted rowans and then to myrtle; the land grew browner, softer, the grass sparse. For a time the track was there and Favorita, my good grey mare, hurried on eagerly with pricked ears and bright eyes.

She had seen so much: a wild and angry sea at John O'Groats; the cold April sleet falling on the long straight road from Wick; Dunrobin Castle white as icing sugar, shuttered and turreted, a landmark for sailors. She had slept anxiously in its stables which she had believed haunted and in countless alien fields, stables and stalls. She had come through Drumochter Pass and stared wonderingly at the lofty Grampians and the naked hideousness of the hydro-electric developments. She had waited impatiently outside shops while we bought provisions, drunk deeply from burns and rushing rivers and buckets brought by well-wishers on the way. Now her Arab blood from the Royal Stud of Hungary which gave her courage, intelligence and a strong, impatient will, was to be tested in the wild, bog-ridden country that lay before us. But, although she could not be expected to have the native sense of an Exmoor or Fell pony, she had learned stoicism as a second whipper-in's horse, turning back into woods to bring out lost or lagging hounds while all her friends galloped on. As a brood mare she had gained a certain calmness and, in dressage tests, some self-control.

Presently the Roman road narrowed, becoming, I thought, too winding and uncertain to be genuine, and,

when we had covered about seven miles, it petered out. Now the shadows were lengthening with late afternoon. Round and beautiful, the sun was drifting behind clouds in the western sky. There were great gullies – the dips in the corrugated cardboard – which were to plague us all the way, and then, quite suddenly, quite horribly, a shining, glinting, brand-new barbed-wire fence stretching like a thin silver scar to right and left across the landscape as far as the eye could see.

I felt a sudden catch at the heart, as you can guess. Should I turn back and retrace the seven miles to that horrible road? No, I hate turning back. It goes against the very core of my nature. But if there was no path, how could I find my way across the moors? Supposing night came down and I rode in mad circles? Well then, I should come back here to the fence and perhaps pick up the track again and then the road, guided by the lights of the long-distance lorries making their way to England. A compass? I realised then, with a twinge of anger at myself, that I had left it with Ailsa. Determined to travel light, I had emptied a heap of belongings from my saddlebags for her to take in the horsebox. But I had a map, two miles to an inch; the sun was still visible in the changing sky, and my watch still ticked.

"When in doubt, go *on,*" I told myself. "Never turn back."

The posts rose twenty centimetres above the wire, and I knew what to do to lessen the chance of an accident. I fished Favorita's halter out of a saddlebag and tied it from one post to another where the ground seemed firmest. Then I unrolled my mackintosh and hung it over the halter, making that part of the fence into a formidable-looking jump. The top was now some fifteen centimetres higher than the highest strand of wire and if Favorita made a mistake, which wasn't likely, she would probably hit the rope, which might cause her to fall but would not cut her. The obstacle had a solidness which would make her stand back and take care. She had never yet hit any jump hard enough to bring her to her knees. And she was no fool. If anything, she was over-careful.

I mounted her again and, without waiting for any command, she swung round and took me over the jump (for had she not in her youth waited many a time while I made her obstacles out of petrol cans and rustic poles?). She landed heavily and the soil under her hoofs gave way with awful sucking noises, but she righted herself and with an effort pulled herself out and waited to be congratulated with a pat and word of praise.

Halter and mackintosh back in their places, we continued on our way, stopping every now and then to consult the map, sun and watch. It was now ten minutes past five, so I presumed the sun would soon be due west and chose my direction accordingly, but the contours worried me, and I wished I had listened more carefully during geography lessons at school. Perhaps if I had grasped the nettle of longitude and latitude more thoroughly I could have found the map more useful now that I was lost.

There only seemed to be crazy sheep paths that wound here and there and took us nowhere, the sheep who made them having been concerned with picking the best fodder and not with finding their way to Moffatt, or anywhere else for that matter, except perhaps to water when the hot August sun beat down on the shadeless acres. We were forced to make our way across untrodden land, where the ground grew softer the further we went until it squelched under us like a sponge being squeezed of water.

Frightened of bogs, and already seeing Favorita sinking from sight before my very eyes, I dismounted and walked ahead, testing the ground as we went. But she was impatient to finish the journey and enjoy a feed of oats. She felt the first whispers of night in the soft air and heard it in the last eerie calls of the curlews. It was all I could do to keep her behind me and she made the most ridiculous suggestions about which direction we should take, not aware that we were heading for Moffatt – or so I hoped. It is amazing how small and solitary you feel when lost in open landscape, how wide the sky seems and how quickly dusk comes.

I wanted to keep the great curve of the highest hill to my left. I wanted to see another road, marked on the map as leading down into Moffatt, but there was nothing except the corrugated cardboard and the sky, now empty of birds and the golden glow of sunlight. Hues of grey and brown don't lighten the spirits and lift the heart. My thoughts became gloomy and Favorita only wanted to be off the moor and heading for – where? Home, I suppose, still hundreds of miles away.

The gullies grew deeper, sharper and more frequent, their steep sides made hazardous by boulders. Little streams of peaty brown water gurgled fitfully through their bowels. Myrtle grew on their banks.

I hated them, each one seemed worse than the last and the descent was always difficult with Favorita on my heels. Her patience was almost at an end. She wanted to go first, knowing she could manage the boulders without my guiding hand, and, after a while, I let her loose, to find that she always waited for me on the other side, taking the opportunity to pull at the heather and the sparse, nearly colourless grass.

I do not know how many miles we covered in this manner or whether I always kept in the direction I intended. When the ground was firmer I rode, and we made better time. Our side of the world passed the sun's rim, and the sky became blank and greyer still with the approach of night. The moors lay silent before me, hateful, treacherous and cruel, a place where people could die for lack of shade or shelter and sheep lay in winter deep in snowdrifts. With two sweaters under my coat I was warm, and, with spring far advanced, I was not much afraid of a night in the open, but I thought of Ailsa with None The Wiser dragging her around at the end of his halter rope on that little road beyond Moffatt. She would be waiting outside Oakridge Farm, just a name on the map to us and the point we had chosen as our meeting place, perhaps thinking of search parties. And how tiresome to be the cause of a search party, to be so inefficient that people had to forsake their leisure hours to comb the moors for someone who should have known better than to venture there alone without a compass. We had eaten digestive biscuits and cheese for lunch, but now, with my stomach rumbling, hunger added to the gloom.

My map reading was a failure. The road I wanted was not even on the skyline. Even allowing for obstacles and a break of fifteen minutes to rest I should have crossed the moors by six o'clock. It was now half past, and the moors seemed endless. The very sight and smell of them began to fill me with disgust. And the brown hill on my left was a traitor, not being where the map told me it should be.

My mother was fond of saying, "Always darkest before dawn," and it was this thought which consoled me as I rode down yet another gully, skirting the boulders, hitting angrily at an innocent twig of myrtle with my stick. As I came up the other side, I felt my heart lift again, for there, a few hundred metres away, was another road, black and stretched out across the landscape like a snake reaching to snatch its prey.

Never have I welcomed a road more ardently. Standing in my stirrups, I could see a few cars passing along it like insects on a curve of black earth, and, now and then, a lorry. I patted Favorita's firm, freckled neck.

"You'll soon be gobbling oats, and thank you for being so good," I said.

She wouldn't wait for me to look at the map, or rather I could have *made* her, but I didn't. After all, she had suffered enough already on the long and tedious journey over terrain for which she had not been bred. I would still be late, but probably only an hour or so and I would reach Moffatt well before dark. The ground seemed firmer to my now optimistic eyes, and I pushed Favorita into a trot so that we soon reached the road, which was wide and curving with a white line down the middle. And then my heart went down again, for I saw that my old enemy was there, older than the last one of its kind and rusty here and there, but firm – another barbed-wire fence. And I couldn't jump Favorita over this one because there was no verge to the road and that meant we would have to land on the slippery tarmac.

Dismounting, I walked up and down, rocking posts to see if one was loose, but they were all strong and resisted me like rocks. I wished I was a huntsman with clippers attached to a dee on my saddle. I would have to follow the fence until I found a gap or a gate, but would I find one? And which way to go, right or left? And which road was it on the map, this or that? I felt bemused. Had I started to go in circles? Could it be the road I had left just after half past two, or the one I wanted? And which hill was that? All at once my self-confidence had gone. I waved to the motorists in the hope that one would stop and offer help, but although some waved back gaily, others ignored me and none stopped. Favorita dragged at the reins, then rubbed her head against me, nearly knocking me over. My legs began to feel like lead, and my heart scarcely lighter, when suddenly Favorita's head went up and I heard a welcome sound.

It was like hearing the bark of a lost dog and knowing that he is still alive, such was my relief. Looking into the brown distance, I saw a two-legged figure coming down a hillside and, on his left, pale dots which were the gathering sheep.

"Hi, help! Hi, help!"

The wind was against me, pushing back the sound.

"Holt, holt," called the shepherd.

I turned Favorita round to face those specks in the distance. "A grey horse is a wonderful landmark," I said, as she stood like a statue, watching, her head very high, clean-cut in profile, with a wide cheek and a forehead so broad that a brow band had had to be made specially

for her. Her face tapered sharply to a delicate muzzle the colour of the underside of field mushrooms, pinky grey, soft and plushy. Now her nostrils were wide and her breath came quickly as she sniffed the air and listened to the shepherd whistling to his dog.

I remounted, waved with both arms and gave a loud holloa, for suddenly the shadow of dusk had fallen over the hills, heralding the darkness which was soon to come. Should I ride down and meet the shepherd, or wait for him and rest my horse? Favorita, excited by the new hope she felt in me, the whistling and the moving sheep, decided the matter by breaking into a brisk trot. And that was our undoing for, before I had even picked up the reins, I felt her sinking and heard the ominous squelch of ground sucking us downwards.

In such moments I die a thousand deaths, and now in my imagination the treacherous peaty substance was in my mouth, the liquid blinding my eyes and stifling my breath, and the sounds of life were dimmed for ever in my ears.

But instinct always comes to the rescue. Without conscious thought, I flung myself clear, landing on squelchy ground yet out of the bog. But what of Favorita? Her dismayed dark eyes were looking straight into mine and there was no fight in them, only that pained surprise, as though she was saying, "Where have you taken me *now?* What have you done?"

"Up, up, Favorita! Come on, up, up."

In that wide expanse of land and sky my voice was a sad trickle of sound. "Up, up!"

As I had flung myself clear I had at least had the sense to bring the reins with me, and now I pulled on these by way of encouragement, my heart hitting my ribs in hammer blows.

"Come on, up, up!"

But the sludge was rising higher on her flea-bitten grey sides, over the elbows it went and above her stifles. Was there no bottom? Were bogs without end?

Here, disappearing before my very eyes, was the horse I had bought as an iron-grey four-year-old, a mare sold cheap because she was going to be difficult to break, having an awkward temperament, it was said. And now she was more than a horse to me, because over the years we had shared so many adventures. She was a friend struggling for her life, far from home and those kinder Chilterns where she had spent the greater part of her life.

I loosened the reins, thinking she might wish to use her neck as a pivot, and said a silent prayer, and she sank further so that the sludge rose to the bottom of the saddle flaps.

"Up, up, Favorita! Come on, up!"

I made as though to hit her, and suddenly the light in her eyes changed, the heavy look of dismay vanished and was replaced by one of fear, then terror. She began to kick and to struggle as though she had come out of a dream into terrible reality. She threw her head about. She floundered and heaved and puffed and panted, her nostrils wide, her sides heaving, and somewhere she must have hit firmer ground, for all at once I saw her chest again. She moved forwards as well as upwards; her girth was visible, her elbows, dark with the liquid of the bog; her knees chocolate brown. Never have I been gladder to see knees, tendons, and a pair of fine fetlocks.

Then she was free. She was out, scrambling to firmer ground, her breath coming like air from a blacksmith's bellows, her eyes protruding like great marbles, glassy with fear.

"Oh, Favorita. Oh, Favorita!"

What does one say on such occasions? I patted her a score of times. I put my arms across her neck and cuddled her. And then I noticed the dark blood like blackcurrant juice oozing from a puncture by a tendon. A punctured vein? How many more trials were to be sent to us? Had I a good strong handkerchief, a pencil or a stick to make a tourniquet? I put my thumb on the wound and pressed, and after a time the bleeding stopped. The puncture was deep, but the vein was uninjured as far as I could see.

Now the whistling of the shepherd was louder. Looking round, I saw he was a couple of hundred metres away and coming at last in our direction. I waved my arms and shouted. He left the dog looking after the sheep and came striding towards us with that spring in his step which belongs only to men who spend many hours on the hills walking across heather, and moss and myrtle. Handsome and aquiline, with a crook in his hand, he stood looking down on me as though I was a freak gone wilfully astray.

I was beginning to feel a little incoherent.

"She's cut her leg. We landed in a bog. Can you help? I want Moffatt. I have a friend to meet in Moffatt."

His dark angular face showed no emotion, as though people like me were common and tiresome occurrences that interrupted an honest and hard-working man's work.

"Is it far – Moffatt, I mean?"

"It's a wee way to be sure, nine miles when you reach the road."

"Nine miles!"

"Och, maybe a little less."

"And how can I get on to the road? I mean – the fence . . . I want to be quick because of my horse's leg. You see it's swelling already."

"I saw you earlier. I thought you knew the way."

"So did I."

He wasn't a horseman. He couldn't have been, because he didn't even glance at the wound. He waved a long arm.

"Go up that way, and at the top of yon hill there's a gate which will take you out on the old Edinburgh road."

"Like that, diagonally?" I pointed.

"Yes, and when you get through the gate, follow the fence down to the road, and keep going down all the way to Moffatt."

"How do I avoid bogs?"

"Keep to the sheep paths."

"But they wind this way and that."

"Och," He gave a gesture of impatience, a frown lying like a ridge across his weather-tanned Celtic brow. "Keep to the dry land."

"Thank you."

"Avoid the brown patches," he added, allowing the smallest of smiles.

"There was a brand-new barbed-wire fence across the right-of-way," I said, encouraged.

"Put up a month back," he replied.

"Well, goodbye then."

We set off up the hill, which was steeper than it looked, and as we climbed the land grew firmer, but Favorita was lame so I would not ride. At the top there was no gate, only the same rusty fence.

I felt near tears. Nine miles to go when we reached the road, and tomorrow sixteen miles to Lockerbie and then Gretna Green, and my horse was lame! The total journey to Land's End was to be between eight and nine hundred miles in all and we were not even halfway and . . . and . . .

But what was the use of letting one's thoughts run in that vein? "Deal with the matter in hand," I told myself. And then I was lucky, for I spotted a broken strand of wire and saw that a slim verge ran along the road on the other side. The highest remaining strand was only about eighty-five centimetres off the ground, so I draped my mac across it and tried to make Favorita follow me over, but she jibbed. In exasperation I mounted, and then she jumped it at once, lame though she was.

At last we were on the road. Dusk was far advanced and passing cars had their lights on. My feet were blistered but I wasn't tired once I knew I was on my way to Moffatt. The sticking-plaster was with Ailsa, but in a saddlebag I had a pair of socks with leather soles which someone had given me, and I quickly exchanged these for my jodhpur boots. The air was fresh, the cars were few and, far away down in the valley, I could see lights coming on like the first stars, golden and twinkling. Favorita was limping but cheerful, and occasionally she stopped to snatch some grass. Eight o'clock came and I

had a look at the map, to see that I had come from Bog Hill and that on my left was the Devil's Beef Tub, a black abyss surrounded by four hills where the Annandale loons used to hide their stolen cattle. Here, too, in 1745, a Highlander had escaped capture and almost certain death by wrapping himself in his plaid and rolling like a hedgehog to the bottom of the Tub. I did not envy him the journey down.

Eight o'clock, nine o'clock, and there was a police car, climbing the hill towards me. It drew to a halt.

"Miss Ravencroft's companion?"

"Yes, I suppose you could call me that."

"She said if we met you to say she was settled in at Oakridge Farm. Everything is arranged. You take the right turn the other side of the town."

"Thank you. How far?"

"A mile and a half to the farm."

"But to Moffatt?"

"Four or so."

"Four!"

"Well, maybe a wee bit less, three and a half, perhaps."

"I shall need a vet."

"The farmer will help you."

They drove away, and below me lay the valley, where I could now make out whitewashed cottages, dark firs, with the lights increasing as the curtain of darkness came down from the hills. I let Favorita graze for a time, taking the bit out of her mouth, and then we continued on our way.

Those last four miles seemed interminable, and my legs began to ache. But at last we were in the sleepy town and, catching sight of myself in a shop window, I realised how ridiculous and bedraggled I looked. Vanity made me put on the boots again, drag a comb through my hair and set my crash-hat straight. I took the right turn and passed through kinder, domesticated country with large trees, then I saw an old car approaching and, beside the moustached driver, a familiar face.

"Found at last!"

Ailsa stepped out, blue-eyed, blonde, with her thick hair plaited into a pigtail. "What happened?"

"My mother has everything ready for you," said the man with the moustache. "The beds are made up and tea is on the table."

The man's name was Cameron Rankin, and he had a bull-pen waiting for Favorita to share with None The

Wiser, and in no time he was bathing her wound, while she was deep in a bucket of the best Scots oats.

So the long day ended by a warm fire with high tea at half past ten at night, boiled eggs and scones, baps and cakes, and Cameron Rankin's father telling us tales of Nottingham where he had been brought up.

I learned that they had found Ailsa at the gate and offered hospitality, having read about our journey in the newspaper, and would accept no payment. In the morning, the vet came and packed Favorita's wound with penicillin, and bandaged it, and injected her against tetanus, and by afternoon we were on our way, for I was told that walking would stop her leg stiffening. I led her the sixteen miles to Lockerbie, and we put up at a large hotel, a once-only extravagance, with a park in which the horses spent the next morning.

The following day Favorita was sound, and we rode on to Gretna Green – where not one of the famous blacksmiths knew how to shoe a horse.

It was summer when we reached Land's End on schedule, forty-two days after we left John O'Groats. While we admired the great white-crested waves of the Atlantic, an uninvited RSPCA Inspector looked at the horses and declared them very fit.

There had been many fearful, happy and moving experiences on the journey. But the most frightening still exists for me in those moments, when a dismayed Favorita sank down in the bog and I stood by utterly helpless, holding the reins.

The Night Coach Comes In

Christine Pullein-Thompson

Luke crouched in a corner of the yard, his back covered with a rough hemp sack, for rain was falling in torrents on to the rough cobbles.

Thirteen years old, thin and undernourished with a greasy cap on his louse-ridden head, Luke was a middle child in a family with thirteen children. He had been working at the King's Head for almost two years as the ostler's servant and errand boy, and the picker up of dung dropped by the countless horses which came in and out of the yard all hours of the day and night, for the King's Head was an important staging post for both the mail-coaches and stagecoaches.

Presently Luke could hear a coachman's horn, followed by the sound of hoofs. Almost at once lanterns appeared from all directions as though by magic, while a fresh team of horses champed their bits and pawed the cobbles, anxiously awaiting the changeover.

It was a dark night and the night team was always a sad one, the wheelers usually unsound, the leaders with broken winds or knees. For most of them it was the end of the road – a few more weeks and they would be going for the dogs. In the meantime, because of the darkness, no one could see their sad condition.

With a final triumphant blast on the horn, the stagecoach entered the yard. The passengers who had sat outside were only too glad to get down and stamp their frozen feet, and go inside for a quick toddy.

"Take the grey mare, boy, and hurry," the head ostler told Luke. "We haven't got all night."

Luke knew the grey mare; almost blind, she was gentle and had to be coaxed to eat. Now she was wet through as he led her to the water trough, then, when she had drunk her fill, into the warmth of the stable, talking to her all the time as his mother talked to the baby at home which had arrived just three weeks ago.

The mare had no name, but Luke called her Princess and the ostlers mocked him for it. "If she's a princess, I'm a duke," said one.

"And I'm the King of England," said another.

But Luke did not care what they said. He loved the mare.

Soon there was a clatter of hoofs as the new team sprang into action, then the night coach was gone, its lamps shining in the dark.

"Steady there. Eat up, Princess. You won't get any more," Luke coaxed. But the mare was restless. Unable to see clearly she turned her head and snorted, and at the least sound whinnied nervously to the other members of her team, afraid to be left alone, always in semi darkness. Luke's heart ached for her. He knew his voice soothed her. She felt safe with him. They were friends, and Luke had no other friends.

"Eat up, you'll be going out again tomorrow night,"

he told her, rubbing warmth into her ears with chapped hands.

But the head ostler was shutting the heavy doors for the night. "Have done, Luke. She'll do. It's time you hit the sack," he said.

Luke slept in a chair in a room beyond the kitchen. Now he covered himself with a blanket and lay back fully clothed, missing his home where he had shared a bed with six brothers and sisters, all clinging together for warmth. He had no idea of time for his life was governed by a rough shake in the morning and an order to go to bed when the day's work was done. Only Sunday was quieter. Luke's meals were taken with a stableboy called Harry in the public bar when the customers were gone; mostly it was leftovers, sometimes only bread and cheese.

Tonight Luke could not sleep; he was missing his family and could not bear to be alone, so presently he went to the grey mare, opening the big doors and slipping unseen into her stall. She was awake and whickered softly to him. The stable was warm and there was a comforting sound of munching. Luke sat down in the straw beside Princess and she put down her head and blew softly into his face.

"You won't be here much longer. You know that, don't you, Princess?" Luke told her with tears of exhaustion running down his grimy cheeks. "You'll be for the dogs, Princess; they'll eat you and your hoofs will go to make glue."

Luke was nearly asleep, hunched in the straw, when a voice asked, "What the hell do you think you are doing here, boy? Have you no home?"

Luke blinked in the light of a lantern and felt fear running down his spine like a cold gust of wind.

"Just looking at Princess, sir," he said, scrambling to his feet and touching his cap, adding, "I'm sorry, sir. She can't see very well. It makes 'er restless. I weren't doing no 'arm, sir."

"Princess! Is that what you call her? Who are you anyway?" asked the gentleman who held the lantern.

"Luke Hall, sir. I works 'ere." Luke stood to attention, trying to stop himself trembling.

The gentleman was dressed in a cape, pale breeches, long boots, and wore a hat. "I've been looking for this mare for some time. It seems I'm only just in time," he said. And he started to talk to Princess, to stroke her nose and whisper endearments into her ear, while Luke stood speechless with surprise.

"She'll be for the dogs soon, you'll 'ave to be quick, sir," he said at last.

"I know. Now you get back to your bed. I want to see you in the morning – six-thirty sharp," he said.

Luke scuttled back to his room and lay shaking with fear. If the gentleman wanted to see him it could only mean bad news. He might be about to evict Luke's mother from her cottage. Or send Luke to prison! He was obviously a gentleman and they were capable of anything, everyone knew that. Luke imagined his mother being dragged from her cottage and being taken to the poorhouse. At last he fell into a troubled sleep and the next thing he knew was Harry shaking him awake.

"'Is lordship wants to see you. Been stealin', 'ave you?" asked Harry.

"I can't see 'im. I can't," cried Luke.

"'E's waiting in the front parlour for you." Harry grinned before hurrying away.

Luke washed himself under the pump in the yard. Then almost ran home. Then found himself by the door of the front parlour, then back in the stable talking to Princess whose morning feed was uneaten. The yard was in chaos with the stagecoach expected in half an hour. But the head ostler saw Luke and dragged him to the front parlour saying, “Lord Crenshaw wants to see you. Gawd knows what you’ve been up to, and him a county magistrate.”

And then Lord Crenshaw appeared, and closing the door after him said, “I want you to work for me. Is that possible, Luke?” He looked taller in the daylight and more distinguished.

“I’ll ’ave to ask my mother, sir,” answered Luke, staring at his boots which were only held together by their laces.

“We’ll do that immediately then. Lead the way,” said Lord Crenshaw.

“But there’s my work, sir,” cried Luke.

“Damn your work, boy, this is much more important,” replied Lord Crenshaw.

So Luke led the way down the street and across the green to the small thatched cottage where his mother lived with nine of her children. As they approached she came to the door with a baby in her arms and her poor, tired face creased with worry. Then, seeing Lord Crenshaw, she curtsied.

“I want to employ your lad,” said Lord Crenshaw, coming straight to the point. “I live some forty miles away, but I will look after him, Mrs Hall, I promise. He’ll have clean lodgings and some schooling. I shall pay him a fair wage and there will be something for you as well, that I promise. Your lad has a way with horses and horses are what I breed and I want him. What do you say, Mrs Hall?” asked Lord Crenshaw.

Mrs Hall was crying now and Luke ran to her shouting, “I want to go, Mother, I want to go. I will visit you reg’lar, I promise; but please let me go.”

"Yes, that will do, m'lord," said Mrs Hall, collecting her poor wits. "I'm ever so grateful, your lordship. Times are 'ard, me 'usband being away at sea, and the baby just born."

"I know, Mrs Hall. And I promise you will see your lad often, not just once a year on Mothering Sunday. I will make a rider of him, perhaps even a jockey. But first we must get him cleaned up, then we'll be off." And he took off his hat to Luke's mother and bowed as though she were a lady before Luke kissed her a fond farewell, and then they set off together across the green towards the King's Head.

"Princess is not eating, sir," Luke said as they entered the yard.

"She will when she returns home. I bred her, Luke, so she'll know her way about and maybe she'll have a foal, because she's not so old and with special care she may get her sight back. We can hope, Luke, and while there's life there's hope," said Lord Crenshaw.

And Luke thought that was the truest thing he had ever heard.

"So don't worry, Luke," continued Lord Crenshaw. "Just get packed up, there's a good lad, we've got a long journey ahead."

But Luke had nothing to pack. So quite soon they left together in a dogcart, the lord and his man in front, Luke facing backwards, holding on to the grey mare whose real name was Mermaid and whose love had changed his life.

Tarragona

Diana Pullein-Thompson

Horse dealing in our childhood was a dicey business and none too honest. There weren't so many rules about fair trading in those days, and, at certain sales where rules were laid down, there was little comeback if you were done. You simply had to be careful and knowledgeable.

The horse dealer who had sold our parents an aged pony saying that she was seven years old used to bring us ponies to try out for him. We would keep them for a while, school them and ride them in local gymkhanas, and he would bring his possible buyers to see them at our place. We made no charge for the schooling. We gained experience from it, and some of the ponies we could use later on for our pupils. If we managed to sell one of the dealer's animals for more than his asking price we were allowed to keep the change.

There was one pony called Tarragona, whom we particularly liked. She was fourteen-one hands high, very dark bay with black points, with a head that was a little too long to be beautiful. Tarragona was wilful, intelligent and quite unstoppable, but she looked as though she could be turned into a good jumper. At the second show

I rode her in she jumped me out of the ring over three rows of chairs, fortunately unoccupied at the time. Once, when I was riding her bareback in a headcollar through our village, she was frightened by white rags tied to barbed-wire and took me for a John Gilpin ride at full gallop. I thundered past our house and stables, down a steep hill and across a main road, before another steep hill on the main bus route forced her to lessen her speed and I was able to turn her into a driveway.

On another occasion, when coming face to face with a lorry she didn't like on the Reading to Bath road, she leaped over a hedge and landed beside a row of tables

in the garden of a café called The Wee Waif. The café's customers looked rather alarmed, but I had ridden her out again through the exit before they had time to say anything.

Yet, in spite of all her shortcomings, we liked Tarragona and we wanted her for ourselves and to use in the riding-school which was growing rapidly in size. But we could not, at that time, afford the twenty-five pounds which the dealer was asking for her.

As the days went by, Tarragona's mouth and manners improved. She quickly learned simple dressage movements and, although her action was not free enough to make us suppose that she would ever be top class, it was obvious that many riders could learn much from her. She had one failing, however, which no amount of schooling could cure.

It was a matter of temperament, something deep-rooted and unusual, which we found rather endearing. She could not bear people laughing in front of her. A smile was just bearable, but a laugh would turn her face ugly. In a trice she would lay back her ears and sink her teeth in the part of the laugher that happened to be nearest to her. Of course, such eccentric behaviour could be dangerous, and although the tactics we used could be called dishonest, they were also protecting a possible buyer from landing himself with a biter whom he might not understand.

We were young – most of our friends were still at school – and we were hard-up. There was an obvious way to reduce Tarragona's price, which we could justify by telling ourselves that she would be better with us where her particular weakness was well understood and not in any way resented. We informed our dealer that she was inclined to bite (which was part of but not the whole truth). He looked at us with his faded blue eyes set deep in a face the colour of tripe. A watch chain lay across his plump belly; his pale moustache twitched. His rather podgy hands came out of his pockets, where they had been jingling coins.

"As long as she won't hurt any kiddies . . ."

That was his rule. He would lie about the age of ponies, about their origins; he would put boot polish on a scar and keep quiet about a jibber. The unwary would pay him twice as much as a pony was worth if they weren't careful, and he wouldn't turn a hair. So long as he felt the pony was not dangerous for children to handle. Any animal he considered truly vicious would be sent by him to Reading market to be auctioned without warranty.

"No, she might bite one, but she wouldn't kill it," we replied, very matter of fact and down to earth.

"We needn't mention it," he said.

And a few days later he brought a thirteen-year-old girl with middle-aged parents to see Tarragona. We didn't like them; they seemed dull and stodgy, without sparkle, but we rode Tarragona as well as we could. The girl, we thought, was weak – a spineless child. She needed a more reliable pony.

"A fine little jumper," the dealer said, after we had popped Tarragona over a pair of hurdles. "A lovely pony that, a real winner."

The parents spoke little, seeming to communicate through glances at one another. The bun-faced girl showed no special enthusiasm. After a while we returned

Tarragona to her loose box, and then, as the parents leaned over the door to take another look at her, we laughed. In an instant her head came up; her ears flashed back and she bared her teeth. Her head, ugly in anger, shot over the door, and the prospective buyers leaped back only just in time.

"She would never have suited them. She would have been quite miserable with them and sooner or later she would have got the upper hand and started to run away with the girl," we told each other afterwards. And we were probably quite right.

And so a pattern was set. Each time a buyer came we laughed at some opportune moment when we were almost within reach of being bitten, although we always dodged away in the nick of time. The sight of those flattened ears, flashing teeth and sneering nostrils were guaranteed to send any possible purchaser home.

After a while our dealer friend began to despair a

little. What could he do with her? He supposed we wouldn't want her by any chance? We offered him fifteen pounds, and he said he would let her go for twenty. He stood in our yard in his checked suit and laced boots, a shortish, plump figure, a greengrocer who hadn't ridden himself for years, if at all. He wasn't fond of horses; they were simply part of trade, although he had a special love for coaches and carriages. Bargaining was part of that trade. It was the breath of life to him.

"Seventeen pounds," we said.

He agreed. We shook hands. He watched me write the cheque.

"Not like that," he said. "Never leave a gap there. Someone could put a one in front of the seventeen and make one hundred and seventeen. And don't leave a space there either or a sharp customer could add nineteen shillings."

Tarragona was the first pony we bought outright. The earlier ones had been paid for by instalments as we earned the money we needed. We owned her for many years until we gave her away to a good home when she grew too old for riding-school work. She won scores of prizes at local gymkhanas, first with me and then with our cousin, Paulla, and various pupils. She helped all sorts of people to improve their jumping and learn elementary dressage. But we respected her sensitive feelings, her hatred of what she must have seen as ridicule. Laughing was banned when she was around, except once in a while when somebody could not believe that she lacked a sense of humour, and then her demonstration was fierce enough to settle the matter once and for all.

A Sixth Sense

Diana Pullein-Thompson

"Ricky must have a ride," Mum said. "Thunderbird is his pony too."

"Yes, of course, I know," I said. "Do you think we should meet somewhere so he can ride the last bit back? I'll walk beside him."

I was thirteen and Ricky seven. I had been riding for three years at the riding-school, my brother for three weeks. And, since Thunderbird was thirteen-two and lively, I was terrified Ricky would fall off and get hurt.

"Good thinking, Chris," Mum said. "Let's meet by Morgan's Garage. At six o'clock. Yes?"

"Fine, thanks." I mounted. "No problem. See you then. Bye, Rick."

It was a beautiful June evening scented by the last of the lilacs and the wild yellow honeysuckle and, as I rode past houses, every lawn seemed to smell of warm, mown grass. Thunderbird, who is black as Dracula's cloak, with a triangular white star on his forehead and one white sock, was longing for a gallop and tried to take off whenever his hoofs touched turf. I waited until we came to a grassy bridle-path which ends in a hill and then I let him canter, then gallop, and the balmy wind rushed past my cheeks while the sense of being one with my pony and the ecstasy of speed drove away all my memories of a bad day at school. On Thunderbird I was queen. I was higher than the hedges, higher than the walkers we met and the cars that raced past us when we reached the road. I wished Thomas, the boy who sneers at me at school, could see me now as I held between my hands and legs the beauty and the power of my pony.

"Hallo, big-bum," his usual greeting, would be met by a charge, which would force him to back away and then to run, and my voice would follow him:

"Weed, coward," I would shout.

For a moment this seemed a just revenge, and then the next it seemed petty. "Why sink to his level?" I asked myself, letting Thunderbird trot on the verge where wild flowers tossed their creamy blooms in the summer wind and rabbits scattered with white scuts bobbing, while in the trees the blackbirds sang. Thomas's taunts didn't matter. Anyway, I had a new friend at school now, called Selina, who was coming next week to ride with me. She was very bright and had promised to help me with maths.

Thunderbird had belonged to a rather bossy girl called Carol I met at the riding-school, a teenage expert who won most of the prizes at the local gymkhanas and was expected to be in the Pony Club One-Day-Event Team next year. Carol had already replaced him, with an Anglo-Arab called Mermaid, when her parents let us have him cheap because we were nearby and not well off. "I can keep a steely eye on you," Carol had said and, although she laughed, I knew she meant it.

Afterwards I was afraid of meeting her in case I had done something wrong for, instead of hoping she would teach me something, I was stupidly afraid of displaying my ignorance.

But now, riding down our quiet lanes this June evening, life seemed perfect. Tomorrow I would school and jump Thunderbird in preparation for the next local horse show and afterwards I would help Ricky learn to circle at the trot. And I would try harder at school, because if I wanted to continue riding I'd need a good job when I left, as ponies are very expensive to keep. Soon, after a brisk trot, I dropped my hands and let Thunderbird walk on a long, loose rein while my thoughts wandered. And then suddenly, without warning, only about a quarter of a mile from where I was to meet Mum and Ricky, he stopped.

"Walk on." I tried to speak in Carol's commanding voice. But he swung round and started to gallop back the way we had come. And at that moment – you've guessed it – Thomas came pedalling along on his mountain bike.

"Hallo, big-bum! Can't manage your nag? Oh dear, oh dear."

"Go away! Get lost!" My voice was a degrading wail. Then I brought Thunderbird to a halt and, ignoring Thomas, tried again.

Trembling, Thunderbird dug his toes in and then swung round and started to back up the lane. Thomas threw his bike down.

"Can I help?"

"No, thank you. Steady, whoa!" I said as I patted Thunderbird's sweat-soaked neck. What was wrong?

Why was he staring down the lane as though a monster lurked there, waiting for us? "It's all right, it's all right."

"Black Beauty sees a ghost," chortled Thomas. "Why not buy a mountain bike, they keep going."

"Shut up."

"Only trying to help. Can't we be friends, Chris?"

"No. You sneer."

Thunderbird was like a spring under me, ready to leap at the slightest excuse. Feeling his pent-up energy I tried to make him walk in a circle, but instead he gave a half-rear and attempted to bolt back up the road. Then I heard a car and there, horror of horrors, was Carol with her mother.

"What's up? Why's he jibbing? He never jibbed with me." Carol got out of the car.

"I don't know. Something's upset him." I dismounted. I stroked his neck "It's all right, Thunder, it's all right."

"We never shortened his name," Carol said. "Have you been jagging his mouth?"

"Certainly not."

"Riding him on a tight rein?"

"No."

"He's homesick and wants to return to us."

"No, no, he loves Jericho."

"The donkey who shares his field?"

"Yes. He's happy. He whinnies whenever he sees me." Struggling to hold Thunderbird, who was treading on my toes, I shouted.

Thomas started to sing, "I had a donkey and it wouldn't go. That's it," he said triumphantly. "Problem solved. The donkey's taught him to stick his toes in."

"I'll try." Carol snatched the reins from me. "Walk now, walk."

But Thunderbird threw up his head, rolled his eyes and continued to back up the lane, away from Morgan's Garage. I took the reins again, patted his neck. "That's it," I said. "I'm going home the long way." I looked at Carol and Thomas, "And thanks for all your help and advice."

"Don't give in," cried Carol. "Never give in. You must be boss. Wait. We'll nip back and get a lunge rein." She jumped into the car and drove off with her mother.

Thomas looked at his watch, then picked up his bike. "I meant to go down to Morgan's Garage to dig out Pete Connor, but I'd better be getting back," he said; and he pedalled away.

I decided not to wait for Carol, partly because I hated her interfering, which was silly because she only wanted to help, and partly because I wanted to save Mum and Ricky a useless wait. I led Thunderbird a few metres in the direction he wanted to go and then remounted. And, realising I had given in, he quietened down at once. We trotted slowly until I saw a phone box and, grateful for Mum's insistence that we never go anywhere without money in our pockets, I rang home. When I told Mum I couldn't meet her by the garage she asked, "Why ever not?"

"I don't know. Thunderbird's gone crazy and won't go down Farm Lane."

Mum, who's not a patient person, cried, "Oh, for heaven's sake, you're only just in time. We were walking out of the door when the phone went."

"Sorry, sorry, sorry," I shouted. "I'll take Ricky out on Thunder when I get back. Must go – he's pulling at the reins."

I remounted and we trotted off down the longer road to home. A few cars passed, then minutes later Thunderbird leaped two metres or more as an explosion rent the air, followed by flames on the other road and then a plume of smoke. And the sound of barking dogs.

"Steady, it's all right."

Remembering you must always hide fear within yourself when riding, I tried to sound calm. The grey plume became a pall of black smoke. And, straining my eyes, I located the place – Morgan's Garage! The thought turned me cold. Supposing Mum and Ricky had gone there after all? Thunderbird quietened. A siren

screamed – ambulance, fire engine or police? Then suddenly, in a flash, I understood. I looked at my watch. It said five past six. I leaned down and patted him. "You knew. You saved us all."

A man on a tractor came slowly by. I asked what had happened. "A bomb, I reckon," he said.

Then my mind back-tracked and I remembered years ago a wise old blacksmith telling me some horses were psychic. "They see ghosts and things we can't see, and happenings before they happen," he said. "They ain't lower beings, you know, their senses are better than ours. That's wot 'tis."

And I remembered a religious teacher telling me we "see through a glass darkly", and a maths teacher saying people see things in three dimensions, whereas there are apparently at least five. That thought was more than I could grasp. But the Connors, who ran Morgan's Garage, were real. Then I was home and Mum was standing at the gate.

"Thank God you're safe."

"And you, too," I said, dismounting. "Was it a bomb?"

"I don't know, but if you hadn't telephoned us in time . . ." Mum paused as she looked at Ricky before telling me she'd seen a police car drive past on its way to the garage and, shortly afterwards, an ambulance. "It sounded too small to be a bomb. Anyway, who in the world would want to bomb the Connors? This is the English countryside!"

"We might all have been injured and perhaps Carol and Thomas Mason, too," I said. "They were heading that way when Thunderbird dug his toes in." I threw my arms round his hot black neck. "You saved us all, and we thought you were being naughty."

At this moment a woman appeared. "A car and lorry collided, an engine exploded, burst into flames," she said. "Terrible mess, both burnt out. A bystander blown off his feet. Could have been me if I'd been ten minutes later."

"Anyone seriously hurt?" Mum asked.

"I don't know. There's a fire engine there and an ambulance. I couldn't look. I felt so queasy. The lorry was carrying propane gas. Terrible! I just had to tell someone."

"Good grief! Must we have big lorries like that down our lanes?" exclaimed Mum. "Soon there won't be anywhere safe for the children to ride."

"Thunderbird will look after us," I said, feeling slightly sick.

"Well, it's the little old cottages which need the gas, isn't it?" the woman said. "Local people."

"Want a ride?" I asked Ricky.

"Not now. What's propane gas?"

"Sorry, I don't know. Same as calor, I suppose," I said, "which is used for cooking and heating."

Leading Thunderbird back to his field, where Jericho waited for him, I didn't want to think about the awfulness of the accident because it would make me miserable and there was nothing I could do to help the victims. I only wanted to think about Thunderbird and his sixth sense, which had almost certainly saved some of us from horrible injuries.

"We owe you so much," I said as he wandered across the field to have a roll.

The Gentle Giants

Diana Pullein-Thompson

Great dark horses they were, brown as mahogany, with huge feathered legs and splashes of white on their faces, as though a bucket of milk had been thrown at them. A gelding and a mare, called Moses and Rebecca, nine years old and enjoying their last summer. All day they stood under the trees head to tail, keeping the flies out of each other's eyes, never dreaming that their lives might soon end because they were no longer needed.

Autumn came with mists and drifting rain and leaves falling everywhere, and each day the two great shire horses expected to be taken into the yard to be groomed and harnessed to cart, harrow or plough, but no one came for them. Instead they watched farmer George Clipper mount his tractor, whose fuel smelt abominable to the horses, and drive it to do the work they had once done. They would raise their heads and stare at him for a moment with their large dark eyes, which were soft and warm under their black forelocks, and then go back to their grazing or a quiet life under the forest trees.

George called them his "Gentle Giants" and longed

to keep them, but he worked now for a company whose senior director lived up the road in a big old house and bothered more about balance sheets and making money than about animals.

"Horses have no place in farming these days," this fat boss in a dark city suit said, standing well away from the mud. "They've got to go, George; big ones like them eat a lot of fodder – it's cash down the drain. Can't have that, can we? If they can't be sold for work, they'd best go for meat."

Sadness made George's throat so dry he couldn't reply.

The winter came, mild at first and then in early December bleak and cold as the Arctic; it was England's coldest winter for decades. For days and days a biting east wind blew across the frozen landscape. And then, suddenly, snow fell quickly in huge flakes and in a moment paths and trees and fields disappeared under a blanket of white. The cattle came into the stockyard; the horses into the stable. The humans drew their curtains early and the cats stayed in the barns.

On the way home from the station the boss's car stuck in a snowdrift and was soon buried. His wife, a pale, petulant woman with ash-blonde hair and pleading blue eyes, was distraught when he did not arrive for dinner. She telephoned the police.

"This is Mrs Lamont-Brown speaking," she announced in her grandest tones. "Please would you send a search party out for my husband, who is lost in the snow somewhere between Wickley station and our house, Mackstone Abbey."

"Very sorry, madam," said the policeman on duty.

"All our patrol cars were recalled an hour ago."

"I don't believe it!"

"It's true, madam, every road is impassable."

"A helicopter?" she suggested weakly.

"Too many calls on their time. They're putting the sick first."

"He'll die," shrieked Mrs Lamont-Brown, "and he's a very important man."

"He should have heeded the radio warnings, then," the policeman said, calm as stagnant water. "This is the worst snowfall in living memory. Why didn't he spend the night at Wickley?"

"I phoned the station and they said he had left in his car."

"He's most likely lost between you and the motorway, then. I must go, madam. I have urgent calls coming through."

"But this is urgent," shrieked Mrs Lamont-Brown, "my husband . . . " After the policeman hung up, Mrs Lamont-Brown called an old servant, who cleaned the shoes and looked after the conservatory to supplement his pension.

"Please fetch George at once," she said. "The master is stranded somewhere between the motorway and here."

"He should never had set out. He should have more sense." The old man lit his pipe.

"Do as you're told," snapped Mrs Lamont-Brown.

"Can't get to the farm; snow's too deep. I reckon the master's buried in a snowdrift. In 1963 . . . "

"I don't want to hear your horror stories," cried Mrs Lamont-Brown, for desperation had made her lose the last of her manners. "I'll phone the farm then."

"I'll do my best," said George in his slow, agreeable voice. "I've been busy keeping a path clear and seeing to the cows. But I can't promise anything. It came down so quick."

He tried to start the tractor, but its fuel had turned to jelly and the engine wouldn't start, however much he tried and however often he cleaned the filters with his cold hands.

Mrs Lamont-Brown phoned the farm again.

"What's happening? While George messes about my husband will freeze to death or he may try to walk and that will be a disaster. Surely you can do *something.*"

"My George is doing his best," replied Mrs Clipper with gentle firmness.

"It's not good enough," snapped Mrs Lamont-Brown, her blue eyes brimming with tears.

"The tractors are useless once the diesel oil is frozen," said Mrs Clipper, who knew about such things.

"You're letting a man die," shrieked Mrs Lamont-Brown.

Then George left his tractor and went to the harness room, turned on the light and took a collar, breeching, traces and a bridle and walked the short distance he had cleared of snow to the stable, a flashlight in his hand. "There's a job for you. Which of you shall I take?"

And the two horses, who were loose, sniffed his head; he could feel their long whiskers and the white hair that sprouted from their lips running over his scalp, and their warm breath on his neck. He was very tired because he had been fighting the snow for the past two hours and when Mrs Lamont-Brown phoned he had been trying to keep it from the milking-parlour door.

"Moses," he said. "Let's take you."

The gelding pushed his head through the collar and looked at the silent, white world which only two hours earlier had been full of different colours and, for him, loud with the distant roar of traffic on the motorway which carved its way through the landscape only a mile from the farm.

"Mrs Lamont-Brown wants you to go to see her," called Mrs Clipper from an upstairs window.

"Tell her I'm off to find her husband," shouted George, grabbing a shovel before climbing from an old mounting block on to Moses' back.

The sky had cleared and a moon rode high above the trees, lighting the land around them. The snow reached the horse's belly, but he waded through it and, instinctively knowing what was wanted, made his way to the road. Here the snow balled on his feet, so sometimes he seemed to be walking on stilts, but, because he wasn't shod, it soon fell off and then for a few moments he would walk normally again. The road dipped here and there and in every dip there was a snowdrift to be negotiated and at times Moses seemed to be swimming, his huge body pushing back the snow. When they came to the fifth drift, they saw a stick sticking out of the snow and stopped. Leaning down, George shovelled snow off what was, as he had expected, the roof of a car.

"Mr Lamont-Brown, are you there?" he called, but his voice met only the uncanny silence of the snowbound night.

Then he slipped off Moses and stood on the roof

and called again, and a voice answered, saying, "That's me," softly like the last whisper of a dying breeze.

"Hang on, sir," said George. "We'll soon have you out of this drift."

He shovelled and shovelled, clearing the snow from the roof of the car and then from the sides of the car and at last from the ground. Then he fixed Moses's traces to the front of the car, climbed on his back from the bonnet and shouted, "Up there, for'ard," slapping the horse's flanks with his cold hands. Moses pulled and pulled, throwing his weight into the collar and dropping his head, and then the car moved. It slipped out of the drift, and George shouted "Whoa!"

He climbed off Moses, undid the traces, opened the car door and half lifted out his boss. He got him on the bonnet of the car and then on to the horse, so that he was lying across the withers. "Can't pull it all the way home, sir," he said.

"I made a hole with the stick so I could breathe," whispered the half-frozen man as George jumped off the car and sat behind him.

Moses, who could hear Rebecca neighing forlornly, retraced his steps, while George held his boss firmly. At last, standing at an upstairs window, Mrs Lamont-Brown saw in the moonlight Moses' head, big and proud with shining eyes, his mane flecked with snow, which clung also to his feathered legs. She told the old servant to fetch the master, but it was George who carried him in.

"Let him thaw out slowly," he said. "No hot-water bottle, mind, but plenty of blankets, and warm sugared tea when he wants it." He laid the man on the sofa and rubbed his hands and then, after taking off his expensive shoes, his feet, while Mrs Lamont-Brown leaned over them both, fluttering her hands.

"Oh, my poor Andy! So terribly white! A doctor!"

"Doctor can't get through," said George, as the old servant fetched blankets.

"Will he live?" Mrs Lamont-Brown's voice was full of awe.

"I thought I was finished," whispered her husband. "Done for. I stuck that stick up for passers-by to see and to let the air in, but I didn't think anyone would come. I thought I would die of cold."

"Oh, my poor darling!" cried Mrs Lamont-Brown, starting to wrap him in blankets.

"I'd take off his damp coat first," said George. "Yes, sir, the stick and the horse saved your life."

"He's waiting outside. Look," Mrs Lamont-Brown went to the window. "He's better than a tractor."

"Ah well," said George. "Them tractors are only machines, aren't they? No brain, no heart."

"Why's he waiting?"

"The last folks here, the ones before you came, used to give him and Rebecca sugar-lumps, so he's hoping. Horses don't forget," George said.

"Tom," said Mrs Lamont-Brown to the old servant, who had taken on her wrapping-up job, "go to the kitchen and find the best lump sugar."

The next morning was dry. When George had cleared the path from the farm to the house, Mr Lamont-Brown tottered round to the stable. He looked at the horses and stroked Moses' nose.

"The world doesn't change much, does it?" he said.

"I don't get your meaning," confessed George.

"When things go wrong it's back to horse power. Their fuel doesn't freeze. Don't sell them," said Mr Lamont-Brown, looking weak, white and tired. "After what happened yesterday I want them to stay here for life – and you too for that matter. Use them when you can and bring them over to the house for sugar every Sunday. And here, for you." He handed George a bottle of expensive whisky. "Just a token. I can never thank you enough, you know that. Perhaps an increase in salary."

"I'll be glad to drink your health, but money's nothing to do with it," George said. "It was Moses did it. Keeping the horses is thanks enough for me."

Lettie Lonsdale

Diana Pullein-Thompson

We live in Cherryford, an old village with an old bridge that crosses the shallow waters of the river Lynne; a village of low-roofed cottages and dreaming houses and quiet sheltered gardens, unfound by townsmen or modern house-builders, a long, low village of trees and mossy walls and cobbled yards.

Our house stands on the left bank of the Lynne, and all day and night we can hear the murmur of the water amongst the rushes. And in the summer when we take tea in the garden two stately swans drift by our lawn and beg for food. We have christened them the Lady of Shalott and Sir Lancelot.

Our house is a shabby pink – badly painted because Mum and I were the painters. The outside woodwork is an unusual colour; neither light nor dark it resembles Picasso's blue. By the back door there are two pink loose boxes, standing in a small cobbled yard that is rough and uneven and difficult to sweep. A white five-barred gate leads from the yard to a little crooked orchard, fenced by green hedges which are kind to the eyes and harbour the birds in spring.

I brought Martini to Cherryford in the dusk, when the Lynne's waters were darker than the darkening skies, and the river meadows drifting into slumber.

I had ridden her from Stringwell Market, bareback in a plain snaffle, and I already loved her long stride and lively carriage. She had shied and jogged in the town, but out in the open country she had become calm, as though quietened by the stillness of the evening, and had walked on a loose rein.

Our village is very interested in the movements and behaviour of its inhabitants. Nothing goes unnoticed. As I rode down the old and lovely street, people came to their windows and doors to watch me on my way.

Tatters, my wire-haired terrier, was waiting for me in the yard. He's a disreputable character, always rabbiting and tearing his ears and getting stuck in holes. But he is very brave and very sporting. One winter he had quite a battle with a fox in an earth in Duke's Wood.

He's fond of horses and I was glad to see that he took a liking to Martini.

My mother came running out of the back door. "Here you are at last! We wondered if you were ever going to get here. Push her into the loose box. Nick and I have put some hay and water ready. And then come in and have some supper. There's ham and salad and cider."

At that moment my seven-year-old brother, Nicholas, came through the window.

"She looks jolly good. I expect Pablo will be pleased. Why did you ride her without a saddle?" he asked.

"Because Pablo's wouldn't fit her," I said.

"Why wouldn't it fit her?" asked Nicholas.

"Because it is too small."

"Why's it too small?"

"Oh, do stop asking questions. Why are your old clothes too small for me? Because I'm larger than you, being older," I said, feeling exasperated.

"Is Marty older than Pablo? And will Pablo grow bigger like me?" asked Nicholas.

"No. Now do stop. I want to settle Martini," I told him.

"When are you going to introduce Pablo to her?" he asked.

"Tomorrow."

"Why not now?"

"Because I'm not."

"Why's she sleeping in the stable? It's so hot."

"Because she's been in since the autumn."

"In where?"

"A stable."

"Which stable?"

"Pip's and Lydia Pike's stables."

"Who's Lydia Pike?"

"You know perfectly well, Nicholas. We've been talking about Lydia Pike for days."

"*I've* never heard you."

"That's because you never listen to what people are saying."

"I do."

"You know, it's your bedtime," I said hopefully.

"No, it's not. Mummy said I could stay up ever, ever so late tonight."

"All right. Let's go in to supper now," I suggested,

giving Martini a last pat and turning towards the house.

"You've forgotten to say goodnight to Pablo."

"No, I haven't. I'll do it later when I shut up the hens."

Indoors we all talked about Martini. At least my mother and I talked and Nicholas asked questions and my father listened.

Riding back from Stringwell I had laid my plans. I knew that Lydia Pike's rough handling had made Martini frightened of her mouth, constricted and excitable. I would start to cure these faults by hacking her quietly in a snaffle on a loose rein.

It was term-time and I had to go to school every weekday, but my homework was not difficult and I could spare an hour for riding in the long summer evenings.

"If you get into real difficulties you can write to Pierre," said Dad.

I think I must explain now that Monsieur Pierre de St Denis, the well-known French horseman, is a friend of my father. Last summer he asked my parents and me to stay at his estate on the outskirts of Fontainebleau. He lent me a little grey mare called Chiffon to ride, and instructed me in the art of equitation. It is from him and the books he recommended me to read that I have learned most about riding and schooling. And I shall never forget those six wonderful weeks in France.

After supper I paid a call on Martini and then wandered out into the orchard to say goodnight to Pablo, the little black pony on which I first started to ride. He was lying against the hedge in a corner, looking very snug and sweet. The night was cool and clear. The moon sailed high amongst her stars, touching the cherry boughs with silver and casting great pools of silver by the gate. I could see the Lynne, drifting before the breeze with barely a ripple. I could see the noble outline of Martini's head above the loose box door. "Pablo," I said, "one day I'm going to be a famous equitation expert. I'm going to jump for England, in Dublin, in Nice, in Rome, in New York, all over the world."

I put an arm round the little black neck and looked at the moon and stars, so clear and lovely in the evening sky. I wished that I could express my feelings in oil on canvas. The pools of silver and darkness . . . the cherry boughs . . . the dead elm, sharp and naked, etched against the sky . . . the stillness and the winding river . . . the old pink house silent amongst the trees . . . the stable roof . . . the curving lawn . . . the sleeping flowers. The beauty of it almost hurt me. My ambitions faded. I patted Pablo and then wandered slowly to bed.

I gave Martini one day in which to settle down and then I started schooling her in earnest.

At half past four each day I would return from school, gobble my tea, do my homework and then ride till darkness fell. The weather was perfect; the evenings warm and fine. Those last hours before nightfall always passed too quickly.

My efforts were well rewarded. Each day Martini seemed quieter and more confident. She shied less often, she became steadier on the bit; she learned to trot on a loose rein. But I had vowed not to canter her for a fortnight. I wanted the rides to be as peaceful and calming as possible. Often I would stop and, dismounting, let her graze while I admired the sunset – golden sands and red-tipped rocks and a darkening sea of blue.

Sometimes when we turned for home all the world seemed asleep. Dusk had fallen and the birds' last songs had faded. The wild flowers in the woods and at the roadside were shut in slumber. The fields lay silent in the gathering darkness. The trees loomed dark and eerie, watchful sentinels of the night. Far away beyond the river an evening star was shining and a great stillness descended on the land.

Presently May turned to June and all Cherryford was bright with blossom and sweet with the scent of hay. Old Bob Silver, the boatman, did some trade with his boats and Nicholas started to learn to swim.

I cantered Martini during the first weekend, and a few days later I started to school her in a corner of the orchard. I was disappointed to find that balancing exercises excited her. She seemed to forget all that I had taught her on those evening rides and would barely walk a step.

Nicholas was exasperating. He made a point of watching me from his bedroom window, which looked out on the orchard, and he asked endless questions.

"Why doesn't she walk?" he would call.

"Because she's overexcited," I would answer.

"Why's she excited?"

"Because Lydia knocked her about when she schooled her."

"Who's Lydia?"

"Lydia Pike."

"Why did Lydia Pike knock her about?"

"Because she is a horrible girl with a bad temper."

"If I was Lydia Pike's mummy I would hit her ever

so hard. I would make her black and blue. Wouldn't you, Lettie?"

"No, I wouldn't. Now stop asking questions and let me school in peace."

But it needed Mum to stop Nicholas. He would never take much notice of me.

During June I schooled Martini four times a week and hacked her twice a week. I kept strictly to a programme when schooling. It was as follows:

Ten minutes walking and trotting on a loose rein, to loosen her up. Thirty minutes balancing exercises at the walk and trot, including work at the ordinary walk, the ordinary, and slow and extended trot, reining back, halting, turning on the forehand and circling. Five minutes cantering and five minutes walking over a pole on the ground.

Her halting was very bad. She tried to swing her quarters to the right, she snatched at my hands instead of accepting the bit and relaxing her lower jaw, and she stood with her legs all anyhow. Hacking, her tempo seemed good, but in the orchard she was nervous and jumpy and there was no cadence in her trot. At first she had only to see the pole lying on the ground to start bucking and plunging. In fact she became so upset that I had to dismount and lead her over it in the first two lessons. But gradually she became more sensible and eventually she paid no attention at all. Cantering, she was difficult to control, and several times she tried to take me over the orchard hedge. She was very fussy in the mouth and at times I found it impossible to stop her in a plain snaffle.

The people at Cherryford were very interested in Martini. The baker and the blacksmith gave me advice, and Bob Silver told me to stick to boats. And many were the compliments passed on her appearance. Each day I was encouraged by her improvement. And then something awful happened, which gave Cherryford a topic of conversation for weeks.

It was a Saturday in the third week of June, and for the first time Nicholas was allowed to come riding with me. He could canter now and Pablo, although obstinate in the orchard, was very good and obliging on the roads.

It was a bright, windy morning. There were little rustles in the hedgerows and the elms round our house creaked as the wind tossed their branches to and fro. The Lynne sparkled with dancing waves and in Duke's Wood a cuckoo called.

"We will go for ever, ever such a long ride, and

when we get home we'll be so hungry that we'll eat all the lunch," said Nicholas.

"Don't tire him, Lettie," said Mum.

We went out in high spirits, taking Tatters with us. For a couple of miles we rode quietly by the river. Then we went through the treasured, old-world village of Ferryfields, climbed a long, steep hill and entered the large, overgrown woods that lie between Ferryfields and Grayley. Martini was walking well with a long free stride, and every now and then I had to wait for Pablo. It was a new piece of country to Nicholas and he was so interested that he would not hurry. It was very quiet in the woods; only our hoofs on the hard pathway and the whispering of the wind amongst the trees broke the stillness. Tatters was in heaven. Far below us in the valley he hunted rabbits, but the sound of his barking drifted away from us to the river. Presently we trotted and Martini shied at shadows and birds. On two occasions she all but unseated me. Nicholas thought her very silly.

"Silly old Martini. Fancy being frightened of little things like that. Pablo isn't," he said, and then he started to chant his pet nursery rhyme:

"Solomon Grundy,
Born on a Monday,
Christened on Tuesday,
Married on Wednesday,
Fell ill on Thursday,
Worse on Friday,
Died on Saturday,
Buried on Sunday,
That was the end of Solomon Grundy."

And at the same moment Martini began to misbehave. We had reached a windy part of the wood, in full view of a magnificent roll of downs. There was an exhilarating freshness in the air and the great stretch of uncut hay before us rippled like a summer sea. Little clouds raced madly in the deep blue sky. Martini began to sneeze and pull and kick up her heels. I sat down hard in the saddle and tried to collect her, but in a plain snaffle it was difficult. Nicholas continued chanting the rhyme.

Our pathway ran beside the downs. If we started galloping we could gallop for miles over all those rolling acres of grass and wheat, oats and barley. I could feel Martini tingling as she sniffed the air. I sympathised with her, but I dared not canter in the open country with Pablo and Nicholas. Nicholas, of course, did not realise that I was in difficulties. After he had repeated the wretched nursery rhyme several times, he began to ask me riddles.

"Lettie," he shouted, "how can you say hungry horse in four letters?"

"I don't know and I haven't time to think," I shouted in reply.

"I've got you! You don't know. Silly old Lettie. Shall I tell you?"

"Later, when we get home." I used my legs and raised Martini's head to prevent a buck.

"MTGG," called Nicholas triumphantly.

"Oh, jolly good," I said.

"Why does a thirsty woman carry a watch?" he asked.

"I haven't a clue," I yelled, trying to straighten Martini, who was dancing sideways, with my legs.

"You might try," pleaded Nicholas.

"Well, catch up. Then I might be able to hear you," I said, hoping that Pablo's presence would calm Martini.

"Okay. Now," said Nicholas, when he had caught up, "why does a thirsty woman carry a watch?"

"So that she knows when the inns are open," I replied.

"Wrong. Wrong. I've got you ! You don't know, do you? Because it's got a spring in it. Now I'll ask you another."

"No," I said. "Please don't. Can't you see that I'm having a job with Martini? She's bucking and playing up."

"Why is she bucking?"

"Because the open fields make her want to gallop."

"Why? Why do the open fields make her want to gallop?"

"For goodness sake, be quiet for a minute or I'll never take you for another ride as long as I live," I said, as Martini gave a whopping buck which nearly sent me over her head.

The remark silenced him for a few moments, and then luckily the pathway turned back into the wood and Martini became calmer. Soon we entered a lane and turned for home through Grayley, which is a little hamlet with a few thatched cottages, a tumbledown farm and a well.

It was here that Martini first became really frightened; a child was rolling a metal hoop along the lane. It made an awful rattling noise. Martini stopped dead and watched, with quivering nostrils and fast-beating heart. Nicholas, of course, didn't notice her fear, shouting "What are you stopping for? I'm hungry. Come on."

I called to the boy to stop rolling the hoop for a minute, but he didn't hear. Each moment brought him nearer and nearer with the terrifying object turning in front of him. Martini stood stock-still with arched back, raised tail and shaking sides. Then, as it came within ten metres of her, she swung round and galloped back up the lane as fast as her legs would carry her. At the top by the wood she stopped and, turning, gazed down to Grayley where Nicholas and the boy with the hoop were talking. I patted her and lectured her, and then gradually

I persuaded her to go back down the lane and walk past the boy.

"What on earth are you doing? I thought you didn't like galloping in lanes," said Nicholas.

I told him about the hoop and then we walked on in silence. Martini was still nervous. She hesitated at every corner and sidled round every object in the hedgerow.

"She *is* a silly horse," said Nicholas.

"She isn't. She's been knocked about and she's highly-bred and highly-strung," I retorted. I was fed up with Nicholas.

There were fields either side of the lane now, untidy fields with old, rusty water troughs and broken carts and tins lying about. Martini found plenty of things to frighten her. She walked with quick, springy steps. Then suddenly she stopped dead, turned round and uttered three piercing snorts.

"She's a wild mustang!" said Nicholas.

There were a dozen pigs in the field, fat pink porkers. They were grunting and snuffling in the ground. They looked very greedy and very wicked. Martini stood stock-still, her eyes fixed on them. I could feel her heart beating and her flanks heaving. I spoke to her.

"What's the matter now?" asked Nicholas in exasperated accents.

"Pigs," I said, and, as I spoke, all the pigs saw us and of one accord came racing down the field towards us, making the most hideous grunting noises.

I shall never know why they made that charge. Perhaps they thought we were going to feed them. They were a monstrous sight and they shattered Martini's nerves. She gave them one terrified stare and then galloped for home. I sat down hard in the saddle and tried to collect her, but to no avail. I pulled at her mouth. I tried to turn her into the hedge. I said, "Whoa, steady. It's all right. Whoa, whoa, walk, silly, walk, Martini. Pigs won't hurt you," in what I hoped were calming tones. But everything failed. We galloped on.

I had never been so fast before in my life. The fields flashed by. Each moment brought us nearer home. I was a little worried about Nicholas. Looking back, I could see Pablo was following Martini. Nicholas rode jolly well considering his age, but I was afraid he could not stand a long gallop and the ground was hard here for falling, hard and rough with big jagged stones. I tried pulling at Martini until my arms ached, and then I tried sitting still and talking to her. I especially wanted to stop before I reached Cherryford. But as the minutes passed, and Martini's gallop was as fast as ever, my hopes faded. I must say she was a beautiful mover, and if the lane had not been so rough and Nicholas and Pablo had not been following at their own breakneck speed, I think I would have enjoyed the gallop.

Presently we turned a sharp corner and saw Cherryford lying in the valley. Red and brown rooftops, apple blossom, and the river winding silver in the sun. And there was our own pink house, just visible through the trees. What will our mother and father say, what will Bob Silver say, when Nicholas and I go galloping down the street? I asked myself. And of course I had yet to know the answer. And then the dreaded moment came. I passed the signpost that points to Ferryfields, Longhatch and Grayley, and raced down the street for home. With all my heart I wished our hoofs did not make such a clatter on Cherryford's partly cobbled street. But I wished in vain. Doors and windows were flung wide. People ran to the side of the road out of our way. A car stopped abruptly. Jack Hill, the farrier, hurried to his gate. Mrs White, the grocer's wife, left her counter. John Hayward left his baking and Bob Silver left his boats. All to see us go clattering by.

"I'm John Gilpin!" cried Nicholas.

Then there was only the bridge between us and home. A child heard our hoofbeats and ran screaming down the road past our house. Three people in a canoe stopped paddling and watched our wild approach. Martini reached the bridge and took it in three bounds. Our white five-barred gate was shut, but she did not hesitate. She jumped and hit the top and fell. For a moment I saw the drive rising to meet me, then I had hit the gravel and Martini was lying on my leg – I marvelled at her lightness – and then with a flash of silver shoes she had scrambled to her feet and was standing shaking in the drive. I rose slowly. I was not hurt, but I had to collect my thoughts. I took hold of Martini's rein and patted her. She had scraped her side and one leg.

"Silly girl," I said.

Then I saw Nicholas opening the gate behind me.

"Are you all right, Lettie? I thought you were killed," he said.

Mum came out of the house with Justice and Jasper at her heels. She had been painting. She still held a palette in one hand and her trousers had red paint on them. "What on earth are you doing?" she asked.

"We had a bit of a runaway. Some pigs upset

Martini. Nicholas was jolly good and galloped all the way from Grayley. Where's Tatters?" I said.

"Here he comes," said Mum, and at that moment a very bedraggled Tatters came panting through the gate.

"Poor fellow, you have had a chase, haven't you?"

"What actually happened? Don't be so frightfully mysterious," said Mum.

"Look, I must bathe Martini. She's got several nasty scratches. Do you mind if I wait and explain at lunch?" I asked.

"All right, but buck up," my mother replied.

My parents were at first rather alarmed by the tales they heard of my gallop from Grayley to Cherryford. Nicholas gave a vivid description at lunch while I bathed Martini. Mrs Wise, who helps us out sometimes, came hurrying round at two o'clock to find out if either of us had been hurt, and then told my mother what she had seen.

She said: "I was indoors, dishing up the dinner, when all of a sudden I 'eard their 'oofs come clattering down the road. 'What on earth is that?' I called to Arthur. And then I could tell it was 'orses like and I ran outside and there they were tearing down the road like a couple of mad things. Never seen ponies go so fast before, that I 'aven't. Thought they were going straight through Mrs White's, 'onest I did. And poor old Nick looked as though 'e was going to fall off any moment. And then they 'eaded for the river. And I thought, *they've* 'ad it. My 'eart leaped into my mouth as young Lettie galloped up the bridge and then I could see neither 'er nor Nick no more. 'Arthur,' I said to my 'usband, 'directly I've finished my dinner I'm going down to see what's 'appened to them Lonsdales – poor little mites.'"

Bob Silver gave his own special version to Dad in the street, and on Monday Jim Hayward and Mrs White compared notes on our doorstep in Mum's hearing.

But in the end my parents were jolly decent and sensible. They just said that I was not to hack Martini again until she had benefited from another week's schooling in the orchard. I was surprised and pleased by their decision, and on Sunday, filled with hope, I rode her for an hour and a half in the orchard. Then on Monday the weather changed. It rained and rained and rained. And I was sick and had to stay in bed, which was absolutely maddening. Mrs Wise said I was sick because of my gallop and fall on Saturday. "Delayed shock, that's what it is," she kept saying. Dad said I was sick because I had eaten too many unripe cherries. Nicholas said I was sick because it was wet and I didn't want to go to school, and Mum said I was sick because the change of weather had upset me. Meanwhile Martini spent two days resting in the field.

On Wednesday Mum said I need not go to school, but I was well enough to go out so I planned to ride Martini in the morning and afternoon. It was a cold damp day, raw for the time of year and muddy underfoot. The Lynne looked dark and dirty. The trees were still weighed down by the water on the leaves. The skies were dull and grey and threatened rain.

Directly after breakfast I caught and groomed Martini. The rest had made her nervous again. She jumped whenever I put a hand near her head. She must have been struck over the head at some time or other, for she was always frightened of a raised hand or a riding-stick. Mum, Mrs Wise and Nicholas came to watch me schooling and their presence filled me with trepidation. Martini was very excited and some time passed before I managed to make her stand still to be mounted. She jogged through the white gate into the orchard with her head and tail very high. She shied and goggled at Jasper and Justice, who were lying panting in the grass.

"Be careful now," warned Mum.

I felt as though I was riding on a spring that would suddenly shoot me high up into the skies. Martini simply would not let me into her back and I was sure that I had never felt so insecure in the saddle before.

"For goodness sake be careful, duck. She looks wicked this morning," shouted Mrs Wise.

"She looks terribly fresh," said my mother.

I shortened my reins and Martini tugged impatiently at my hands. Then she heard a rustle and shot into a gallop. I used my legs and pulled at her mouth, but she stuck her nose in the air and took me to the gate into the stable yard.

"Do be careful, darling," said Mum,

"That pony will be the death of you, that she will," called Mrs Wise.

"Why did you go to the stable yard?" asked Nicholas.

I turned Martini round, but she didn't want to go back to our schooling corner. She bucked and plunged and ran backwards and pawed the ground.

"Lettie, I think you had better dismount right away," shouted Mum.

"Else you'll 'ave another accident," added Mrs Wise.

Suddenly I felt angry. "I'm certainly not going to give in to her. She's going to do as I say," I shouted.

"Ride a cockhorse to Banbury Cross," said Nicholas.

"Don't be silly, Nick," said Mum.

I hit Martini, and she bucked and dug the ground with each front hoof in turn, almost kneeling at the same time.

"You mark my words, that pony's wicked, that she is," called Mrs Wise.

I used my legs and hit Martini again, and she swung round with a half-rear and faced the gate again. I turned her once more, thinking, This is awful. I must win or they'll make me sell her, and I set into her with my legs. And then suddenly she trotted forward.

"Oh, well done, Lettie. Jolly good. You've won!" cried my mother.

But she spoke too soon. For the next moment Martini heard another rustle in the hedge. She bucked, dropped her near shoulder and then swung round and galloped back towards the gate. The buck unseated me a little and I lost my stirrup, and the swing round threw me on to her neck. I mustn't fall off, I thought, I mustn't. Then the gallop threw me off all together and I landed on the wet, cold grass in a sprawling position.

The next moment Tatters was licking my face, and Jasper and Justice were looking at me with doleful eyes and wrinkled, worried brows.

I leapt to my feet at once, saying, "It's all right, dogs. I'm not hurt."

"Gracious, child, are you sure you're not 'urt?" cried Mrs Wise.

"Are you all right, Lettie?" asked my mother in calmer tones. "You landed awfully neatly. It was the devil of a buck."

"Yes, I'm all right, thank you," I replied. Then I saw Nicholas had caught Martini (he's always good in an emergency). I mounted her again and started to trot her round the orchard. She was thoroughly excited now and very awkward. Her back was up and she either tugged at the reins or stuck her nose in the air to evade the bit. Again I met with disaster. This time Minnie, our tabby cat, frightened her and she gave three bucks instead of one. I landed on my feet and wrenched my little finger trying to hold on to the reins.

"Lettie," said Mum, "you've done enough riding for today, and that's flat."

"But I can't give in to her," I cried.

"No arguing," said Mum.

"But you don't understand," I said.

"Yes I do. I understand terribly well. And you are to turn that pony out into the orchard and come indoors at once. It's nearly lunch-time anyway." The firmness of my mother's voice depressed me.

"Oh, Mummy, don't be mean," whined Nicholas.

"And you can come in and help me fry the omelettes, Nick," she added.

Of course I had to do as I was told. I caught Martini and scolded her, and then I turned her loose and leaned on the gate and looked at the dripping trees and the monotonous grey sky.

It's a miserable day, I thought, and I should hate to try and paint it. I don't wonder Martini was in a miserable mood. One shouldn't ride when the weather is so awful and one has only just recovered from a bilious attack. It shows a lack of imagination.

Then I fell to wondering why Martini was getting worse instead of better. What was I doing wrong? Should I change her bit? She ought to enjoy being ridden. Perhaps I was too rough with my hands. I mused until my toes and feet and nose were cold, and then I remembered that I should be having lunch, and hurried indoors feeling very apprehensive about what my mother would say on Martini's behaviour.

She actually said very little and could offer no practicable suggestions, and I felt very depressed.

It started to rain really hard after lunch. There was a leak in our roof and the water came dripping through the ceiling in the passage upstairs, and downstairs we could hear it rushing madly into the well under the scullery floor. Nicholas said:

"Rain, rain go away,
Come again another day,
Nicko wants to make some hay."

Tatters returned soaking wet from a ratting expedition. Jasper and Justice gazed dolefully out of the window. I was sunk in the deepest despair. What *was* I to do with Martini? I collected all of my books on schooling horses and, shutting myself in the dining-room, tried to solve the problem.

It was *Difficult Horses* that first gave me an idea. I found that James Findlay, the author, in his chapter on *Bucking . . . The Causes and Cure,* gave the following advice: "Several weeks in a drop nose-band and running

martingale will often work wonders with a bucker. Used with a plain egg butt snaffle with two reins – the martingale should be fixed to the bottom rein – this combination will put the rider at an advantage and gives him more control than he would have in a double bridle without any danger of the horse becoming constricted or afraid of his mouth."

It was food for thought. I sat thinking in the dining-room till teatime. The first question which arose was, from where could I borrow a running martingale and drop nose-band? Most children in my predicament would approach their Pony Club, I decided, but I had a guilty conscience where my branch was concerned because I had not attended any rallies during the past year. To tell the truth, I was disheartened by previous experience. You see, I was always put with the "little ones" and instructed by Miss Fipps, a hard-faced, elderly lady with grey hair permanently encased in a most unbecoming net.

Miss Fipps was one of the old school. "Lift him, Lettie," she would cry, as I approached a fence. And, "Put your legs farther forward and your stirrups right home, and bend your wrists," as I was schooled in the field. And she would tell my parents that my position in the saddle was absolutely incorrect. Once she pulled me out in front of the other "little ones", who were all under ten, and said, "Now, this is exactly how you shouldn't sit. You see how Lettie rides. Her reins are too short; her legs are too far back; her feet are not far enough in the stirrups and she sits too far forward in the saddle. If she had to ride a more difficult pony she would come to grief in no time. With her position she couldn't hold a pecking horse up for a moment."

I didn't really mind these criticisms very much because I had complete faith in Pierre St Denis, who had spent hours correcting my "terrible English seat" and teaching me all that Miss Fipps objected to so strongly. If only I could have been put with the "bigger ones" I think I might have improved, for sometimes they had fairly well-known horsemen to instruct them, but Miss Fipps was sure that neither Pablo nor I were up to cantering circles or jumping anything above one foot high, and so we seemed doomed for ever to her class and I became disheartened.

Sitting now in the dining-room, I recalled long hacks home from rallies, when I had dreamed of the day when Miss Fipps would see me winning the Open Jumping at the White City, or the Prix Caprilli or the

British Dressage Championship. But these reminiscences brought no solution to my problem, and presently I fell to thinking of all the people I knew. And then I remembered a girl at my school called Megan O'Connor. She was Irish and her father owned several horses, including some youngsters, and most Irishmen use running martingales.

During tea I told my mother that I had found a cure for Martini.

"All right, darling," she said, on hearing my plan. "Try it by all means, but be terribly careful. I simply can't bear all this falling off."

"Why did Lettie fall off?" asked Nicholas. "Because she wanted to hit the ground. That's a good one! Mummy, Mummy, don't you think that's a good one?"

"Oh, Nick," said my mother. "You really are too senseless."

"Lettie, why did the chicken cross the road?" asked Nicholas, quite unperturbed.

"Can't remember," I said.

"Got you! 'Cos it wanted to get to the other side, of course. Do you know this one, Lettie? Why did the cow look over the wall?"

"Because it wanted to get to the other side," I replied.

"No, silly. 'Cos it couldn't see through. I told you that one yesterday. Do you know this one?"

"No," I interrupted, "and I'm going to go and wash up and make the dogs' dinners."

"Oh, Lettie, you are too mean," wailed Nicholas. "It's such a good one too."

After tea I rang up Megan and she promised to

bring a martingale and drop nose-band to school next day, which was jolly decent, because we were really no more than acquaintances.

Next day I gobbled my tea even faster than usual, and at five o'clock I was adjusting the martingale and drop nose-band in the stableyard. I measured the martingale to the withers and adjusted the nose-band so that it was just below the bit and I could fit three fingers between it and the curb groove. Then, full of hope, I mounted and rode into the paddock. I had only Tatters to watch me this evening, for which I was glad.

Martini was fresh, her back was up and she was nervous. She was listening for rustles in the hedge and her eyes were searching for unfamiliar and frightening objects. Presently I told her to trot and then the trouble began. She bucked and swung round and tried to gallop me to the gate. But previously she had succeeded by sticking her nose in the air and opening her mouth, whereas this time I brought the martingale, which forced her head down, into action and the nose-band prevented her opening her mouth as wide as she wished. I lost a stirrup when she bucked, but I quickly regained it, and in a couple of strides I had brought her to a standstill. I was convinced that Martini was not really afraid of anything. She was just playing up. So I made the most of my triumph and, turning her, used my legs and stick and drove her forwards in the direction I had first told her to go.

We trotted twice round the orchard and then she tried her bucking trick again, but I was ready. I managed to prevent her swinging round, and sent her into a brisk trot. I kept her trotting in the orchard for twenty minutes and then I started schooling her in earnest. I practised transitions from the slow trot to the ordinary trot and the ordinary trot to the extended trot. I practised halting, and circling, at the walk and trot. I practised trotting over a pole resting on two boxes and walking in a straight line. She did not attempt to buck again. She responded to the action of the drop nose-band and I began to understand a little how it worked. She would open her mouth to resist the bit when I used the reins, and the nose-band would immediately press on the front of her nose and on the curb groove. She would then drop her nose and relax her lower jaw, and the nose-band would automatically stop pressing her.

I was delighted and, as though sharing my happy mood, the sun came out and a bird high amongst the apple branches burst forth in a song. A window in the house opened and Nicholas's untidy fair head appeared.

"She looks lovely, like the horse in the circus. Look at the sun. I don't see why I should go to silly old bed, it really is too senseless . . .

"The sun has got his hat on,
Hip, hip, hip, hooray.
The sun has got his hat on,
And he's coming out today."

I thought of coming shows and then I thought of Lydia Pike, who had made Martini so difficult. I remembered that she looked a bad-tempered, lazy girl and I knew she was a very rough rider. Mum said she was a selfish girl, the sort of daughter who would leave her mother all the washing-up to do. I thought of Pip Cox, whom I had met at a children's party and at a gymkhana a year ago.

"Poor Martini," I said, "you've had a rough time of it, haven't you? Never mind, you'll be all right soon."

Then Mum called that I had forgotten to make the dogs' dinners, so I left the sunlit orchard and turned Martini loose, and went indoors.

From that day onwards Martini began to improve. She must have had some concentrated schooling at some earlier time in her life. Perhaps her breaker-in was a wise man, for now she learned very quickly. She stopped fighting against the bit. She became more supple and more attentive to the aids. My parents were very pleased, and soon I started to hack her again.

Then a marvellous thing happened. At the beginning of July my school had an epidemic of measles and had to close. I had all day and every day free for riding.

I was sure that Martini needed plenty of quiet work, so I gave her an hour's schooling and an hour's hacking a day, and within a fortnight she was jumping two feet six out of a trot. She was nervous of triples and parallel bars, but I knew this was Lydia's fault. Lydia had strapped her head down so that she could not extend herself, making it terribly difficult for her to clear any broad obstacles. And Martini had developed a cat-jumping habit because Lydia did not give her enough freedom over the jumps, and she had become afraid of her mouth. So now I jumped Martini on a very loose rein and soon discarded the martingale, and gradually she became more confident. She lost the habit of kicking whenever she hit a jump, and she lost the habit of rolling back her eyes to see what my stick was doing. She began to look more at her fences when she approached them, and as a result she hit them less often. We had one or two quarrels, but if any difficulties arose or she started to excite herself and plunge and paw the ground, I always lowered the jumps at once. I found this method very successful.

Mum and Nicholas were very decent and helped me make fences out of some wood I had bought for very little, with my pocket-money, from a nearby woodyard. I found some three-ply in the garage and made letters, and marked out a dressage arena, like Pierre St Denis's arena.

Towards the end of July I received my Pony Club's fixture list. They were holding a show and gymkhana on the first of August. I decided to enter Martini for the equitation and jumping classes. I told Megan of my decision when I returned her martingale – I was still using the drop nose-band – and she said I could ride over one day and practise over her jumps. I accepted the offer and a week before the show I had a rehearsal at her place. Her fences, built by her father's men, were solid and formidable, but well winged. I was able to take them fairly fast and Martini jumped magnificently. Megan was riding a green youngster which bucked between the fences and tried to run out. However, she only laughed at his misbehaviour. She was not interested in schooling or dressage or showjumping. She was only interested in riding with the hunt and point-to-pointing. Her great ambition was to win a point-to-point.

Then July the thirty-first arrived and I took Martini for a quiet hack in the morning. It was a very hot day.

There was hardly a ripple in the river, so slight was the summer breeze, and the flies buzzed ceaselessly round the ponies' heads. The dogs would not venture from the shade of our garden except for a dip in the Lynne. Mum set out early with her easel, canvas, brushes, paints and palette to start a landscape, a picture of the rolling fields of corn by Grayley, a picture of blue and gold, of sunshine and the clear hot skies.

Nicholas was riding in the egg and spoon race for children under ten at the show, so after lunch I helped him groom and trim Pablo and clean his tack, on the condition that he asked no riddles or questions. Pablo and Martini are encouraging ponies to groom because you can get a wonderful shine on their coats. Soon Pablo shone like polished ebony and Martini shone like polished oak, and by teatime we had finished grooming

them. We kept them in the stable till dusk because the flies were so awful, then Mum, who had insisted that I should go to bed at half past seven, turned them out.

The night was so stiflingly hot that I slept little, and I felt so sleepy when I wakened at six in the morning that I had a swim in the river before catching the ponies. It was a wonderful morning. An early haze lay over the fields and the sleeping cottages of Cherryford, but above the sky was blue and in the east a great golden sun rose slowly, lighting the treetops and the rooftops with gold. A summer breeze, rich and warm, stirred the grasses. In the boughs of the elms and in the green hedges the birds sang their welcome to the day.

And so, I thought, another August begins. A month of holidays and hopes, a month of fêtes and horse shows, of crowded trains and coach parties. For me, this year, a happy and exciting month. And then at once my mind was filled with doubt . . . would it be happy? Might I not disgrace myself today? Gallop like a mad thing from the ring? For a few moments I saw myself as I had seen Lydia at the Stringwell Show, and then, in my imagination, I heard my father say, "The pony must go, Lettie. She'll only break your neck. I'm sorry, but there it is," and I felt a wave of disappointment and sadness, a sickening tug at the heart. And then I remembered that this was only make believe. The show was not over but soon to begin. I must hurry, not waste time in dismal daydreams.

I ran indoors and changed from my swimsuit to my shorts and T-shirt and trainers. A moment later I was in the orchard catching the ponies, which were damp with dew and sleepy-eyed. There were two rabbits nibbling the short, sweet grass under the white-heart cherry tree, and Tatters, yapping wildly, chased them to their burrows. It was the first sharply penetrating noise to shake the morning air, and it made me wide awake at last.

I washed the ponies' tails and presently Nicholas came out from the house.

"I say," he said. "I'm awfully sure I shall be last. My hand's shaking. I shall never hold a spoon."

"Nonsense. Come and help me groom. Grooming will make your hand steady again," I told him.

At eight o'clock I started plaiting the ponies' manes. I am not nimble with my fingers, and my plaits looked loose and floppy. Martini made matters worse by constantly shaking her head. Nicholas asked questions until in exasperation I sent him in to breakfast, and Tatters yapped and yapped because Minnie was up a tree and for some unknown reason he doesn't think Minnie should be allowed to climb trees. By nine o'clock I was nearly demented. I vowed secretly that I would never again enter for a horse show and I snapped at my mother when she called "Breakfast" for the fourth time.

At long last I was indoors eating and dressing. I recited poetry to take my mind off the equitation class.

"I strove with none, for none was worth my strife.
Nature I loved, and, next to nature, Art:
I warm'd both hands before the fire of life;
It sinks and I am ready to depart."

I felt that I had already striven too long. Why do I strive? I wondered. Why not stay at home whenever possible, in peace and quiet?

I wondered how other children felt before horse shows. Did they wish they had never entered?

And then it was time to go.

It was a long, hot ride to the showground, and the ponies were very quiet. We had two miles of roadwork at the start, and very dusty miles they were too, and then we took a bridle-path that led us through fields high in corn and pasture that smelt of burnt grass and hot clover, and a fir-wood that smelt dry and harsh as all fir-woods do.

After a little while we reached a rough hillside dotted with gorse and broom, and we dismounted and rested the ponies, for Pablo was showing signs of weariness. There came to us the scent of thyme and the hum of bees, and, from the tall bitter grass, the burr of grasshoppers. We looked down into the valley where we had ridden only a few moments before, to the rolling acres of gold and the brown pastures, to the winding track, dusty and grey, which had guided us so faithfully towards our destination. And we looked to the horizon of blue, to the deep blue sky.

"What colours!" I cried. "They are like van Gogh's Provence. Never have I seen such gold before. How I wish I could paint! Or even write."

"Oh, that reminds me. Do you know this one, Lettie? Why is an author a peculiar animal?" asked Nicholas.

"I don't know," I said without troubling to think. "Gosh, it's a quarter to eleven and we've two miles to go. We must push on."

"Because his tale comes out of his head," said Nicholas.

"Whose? Oh – the author's – sorry. That's quite a good one. Come on. Hop up."

A mile of grassland and twenty minutes' ride down lanes and roads bought us to the showground, where the first class, an equitation competition for children under ten, was in progress. Our mother and father had arrived. I could see our three dogs and our battered car over by the collecting ring. Bob Saunders, who is a Pony Club member though he never attends rallies, was cantering Nobby Boy in circles. Nicholas dismounted.

"Poor Pablo's tired already," he said.

Mum appeared panting at my side.

"Lettie, you are terribly late. Do hurry. Your class is next," she said.

"We had to stop on the way, 'cos Pablo was tired. We've had a lovely ride, Mummy, through corn and hay-fields. We've come ever, ever such a long way," said Nicholas.

I loosened Martini's girths, took her to the car and brushed her over and oiled her feet. When I mounted the megaphone was calling all competitors for class two, and then I realised that I was riding in a snaffle and drop nose-band instead of the double bridle as I had intended. I cantered back to the car and, with Nicholas's help, changed my bridle, and then it was time to enter the ring. Miss Fipps was at the entrance.

"What's that you are riding? Not a bad-looking brute, is it?" she asked.

I paused. "Yes, I think she's quite nice-looking, but I don't know how she'll behave," I answered.

"What have you done with that dreadful little black animal?" she called, but I was walking into the ring and, because I thought her remark about dear little Pablo rude, I pretended not to hear.

There were two judges, both men. They were not the usual ones we have for our Pony Club show, in fact I was sure I had never seen them in my life before. There were about fifteen competitors in the class, which was open to members of ours and our neighbouring Pony Clubs; nearly all of them rode with their legs well forward. Presently we were told to trot and then to canter. We were going round to the right and three riders were sent out of the ring because they were leading with the wrong leg. Fortunately Martini was calm, and when she is calm she never makes a mistake when told to canter. Presently we were sent round on the other rein and four more riders were asked to leave the ring because they led off on the wrong leg. Then the eight of us that remained were lined up. The oldest judge, who wore spectacles and looked too old and decrepit to ride, explained that he wanted each of us in turn to trot up to the brush fence and canter back on the off leg, and then halt in front of his co-judge and himself, and rein back three steps.

Maureen Fielding, a red-haired girl who, according to Miss Fipps, has a perfect seat, went first. She bent her pony's head outwards when she turned at the brush fence and pulled on the reins when she backed, relaxing her hands for a second each time the pony took a step. Next a boy on a piebald tried the test and was sent out because he could not make his pony canter. He was followed by a tall, elegant girl on an obviously schooled and balanced hunter. I thought she rode well, with a style that would have pleased Pierre St Denis. Her horse gave an excellent show. He carried himself with an air; he flexed his head inwards when he turned the corner and led straight off at the canter. Someone whispered that the tall girl came from a Pony Club in Oxfordshire or Berkshire and that she had been placed in dressage tests. Now it was my turn. A steward beckoned to me. For an awful moment I panicked; I could not remember what I was supposed to do. I looked helplessly at the judges and then suddenly the test came back to me. I collected my thoughts, shortened my reins and trotted up to the brush fence. Martini was nervous and hesitant and, as a result, she was not trotting straight. I used my legs and then, as we turned, I lowered my outside hand and used my outside leg just behind the girth and my inside leg on the girth. She led off correctly, and with a feeling of tremendous relief I cantered back to the judges. Although I used my legs, she was rather on the forehand when I halted and she did not back quite straight. However, the old judge looked fairly pleased and said, "Well done," which was heartening.

Only four riders survived the test. The others were sent out for not cantering at all or for leading off on the wrong leg. Presently we were told that we were to trot and canter a circle to either hand. I began to feel sick so I didn't watch my fellow competitors. Instead I looked at the spectators. They were a drab crowd on the whole. Mum was the only brightly-dressed adult that I could see. She was wearing a plain yellow-checked dress and a blue jacket and a large straw hat from Sorrento. Miss Fipps was wearing a very dreary coat and skirt; it drooped terribly and its colour bore a strong resemblance to mud. I fell to wondering why she liked such dreary shades. And then the tall girl said, "The judges want you to go next," and with horror I realised that I had been sitting gaping at the ringside while the decrepit judge had been speaking to me.

"I'm terribly sorry," I said, hurrying Martini away from the other ponies.

"All right," the younger judge said. "Take it easy. Don't get fussed."

Martini went well with a nice even tempo at the trot, but cantering she rushed a little and my circle became larger than I intended. She was a little worse to the right than the left, and at one moment she was very heavy on my hands. I decided that I might be placed fourth and wondered vaguely whether my rosette would be white or green and whether it would say fourth or reserve. Then I looked at the judges and noticed that the other riders were moving.

"Come on," said the tall girl. "You've got second."

I hurried forwards and stood beside her, making Martini look as nice as I could.

"Your pony goes well into her bridle. And her tempo's good. Give her some more schooling and then try her in some elementary or novice dressage tests later on. She might win something. Where did you learn, by the way?" said the decrepit judge, handing me a blue rosette.

"Thanks awfully. Pierre St Denis taught me all I know about dressage. I think he's frightfully good," I told him and wished I hadn't said *awfully* and *frightfully.*

"You lucky girl!" said the younger judge.

"Couldn't find a much better instructor," remarked the decrepit judge.

"Thanks frightfully," I said, and then, as I couldn't think of anything else to say, I turned and followed the tall girl who had won first and cantered round the ring. I had an awful desire to grin broadly, but I quelled it because I did not wish to appear triumphant or smug or self-satisfied.

In many ways it is easier to be a good loser than a good winner. I have so often lost in races and competitions that I never expect to win, and therefore I am never disappointed or annoyed when I lose.

My parents were very surprised by my success. Dad had not watched all the equitation class, and he was amazed to see my blue rosette.

"Good lord!" he said. "You don't mean to say you've *won* something. Janet, Janet, Lettie's actually won something. Old Miss Fripps will die of shock."

"Not Fripps, *Fipps.* I think Martini's been jolly clever," I said.

Mum gave Martini six lumps of sugar, and then the megaphone called me into the collecting ring for the children's jumping. There were nine entries in this class including Bob Saunders with Nobby Boy.

Pierre St Denis would not have approved of the course. The jumps were narrow and flimsy and fell too easily. But the Pony Club members liked them because they were well winged. Because the Pony Club members rode with their legs too far forward, they could never keep their ponies straight at unwinged obstacles. Two of the older members were complaining now about the judges.

"Can't think why Miss Fipps asked such awful judges. One of them is not even English. And he learned at some cavalry school in France. Like to see him hunting in this country."

"Don't worry, Jane, he wouldn't. He would be scared of the fences. But I know why Miss Fipps got them here. It's this Pony Club Inter-Branch Competition. They are experts on that sort of thing and she wants to know what they think of us."

The standard of jumping was very low, and the first two competitors each had three refusals and were disqualified. Then Bob Saunders jumped his usual clear round with Nobby Boy. He's a very rough rider, but he's fairly successful with his cobs. Then it was my turn. Martini was nervous and up to now I had kept her walking about. She was trembling when I entered the ring. I remembered Lydia's dramatic exit at Stringwell and decided to take her slowly. The first jump was a brush fence. I took it from a trot and then increased to a canter for the second – a pair of hurdles – and then slowed down for the third – a gate – which was the nearest to the exit and entrance.

As Martini landed she tried to put on a spurt, but I was ready and collected her in time. We passed the entrance at a slow canter and knocked the stile, which was the fourth jump and very flimsy indeed. Only three more remained: some rails, a very poor imitation of a red brick wall and a narrow triple. We cleared them all, and faint applause accompanied us from the ring.

Outside, I dismounted and patted Martini. Mum came hurrying across the showground. Nicholas was waiting for the egg and spoon race, which was the next event. I could hear him talking to the tall girl, whom he admired tremendously. He was saying, "Why did the chicken cross the road?" I wished he would not bother people with his silly riddles.

"Well done, Lettie," said my mother. "You were terribly good."

"I took her too slowly at the stile. It was my fault she hit it," I said.

Presently I loosened Martini's girths and lay in the long grass looking at the cloudless sky. I thought, I mustn't forget this day; it's one of the happiest in my life. I don't mind if I don't win anything in the jumping. I know she's improving, and that's all that matters. One day I'm going to school some of the best horses in England. I'm going to be an expert. Today is the first step up the ladder to success.

And I gazed at Martini and thought, She's lovely. Look at those long forearms and those neat, short cannon bones. Look at her head, so well-bred and intelligent. I wish I could paint horses . . . I am really the luckiest child here. No one else has such a marvellous pony.

I was so hot that I couldn't watch the other competitors, but I had seen most of them jump at rallies and I knew they were not particularly good. I was not unprepared when I heard my number called over the megaphone. This time I was half expecting to win second or third, though I was surprised when I was handed the blue rosette and I realised that I had beaten the tall girl, who told me that she had knocked the rails and stile. We cantered round the ring and then Bob Saunders, the winner, shoved Nobby Boy into a cattle truck and dashed off to another show.

I ate lunch while the egg and spoon race was in progress. Nicholas was last in his heat because he dropped his egg three times.

Then, after Nicholas and the ponies had eaten – Martini waited for Pablo – we left for home.

Nicholas was cheerful. "Never mind," he said. "I expect I shall win something one day. P'raps when I'm an old, old man. And now you've got enough to buy Martini a bridle, haven't you? With the money you've won?"

We rode very slowly because the weather was so hot, and it was past teatime when we reached home.

Towards evening the telephone rang. I answered and a voice the other end said Miss Fipps wanted to speak to Lettie Lonsdale.

"This is Lettie speaking" I replied.

"Oh, yes, well," said Miss Fipps. "You know the older of the two judges today? He's my brother-in-law.

He's got all sorts of crazy notions about riding – always did have them. Thinks you should lean forwards downhill . . . simply ridiculous . . . But he's supposed to be an expert on this dressage stuff. So I told him to come today and judge and tell me who was best to ride in a team for this Dressage Championship – Branch Competition or whatever it's called. Never could remember the name of the wretched thing. Anyway, he picked on you, first of everyone. Likes your pony. Says she's well schooled and can jump and he'll train you. Are you interested? Seems to me simply ridiculous – all this bothering about angles and flexions and cadence. What does it all matter as long as the horse goes?" She paused for breath.

"I should love to be trained," I said quickly.

"He says we must enter a team even though the other two won't have a chance. But you can ride as an individual as well. He thinks you might have a chance – might get high marks or something." said Miss Fipps.

"When do I start being trained?" I asked.

"He's staying with me and you're to come the day after tomorrow."

"By the way, what is his name?"

"Peter Venten. He's Belgian, you know. I suppose that's why he has such odd ideas."

"Not the author of *The Training of Mount and Man*?" I asked.

"Yes, I think his book's called something like that."

"But that's wonderful!" I cried.

"Well, he will give you three weeks' teaching. Goodbye," said Miss Fipps, and she rang off abruptly.

For a long moment I sat perfectly still, holding the

telephone. Peter Venten, I thought. The Belgian expert! It's too good to be true . . . Three weeks' training – and he thinks I have a chance . . . It's like a dream, a marvellous dream.

Mum's voice came to me. "Anyone interesting?" she called. I ran upstairs and told her all.

"The Pony Club Inter-Branch Competition! It's marvellous," I finished.

"Some people are born with silver spoons in their mouths," said Mum.

Nicholas came out of his bedroom in his pyjamas. He said, "Who was born with a silver spoon? Not Solomon Grundy." And of course he had to chant:

"Solomon Grundy,
Born on a Monday,
Christened on Tuesday,
Married on Wednesday,
Fell ill on Thursday,
Worse on Friday,
Died on Saturday.
Buried on Sunday,
That was the end of Solomon Grundy."

"I'm going to tell Martini," I said.

"Give Pablo an apple and a pat from me. It wasn't his fault we were last," said Nicholas.

I went outside and looked down to the river. The last pale light of day lay on the water meadows. A solitary swan, white as snow, paddled by our lawn. The scent of hot earth and burnt grass lingered on the evening air.

I wandered to the orchard and found Martini and Pablo grazing side by side. They raised their heads at the sound of my voice and, while they ate apples from my hand, listened to my story of days to come.

"You see," I finished, "I've lots to learn. But this is the beginning. When I am seventeen or eighteen I shall compete at Badminton. Later I shall jump for England on a horse that I have trained myself."

I saw a show ring in Paris, by Auteuil. The white jumps with green shrubs either side; the stands decked

with flowers; the chic Parisian spectators with exotic hats and gay accessories. I saw Rome, as I had read of her. The great quiet churches; the priests with long robes and sandals on their feet; St. Peter's; the jangling trams in the main streets; the Tiber, hot and muddy in the summer sun.

"I shall take a day off to look at pictures," I said.

But the ponies were no longer listening. They had left me and were grazing under the white-heart tree.

The air was cooler and night was falling. The sky was a dark and inky blue with one brave star shining high above our tallest elms. I thought, For years we strive to satisfy our vanity, to achieve our small ambitions, to shine in the eyes of others or better the world. But all the great things are here without the asking. The silhouette of a tree against the starry sky; early sunlight on hills; the ripple of river water between fingers, springtime in England and the song of the birds. And yet these are not enough. There is for ever the urge to improve and create.

"And all my life," I told the sleeping orchard, "I shall paint pictures and improve horses."

I'll Never Pass

Josephine Pullein-Thompson

"What are the most important things to remember about feeding?" asked Jenny as they left the Ridgeway and turned down Ansell Road.

Pippa's mind went blank.

"Hurry up," said Jenny.

"Grass in summer, hay in winter and lots of pony nuts and oats if you want to liven them up," answered Pippa.

Jenny sighed. "You're supposed to say basic things like, 'Always water before feeding; feed little and often; allow at least an hour to digest before fast work.' Now, here's an easy one, which is the best straw for bedding?"

Pippa's mind went blank again. "I thought it was just straw, otherwise you use shavings or peat."

"It's wheat straw," Jenny told her impatiently. "You *must* read the manual, Pippa, or you're going to fail again."

"Yes, I know, I'm hopeless at exams. I'll never pass." Pippa tried to sound lighthearted, as though she didn't care, but secretly she cared a lot. Nearly all her friends had passed C test and the last two, Jean and

Charlotte, were certain to pass tomorrow, while she would fail for the third time.

"You'd better read the sections on feeding and the aids before you go to sleep," suggested Jenny, "That's what I do when I want to remember something."

Pippa stopped dead and said, "Oh help! I've left the book at the stables. Well that settles it, now I'm bound to fail."

"I'll go back with you," offered Jenny.

"Oh, we can't, not all that way," moaned Pippa. She looked at her watch. "Besides there's not time, I promised to be home for tea."

"Okay, it's up to you." Jenny's voice was cold and hostile. "I may as well go home by the quick way," she added, and turned into Chadwick Road.

I can't help it if I'm useless at exams, thought Pippa, walking on alone. I've always failed everything. It's so unfair that I'm the stupid one. Nichola and John were older, but they had always been successful. Sailing through exams, always coming top, passing with honours; getting into teams, winning matches.

Luckily Mum doesn't mind, Pippa consoled herself. She says I have other virtues. Dad minds a bit, though he tries to hide it with jokes about my being a dumb blonde.

One reason she'd taken up riding was that you didn't have to be competitive, but now it was going to be very grim if all her friends moved up into the C ride and she was left among a new lot of D plusses.

All through tea the thought of growing older and older and still being in D+ haunted her and, afterwards, she told her mother that she simply *had* to go back to the stables to fetch the book she had forgotten.

The spring evening was warm. The gardens were festive with flowers and the scent of the blossoming trees filled the air, but Pippa, struggling to remember the aids for everything, barely noticed. It wasn't until she had crossed the Ridgeway and was walking up the stable drive that she realised that the smell had changed and become an autumn one; fallen leaves and bonfires, she thought.

All the horses were looking out, they whinnied urgently when they saw her. That's strange, she thought. Surely they've been fed. She looked over Prince's door, his haynet hung from the ring, reassuringly full. There was no one about, no sign of the three instructors who lived at the stables: Chris in a converted loft above the office, Maureen and Jane in a shared caravan. The tack room door was locked but she saw that her book had been put on the shelf outside, they had guessed she might come back for it.

As she picked it up and turned to go, she realised that the bonfire smell was growing stronger and she could see a column of smoke billowing up from the lower yard where the small ponies were still stabled, waiting for the grass to grow before they were turned out for the summer.

She wandered down to investigate, holding the book open and muttering the points of the horse, until an extraordinary roaring noise filled her with sudden fear. She ran past the ponies' stable to the open-fronted forage shed and saw that the stack of bales was alight. The flames had just burst out of the hay and were roaring ferociously as they devoured the wooden walls and found their way into the dry timber of the roof. As she stood watching in horror they spread, engulfing the whole building with terrifying speed.

Dial 999, she thought, but the telephone was in the office and it was bound to be locked. And, looking from the inferno of red and roaring flames, and black acrid smoke to the pony stable, she knew there wasn't time. It was only a matter of moments before the stable was ablaze, and with seven helpless ponies tied inside.

They stood in stalls. Pippa ran to the end of the long, narrow building that was nearest the fire. Grey Sixpence was frightened, he whinnied nervously. She grabbed his rope and pulled the end. The release knot undid smoothly; dropping the wooden block she pulled the rope through the ring, turned the pony and hurried him out.

The air was full of smoke and sparks and Pippa wondered what to do with him. Then, looking back at the stable, she realised that there wasn't a moment to loose. The hungry flames were already darting across the small gap between the two buildings, licking at the wooden wall of the stable. She swung open the gate into the jumping paddock and left Sixpence to look after himself.

Patrick, a narrow little bay, was trembling, and the stable was hot and full of smoke. Pippa decided to try and take two at once. Tansy, the skewbald Shetland, was already tugging at her rope and the moment she was free she trotted down the passage ahead of Patrick. Outside they hesitated, but then, from the paddock, Sixpence neighed and they went to join him.

Pippa turned back. Now it was the turn of the stout

cob, Blackberry. She stood on Pippa's foot in her rush to get out, but there was no time to feel pain for the crackling and roaring of the flames was growing terrifyingly loud and near.

Suppose the roof falls? thought Pippa and forced herself to say calming words in an unconcerned voice, for chestnut Minty was panicking, rearing and plunging wildly in her stall.

"Whoa, whoa. It's all right. We'll have you out in a second," she soothed as she struggled to snatch the wildly swinging wooden block. The moment the pony was free she turned and fled, crushing her rescuer against the side of the stall.

The stable was dark with smoke now and the heat was intense. Wracked with coughing and almost blinded by the tears that poured from her smarting eyes, Pippa told herself that there were only two left.

"Only Pepper and Carlo," she cried aloud as she fought with her desire to run. She couldn't go on. Why didn't someone come? Where were the instructors? She needed help.

Pepper was easy. Though shaking with fear, he stood calmly and she had him through the door in moments, but Carlo's frantic struggles had pulled his knot tight and, jammed in the block, it refused to release. Pippa pulled at it with all her strength, but it wouldn't give. Blindly she tried to loosen the knot itself. Then there was an appalling crash. The far end of the stable had collapsed, an orange glare dazzled her stinging eyes, the roaring grew louder and nearer. The fire was almost upon them.

Carlo gave a terrified whinny. Pippa fumbled for his headcollar and managed to unbuckle it. She took hold of his mane and tried to lead him out. He stood stock-still, afraid to move.

"Come on, quickly," she screamed at him. The heat

was growing unbearable, they were going to be burned to death. She *must* leave him. Petrified with fear, the pony stood rock-like and immovable. Pippa struggled with her own terror. She produced a small handful of pony nuts from her pocket. "Come on, good boy, a few steps and you'll be in the paddock with your friends," she told him in a coaxing voice. He didn't take the nuts, but the normality of her manner seemed to calm his terror, and then mercifully one of the ponies in the paddock called to him and he found the courage to follow Pippa out.

She steered him into the paddock and, checking that the other six were there, slammed the gate. Then, mopping her streaming eyes on her sleeve, ran to the office. The door was locked. She kicked and banged, and then looked round for a shovel or a brick; something to smash the window. She was crying again, this time they were tears of frustration. She *had* to get help before the fire spread, before one of that mass of flying sparks found its way into the main yard.

Then suddenly a car raced up to the gate, it was flung open, and Chris and Maureen and Jane came running across the yard.

"I couldn't telephone," cried Pippa desperately. "The office is locked."

"We've sent for the fire brigade. We saw from the hill," shouted Chris. They ran towards the fire.

Maureen was crying, "The little ponies! Oh the poor little ponies!"

"It's all right, I got them out," Pippa shouted. "They're all in the jumping paddock."

She could hear the sound of sirens blaring along the

Ridgeway. Suddenly she felt deadly tired. I came for my book, she remembered, and realised that it no longer existed – she had put it down as she untied the first pony. Well, I'm certain to fail now, she thought, as the leading fire engine swept into the yard; but it didn't seem important.

She watched as the hoses were run out and torrents of water began to sluice down on the burning ruins of the lower yard.

The instructors came back. "The ponies are all okay, except for a few minor burns," said Jane.

"Pippa, how did you do it?" asked Chris. "How on earth did you get them all out on your own?"

"You're all black, your hair's singed and you're probably suffering from shock," said Jane.

"It must have been terrifying," added Maureen, giving Pippa a long hug. "I was so frightened, I thought all the little ponies were dead."

They sat Pippa in the office, her burned hands in a bucket of water, while they moved the horses out of their boxes and the fire brigade damped down the roofs of the stables. Then an ambulance came.

"You have to go to hospital for a check-up. Nothing serious, but you swallowed a lot of smoke, as well as burning your hands," Maureen explained. "I'm coming with you and your mum will meet us there."

As she listened to Maureen telling the ambulance crew how brave she, Pippa, had been, a mild pride began to fill her. It was certainly a really scary test, she thought, far worse than any exam, and I didn't fail the ponies.

The Runaway Boy

Josephine Pullein-Thompson

It was a dampish April day with the sun making feeble attempts to shine and the green, earthy smell of early spring that fills the air before the primroses take over and the sun gets really warm. We walked along the road with the moor, still brown from the winter's frosts and snow, stretching away on either side of us. We passed Chapel Cottages, the church, the chapel and the post office, which is just about all there is of St Dinas, and then we turned left along the lane to Black Tor Farm. It's a small farm with poor land that was once barren moor and the Jacksons all have to struggle hard to make a living.

The notice-board announcing BLACK TOR TREKKING CENTRE had been retrieved from the nettles where it had lain all winter and nailed back on its post. It must be Mick's work, we decided; Mr Jackson never mends anything. He's a real muddler who drives his children mad. He's always booking more trekkers than they have ponies, mixing good riders with complete beginners, buying saddles with broken trees and ancient, rusty bits and stirrups because they're cheap.

We could see Heather instructing some pupils in the school, a patch of moor from which they've cleared the stones, building them into a low wall in the traditional way, and we found Mick standing in the middle of the yard looking worried. His face brightened when he saw us. "Have you come to join the search party?" he asked.

I groaned. "Who's lost?" I asked. The visitors and tourists in our part of the world are maddening. They are always going out on the moor in the wrong clothes and without maps, they fall down, they lose themselves and then the locals are expected to stop whatever they are doing and go out in search parties.

"Danny, Danny Kyle," answered Mick. "He's not exactly lost, we think he's run away; he had a bit of a dust-up with his mum and walked out last night. Hasn't been seen since and she's getting worried."

"He's the boy Heather's been teaching, the one she said was a natural, who's just come to live at Chapel Cottages?"

"That's right; they've rented Mrs Grant's two rooms. I'm waiting for Heather to finish and then we're going out on the moor to look for him. If he fell in the dark and hurt himself he could be lying out there somewhere; that's what his mum's afraid of. The police think he may be trying to get back to Reading, where they came from."

"I can't imagine leaving St Dinas for *Reading,*" said Louisa, "especially if he's horsey."

"His grandparents live there," explained Mick. "It's his grandma who pays for his riding lessons."

"What did Danny and his mother quarrel about?" I asked.

"Oh, I dunno. He doesn't have much of a life; no father, mother at work, so, in the holidays, he's on his own all day. Heather reckons he could be useful to us. Now that Tracy's always over at Dawn's helping with the baby we've no one to school the little ponies and, though he hasn't ridden for long, Danny's quite good. He's plenty of nerve. Trouble is Dad takes so long to make up his mind about things . . . "

Heather's pupils came riding into the yard at that moment and Mick broke off as he went to help them water and unsaddle their ponies.

"Hullo, have you come to search?" asked Heather, looking pleased.

"Not on Spider," said Louisa firmly. "Look, my feet are nearly touching the ground. It's cruelty to ponies, so unless you've one that needs exercising . . . "

"We have," Mick interrupted, "take your pick; they've all to be got fit for the summer." As he and Louisa vanished into the long stable, I tackled Heather about our horse situation and asked her to ask Mr Jackson to see what he could do. She said she would, but I didn't think she was really listening, and as soon as I stopped talking she went back to the subject of Danny.

"If you and Louisa would do West Moor it would be great," she said. "Mick and I are sick to death of riding there and Middle Moor will make a change. No one knows which way he went."

I agreed to search West Moor, but a bit reluctantly because Penhydrock, where the Hamiltons live, and Chilmarth, the Mitchell's house, are on opposite edges of Middle Moor and I would have been quite glad of an excuse to ride round and see if they were back for the holidays yet. Felix, Toby and Huw all go to a very progressive school in the Home Counties near where they used to live, and the Mitchells, whose father has a large and prosperous farm, go to conventional boarding schools at vast expense. The rest of us go to local schools in Tolbay or Baybourne.

"What about Jane?" I asked. "Will she help?"

"I doubt it. Now she's made friends with Marion Brewster she's gone right off riding."

"Well, we'll start as soon as we've collected some lunch and a first-aid kit," I told Heather as Louisa emerged from the stable mounted on Crackers, black, strong and obviously as fiery as ever. I quite like riding him, but he doesn't suit everyone and Mr Jackson had failed to sell him at the end of the last trekking season.

"Will you lead Spider home?" asked Louisa, already sounding breathless as Crackers, refusing to stand still for a second, twirled her round the yard.

Mick gave me Spider's reins and said, "Ring the post office and the Tolbay police station if you have any luck." I set off after Louisa who had vanished down the lane.

At home, we left Crackers twirling in the stable while we put Spider in the field and found some lunch. We packed bread, cheese, apples and biscuits into the first-aid rucksack and left a note for our mother, explaining what had happened.

I held Crackers down while Louisa mounted and then we were off again.

Two people can't possibly search West Moor properly, but we decided that if we rode out along the Old Dog side and home along the Black Tor side we'd have a fair chance of seeing or hearing Danny if he was lying in the heather with a sprained ankle or a broken leg. We had just separated and were riding along parallel to each other when we heard a voice calling "Danny", and saw a figure coming towards us along one of the small, winding sheep paths. We trotted to meet her.

"Hullo," I said. "Are you looking for Danny Kyle too?"

"Yes, I'm Cindy Kyle, his mother." We looked at her with interest. She was very pretty in a gypsyish way, with curly dark hair, fairly long and tangled, and brown eyes; and she wore gold earrings and a longish green dress with strange patterns that I guessed was Indian.

"We're going right down to Tolkenny Castle and then back up the other side," I explained. "The Jacksons are doing Middle Moor. How far have you been?"

"I've only done this top end, across to the farm and back. I'm not supposed to go too far from the post office in case there's any news. I'm sorry Danny's causing all this trouble. He's usually so sensible and though he's run away before he's always come back in two or three hours. He's not a sulker, that's why I'm afraid something may have happened to him."

We separated again and rode on, calling "Danny" at intervals and then waiting for an answer, but only the sad voices of a pair of curlews wheeling overhead replied. We rode on and on, past Old Dog, past the dark conifers of the Barley Bog plantation. The day had turned out well; warm and fitfully sunny. Redwing's long stride beneath me made the boredom of the search quite bearable, but I could see that Louisa was having a rough time on the jogging, overfresh Crackers. I was wondering if I ought to offer to change with her when, to one of our shouts of "Danny", there came a faint answering cry.

We shouted again and searched the miles of brown moor with our eyes. Suddenly Louisa pointed. Far away on our right something moved. We turned and began to ride over the rough, stony, boulder-strewn ground looking for a path that led in the right direction. We tried to hurry but the paths kept petering out, leaving us to make our way as best we could across the treacherous, pony-tripping stones and heather.

As we drew nearer we could see a small, toiling figure, apparently bent double under some burden, and followed by a pony. As we got closer still we saw that it was a boy carrying a young foal over his shoulders and we knew that the little bay mare who followed him must be its dam.

"Are you Danny Kyle?" we both asked at once.

"Yes, look at this. He's got a great cut on his leg and he looks dreadfully ill."

"They're Jackson ponies, aren't they?" I said, trying to remember.

"Yes, it's Poppy." Louisa dismounted and flung me Crackers' reins. Carefully she helped Danny lay the foal down. He was obviously very ill for he made no struggle or protest. Poppy nuzzled him anxiously. Redwing, who loves foals, gazed at him with a worried maternal face, but Crackers began to twirl round impatiently and trod heavily on my toe. I was trying to struggle out of the first-aid rucksack so I slapped him hard and told him that this was an emergency and he must behave. He looked surprised but stood quite meekly while I opened the rucksack and searched for cures. "It's not bleeding," said Louisa. "I think it's an old cut that's become infected; his leg's all swollen up and very hot. Here, you look, Frances." She took the ponies.

"You're the expert," I told her, because she means to follow in Daddy's footsteps and be a doctor, but I looked all the same. The leg was huge and hot, the wound gaped open and was yellow round the edges.

"He's going to die," said Danny, "I know he is. We must get him to the Jacksons' quickly; help me get him on my back again."

"No, carrying him will take hours. We need Mick and the Land-Rover."

"And an antibiotic injection," said Louisa. We looked at each other. "Do you want to go or stay?" I asked.

"Stay, only Crackers is such a bore to hold."

"Okay, I'll leave you Redwing. And food. Danny, have you had anything to eat?"

"Not lately, but it doesn't matter."

I divided the bread and cheese into three and started on my share as I let down Crackers' stirrups and mounted.

"We could carry him to meet the Land-Rover," suggested Danny. I looked at the foal lying on his side with glazed eyes. "I'd put the antibiotic ointment on and let him rest," I answered. "I'll be as quick as I possibly can."

"Don't forget to tell the police and the post office," Louisa shouted after me.

I found a small path heading north and let the ever-eager Crackers break into a canter. I knew that we weren't far from the track that leads along the Black Tor side of the moor and right up to the Jacksons' farm. When we joined it, just below Black Tor itself, I was able to give Crackers his head and we shot off at a tremendous speed. He isn't quite as fast as Redwing and he thunders rather than glides, but his fire and enthusiasm and his rough knee action give a great feeling of speed. It was a pity Louisa didn't like him, I thought, as I took the wall into the Jacksons' land at its highest point. He hurled himself over. The next one was tame in comparison. As we came towards the yard gate I could feel Crackers sizing it up. He was quite willing to jump it too. I decided against such recklessness; it was well over a metre and Mr Jackson would be furious if we demolished it. I called for Mrs Jackson, Mick, Heather and Tracy as I rode into the yard. A lean cat fled, chickens scratched, ponies whinnied, but there were no people and no Land-Rover. I tied Crackers in the long stable, headcollar over his bridle, and ran to the house. The kitchen was empty except for a row of dogs and cats warming their backs against the Aga.

"Mrs Jackson," I yelled up the stairs. There was no reply. I decided to telephone. I rang the post office and told Mrs Merton that we'd found Danny trying to rescue a sick foal on the moor; she agreed to tell the police as well as Mrs Kyle.

Then I dialled the Hamiltons' number; the Jacksons would have called in to ask for their help and might still be somewhere near. Huw, the youngest of the boys, answered. He said that they had only arrived home from school the night before and they were waiting for Charlie Cort to come and shoe the ponies. Then he called Felix. It's always a bit unnerving at the beginning of the holidays when you have to meet people, especially boys, who have been away for a whole term and may have changed completely, but now I was too fussed over the foal to worry.

I explained that I was at the Jacksons and needed transport for the sick foal, that if I could get hold of Heather or Mick they would know where their father was with his Land-Rover or they might be able to send their Uncle Geoff with *his* Land-Rover or even Dawn's Chris with his van.

Felix said, "Hang on a minute, I've an idea. We've just bought a Range Rover. It's about third-hand and it costs a fortune in petrol, but it's meant for this sort of emergency. The trouble is I can't take it on the road. Hang on a minute, I'll see if my mother can help."

I like Mrs Hamilton but we don't see much of her

in St Dinas because her husband is Stewart Hamilton who explores and travels in remote places and then does programmes about his journeys on the television. In fact they only seem to live at Penhydrock in the school holidays and even then they are always dashing up and down to London.

Felix came back. "We'll be with you in five minutes. You did say you were at Black Tor Farm, didn't you?"

I said "Yes" and began to thank him, but he'd rung off. Then I telephoned Mummy and told her what had happened so far. She said Spider was neighing indignantly and what was Louisa riding? I explained.

There was still no sign of the Hamiltons so I wrote a note for any Jackson who returned, explaining about Danny, Poppy's foal, and the urgent need for an antibiotic injection.

If it had been one of our ponies I would have telephoned for the vet, but the Jacksons have so many animals that they can't afford too many vet's bills and usually doctor theirs themselves. Then I went out and sat on the water trough until I saw the green Range Rover coming slowly up the lane. Felix was at the wheel looking very serious and intent. Mrs Hamilton and Toby sat beside him. I ran for Crackers, mounted and, waving at them to follow, opened the gate into the fields. After that there was one of Mr Jackson's maddening arrangements of sheep hurdles and barbed wire to be dismantled before we were out on the moor. Toby came to help me. He'd grown enormously and looked very strong. He's always been broader than Felix, though he's two years younger.

"Felix drives like an old lady of ninety," complained

Toby. "He dithered so much it took him ten minutes to get up the lane. I'm not allowed to *start* until next year; it's not fair, I *know* I wouldn't be as hopeless as he is."

"No, you'll be tearing round the moor roads killing ponies and squashing hedgehogs," I said disagreeably.

"I won't. Fast drivers are more efficient, it's the ditherers who cause all the accidents." The gateway cleared, he ran back to the car and I cantered on ahead of them, annoyed that I hadn't crushed him with some brilliant reply.

I cantered until Crackers began to flag, then I slowed him to a walk and let Felix, who seemed to me to be driving at a very sensible pace and quite fast enough for a rutted moorland track, come alongside. I explained where the foal was and that they would have to leave the Range Rover on the track and walk the last bit. Then they went on ahead. After a bit I took a small narrow path, hoping that it would lead me diagonally to Danny and Louisa. It did, with a few diversions, and I reached them just before the Hamiltons arrived.

Louisa was sitting on a boulder, holding Redwing and looking very worried. The foal still lay on his side with glazed eyes, but he seemed to have shrunk while I was away and I could see by the rapid rise of his flank that his breathing was very fast. Poppy stood with her head hanging over him and an anxious look in her soft brown eyes. Danny knelt in the heather, tears trickling down his face as he gently stroked the foal's neck.

"Oh dear, he *does* look sick," said Mrs Hamilton. "We ought to have brought a rug to carry him on."

"I carried him over my shoulders," Danny told her.

"He looks to me like a stretcher case," said Felix, taking off his anorak. "He's very small. Do you think we could carry him on this?"

It was one of those huge, loose anoraks and the foal fitted on it easily; with four people, one at each corner, they lifted him without any effort and set off towards the car. Louisa and I followed, leading our ponies.

They loaded the foal in the back and decided to leave the lower part of the tailgate open so that Poppy could see him as she followed them home. Toby said he would sit beside the foal and restrain him if he suddenly revived and tried to jump out, but I could see that Louisa didn't trust him and wanted to go too, so I offered Danny a ride home on Redwing. He jumped at the offer so Louisa lent him her crash-cap, which was only slightly too big, and when we'd watched the Range Rover move steadily away up the track with poor Poppy trotting behind, I legged Danny up and insisted that he put his stirrups at the right length before we started.

With so many competent people looking after the foal there didn't seem any need to hurry and even Crackers seemed happy to amble along at a gentle pace. Danny cheered up and seemed very pleased to be riding Redwing. He patted her several times and said she had a very long stride. He looked, I decided, almost exactly like his mother. The same dark, tangled gypsy hair, the same brown eyes, the same pretty nose and mouth; in fact he was too pretty for a boy. The only difference lay in their expressions. Danny had a very determined look.

After a bit, I suggested a trot and then a canter. I didn't risk a gallop because, though as Heather said, he was a good rider, he was too small to control Redwing if she really got going.

When we were walking again I asked, "Why did you run away? Don't you like it here?"

He looked embarrassed. "I had a quarrel with Mum." He changed the subject. "That foal looks really bad. Do you think he's going to die?"

"We might be just in time. He would have died if

you hadn't found him. Quite a lot do every year; the farmers don't look at them often enough, they're too busy. Where did you sleep last night?" I asked after a pause.

"In the shed in the churchyard, where they keep the watering-cans and things; it wasn't locked."

"The police thought you might have gone to Reading to see your grandparents. Your mother and the Jacksons thought you might have fallen and hurt yourself. People do on the moor; it's not a very good place to go wandering on your own."

Danny stared straight ahead with a fixed expression. I could see he wasn't going to talk about it, so I suggested a trot. When we reached the farm we found that Heather and Mick were back. Poppy and the foal were bedded down on fresh straw in one of the little stone houses meant for sheep and Sam Parsons, the vet, was on his way.

"We've got a cow that's poorly as well," explained Mick. "Dad's been dosing her for a week with no results whatever. He was talking of getting Sam to take a look at her yesterday so now we've done it."

"We'll show him Juniper's warts while he's here," added Heather, "*and* he could take a look at that old ewe. I know Dad says it's just age with her, but you never know."

I watered Crackers at the trough and Louisa took Redwing from Danny while Heather pushed him firmly towards the back door, saying that his mum was in the kitchen having a cup of tea. At that moment the door opened and Cindy Kyle appeared. "Oh, Danny!" she shrieked, holding out her arms. As she hugged him we could hear her saying, "You're a real meany. You had me worried stiff, Danny, absolutely petrified. We all thought something really dreadful had happened to you. It wasn't a very kind thing to do, was it?"

In the end her reproaches dragged a muttered sorry or two from Danny.

"Never mind, my dears," said Mrs Jackson, who seemed unusually calm and motherly. "He's saved the life of Poppy's foal, so it's an ill wind that blows nobody any good. Come on in, now, Danny, and have something to eat."

Louisa and I took a last look at the foal and wondered if it *was* going to survive and then, agreeing to take it in turns on Redwing, we set off for home.

The Failure

Josephine Pullein-Thompson

We rode through the newly green woods: Jan Mason, my sister Francey and I. I was hating them because they were happy and successful and I was a failure.

It was spring. There were primroses in the clearings and along the banks of the stream; the pale blue sky showed patchily through the trees, the sun shone and after the rain the countryside smelled warm and earthy and sweet.

Usually I love April, but this year my hate spoiled it all. I hated the primroses and the singing birds almost as much as I hated Francey and Jan. I felt out of accord with everyone and everything, even with my treasured golden chestnut, Ripple. I'd been in this black mood for four whole days, since Monday when I had been dropped from the Pony Club mounted games team.

Elizabeth Brent, who trained the team, had done her best to be tactful. "Look, Gillian, it's not really *you,*" she had said. "I mean there's nothing to choose between you and Francey, it's just that Ripple's a bit large for mounted games; Ringo and Chippy are perfect."

But I knew it wasn't really Ripple's size – after all

he's only a hand taller than Jan's Chipmunk. I knew that it was my riding and, if there *was* nothing to chose between Francey and me, there ought to be, for I was two years older. Eight of us had trained for the team, but Jean's pony had gone lame and John Morgan was being kept on as reserve. I was the only one to be dropped.

It was towards the end of the previous summer that Francey had first begun to shine. Until then we'd both been the sort of people who are overjoyed at winning a single, pale rosette. The first time she had acquired a collection of firsts and seconds at a gymkhana it had seemed a wonderful piece of luck, and I had been almost as delighted as Francey. But, when it gradually transpired that this was no fluke and winning became a habit, my attitude changed. I ceased to be contented with my single third or fourth and only the end of the summer holidays saved me from an outburst of jealousy. Now she was in the team and I was out, and something inside me had burst. Our parents guessed how I felt and tried to comfort me.

"You're a dreamer, Gilly, not a doer," my mother said. "One isn't better than the other, they're just different and there's plenty of room for both in the world."

"Well, I'm delighted that you're not both in the team," added my father. "One daughter talking exclusively of regions and zones and finals is quite enough for me. And surely an intelligent girl like you doesn't want to spend days on end practising garbage collecting or racing up and down with flags?"

But it wasn't any use. I wanted to be in the team and I couldn't bear the thought of having to watch my sister being successful while I moped at the ringside.

It was just jealousy. I realised that, but realising didn't help, in fact it made things worse. I hated myself for being so ignoble and for spoiling Francey's fun. She did her best to be tactful. She tried hard to subdue her elation and to avoid all mention of the team, but the better she behaved the more my feelings shocked me, and the more miserable I felt.

The next team practice had been arranged for Wednesday. "Do come along if you feel like it," Elizabeth had told me. "I can always do with some help." But I had no intention of going near them. I pretended to sleep through Francey's alarm-clock and kept up the pretence until she made a really determined effort to wake me. Then I snarled disagreeably that I didn't feel like getting up and demanded that she should mind her own business and leave me alone. Later I heard the sound of Chippy's hoofs on the road and Jan's voice calling from the gate and then Ripple's indignant neighs when he found he'd been left behind.

Presently my mother came to ask if I was all right, or if I felt ill or anything. This filled me with unreasoning rage. "Surely a person can stay in bed late in the *holidays* without a lot of stupid fuss," I demanded angrily.

When she had gone, I tormented myself with mental pictures of the championship at Wembley. I visualised huge rosettes, Francey and Jan holding the Prince Philip Cup aloft, television cameras. I was crying angry tears into my pillow when I heard my mother calling that Ripple was out.

He had jumped the paddock railings and, by the

time I had pulled on jeans and a sweater and shoes, there were hoofmarks all over the garden. I caught Ripple quite easily, and then I spent the rest of the morning with a fork, lifting his hoofprints out of the lawn.

When my father came home that evening he only complained mildly about the state of the lawn, but he said that in future I *must* take Ripple out at the same time as Ringo.

"You don't have to go with Francey," he told me, "but obviously the pony can't be left in the field on his own. It's not only the garden, he could easily damage himself."

So on Friday I had to get up. I hadn't meant to ride with the others, but Jan nagged me. "Oh, come on, Gillian. You may as well ride over with us even if you don't stay. If you go on like this everyone's going to think you're sulking. Anyway, what *does* it matter? We're not even going to get to the Zone, we're certain to be knocked out at Denley."

Grudgingly I agreed to ride with them. At first Jan tried to talk to me, but growing tired of my bad temper and monosyllabic answers she gave up, and, dropping back, chattered to Francey instead.

At the end of Chorley Wood the track crosses a couple of fields and then brings you to a gate into a lane. As I opened the gate Francey said, "Look, there's that ghastly child we met on Monday, the one who can't control her pony. What does she think she's doing?"

I remembered the small girl. The pony had tried to follow us and in the end she had to dismount and drag him away. She had dismounted now, but this time the

pony was winning the battle and dragging her towards us. She began to shriek and whack at him with her whip. He was a dear little grey pony and he was holding his head as high as he could to escape her blows.

"Stop that!" shouted Francey as she and Jan turned into the lane. "You're not fit to have a pony if that's how you treat it."

"You should be reported to the RSPCA for cruelty," added Jan in threatening tones.

By the time I had shut the gate the little grey had dragged his owner right over to us and was sniffing noses with Ringo. The girl – she looked about nine – was red in the face and large tears were trickling down her cheeks.

"I can't help it," she wailed. "He won't do anything

I want. He's a horrible, obstinate pony and I wish we'd never bought him." Her sobs grew louder, and we sat on our ponies feeling rather embarrassed and wondering what to do.

Jan spoke first. "Oh, come on," she said. "*We* can't do anything and you know Elizabeth asked us not to be late for the practice; she's going to a show this afternoon." The little girl sobbed louder, she had obviously hoped for help. The grey pony was nuzzling Chippy, and he didn't look horrible or obstinate. He had large brown eyes, a wide forehead, a slightly cheeky expression and a tiny mouth.

"Yes, come on," agreed Francey. "You hold him until we're out of sight," she told the small girl, "then you'll be all right."

"But I couldn't get him to go home for hours after we met you on Monday," wailed the small girl. "I kept turning him round, but he kept cantering after you. We went right up to the main road and then a man on a bicycle helped me. And yesterday he bolted with my brother."

"Well, we *can't* stay. We're in the mounted games team," said Jan importantly, "and we have to get to a practice."

Suddenly I realised that there was absolutely no reason why I shouldn't stay. "I'll ride home with her, I don't have to practise," I reminded Jan.

Then I dismounted and took the pony's rein. "We'll wait," I told the small girl, "until the others are out of sight."

Jan and Francey looked at me. "Are you sure?" they asked.

"Yes. It can't be more boring than watching you practise."

"Okay. See you later then," said Francey and they trotted away looking relieved and happy.

The grey pony was nose to nose with Ripple and the small girl was searching her pockets for a handkerchief. "What's your name?" I asked as I held the pony and she mounted.

"Joy," she answered, "Joy Fraser." I looked at her critically. She didn't seem old enough to be a villain or the sort of person who should be reported for cruelty to animals. She wore jodhs, a blue anorak and a riding-hat, she had long, straight, fair hair, blue eyes and a worried expression.

"What's your pony's name?" I asked as I mounted.

"Dream," she answered. "It's a silly name, but Mum chose it."

Dream was obviously delighted to be with another pony. He copied Ripple's actions carefully, trotting, cantering and pulling up exactly when he did. I pointed this out to Joy, who had stopped tugging and kicking and was beginning to look more cheerful.

"Yes, it's much nicer now you're here," she told me. "Usually he won't do a thing."

"I think he's very young and I don't think he's obstinate; if he hasn't been taught the aids he *can't* have any idea what you mean when you use your reins and legs."

The Frasers lived in a very modernised cottage, newly painted white. Chorley Wood was on one side of it, a field on the other and an overgrown orchard at the back. A new wooden loose box had been erected close to the garage; it looked a lovely place to keep ponies.

Mrs Fraser came out of the cottage at the sound of our hoofs and with her was a boy with red hair and freckles. "That's Mum and my brother Ian," said Joy.

"How did it go this morning? Was he any better?" called Mrs Fraser anxiously as she came down the path.

"He was really awful until we met Gillian, since then he's been brilliant," answered Joy. "Gillian says he's only a baby and hasn't been taught the aids," she went on. "That's why he doesn't do what we want; he's not obstinate." It was a bit embarrassing to be quoted like this, but I was glad, for Dream's sake, that my lecture had sunk in.

"It's been such a disappointment to us all," said Mrs Fraser. "We called him Dream because we'd always dreamed of having a pony, but it's more like a nightmare, really. You see, my husband and I are both fond of animals, but we've no experience of horses."

I dismounted and looked in Dream's mouth. In the centre of each jaw he had four shining new teeth, but the four corner ones were shabby little milk teeth. "He's only just four," I told the Frasers. "He must have been three when you bought him."

"We knew he was young but we thought he'd grow up with the children," Mrs Fraser explained. "The dealer assured us that he was used to children and absolutely trustworthy, but Joy and Ian don't seem able to manage him, yet they rode the pony at the farm in Wales last summer with no problems at all."

"I'm going to show you just how obstinate he is," announced Ian, scrambling into the saddle. "You put up the jumps, Joy."

I followed them into the field. Joy erected a few flimsy beanpoles on small piles of bricks, while Ian, trying to urge Dream into a canter, was horrible to behold. He kicked and flapped his legs with such energy that his whole body contorted. This made his elbows wave madly and caused his hands to jerk at the poor pony's mouth. When Dream trotted over the beanpoles, dragging his legs through them and knocking them down, Ian began to use his whip.

He was older and stronger than Joy and one particularly hard blow was too much for Dream, who stopped dead and bucked him off. Ian got up, red in the face and very angry. He looked as though he intended to set about Dream, so I stopped him quickly.

"It's no use your getting in a rage with him," I said. "You might as well get angry with a Russian boy because he doesn't understand English. A trained pony doesn't need kicking and hitting, but Dream isn't trained; he hasn't been taught to answer the aids and you and Joy don't ride well enough to teach him."

"They ought to be *born* knowing what we mean. And I'm sure he does know; he's just obstinate," argued Ian.

That made me angry. "He can't possibly understand what you mean, because you ride so badly that you give the aids to go faster and the aids to stop at the same time," I said sharply. "Do you pedal your bicycle with the brakes on? Because that's how you ride your pony."

Ian looked rather crushed by my words but, having re-erected the bean poles, Joy asked brightly, "Will you show us how to jump on Ripple?"

"Not over those, they're far too flimsy," I answered,

looking round for something solid. "I could jump the hedge into the orchard, if that's okay."

Mrs Fraser assured me that it was, so, when I had checked for wire, I cantered a circle and jumped the hedge and then came back over a post and rails in the corner. Ripple loves natural fences and he jumped them both smoothly and easily. The Frasers seemed impressed.

"What a beautiful jumper," said Mrs Fraser.

"Isn't he brill?" added Joy.

And Ian said in dissatisfied tones, "I wish Dream would jump like that."

"But Ripple's eight," I told him. "He already knew how to jump when we bought him and we've been practising together for two years. You can't train a pony in five minutes."

"You wouldn't give Ian and Joy lessons, would you?" Mrs Fraser looked at me anxiously to see if I minded being asked. "But I expect you're very busy," she added disconsolately.

I thought. No team practice meant that I had time on my hands, I didn't like Joy and Ian much, they were so foul to their pony, but then they were unhorsey; they couldn't be expected to understand, and most of us become bad-tempered and horrible when things go wrong. Then there was Dream, he was a sweet pony, I'd like to help him.

"Yes," I said, "I think I could manage that."

Joy gave a little skip. "Oh, when?" she asked.

"Tomorrow morning?" I suggested. "I could be here by half past ten."

"Could you really? That would be *wonderful,*" said Mrs Fraser. "We'd all be so grateful. You've no idea how frustrating it is to stand by and watch everything going wrong and not have a clue how to put it right."

I told my mother and Francey about my adventures at lunch.

Francey said, "You've certainly let yourself in for something. *Can* you teach riding? I mean I know what to *do,* but I couldn't explain it to someone else."

"Of course she can." My mother spoke confidently. "Gill's very good at explanation. I never understood dressage until she took me in hand, now I'm an absolute authority on correct bends, rhythm and impulsion."

"The point is," I said, ignoring this flattery, "that it's going to take ages to improve them if they have to take turns on Dream, and anyway, they need to ride a reasonably well-schooled pony so they get some idea of what it feels like. Do you think the Bedlows would lend me Pip?"

"Yes, I'm sure they would. Even Annabel's outgrown him now. Give Mrs Bedlow a ring," my mother encouraged me.

When I explained about the Frasers' desperate need for lessons, Mrs Bedlow said that she would willingly lend Pip. "You wouldn't be an angel and teach Annabel at the same time?" she asked. "I think she's finding the change from Pip to Crumpet a bit frightening. She doesn't seem to enjoy riding like she used to. And Liz is in France for the whole holidays so she can't take her out and Juliet and Annabel don't really get on."

So, on Saturday, I found myself standing in the centre of a hastily marked out school and instructing three pupils. The Frasers were very uphill work at first. I spent my time saying, "Don't kick, *press*." And, "You're pulling, you must only *feel* the reins." Sometimes I shouted, "*Sit still*, you're not whirlwinds!" Or, "Keep your legs back, your toes mustn't be in front of your knees," in Elizabeth Brent's voice.

Annabel cheered up when she saw how badly the Frasers rode and when the lesson, which had to be sedate, calmed Crumpet. She is a gentle rider so I soon had her demonstrating the aids for the halt and the turn on the forehand to the Frasers.

When I thought my pupils had had enough schooling, I arranged bending and potato races at the walk. And, when the Frasers controlled themselves and gave up kicking and tugging, we graduated to the trot. Dream seemed to be enjoying himself, he watched the other ponies carefully and trotted up and down with pricked ears and a smug expression.

After that I found myself booked for a lesson five mornings a week and I acquired two more pupils, friends

of Annabel's called Toby and Harriet. They were boring sometimes, especially Ian, but it was tremendously exciting and rewarding to watch them improving. In a way it was a voyage of discovery. I corrected what I thought was wrong with them and sometimes it worked, and sometimes it didn't and I had to try something else. I found that, in teaching, I was also learning a good deal about riding.

I was so busy that I forgot about the mounted games and the day of the regional competition came almost as a surprise. A huge gang of us went to watch, including my five pupils. We cheered ourselves hoarse and were delighted when our team qualified for the next round.

As the teams were given their rosettes Ian, who was standing beside me, said, "I want to be in the team. In two years I ought to be good enough."

"You might make it," I agreed. "You're competitive and good at vaulting; you might be just the type if you improve your riding."

"I'll never be in a team," said Annabel despondently. "I've been riding since I was five and my only rosette was third in a leading-rein class."

"But winning doesn't matter," I told her. "You can get masses of pleasure from riding without going near a show. You just have to discover what suits you; it may be schooling horses or teaching people, it could be long distance riding or dressage or jumping, or just having a pony to look after at home."

Sour grapes? I wondered as I ran to congratulate Francey and Ringo. No, just the truth, I told myself, for I didn't feel jealous at all.

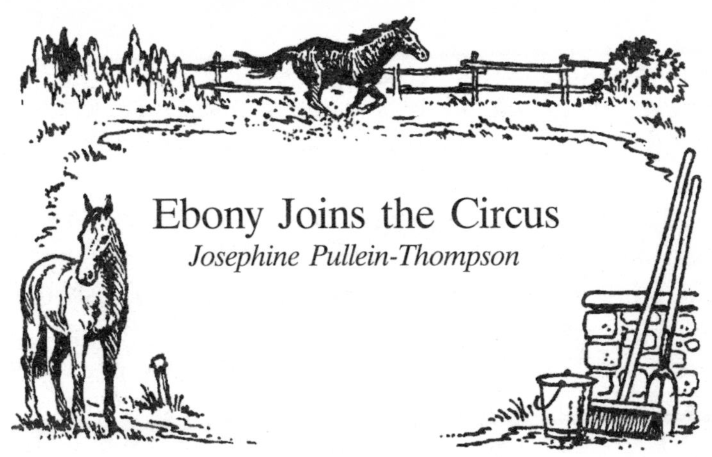

Ebony Joins the Circus

Josephine Pullein-Thompson

When I left Clarendon Mews I wasn't the clean and elegant horse that I had been on arrival. In fact I was dirty and unfit, with a staring coat and a mane and tail that needed pulling, when Percy put an old rope halter on me and led me to the horse sale.

I was tied to a ring in the wall between a shivering and half-starved pony and a stout cart-horse, and a round paper with a number on it was stuck to my quarters. I turned as far as my rope would allow me and watched the scene. There were a great many people, mostly farmers and tradesmen, but also some very rough-looking men and boys who swore and spat a good deal.

The noise was very great. The sellers were telling everyone what good animals they were offering. The frightened horses were all whinnying and there was an endless clattering of hoofs and cracking of whips as they were run up to show their paces to likely buyers. There were a few men already drunk, though it was not yet twelve, and they were shouting and singing.

It was very unpleasant having my mouth forced

open by complete strangers who wanted to see my teeth. Some of them felt my legs, slapped my flank and pulled out my tail as well, before making a disparaging remark about my age and walking on.

The farmers all thought me too well-bred. "You got to cosset that sort," they said, or, "I 'aven't the time to look after a blood-'orse." The tradesmen all asked if I was broken to harness and Percy, who didn't know any better, said no, I was a hunter. The occasional person looking for a cheap hunter was always horrified by my age. The cart-horse next to me was having a better time. The farmers all said that he was "a likely sort". He told me that he'd been working on the canals, towing barges. He enjoyed the life, but more and more goods were going by rail instead of by water so he, and many more like him, were out of a job. But, he added placidly, he would be quite happy to work on a farm.

At last two men came who didn't dismiss me as useless. The younger was tall and thin with an eager, handsome face, the other short and fat, wearing rather old-fashioned clothes and smoking a cigar. The young one, Felix, stood back, studying me carefully, and then said, "I think we've found him, Alf. He's got presence, look at him, and breeding. Trimmed up a bit, well-groomed, he'd be exactly right; stupendous!"

"Except that he's not a mare," said Alf. He looked at my teeth. "Past his second youth. Is he sound? That's the question. And can he jump?"

"Oh yes, he can jump all right," said Percy, coming forward.

Felix laughed a lot. "There you are, that clinches it," he said. "I knew at once he was the horse for us.

Personality, looks quiet, friendly; a great jumper and any amount of character."

Alf seemed less certain. "We'll see what he fetches; I'm not paying much for a horse of his age. Here, boy, trot him out and let's see how he moves."

I liked the look of Felix, I felt that he would be a considerate master and all that talk of jumping was music to my ears, but I hoped that he didn't want to hunt me in a fast country for I knew that I wasn't up to that sort of work any more.

Presently my turn to be sold came. I was walked and then trotted up and down amid a sea of white faces and brandishing whips, while the auctioneer called for bids. There was no great eagerness to buy me. A few of the people who'd looked at me bidded; one sounded like the undertaker, another voice could have belonged to the cat's-meat man, the third was obviously a farmer. Then I saw Alf waving his catalogue in a lordly manner. At last the auctioneer's hammer fell and I was led away and tied up. The half-starved pony was being sold; I hoped he would go to someone who would give him a square meal, and not for cat's-meat. Then Felix came up carrying a saddle and bridle. "We got you for a song, old horse," he told me. "Now, where's that boy? I want to know your name." Percy seemed pleased that Felix was to have me and told him that my name was Ebony. He put on the saddle while Felix adjusted the bridle to fit my head, then he sobbed a tear or two as he stroked my neck, but Felix gave him sixpence and told him I should have a good home.

As Felix mounted and rode out of the saleyard I knew that he was a good rider. He felt confident and easy, he didn't attempt to impose his will on me but just rode me quietly forward while he learned what I was like. In no time we were partners, it was as though I had Fanny or Ned back again and my heart rose as we left the town.

It was a frosty day but the sun was high and warm and had already thawed most of the bone from the ground. Felix sang as we walked and trotted along and altogether he seemed very pleased and cheerful.

We passed through several villages and then we cantered over a short stretch of moor and came to a long lane, between stone walls, that brought us down to a grey stone farm in the valley.

It was rather a tumbledown place and the yard, instead of being full of pigs or cattle, had a whole collection of caravans within its walls; like gypsy vans they had little chimneys, two windows, and shafts for the horse, but the people who came to greet us weren't gypsies, though there may have been one or two among them. There were a great many children playing everywhere and a smell of paint and cooking filled the air.

Felix led me into a stable. I saw with pleasure that it was quite a large loose box and when I looked over the low partition into the next box I found the smallest pony I had ever seen. He was skewbald and much smaller than The Giant. He could not have been more than eight hands. He said at once that his name was Tom Thumb, that he was the smallest pony in the world and came from the Shetland Islands. Felix was rubbing me down, someone was spreading straw, someone else brought a bucket of water and yet another came running with a rug so I was soon very comfortably settled. When the humans had gone away and I had eaten my feed, Tom Thumb asked me what I did. I answered that I was a hunter, an answer that he didn't seem to find at all satisfactory.

"I wonder what you'll do here, then," he said. "Oh well, I suppose they'll teach you something. I jump through hoops, lie down, take handkerchiefs from my master's pocket, chase a boy round the ring and do numerous other tricks. I'm billed as 'The Clever Pony' as well as 'The Smallest Horse in the World'; people pay good money to watch me."

I felt rather alarmed at this, but Tom Thumb, who seemed very pleased to have a companion, talked on and on. It seemed that he and his master, Andrew, had belonged to a circus, but there had been a fire and the equipment had all been lost so now they had joined this fair and soon we would all be travelling round the countryside performing.

I asked if he knew what Felix did and he answered that he was an actor and that sometimes a whole company of them went round with a fair, but he thought that Felix was the only one and he had been talking about an equestrian act. Then I asked about Alf, and Tom Thumb said he was the Guv'nor and usually called "His Nibs". He settled the quarrels and arranged the fairgrounds and lent everyone money.

Felix seemed a very thoughtful master. The very next morning he spent a long time sawing and hammering at my door and when he had finished it was in two halves and the top one fastened back and enabled me to look out and see all the activities in the farmyard. I can't describe the pleasure that gave me. Being tied up in a stall is all very well for a short time and it's not so bad for a horse that is out all day doing slow work and only in his stall at night. But when a hunter or hack is condemned to spend twenty-two out of twenty-four hours, six or seven days a week, facing the same blank wall, well, it's no wonder that horses are driven to crib-biting, wind-sucking and other nervous disorders.

After the boredom of the mews I was delighted with my view and made Tom Thumb so jealous with my accounts of all I could see that he began to work on the bolt of the door between our boxes. He got the head up and then slid it back with his teeth and pushed the door

open and came in with me. Of course he wasn't tall enough to see over the door and he had to balance with one toe on the crossbar. When Felix found our two heads looking out he laughed and fetched a stout box for Tom Thumb's forefeet.

For a few days Felix just took me for rides in the countryside. We jumped some walls and hurdles and a gate and he seemed very pleased with me and always told everyone that I was "just the thing".

Then one day he took me into the barn. The floor was scattered with peat and a ring was marked out in the middle; it was rather a small space but I was well enough balanced to canter round it quite fast, which pleased Felix. We practised entering at a wild gallop and stopping dead in the centre. He was very careful of my mouth and threw his weight back as a signal instead of pulling on the reins and, as soon as I understood what he wanted, I did it all on my own. Then we started work on the whole act. After the gallop in Felix would make a speech all about his wonderful mare Black Bess, and then another man called King would come in on one of the caravan horses and he and Felix, who was Dick Turpin, plotted together.

Then a very old coach came in, drawn by four very hairy horses, and it was robbed by Turpin and King, several people fell dead and everyone fired pistols which made us horses jump at first though we soon became used to it. After that the police came and they captured King and he called to Turpin to shoot the men who held him, but Turpin missed and killed King by mistake.

Then a great chase began. I would go round and round the ring at a gallop, rush out and come in again from the other side and the pursuers were doing the same though they never caught up with us. We robbed another coach; it was the same one really, but they put a different name on the doors and dressed the people differently, and there was some more firing of pistols.

The next exciting part was when a toll-gate was put up in the ring. As Turpin and I came galloping in the keeper shut it to stop us, but Felix would give a shout and I would soar over. After that I had to show signs of tiring and when I could only proceed at a weary trot with my head low we stopped at an inn and I was given a drench of brandy or ale or something from a bottle, only the bottle was always empty.

Then we came to the city of York and a large cardboard spire was put up and bells began to ring. I was reduced to a walk and Felix dismounted and led me, and then I was supposed to fall down dead. This wasn't easy to learn. Tom Thumb could do it and I was made to watch him, but I found all his advice very irritating and got on better when Felix taught me alone. He would take me to a nice soft spot and strap up one of my forelegs, then he would tap my other knee with a whip until I bent it and kneeled down. The moment I did it I was praised and given oats or carrots. Gradually I learned to kneel without the strap and whenever he pointed at my knees. All he had to do then was to turn my head towards him and gently push my shoulder until I gave way and lay down on my side. I wouldn't have done it for anyone, but Felix was kind to me and made all my lessons enjoyable, so I decided to oblige.

I soon knew the routine and when we reached York and the bells began to ring, I would watch for the signal.

When I had died Felix would make a long speech over my dead body and then the pursuers would come up and there was another fight. The first time this happened I raised my head to see what was going on, but this caused a great outcry from the watching children and Felix came and told me I had to stay dead.

The next problem was carrying me out. A great yard-door was brought in and slid under my body as six strong men lifted me, then about twelve of them carried me out. I always hated this part but Felix would walk by my head and stroke my neck to keep me calm, so I put up with it because I was doing it for him.

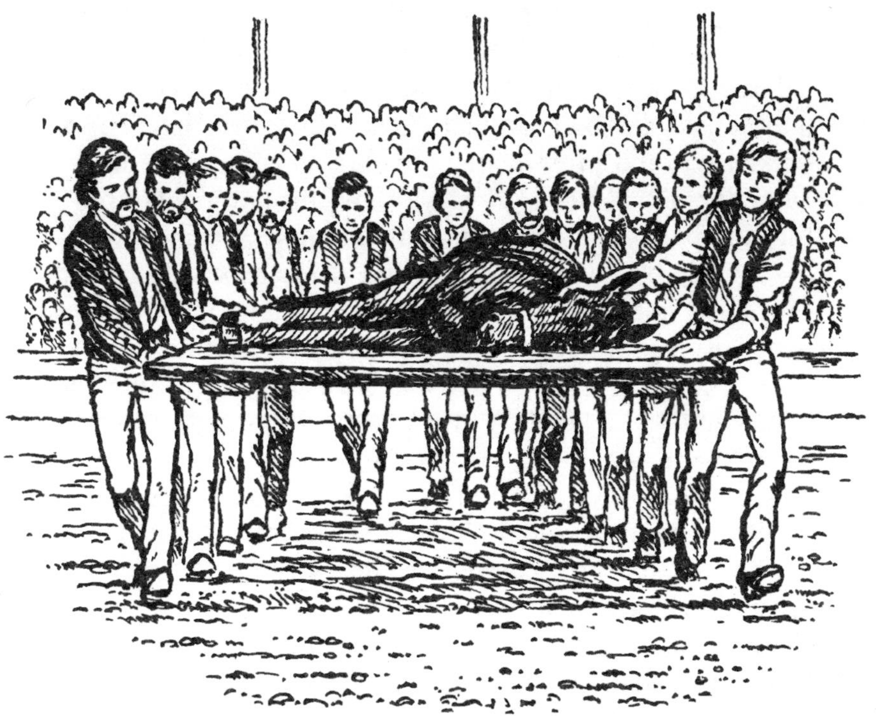

Though there were stablehands among the fair people, Felix looked after me himself and by the start of the season I was a picture. Too round and well-covered to be hunting fit, I was just right for a public performance, my coat shone, my mane and tail, neatly trimmed, were beautifully brushed out and this was just as well, for there were some very extravagant tributes to Black Bess's beauty in the verses Felix had to say.

On the day we moved out of our winter quarters all the carts and wagons and vans left very early in the morning. Felix and I started later for we could take a short cut across country instead of going by the roads.

When we reached the fairground, which was just outside a large town, Felix rode me to a tent which had a large notice about Tom Thumb the Clever Pony and another saying that Captain Felix Fanshawe, late Royal Hussars, would present the stupendous equestrian drama *Dick Turpin's Ride to York*, with spectacular fights and a thrilling performance by his famous horse, Black Bess.

Inside was our usual ring and the cardboard inn and the spire and the toll-gate, and a couple more jumps were all ready at the side. I began to feel nervous but Felix rode me round until I was used to the tent and the lights and then he took me out to see the fairground. There were stalls for hoop-la and ranges for shooting and coconut-shies. There was a huge roundabout with brightly coloured and richly gilded horses and a steam engine to work it. There were many little booths with fortune-tellers and fireproof ladies and fat ladies inside. There was Professor Lopescu's Flea Circus from Romania and a Punch and Judy Show and many slides and swings and entertainments of all sorts.

As it grew darker more and more lights came on and the steam engines sent sparks and smoke up into the dark sky. There was a smell of burning coal and hot engines. Then a great steam organ started up. It was painted in bright colours and gilded like the roundabout horses and the noise from it was tremendous, as though a whole brass band was playing close at hand. I stood looking at the scene, turning this way and that to take it all in, and Felix sat on my back laughing loudly at my amazement.

When we went to the stable tent that I was to share with Tom he was being got ready for his act. He wore a silver and orange bridle, roller and crupper and from his forelock rose a very handsome orange plume. I wondered if I had to dress up, but no, it was Felix who came disguised. He had a curly moustache, a green coat and cocked hat, a belt full of pistols. Andrew was impossible to recognise with his face covered in white, a huge mouth and a false nose; he was dressed as a clown. The small, fat boy Tom had to chase had been made to look fatter than ever by very tight clothes.

When Tom left for the ring one of the stable hands put the finishing touches to my appearance, then Felix stopped brushing his coat and mounted and we walked over to the ring tent and waited in a dark corner.

Tom was pretending to become angrier and angrier with the fat boy and finally he chased him round the ring and out in a ferocious manner. His Nibs, wearing black trousers, a scarlet coat and a top hat, announced Dick Turpin, and Felix took me well back so that we could get up speed for our entrance.

We whirled in and round and came to a dashing

halt in the centre. Felix took off his hat and bowed low, I stared at the lights and the white faces all round me. Then Felix began the verses on how much he loved his bonny Black Bess. As he came to the verse:

Mark that skin, sleek as velvet and dusky at night,
With its jet undisfigured by one spot of white;
That throat branched with veins, prompt to charge
or caress.
Now, is she not beautiful? Bonny Black Bess!

King came riding in and they began to plan robberies.

We held up the coach, the horses were all looking a good deal smarter than they had at rehearsal and the guard had a horn to blow. There were the usual shootings and several deaths and then we made off with some bags labelled MONEY. King had taken too many and could not control his horse, which was why the police got him.

When Felix's shot killed King all the audience groaned in horror but they cheered up when we took one of the extra jumps and galloped away. These brush fences were not very big, but, though I was supposed to leap over perfectly, the pursuers, especially the police, were meant to run into each other, fall off and generally make a hash of things and this pleased the audience very much.

Then we robbed the second coach and came to the toll-gate. It had grown larger at every practice and was now a big jump, about five feet. I took it carefully for the lights were casting strange shadows and made finding the right take-off difficult. The people cheered and

clapped as I soared over. We stopped at the inn and Felix had another long verse to say which ended:

By moonlight, in darkness, by night or by day,
Her headlong career there is nothing can stay.
She cares not for distance, she knows not distress,
Can you show me the courser to match with
Black Bess?

Then I began to slow down and hang my head; soon I was only walking and then as the spire was put up and the bells began to ring, Felix led me. Right in the middle of the ring he pointed at my knees and I fell dead. The audience were very upset; I think some of them thought I really had died. Turpin was very upset too:

"Art thou gone, Bess? Gone – gone!" he cried out very dramatically. "And I have killed the best steed that was ever crossed?"

O'er highway and byway, in rough or smooth weather,
Some thousands of miles have we journeyed together;
Our couch the same straw, our meals the same mess;
No couple more constant than I and Black Bess.

They fought the last fight and I managed to lie still and not look, though it was very hard. Then the door came and they called for volunteers from the audience to help carry out poor dead Bess and I'm certain a great many people went home wondering whether I was really dead or not.

All the fair people thought the performance a great success and Felix kept patting me and saying, "Old horse, you're a natural, a born actor; stupendous!"

After that he became even more ambitious and besides adding new touches to our present act he was always thinking of other acts we could perform in the future and talking about *The Tailor of Brentford* and *The High-Mettled Racer* or *The Fat Farmer,* who wore layers and layers of clothes and undressed as he galloped round the ring.

We seemed to be doing well. We moved from place to place, sometimes only staying for one day and night, sometimes for five. By the summer we had reached the West Country and I was jumping the toll-gate keeper as he ran to bar the way, as well as the gate; we were practising for *The Tailor of Brentford* which called for a lot of acting on my part as I had to push Felix around and make disagreeable faces and pretend to bite him.

In some places our audiences were so large that we had to do Dick Turpin three times over every evening. I did get very bored at having to go through it so often and we had to think of new things to do to keep up our interest. Felix invented that I should raise my head and give my thoughtless master a kiss with my lips before I died; this upset the audiences very much.

In the autumn we came near to London and the idea was that we would work our way north and back to winter quarters, except for those who had special Christmas engagements.

Then one night some men came round to the stable when the performance was over. The stablehand was rubbing me down and Felix was unsticking his moustache. They introduced themselves and asked him out to supper. He seemed very excited and, changing quickly, he went off with them, leaving me to the stablehand.

Next day Felix seemed very thoughtful and he had a long talk with His Nibs. Our show went on as usual but we gave up rehearsing *The Tailor of Brentford.* I sensed that something was wrong and I lost some of my enthusiasm. But he didn't say anything until one morning when we had just come to a new town. Then he came rushing into my tent; he was dressed very smartly in his best suit. He put his arms round my neck and said, "I'm sorry, Ebony, I feel a brute, a complete cad, doing this to you. You've been magnificent, you did everything you could to make the show a success, you never let me down once and now I'm walking out on you. But you see, old horse, it's the chance of a lifetime, you *can't* refuse a part like this. You just can't!

"If I had the ready cash I'd buy you from His Nibs and take you with me, but I haven't and no stable to put you in either. I'm truly sorry, old horse." He gave me a carrot and ran out of my stable. I couldn't believe that our happy times together had ended as suddenly and finally as this. For a day or two I thought he might come back. I would look for him in the mornings and when the time for our performance came, I felt sure that he would come bursting in, sticking on his moustache and telling me some new plan. Sometimes I thought I heard his voice and would whinny excitedly, but he never came.

Then I learned, from the talk of the stablehands, that he had been offered a good part at a big London theatre and might well become rich and famous. For a time I clung to the idea that His Nibs was finding another Dick Turpin to ride me and things would go on much as before, but men appeared who looked at my teeth and felt my legs and had me trotted up so I knew I was to be sold.

"Too old for a hunter," they all said, and, "Who wants a circus horse, he'll be doing tricks in the road." And they haggled with His Nibs over the price.

At last a man with very fair hair came; he said that he owned a large riding-school and livery stable in London and needed a reliable, well-mannered horse for his lady clients and was willing to pay a good price for the right animal. So I changed hands again; and that marked the end of my time as Black Bess and the beginning of a new, but less exciting, life in London.

The Race

Josephine Pullein-Thompson

Mr Brake liked the idea of the island's annual pony race and spent the evening preparing his cameras. The difficulty of reading or playing any of Jeremy's card-games by oil lamp, especially as Mr Brake would only allow the tiniest of flames in case they blackened or cracked the glass shades, drove everyone to bed early, with the result that they all wakened much earlier than usual and were on the terrace eating melon for breakfast and admiring the sun climbing higher and higher over the sea by seven-thirty. By nine they were all waiting round the replacement hire car, which Jeremy said disdainfully was even more of a banger than the first, while Mr Brake assisted Mrs Brake, still limping from her encounter with a sea urchin, into the front seat.

There were no signposts pointing the way to the town. With only one tarred road on the island, winding its way across the centre to join the tiny port on one side to the town on the other, the inhabitants of the little Greek island obviously thought signs unnecessary. But where, close to town, the road divided, a notice announced CAMPING and an arrow pointing along the lower road above the sea indicated the direction.

"Left, Dad, left," shrieked Mandy.

Jeremy was grumbling about the car, "It's burning oil, Dad. Can't you smell it?"

"The brakes work and the clutch works," his father answered, "and that's more than you could say for the first one. The chappie at the garage told me that all the cars here are completely clapped out, it's the roads, or the tracks they use as roads . . . "

Kate Morrison and Fergus Stapleton, Mandy and Jeremy's friends, who had happily accepted the Brakes's invitation to join them on this holiday, were tired of hearing about the car.

Kate dug her elbow into Fergus. "Ponies," she said softly.

"Race horses," said Fergus with a grin as they gazed out at the two long-legged boys riding a grey and a bay.

"They're not as good-looking as Nico," announced Mandy.

"If you ask me the whole thing's going to be pretty grotty," complained Jeremy. "They're all going to be bareback and in headcollars, and those two haven't plaited their manes or anything."

"I think it's rather nice; you obviously don't have to be rich to ride," argued Kate. "Though I agree the ponies could do with a groom."

"Right, Dad," shrieked Mandy. "There it is, beyond the camping field. Look, there are masses of people going in."

They joined a jam of cars. The drivers were excitable, hooting their horns and revving up their engines as a crowd of brightly dressed holidaymakers threaded their way through and a mule, long-eared and serious looking, with four straw bales piled high on his wooden pack-saddle, squeezed past from the opposite direction.

"I'm certainly going to get some pictures today," said Mr Brake in satisfied tones. "No sunbathers on the beach this year, but a slice of real Greek life. Pity about your foot, Cynny, or you could have driven while I shot this lot."

"Dad's dotty, he enjoys looking at his snaps and showing off his films when he gets home much more than the actual holiday," Mandy explained to Kate.

"There's Sophia," said Kate as the car advanced into a sudden space, "and that must be the hippodrome."

"It doesn't look much like an English racecourse." Mandy sounded disappointed.

The field, by far the largest and flattest they had seen on the island, was of golden stubble. The corn had been recently cut and bales of straw lay about everywhere. Some had been arranged as seats around the course, which was square and had been fenced off by stout posts with rails along their tops and more rails, crisscrossed between the posts, filling in the gap below. There was an outer and an inner fence and it looked as though the ponies would race round the track between the two, which had been harrowed to make the rock-hard ground soft and dusty.

"No green turf, no white paint, no grandstands, disgraceful!" announced Fergus, putting on a pompous voice. "Don't you agree, Jeremy?"

"These foreigners have no idea," said Kate, stifling

a giggle. "Whoever heard of a square racecourse?"

"Do stop, Dad; can't you park here? I want to go and talk to Sophia and I don't want a ten-mile walk," wailed Mandy.

"You can't park here, it's in full sun. We'll be roasted alive when we come back. Can't you find some shade?" demanded Jeremy.

"Right, all kids out then. I'm going to drive your mother over to the rails."

They began to run back, dodging through the crowd, to where they had seen Sophia. But there was soon a wail from Mandy. "Wait for me, Kate. This stubble's prickly, it's making holes in my feet."

Kate sighed and waited. "Why must you always dress up so?" she asked. "It's much more comfortable in jeans and trainers."

"She won't learn, she's too thick," Jeremy, walking on, shouted back over his shoulder.

"She doesn't understand that this island is country, real country, with goats and sheep and proper fields, not a suburb like Ralston," said Fergus, waiting for Kate.

"I'm not dressed up; everyone wears dresses and sandals at the seaside," argued Mandy, hobbling after them.

Jeremy had found Sophia waiting with Mya, her pony, but couldn't think of anything to say.

"How's Mya?" asked Kate, patting the pinkish-grey neck.

"She is a little nervous, but I am much worse; I am nervous for myself and for Nico," Sophia answered with a forced smile.

"I've counted twenty-three ponies so far,"

announced Jeremy, "but they look a pretty ropey bunch; nothing that looks nearly as good as Vrondi."

Kate looked round. Most of the ponies were hitched to the sagging barbed-wire which fenced the field: bays, browns, blacks, duns and greys, they stood patiently, with hanging heads and half-closed eyes, dozing in the still, gentle, morning sunshine. Two, who were awake, were giving angry squeals every time they touched noses, others were having their photographs taken by the mainland Greek families who seemed to make up most of the crowd. Doting fathers were plonking little children on the ponies' backs and snapping them with expensive cameras.

"You can't call those two ropey," said Kate, pointing

across the field. Two grey stallions were surrounded by a group of boys who seemed to be inciting them to fight. One stallion was almost white. High-crested and proud in carriage, he was obviously in the prime of life. The other, iron-grey and less powerful in build, looked younger. As they reared up and boxed with their fore-hoofs the boys cheered. The ponies squealed and bit, then reared again.

"It's a good thing they're not shod," said Fergus, hearing the blows thudding home.

"That's Mr Pappas, Vrondi's owner," said Sophia, pointing to a small, swarthy man wearing what seemed to be the farmers' uniform of trousers, short-sleeved shirt and straw hat. He was hurrying towards the boys, shouting at them in Greek. "He also owns Hyóni, the white stallion, who breeds excellent mules. Hyóni is very popular with the farmers, but Mr Anesti, who is the president of the island Horse Society, will not register him in the first grade of ponies because he is too large and has imported blood."

"He looks lovely, rather like the bigger sort of Welsh pony," observed Kate.

"Surely it's time they got started," said Jeremy with an impatient glance at his watch.

"What staggers me is that there don't seem to be any girl riders," Fergus told Sophia. "In England it's the other way round; at least, there's usually about five girls to every boy."

"The island girls do not ride, it is not considered correct; they are very quiet and old-fashioned. In Athens plenty of girls ride, but there it is very expensive. As I am half English I do not count as an islander, so I can do as I please. My grandfather does not mind me riding, but he does not like the idea of the race. He will only let me ride Mya, who has no chance. He has found boys to ride his faster ponies, Libertas and Kima."

"How mean can you get? Now I've heard that I'm really glad I don't live here," decided Mandy.

"It might be fun changing things," suggested Kate. "I'd start a special race for girls and some showjumping classes."

"I like this," said Fergus, who was examining the spoon-shaped piece of leather, decorated with a turquoise ornament, which dangled in the centre of Mya's forehead.

"It's a charm," explained Sophia. "You need them today because all the horrible characters like Andony Komas will be going round trying to put the evil eye on other people's ponies."

"You don't believe that, do you?" Jeremy sounded scornful.

"It happens. They come up and praise your pony, that's the most usual way, and he suddenly goes lame or starts colic. I think I'd better go and put my name down. Will you hold Mya for me?" She looked at Kate. "Don't let anyone admire her. Well, it doesn't matter about the tourists, but not the islanders and especially not Andony."

"Which is he?" asked Kate, looking round anxiously.

"The fat one over there. Fat and quite fair, wearing a red T-shirt and cantering about on a dapple-grey."

Mr Brake appeared, a camera swinging from either shoulder.

"You've got hold of a pony already, that's a bit of

luck. Up you get, Mandy, and I'll take a picture."

"No, we can't ride her, she's just about to go in the race," Kate told him hastily. "We're looking after her."

"Well, stand in a bit closer then. Jeremy, get behind Kate, that's better. Now Fergus, you sit down in front of the pony. Great. All look this way, smile."

Sophia came running back. "We are going to have the parade now," she told them. "We lead the ponies round the track for everyone to see. You must go and find a place by the rails."

"I'd hate to be the only girl," said Mandy as they hurried towards the rails. "The boys aren't paying poor Sophia any attention at all; even Nico's pretending she's not there."

"Oh, it's not that bad. I've been the only male in the ride at Mrs Kark's," Fergus told her.

"That's quite different, you weren't cold-shouldered, made to feel you oughtn't to have been there."

They found Mrs Brake sitting on a bale of straw and looking bored.

"The sun's beginning to get hot," she said, "I wish I had a parasol. Do put on some more sunscreen, Mandy, your nose is catching the sun and the last thing I want is a permanently red-nosed daughter."

"No, that would be the last straw," agreed Jeremy. "Mandy, the red-nosed reindeer," he chanted.

"Oh, shut up." Mandy hit out at him.

"Here are the ponies," said Kate hastily. The riders were now wearing large home-made numbers on their backs, most of them were boys of fourteen or fifteen and they looked very tall walking beside their ponies, none of which was more than thirteen hands.

But there was one boy, a smaller edition of Nico only his skin was even darker and his black curls tighter, who didn't look more than ten and was obviously frightened of his pony, a very pretty, slender youngster, brown with a white blaze.

"They'd all get nought for turnout at the most hopeless Pony Club rally," announced Jeremy scornfully as he looked along the line of riders who were mostly dressed in jeans, T-shirts and trainers. A few wore shorts and sandals, one had bare feet. The ponies, too, had a workaday look; only the charms on their headcollars showed it was a special occasion.

"Yes, and what would Mrs Kark say? Bare feet and not a crash-cap in sight," added Mandy, for once in agreement with her brother.

"Well, I suppose it's not so dangerous as the ponies aren't shod," said Kate. "I mean kicks on the head and having your toes stamped on are nothing like so bad with a plain hoof."

"Who's going to win, that's the question?" said Fergus, looking at the ponies carefully. "Vrondi seems fit and eager to go, which is more than you can say for some of them. That bay, number nine, looks fast, and the taller of the two iron-greys."

"I quite like the look of Andony, whatever Sophia says. At least he's cheerful and talking to everyone," Mandy pointed out. "He's not being silent and stuck-up like Nico."

"Nico's probably got the needle," Kate defended him. "Now what's happening, are they all going out?"

"They're getting into heats; you didn't think they'd race the whole lot at once, did you?" asked Jeremy.

There seemed to be a lot of argument about who should be in which heat and while the boys protested and the officials shouted commandingly, most of the ponies went back to sleep. One enjoyed a very thorough roll in the dust of the harrowed track, only a few, Vrondi among them, seemed at all excited.

"Nico's in the first one," announced Fergus as the argument ended and six ponies came forward and lined up, their riders standing beside them.

Suddenly, at the starter's command, the riders vaulted on and the ponies surged forward. A tall boy, his long legs wrapped round the belly of his bay pony, took the lead. Vrondi, who had started slowly, and an iron-grey disputed second place. Behind them the pretty brown youngster bucked. It was a huge buck. His rider shot into the air and landed on his back with a painful-sounding thud. To Kate's surprise he jumped up, smiling, and pursued his pony round the course. The others raced on. Nico and Vrondi had drawn ahead of the iron-grey, but the long-legged boy on the bay seemed to have an unassailable lead. Then, as they came into the fourth corner, the bay stopped abruptly. Ears back and eyes rolling he began to nap towards the entrance. The iron-grey, going fast and not very steerable in a headcollar, ignored his rider's frantic tugs and cannoned into the bay. The riderless brown vanished through the exit, a stout, dun mare tried to follow him, but was shooed back on course by the crowd. Nico, taking the shortest route on the inner rail, avoided the mêlée and swept on. Followed by a tiny, very white grey, he started the second circuit. The English cheered him loudly as he raced past, but the long-legged boy had got his bay going

again and was gaining on Vrondi length by length.

"The bay's the faster," said Jeremy in an excited voice, "he's going to catch Nico."

"Come on, Nico, come on!" they shouted at him frantically, as he came round the top end and put on a spurt for the winning line. At the same moment the bay swerved towards the exit again. This time his rider was ready for him and whacked him with the rope reins, but Nico, with a quick look back, raced on and won by five or six lengths. The bay came in second, the iron-grey a bad third.

"Well done, Nico," they shouted and, hearing English, he looked round and waved.

An official appeared with a loudhailer; he made an announcement in Greek and the second heat came in.

"There's Sophia," said Mandy. Mya's strange pink colour made her easy to pick out. She was against a cream pony, a black with a star and a white snip on his nose, two bays, one very lively and the other half asleep, and another of the little white greys.

"Mya needs waking up," announced Jeremy. "Sophia ought to get her on her toes."

"How do you know? You've never ridden her," Mandy began, shrill and argumentative.

"I think the lively bay will win," Fergus shouted her down. "What do you think, Kate?"

"The cream," Kate picked him at random, "but I'm going to cheer for Sophia."

The start was very dramatic. The ponies shot forward, swerving and bucking in an entangled mass. In a moment there were three or four riders on the ground, but they were vaulting on as fast as they fell off.

Suddenly Sophia emerged from the scrum and set off at a brisk canter. Finding they had a leader, the other ponies decided to join in, four of them with riders. Sophia held her own on the first circuit, but then it became obvious that Mya was tiring. The sleepy bay and the cream pony passed her and fought out a neck and neck finish, no one seemed sure which had won.

The third heat was a fiasco. Except for Andony Komas, the riders seemed much less experienced than in the earlier heats, and a boy with brown curly hair, who rode a very fast, brown pony, raced round the first circuit with an enormous lead, then pulled up, thinking he had won. The spectators shouted at him but he looked at them uncomprehendingly until the other ponies thundered by, then understanding at last, he galloped in pursuit; but it was too late. Andony's little grey, though carrying much more weight than the other ponies, flew round, neck stretched out, ears back, and won.

The fourth heat started well, but piled up in a nappy heap when they came to the exit corner.

"They don't use their outside legs. Mrs Kark would soon get after them," said Fergus.

"Still, it must be difficult, bareback and in headcollars. I bet you wouldn't do any better," Mandy argued.

"Maybe not, but I'd love to have a go."

"So would I," agreed Kate. "But not on an unknown pony. I'd like Bodkin or Seagull."

"If only Sophia and Nico had been in this heat, they'd have won easily," moaned Mandy when, on the second lap, most of the ponies made for the exit again, allowing an iron-grey with a large head to win at a leisurely canter.

"You can't say that, their ponies might have napped too," Jeremy told her.

Mandy made a face at him, "I can say what I like, and anyway it's true, isn't it, Kate?"

"I'm wondering whether to go and look for Sophia now. I must ask her if there's anywhere you can hire ponies and I might miss her in the crowd at the end."

"Oh, wait till after the final," Fergus advised. "Look at the crowd behind us, and they're six deep all along the rails; you won't see a thing if you move now."

"Now, don't you go wandering off on your own, Kate. We don't want to lose you," instructed Mrs Brake from her straw bale. "And what's all this about hiring ponies? You can all ride in Ralston. Surely we've come here for the beach and the sun and the swimming; the things we can't have at home."

"It would be a different kind of riding," explained Kate.

"I'd love to ride up into the mountains; you can't do that in Ralston," Fergus supported her.

"I don't think I want to ride miles and miles bareback in this heat," objected Mandy.

"Oh, why don't they get a move on?" asked Jeremy in an irritable voice. "What *are* they arguing about now?"

"Let's try a slow handclap," suggested Mandy.

"It looks as though extra people are trying to get into the final," said Fergus, standing on the edge of Mrs Brake's bale and gazing up the course. "Oh, I think he's letting in the two who dead-heated."

They watched the five ponies line up. Nico and then Andony on the inside, the cream pony, the sleepy bay and the iron-grey with the large head grouped together on the outside of the course. This time Vrondi was very keyed up. He knew what was coming and pranced and twirled nervously as he waited for the starter's command. It came, and Nico was quickly away. Andony went with him, the dapple-grey's head level with Vrondi's black flank. The cream stayed within striking distance, but the iron-grey and the bay were soon trailing lengths behind.

"Come on, Nico," Mandy encouraged him. "I want to be able to say I know the winner. I'll get Dad to take a photograph of us talking and drive everyone at school mad with jealousy."

No one paid her any attention; they were too intent on the race. Nico, still on the inner rails, held his lead of half a length, with the cream pony two lengths behind Andony. The rider of the sleepy bay had fallen off when his pony swerved towards the exit, but, as the leading three came round for the second time, he remounted and continued, in front, but a lap behind.

The crowd was roaring. Lying low on their ponies' necks, legs driving, the boys raced on. The dapple-grey was catching up, she drew level with Vrondi, for a moment they raced neck and neck, then she began to tire, strength and youth told and Vrondi started to draw away. The bay was cantering sedately ahead of them in the middle of the course. Andony shouted at him urgently, and the boy hauled on his rope rein, turning the pony towards the inner rails. As they came, galloping flat out for the finishing line, Nico was suddenly trapped – the rails on one side, Andony on the other, the slow pony ahead. He tried to pull out, but Andony urged the dapple-grey to even greater efforts, and Vrondi was going too fast to be controllable in a headcollar. He swept on, apparently hoping to force a way through the rapidly-closing gap between the bay and the rails. Before he reached it, the gap vanished, the black pony braked, there was a crash and a splintering of wood as he met the rails. Andony crossed the finishing line and, waving one arm above his head in triumph, proclaimed himself the winner.

"Foul, obstruction or whatever it's called in racing," said Jeremy. "There ought to be a steward's enquiry."

"I think Nico's hurt," Kate watched anxiously as he slid off Vrondi and then leaned against the pony, his face pale and rigid with pain. Various people ducked under the rails and ran to him. Mr Pappas, looking grim beneath his straw hat, strode down the course to inspect his pony.

Andony, who had been acknowledging the roars of the crowd, sitting on his pony waving his joined hands

above his head, set off on a lap of honour.

"It's maddening not being able to understand," complained Mandy. "Why doesn't Sophia come and tell us what's happening?" A fierce argument had begun between Mr Pappas and the officials; the boy on the sleepy bay defending himself shrilly.

Nico was still massaging his knee but his face had returned to its normal colour. He began to protest too, pointing across the course, arguing vehemently, but he didn't seem to make much impression on the flint-faced officials, and Andony was allowed to continue his lap of honour.

"Poor Nico, what a shame," said Kate turning away. "Why don't we go and find Sophia?" She looked at Mrs Brake. "If we do get lost we can go to the car and wait."

"I wish I could speak Greek, I'd go and join in. Tell them what we saw," said Fergus fiercely. "I'd give anything to know what Andony shouted to the boy in front."

They edged their way out of the crowd and then fought their way into an even thicker one round the course entrance, where all the ponies and riders seemed to have gathered. As they reached Sophia, Nico came limping out, leading Vrondi, and the other riders surged round him, asking questions. Kate and Fergus looked at each other and sighed.

"If I ever come here again I must learn some more Greek," Kate decided.

"We never go to the same country twice, so it's pointless," Jeremy told them. "Besides, most people speak English."

"Not when anything exciting happens," argued Kate.

Mandy had squeezed closer to Sophia and was tweaking her T-shirt. "What's happened? What's going on? Do tell us?" she demanded.

Sophia turned, "Nothing very good. Andony is to be allowed to have things his way."

"Oh, he's not. It's not fair. Everyone saw what happened, they ought to at least rerun the race."

"Hear, hear," added Fergus.

"No hope, I'm afraid. Andony's father is one of the officials and his uncle's the mayor. If Mr Anesti – the president of the Horse Society – was here he wouldn't have got away with it, but no one else is strong enough to stand up to the Komas family."

"What *did* Andony shout at the boy on the bay?" asked Fergus.

"To get out of the way, to get on the rails," answered Sophia.

"Of course Mr Komas says he meant the outer rails, but Nico is sure he didn't. If he had held his tongue they could easily have passed one on either side of Stephan. And then it was at the very moment when it came to him that he was going to lose, that he shouted."

"There must be *someone* you can appeal to," Jeremy sounded very indignant. "A chairman or vice-president or someone."

"Mr Anesti is president, chairman and secretary all rolled into one," said Sophia, shrugging her shoulders hopelessly.

Kate began to ask about hiring ponies. It didn't seem a very good moment, but she had a feeling that this was one of those days when the right moment never comes.

"There is no riding-school or trekking centre on the island," Sophia answered, "but Mr Pappas might hire some of his ponies. How many do you need, one for each of you?"

"I'm not sure about Jeremy yet," Kate told her, "but certainly three."

"I'll find out and let you know. My grandfather might let you have Kima, but he is particular over Libertas. Can you all ride? The island way – bareback and headcollars?"

"Yes, Fergus and I ride a lot bareback. But how will you let us know? Our cottage has no telephone."

"Can you come to my house tomorrow morning, not too early? It is next to the Ionis Hotel, there is an iron gate into a garden. If you cannot find it ask for the Perdikas, everyone knows us."

"Thank you very much," Kate tried to sound as grateful as she felt. "About twelve then."

"Good. I must go now," Sophia explained, "something else has happened. That very dark man over there, the one with the smiling face and many gold teeth, is a horse-dealer from Athens. It seems he is trying to buy some of the little horses and Nico is very worried, he is afraid that Mr Pappas may agree to sell Vrondi."

"Did you hear that?" asked Kate, turning to the others as Sophia pushed her way into the group of boys surrounding Nico.

"Yes, it's awful, because Nico really does seem fond of Vrondi," said Mandy, "but I suppose Mr Pappas must have other ponies he could ride."

"You can't exactly prevent a farmer selling his ponies," agreed Fergus, "I mean, he breeds them to sell and make money; but it's certainly not Nico's day."

Jeremy, silent and suddenly impatient to get away, led them briskly through the fast-dispersing crowd to the car. Mr and Mrs Brake were already there and had opened all the doors and windows in an attempt to cool it down.

"Well, kids, did you enjoy that? I took some really wonderful pictures," Mr Brake told them enthusiastically. "And I met a Greek-Canadian back here on holiday. He told me a perfect place for us to have lunch. A taverna on a sandy beach – not a sea urchin in sight – and right off the usual tourist track. Oh, get in," he added irritably as Jeremy and Mandy began to complain about the scorching state of the car's interior. "We won't have time for a swim before we eat if you keep messing about."

The Bargain

Christine Pullein-Thompson

The dream seemed to last for ever. The bell would not stop ringing though I had already cleared three fences in the junior jumping. Then suddenly I was awake, leaping from my bed, taking the stairs two at a time before picking up the telephone and asking "Who is it? What's happened?"

"It's the Longcoombe Police speaking. I'm sorry to disturb you at this unearthly hour. We have three horses which were straying on the B45. We're told they are yours."

"Thank you, thank you very much. We'll collect them. Where are they now?" I asked, my heart beating at a furious rate.

"We've got them in the corner of a wheat field behind the Three Bells," the voice said.

"We'll be with you in ten minutes," I cried, replacing the receiver before tearing upstairs again to bang on my brother's door and cry, "Wake up, Hugh. The ponies are out . . ."

"All right, all right, I'll be with you in a minute. Hang on," he muttered, his voice muzzy with sleep.

Marian, our younger sister, was in the passage now. "I'm coming too," she told me, pulling a shirt over her head.

"You won't be able to keep up, and we can't wait," I said. Two minutes later we were all dressed and running downstairs. We could have woken our parents, but they would have taken ages asking questions and looking for car keys and the Three Bells is less than half a mile from our house so we did not need transport.

"Who telephoned?" asked Hugh, who is fair and sixteen, two years older than me.

"The police."

Hugh groaned.

We picked up carrots as we ran and headcollars and ropes from the tack room. Dawn was just beginning to break across the sky and there were rabbits everywhere and a hedgehog grunting in the drive.

"They're behind the Three Bells in a field of wheat," I explained.

"They'll get colic then," shouted Hugh, "and we'll be fined for letting them stray. How on earth did they get out. I know we shut the field gate."

We were strung out now – Hugh twenty metres ahead, me in the middle, Marian toiling behind. The road was empty, silent, beautiful. Curtains were drawn in windows; birds beginning to herald another day with song.

Hugh reached the Three Bells first. A police car was parked outside but now none of us had any breath left for words.

"They are over there," a tall, bearded policeman told us. "They seem quite docile."

"They aren't hurt, are they?" I asked.

He shook his head as we walked round the side of the pub. There were three horses standing shoulder high in wheat, but they were not ours.

"They could have caused a terrible accident," the policeman continued. "They were wandering down the middle of the road. Five drivers rang the station."

"They aren't ours," my brother said.

"Definitely not," agreed Marian, not wanting to be left out.

"Who do they belong to then?" asked the policeman after a short silence.

"I have no idea," said Hugh.

The policeman removed his cap to scratch his balding head. Cocks were crowing now, competing with one another, drowning the birdsong.

"Ours are bay, brown and roan, not liver-chestnut or grey," said Marian.

"Well, we can't keep them at the police station, there's only three rooms and the carpark," said the policeman.

"We can take them home, can't we, Hugh?" I asked. "We can keep them until their owner turns up."

"We would be much obliged to you," the policeman said.

The horses were wearing shabby nylon headcollars. Two were liver-chestnuts, almost the same; the other was an elderly-looking grey. They looked kind and friendly, with ribs showing through dull, lifeless coats.

We clipped our ropes on to their headcollars.

Our own horses were turned out three fields from our house and I thought thank goodness it wasn't them, as my brother said, "We'll have to put them in the stable. And they mustn't have a lot of water, or the wheat they've eaten will swell up inside them. Do you hear, Marian?"

"I'm not an idiot," she retorted, going first down the road leading a chestnut, while my brother led the grey.

When we reached home, the horses looked pleased with the stables. I gave them a little hay before we went indoors. Our parents were making tea in the kitchen and we told them what had happened.

"Their owner is sure to ring the police station before long," Hugh said.

But it did not work out that way. The whole day passed without a squeak from anyone. We fed the horses hay and gave them sips of water and watched for signs of colic which did not materialise.

"I wanted to ride," wailed Marian at four o'clock. "But I can't, can I?"

"You can tie Bimbo up," I suggested. Bimbo is her small brown pony.

"He'll be upset. He'll want his loose box," she said.

When Dad returned from work, he wanted to know why the horses were still with us. "We're not a charity," he said. We spent the evening telephoning horsey friends, but none of them knew anything about two matching liver-chestnuts and a dear old grey.

"You can see they've been loved by someone even if they look awful now," I said, as we gave them bulging haynets and buckets of water.

Before going to bed, we wandered across the fields to see our own horses. They were grazing peacefully, unperturbed by the midges that were everywhere.

"Tomorrow we'll put them in the field with the shelter," Hugh said.

"Tomorrow the others must be gone," I answered.

But it was Monday before anyone called and by then we had ridden the three horses gently around the paddock by the house. We had discovered that the grey was well schooled and that the chestnuts could trot at enormous speed. And we had fallen in love with them.

Their owner turned up with two scruffy youths in a big car. He had a red face, a hat on the back of his head, baggy trousers, soft shoes, a flashy tie and teeth patched with gold.

"Where are they then?" he asked getting out of his car heavily, while we stared in horror.

"You mean the horses?" I asked stupidly, my heart pounding, but he had already seen them in the paddock, looking at home there.

"They were to go to the sale on Saturday. The driver called for them, but they weren't there no more, so he thought I must have changed my mind," he explained.

"Why didn't he telephone you?" I asked.

"I was in the North. I'm a dealer, not in horses, in other things, antiques mostly. Got your ropes, boys?" he said. The youths nodded and went across the yard to the paddock.

"They would have gone for meat. Don't you care?" Hugh asked.

The man handed my brother a card which had JACK SWORDER – GENERAL AND ANTIQUE DEALER on it.

"I picked them up at a sale. I wanted the vehicles for clients, a nice little phaeton and a dogcart," he

explained, crossing the yard and leaning on the paddock fence. "They were sold as one lot, horses and vehicles together. Their owners were killed in a car crash. They used them for films and weddings."

Marian was crying. I looked at Hugh. His face was shuttered. He was fighting emotions which he preferred to keep hidden, I thought.

"What are you going to do with them now?" he asked.

"Send them to another sale, or else straight to the abattoir."

"You won't get much. They haven't any meat on them," Hugh said.

"The profit is in the vehicles," answered Jack Sworder. "They were selling everything at knockdown prices."

"We can get more for them as riding and driving horses," continued Hugh. "They are good horses. We might get four hundred for the grey and seven hundred for the chestnuts. And they won't fetch that for meat, not in their present condition, and then there's transporting costs."

"Money doesn't come into it. I've done all right on the vehicles."

"You won't lose anything," my brother insisted. "When we sell them, we will give you a thousand pounds, and if we can't sell them, you can enter them in next month's sale and they will be a lot fatter by then; so the meat men will pay more and everyone will be happy."

"Except the horses," I muttered.

"So it's a bargain whichever way you look at it," finished my brother. The man's eyes were wavering now.

Bargain was probably his favourite word. He was that sort of man, the sort who can't see beyond bargains and money, who lives for nothing else.

"Come inside and have a cup of tea," I suggested.

"Or something stronger," added Hugh.

"And your assistants, I'm sure they are thirsty too," I said. So we all went inside and introduced Jack Sworder to Mummy, and sat drinking tea in the kitchen.

When we went outside again, Jack Sworder shook Hugh's hand, then mine. His hand was large and rather soft. "It's a bargain," he said. "Come on, boys, we're going."

"Now we are the dealers," Hugh exclaimed as the three of them drove away.

"And we had better get cracking before our parents turn nasty," I replied.

Then Mummy appeared shouting, "He's gone without the horses, run after him, Hugh – quick! Don't stand there gawping!"

As though horses were like shopping.

We started to laugh then. "We're the dealers now," cried my brother again. "We are going to make a lot of money."

But I knew that money was not important; it was finding the right homes which mattered, nothing else.

Only a month, but the horses had already had one lucky escape – it was up to us to see that they had another and we would make sure that they did!

The Storm

Josephine Pullein-Thompson

Laura had been counting on her mother coming home. When she had telephoned, it had been some comfort to think that Stephen, her stepfather, was on his way. But now both parents had been delayed and the thunderstorm was crashing round them. Becky, one of the two dogs, was cowering in a cupboard and Lottie was wailing about her headache.

"My head's aching, too," moaned Ben, as the storm flashed and thundered.

"You'd better both have an aspirin," said Anna briskly, taking control of the situation. "Peter, could you fetch them from the medicine cupboard – they'd better have the junior ones. I'll start cooking the chops, if someone will do the veg."

Anna, Peter and Ben were Stephen Dalton's three children; Tom, Laura and Lottie were his wife Carol's three, and they were learning to live together as one family.

"Mummy was going to buy vegetables today, at the market near her office," Laura explained. "There aren't any potatoes left, but there are still some frozen peas."

"I'll cook spaghetti," offered Tom. "Is there any of that ready-made sauce left?" He put a pan of salted water on to boil and then, as the storm grew more violent, went through to the dining-room window. The lightning and thunder were now almost simultaneous.

"It's the worst storm I've ever seen," said Tom as Peter, having handed out the junior aspirin, joined him. "Look at that great zigzag – is that forked lightning?" Peter's answer was drowned in a nerve-wracking crack that seemed to be immediately above their heads.

"I wish you'd come away from that window," said Anna. "I'm sure you could be struck." The boys, a little afraid, moved back without arguing.

"I've found two bananas and one rather withered orange in the larder. Shall I add them to some tinned fruit and make a fruit salad? We could put in some apples too," said Laura.

"Good idea," said Anna. She made a face at Laura. "Ben and Lottie can help you." Laura took the hint, she got Ben opening tins, Lottie slicing bananas.

"Here's the rain," announced Tom. "It's coming down in *torrents.* I'd better shut the upstairs windows."

Peter ran out after him, and Laura called, "You'd better check the sitting-room, too. It would be awful if all that decorating was ruined."

"It's even worse up there," said Peter, when they came back. "And the roof's leaking into the attics."

"We looked out of the windows, but we couldn't see any ponies," added Tom. "I hope they've found somewhere to shelter."

"If they've any sense, they'll be in the hollow," said Anna. "You don't get struck by lightning in hollows."

By the time supper was ready the rain had ceased to fall in such tropical torrents, and the thunder and lightning seemed to be moving away; but now the wind was getting up and the trees and laurels outside the kitchen window were waving and tossing with increasing violence as the gusts gathered force.

"It's beginning to sound like a horror film," said Tom, as doors slammed and the whole house creaked and groaned, and the wind howled outside.

"I hope the roof doesn't cave in," said Ben.

"It's more likely to sail away and land somewhere else."

"Leaving us to get wet."

"Can you see Dad's face if he arrived tomorrow morning and found a topless house?" They giggled weakly as Laura served the fruit salad, dividing it exactly, determined to be fair.

Becky had crawled out of her cupboard, and sat shaking, listening for the return of the thunder. Jemima, trying to comfort her, began washing her friend's ears.

Then there was a sudden sharp crack, followed by a prolonged crash, the sound of a falling tree. They all ran to the dining-room window.

"Can't see anything, it must be in the lane."

"Let's hope it was one of the dead elms."

"Yes, that would save Dad a job."

"Treacle's going to have plenty of work this week-end." They went back to their fruit salad.

"I do wish the wind didn't have such an eerie voice," complained Lottie.

"It's howling worse than a pack of wolves," agreed Ben with a shudder.

"We might all play something when we've washed up," said Anna. "There's no point in going to bed till this racket stops."

"Play what?" asked Ben.

"I don't mind – Monopoly, snap, anything."

Peter and Ben were arguing about which game would be most fun with six players, when there was another crack, the sound of splintering wood, a long rumble of falling masonry, a tinkle of glass.

"Oh, now what's happened?" said Anna irritably as they all ran to the dining-room window.

"It sounded like Mr Hunt's cottage," said Tom.

"We'd better take a look," decided Peter, making for the front door.

"No point in everyone getting soaked," said Laura, holding Lottie back as Tom and Peter ran down the drive.

"Quite right," agreed Anna. "If you want to go, Ben, you're to put on a mac."

Ben and Lottie, seeing the sense of this, went to find macintoshes. Laura and Anna, standing in the doorway and peering out into the gloomy night, heard a shout. The words were whirled away on the wind, but a second shout had an urgent note; they knew that they were wanted and they ran, heads down, into the buffeting wind and the stinging rain.

They found the boys at the corner of the walled garden, where the path led to Mr Hunt's back door. The whole area was strewn with chunks of stone, beams of wood, tiles and broken glass. They realised that the row of outhouses and greenhouses that had stood against the garden wall had collapsed into rubble and, among their ruins, lay the frail figure of Mr Hunt.

"He's hurt," yelled Tom, trying to be heard above the roar of the wind in the storm-torn trees. "He can't get up."

Anna and Laura knelt down beside the old man. "I didn't hear the car," he told them, "so I thought I'd come over to the house and make sure all was well. Then this lot came down, knocked me for six. I felt something snap in my shoulder, but I'm not too bad. If you can find my sticks I daresay I'll be on my feet again soon."

Tom had picked up Mr Hunt's torch; it was still working, so he shone it among the broken timbers and scattered stones and they all searched for the sticks.

"Are we going to take him to our house or back to his own? It's nearer," asked Peter.

"To ours," said Anna, "so we can telephone for the doctor."

The sticks were found, and Mr Hunt insisted on getting to his feet. He was so thin and light that they heaved him up very easily, but Laura saw his face twist with pain. He soon found that his left arm was useless. He could only use one stick, but he started on his slow hobble to the house in a very determined manner.

"I think we ought to find some sort of stretcher," shouted Peter.

"We could easily carry him on a chair with two poles," replied Tom.

"What about a wheelbarrow?" shouted Lottie. She and Ben had joined the group, standing in the pelting rain and watching Mr Hunt's slow progress, not knowing how to help him.

"Some of you run ahead and put the kettle on," he said between two gusts of wind. "I could do with a nice cup of tea."

"Yes, go on some of you," ordered Anna. "And Laura, he needs a sling, do you think you can find one of your mother's scarves? A large square one would be best."

"What about the doctor? Shall I ring him?" shouted Tom.

"No, don't worry him. I'll be better by and by," said Mr Hunt. But Tom was beaming the torch on their faces and he could see how wretchedly ill the old man looked. He flashed it on Anna's face and saw that she was mouthing "yes" at him.

Laura ransacked the drawer where her mother kept her scarves, trying to find one that was large and square; she took the three best and ran downstairs. Tom was shaking the telephone. "It's not working," he said. "There's no dialling tone, just silence. I've tried 999 as well as the doctor, but there's just nothing. Do you think a tree could have fallen on the lines?"

Anna and Peter were helping Mr Hunt on to the sofa, which had been put into the dining-room for watching television.

"Would you like to take your mac off?" suggested Anna. Mr Hunt shook his head. "I think we'll let the arm be," he said. "But if you've got that sling handy . . . "

Lottie brought tea, Ben followed with sugar and milk. Tom had fetched the fan-heater; he arranged it pointing at Mr Hunt and turned it on full. Peter was trying the telephone; Anna went through to the kitchen and tried it too. "One of us will have to ride to the village and fetch the doctor," she said.

"He lives in the red house on the left, doesn't he?" asked Tom.

"Yes, past the shop and the church and the Three Horseshoes. There's a row of old cottages and then a modern house."

"Well, I'm willing."

"So am I."

"We're all willing, but someone must stay and look after Lottie and Ben as well as Mr Hunt."

They went through to the dining-room to tell the old man their decision.

"Wait a bit," he said. "The pain's not so bad now I've got the arm in a sling and I'm resting. You go and get out of those wet clothes and then we'll see what the storm's doing."

They changed, putting on sweaters and jeans, for now that the thunder had passed it seemed much colder. Then they went back to Mr Hunt. He looked ill, his face was very white and he was shivering.

"I've been thinking that you could take me up in the little cart," he said. "Ten to one Dr Hoylake will want to send me into hospital for an X-ray. And the ambulance will never find its way down here on a night like this. Save everyone a lot of trouble if I was up there in the village."

"But what about the jolting?" asked Laura. "Won't it be bad for your arm?"

"And do you think we can get you up into the cart?" asked Tom.

"We'll manage if we take it nice and steady," said Mr Hunt.

"Okay, we'll go and catch Treacle."

"I think three of us had better go," said Anna, following the Brodies into the kitchen. "Someone had better ride, then if there's a fallen tree and the cart has to turn back, the mounted person can go on to the village. You two had better go with the cart and either Peter or I will ride. Shall we toss for it, Pete?"

While the Daltons tossed a coin, the Brodies pulled on macintoshes. Anna won. "Look after Lottie," Laura told Peter. "Don't let her do anything mad."

Tom had opened the back door a few centimetres and was peering out at the pitch black of the raging night. "How are we going to find any ponies in *that?*" he asked, shutting the door quickly.

"Dad's torches," said Anna, feeling on the shelf above the coats. "He always buys these huge, powerful things and now, for once, they're going to be useful." One torch was long and made of rubber, the other red and lantern-shaped; they took them both and went out into the noise and violence of the storm. Lashed by the rain and buffeted by the wind, they collected headcollars and made for the field. At the gate they shouted, calling the ponies against the roar of the wind. They called again and were answered by frantic neighs. Treacle and Ambrose appeared at the canter; they were dripping wet and trembling with fear or excitement.

Anna called again, hoping for a Dalton pony or Sheba but no more ponies came galloping out of the darkness and, when Tom shouted that she wouldn't be too heavy to ride Ambrose just to the village, Anna agreed. "We can't waste time wandering about the field in this," she yelled back.

Both Ambrose and Treacle seemed to be thoroughly unnerved by the storm, they shivered and shook and stared wildly about them all the time they were being saddled and harnessed.

"You must calm down," Laura told Treacle as they led her out to the cart. "You're an ambulance horse tonight, you've got to be very steady."

"I expect they're cold," said Anna. "They'll quieten down once they're on the move."

When they reached the front door, Peter appeared with the small stepladder and, letting down the tailboard, placed it behind the cart. Then Lottie and Ben came out with Mr Hunt. No one spoke much; it was such an effort to be heard against the roar of the wind and the tearing noise it made as it rushed through the branches of the tormented trees.

Tom was having first drive, so Laura screwed herself into the back of the cart and they set off sedately, Anna in the lead, lighting the way with the long torch, while the lantern-shaped one was hooked on the front of the cart. Down the drive the ponies walked with bowed heads, trying to escape the stinging rain. The lane, enclosed between high hedges, was more sheltered, though the sound of the trees groaning and cracking overhead terrified Laura, who expected one of them to crash down at any moment. She wished they could tear along at Treacle's fastest trot; danger seemed less frightening if you were able to flee from it. Crawling along at this snail's pace, with the rain bucketing down, the enveloping darkness and the sound of the tortured trees, she found she was becoming stiff with the effort of controlling her terror.

There were leafy branches torn from the trees and scattered all over the lane. Several times Anna dismounted to move larger ones that could become entangled in the wheels of the cart. Then, at the top of the hill, there was a really large bough barring their way. Anna dismounted and began to tug at it. Laura, delighted to have something to do, jumped down and ran to help. They pulled and heaved, but it wasn't until Tom gave the reins to Mr Hunt and came too that they managed to drag it to one side and make room for the cart to pass.

On the road, the gale seemed to be blowing harder than ever. The wind came in ferocious gusts, almost knocking the ponies off their feet. The road was strewn

with tiles and slates blown from roofs and littered with leaves and branches; the roof of a garden shed lay smashed across a gateway. All the cottages and houses had their lights on, but the noise of the storm drowned the sound of hoofs and cartwheels and no one looked out to see who was riding on such a night.

By the time Tom drove the cart into the doctor's drive, Anna had already found the emergency bell with the light above it and pressed it hard. She also seemed to have thought out what she was going to say, for when Laura jumped down and joined her on the doorstep she was explaining to a grey-haired woman what had happened – and doing it very clearly and calmly.

"I'm Mrs Hoylake," the woman said when Anna had finished. "And I'm afraid the doctor's been called out – a new baby. They came to fetch him – our telephone is out of order too."

"Well, I'm sure Mr Hunt needs to go to hospital.

Isn't there anyone with a car who could take him?" asked Anna.

Mrs Hoylake went back into the house for a macintosh and, putting it over her shoulders, came out to the cart. "I'm so sorry to hear about this, Mr Hunt," she shouted. "Such a dreadful night and the doctor's out the other side of Balton."

"Evening, Mrs Hoylake," Mr Hunt put on a cheerful voice but when Tom held the lantern so that it shone on his face, they could all see that he was obviously in great pain.

Mrs Hoylake became brisk and competent. "Never mind. I can look after you until he comes. I'm a trained nurse, remember? Now, how can we get you down?"

Laura explained about a stepladder, and Mrs Hoylake rushed into her kitchen and emerged with a stool that turned into steps. She and Tom and Laura helped him down while Anna held the ponies. He refused to be taken into the sitting-room, protesting that he was too wet, so Mrs Hoylake sat him down in the kitchen and then joined Tom and Laura on the doorstep.

"He really is quite poorly," she said. "It looks like a broken collar bone to me, which isn't serious, but he's not a young man and I think he's quite severely shocked. Do you think you could go to the police house and ask Mr Fox to call an ambulance? He can radio through to Bruminster police, you see, and they can pass the message on."

Laura and Tom looked at each other. They'd both thought their adventure was almost over: they'd seen themselves trotting home. Now it seemed they had to battle on through the storm.

"Yes, we'll go."

"It's in Upper Milford, isn't it?"

"Yes, next door to the shop. I wouldn't ask you – it's a dreadful night for children of your age to be out – but I've no one else to send and I really think we ought to get him to hospital as quickly as possible."

Laura shouted the purpose of their new errand at Anna as Tom turned the trap. Treacle and Ambrose, thinking they were going home, tore along at their fastest trots, but when they were asked to pass Mill Lane and go on to Upper Milford, they both jibbed. Ambrose's was only a mild protest at the madness of his rider, but Treacle's was outright rebellion. She swerved about the road and ran backwards and was only persuaded to go on when Laura led her, and Ambrose, trotting ahead, began to disappear into the darkness.

It was very dark below the hanging wood. They were sheltered from the worst of the rain but the wind, tearing and rending at the treetops, sounded like a wild and stormy sea. There were constant cracks as boughs were torn from trunks and old trees, no longer able to bend with the wind, split and keeled drunkenly against their fellows. The frightened ponies trotted faster and faster, trying to escape from the dark and terrifying tunnel of wind-thrashed branches. It was a relief to all of them when they emerged and, rounding the bend, saw the lights of Upper Milford ahead.

Tom seemed willing to talk to Mr Fox. "It's your turn to drive now," he said, handing the reins to Laura. Jumping down, he ran up the path and rang the police house bell. Anna followed, leading Ambrose. Laura turned Treacle and waited. She felt very wet and rather miserable. The water had gone down her neck and her hands were cold. She comforted herself with the thought that this was the end of it; in a moment or two they would be trotting home. Tom and Anna came down the path and, with Tom aboard, Laura gave the impatient Treacle her head.

"He's radioing through at once," Tom shouted. "He was a bit doubtful until Anna explained that it was a message from Mrs Hoylake. He said we were to get home as fast as we could and stay there."

"Treacle agrees with him," Laura shouted back.

They re-entered the dark tunnel below the wood. Anna was trotting ahead, swinging the beam of her torch across the road. At the Willow Lane turn she stopped. She shouted something back towards the cart and vanished into the dark.

"Did you hear what she said?" shouted Laura.

Tom shook his head. "Perhaps she wants to go home that way, but it's not much good for the cart," he shouted back.

"Whoa!" Laura slowed Treacle to a walk and as they looked down the lane in the light of Anna's torch, they could see that it was completely blocked by a fallen tree. The huge, silver-grey trunk of a dead elm lay across the lane from crushed hedge to crushed hedge, and beyond the tree they could see the square silhouette of a cattle truck. Tom jumped out and ran to join Anna. Laura turned Treacle into the mouth of the lane – there was just enough room for the cart. She unhitched the lantern torch and shone it down the lane. There seemed to be a second cattle truck, parked behind the first.

Tom was standing on the trunk of the elm. "No

damage done," he shouted. "And it looks like Keith's truck behind. I expect they've gone back to the farm for a saw."

Anna was mounting and Laura had decided she would have to back the cart out of the lane when Treacle raised her head and neighed loudly. From the truck on the other side of the fallen tree a chorus of anxious neighs answered her.

Tom grabbed Anna's torch, slid down the other side of the tree and ran round the cattle truck looking for a way in. Anna took the lantern torch from Laura, who found herself alone in the dark holding both ponies. The ponies in the truck were whinnying; Treacle and Ambrose answered them. Then Tom appeared, shouting and waving his arms and torch frantically. Laura couldn't hear a word, but she knew that something awful had happened. She hitched the ponies' reins round the elm's broken boughs and climbed over the trunk. Anna and Tom were at the rear of the truck. Arms above their heads, they were unscrewing the wing nuts that held the ramp closed.

"Our ponies are inside," shouted Tom. "All four of them. Somebody's trying to steal them!"

"Hurry," screamed Anna. "The thieves may come back."

"See if the keys are in the ignition," Tom shouted at Laura. "If they are, chuck them over the hedge." Laura took the torch from him and ran round the side of the truck, squeezing between it and the hedge. Then she stumbled over something, something soft. She pitched forward and almost fell. Picking herself up, she shone the torch downwards and saw a body – a man's body.

She felt like running, like screaming, but she forced herself to take a closer look. She saw that it was Keith Williams lying there and there was blood on his face.

"Keith," she shouted, pulling at the sleeve of his anorak, "Keith, are you all right?" To her relief he stirred and groaned.

"I didn't hear the clock," he said sleepily.

Anna was holding Jonjo and Sheba in the lane. "Quick, get Rocket," she shouted. Tom was untying Goldfinder. Laura ran up the ramp and as she untied Rocket she told Tom about Keith.

"He's hurt, there's blood on his face and he's lying there half conscious." They gave the ponies to Anna.

"Come on," she said, vaulting on Goldfinder. "We must get away before the thieves come back."

"Wait a sec. Keith's hurt," Tom shouted at her, as he followed Laura round the side of the truck.

Keith seemed asleep again. Laura shook him, with more confidence this time. "Keith, wake up, tell us what happened," she shouted.

He sat up slowly and gazed at them stupidly. "Late again, am I?" he asked.

"We'll have to take him to the doctor's. We can't leave him lying here, he's soaking wet," said Laura, standing up. "I'll take him if you can help me get him to the cart."

"Perhaps Anna could manage the four ponies on her own."

"Supposing the thieves have gone to the farm for a saw and she met them coming back? If you've got two ponies each you could gallop away; but with four she'd be helpless."

"You'll have Ambrose, too, we can't get him over the log. And suppose you come to another fallen tree?"

"If you get the ponies home safely you can come and look for me," said Laura, pulling at Keith's arm. "Come on, Keith, up you get, it's morning."

"I'd better tell Anna," shouted Tom. "She's getting in a state over Jonjo."

Laura managed to pull and persuade Keith to his feet. He kept mumbling that it wasn't all that late and surely he could have another five minutes, but she said "no" very firmly. Then he tried to get into the thieves' truck, and Laura had to drag him away. She told him that his was parked in the road and he had to climb over the log, but he stood staring at it stupidly and said that he was very tired and couldn't he knock off now. Then Tom came. "Quick," he said, "Anna's panicking. She says the thieves will be back any minute and she could be right. Come on, Keith, don't fool around. We're in a hurry."

They pushed and pulled him over the tree-trunk and up into the cart. "I hope you'll be okay," shouted Tom doubtfully as he hitched Ambrose's reins to the tail-board chain.

"I hope *you'll* be okay," Laura shouted back. "Walk on, Treacle." It was very dark without Anna to ride ahead and light the way. The beam from the lantern torch only illuminated the ground immediately in front of Treacle, so they always seemed to be driving into a pitch-black wall of darkness. The wind was still roaring, the trees thrashing and crashing above her head but Laura, driving and watching that Keith, who had drifted back into his semi-conscious state, didn't fall out and that Ambrose was still tied on behind, had no time to imagine or fear things that *might* happen.

She was almost at the village and preparing for a battle with Treacle at the Mill Lane turn when the yellow beam of car headlights lit the road from behind. She drove the cart close to the verge and looked back. It was a police car. She pulled and began waving frantically. She shouted, "Can you help me?" into the wind and pointed at Keith.

The car stopped and the policeman came across to her. It was too dark to see his face.

"If you're Mr Fox, my brother spoke to you about Mr Hunt," Laura shouted. "Now we've found Keith Williams hurt. There's blood all over his face, but I don't think it was the storm. I think the horse thieves must have attacked him – his truck was just behind theirs at the top of the lane." She explained how they had found four of their ponies inside the strange cattle truck that had been trapped by the fallen tree, and how Anna and Tom had taken them home.

"Hang on there a minute, I'll just report this on my radio," said the policeman and ran back to his car.

Laura felt full of relief. At least he would be on the lookout now if the thieves returned with a saw and then tried to recapture the ponies.

The policeman came back. "Right, I'll relieve you of Keith Williams," he said. "I've told them to try and hold the ambulance at the doctor's. We'll keep an eye on the truck and I'll pop down to your house later and check that your brother and sister had no further trouble. Come on, Keith, wakey-wakey. You'll be a lot more comfortable in a real bed."

Complaining that he was never allowed five minutes' peace and quiet, Keith allowed himself to be helped down and transferred to the car. Laura let the car go first and then set off at a steady jog with her two ponies. She suddenly felt terribly tired and prayed that there were no fallen trees across the lane for she had no strength left to deal with new disasters. Then, as the lane seemed only to be littered with small boughs, she began to worry about Tom and Anna and whether or not they had reached home safely.

Treacle and Ambrose kept up their steady jog, even down the hill, and at last they turned in at the drive gate. The lights were on in the front of the house; but no one ran out to meet them so Laura drove round to the stables. A chorus of neighs greeted Treacle and Ambrose, and a whinnying Jonjo dragged Anna across the yard.

"*There*, now you've got your precious Treacle. So for goodness sake stop deafening me," said Anna as the two ponies touched noses. Lottie took Ambrose. Ben and Tom began to unharness Treacle.

"Did you deliver Keith all right?" asked Tom as Laura climbed down. She nodded. She felt too tired to shout against the wind. She waited until Treacle was out of the cart and they were unharnessing in the cow-byre before she explained about meeting the police car.

"I told the policeman about the thieves and how I thought they must have attacked Keith, and he's coming down later to make sure you got home safely. You didn't meet anyone?"

"Not a soul, but we've decided to put all the ponies in Hill field for the rest of the night. There's only the one gate and we can keep watch on that from the house."

"Yes, we've worked it out," said Peter. "You can see the gate from the window at the end of the downstairs passage."

"And we're going to keep all the lights on all night to frighten them off," added Lottie.

"I'm really glad you met the policeman, Laura," said Ben. "Peter says six of us and two dogs could fight off two horse thieves, but I'm not so sure."

The ponies seemed quite pleased to be put out in Hill field and were soon grazing. The rain had slackened and the wind was blowing with less ferocity. Tom led the way back to the house, saying that he was starving and that he hoped there was still one of those huge cans of tomato soup. There was; and as Tom and Anna heated it, Laura sat down at the table and let her weariness take over. Peter was discussing the watches. "Four and a half hours each," he said. "We change over at three. Who wants to be in the first watch with me?"

"Not Laura," said Anna, handing her a bowl of soup. "She's half asleep already. I think the Daltons look the most alert."

"Right, all Brodies in bed," said Peter, "and we'll wake you at three."

"We'll sleep in our clothes," said Tom, "so you'll only have to yell for reinforcements if they do come back."

It was daylight – morning – with bright sunshine slanting in at the window when Laura wakened. The storm, she thought; and then, in a panic, *the ponies.* She was up in a second, searching for her shoes, imagining the ponies recaptured by thieves while she overslept. Tom and Lottie's beds were empty. Why hadn't they wakened her? Shoes in hand, she ran downstairs.

Her mother was in the kitchen, leaning against the cooker and drinking coffee. Tom, Lottie and Ben sat at the table eating. There was a delicious smell of bacon.

"Oh, Laura," her mother hugged her. "Oh, darling, I'm so sorry you had such an awful time and that we made this muddle and left you on your own all through that ghastly storm. We just couldn't get back."

"Do stop feeling guilty, Mum," said Tom through a mouthful of bacon and egg. "I keep telling you we were okay; we coped."

"But the ponies," asked Laura, "are they still there? The Daltons never woke us at three."

"They're fine," answered Ben. "We didn't wake you because Mr Fox came round soon after you went to bed. He said that they were sending another police car out from Bruminster to keep watch for the thieves and there was no need for any of us to stay up. Anna told Tom, but she didn't see any point in waking all of you."

"Here, sit down and eat this, darling." Her mother handed Laura a plate crowded with bacon, egg, tomato and fried bread. "I know you coped, Tom. You all seemed to have been very brave and resourceful, but I still think it was putting far too much responsibility on children of your age."

"We were all right," said Lottie. "Peter looked after Ben and me while the others went up to the village with Mr Hunt. He was very nice. We played Monopoly and he made us buttered toast."

"Where are Peter and Anna?" asked Laura.

"Anna's tubbing Jonjo's hoof – he's a bit lame – and Peter's gone into Bruminster with Stephen. When they've done the shopping, they're going to call at the hospital and find out how Mr Hunt and Keith are. We tried to ring up, but the telephone's still not working," explained Tom.

"It was a freak storm; the worst for fifty years, they said on the news," said Laura's mother. "It hit the whole of the west of England. Dozens of roads are blocked by fallen trees, and practically all the telephones have packed up – we're lucky to have electric light and a roof. I can't tell you how terrified Stephen and I were, coming down on the train and seeing all the damage."

"You expected to find six mangled little bodies in the ruins of Milford House," mocked Tom.

"Shut up, don't be horrible. It's too near the truth for joking."

"And poor Mr Hunt was a *bit* mangled," said Lottie.

When they had finished breakfast, the Brodies and Ben went out to see the ponies. They took the contents of the bread bin and some apples and, when the other ponies weren't looking, they gave Treacle the lion's share; because as Laura said, Treacle had been the heroine of the night.

Oh, Cobweb, How Could You?

Josephine Pullein-Thompson

The Hayford and District annual show was in full swing and almost everyone from the neighbouring villages was there. Some had come to watch, but others were showing their onions, their hamsters or their home-made marmalade. There was a large entry in the competition for the dog with the waggiest tail and for the gymkhana, but the main crowd was gathered round the ring where the jumping events were being held.

The Scotts and the Eastwoods lived in Monksthistle, which was three miles from the showground, and, because they were almost the same age and the only people with ponies in the village, Philippa Scott and Fiona Eastwood were almost forced to be friends; though they were quite different in character and didn't like each other very much.

Fiona, who had curly blonde hair and a plump, pink and white, rather discontented face, was an only child. She had proud parents, who loved to show her off, and masses of pocket money, clothes and possessions. The only thing that Philippa really envied her was Cobweb, a lovely dapple-grey mare, a fourteen-two jumping pony, on whom Fiona competed in shows practically every Saturday throughout the summer. Fiona had had several ponies since she started riding, she had won prizes on all of them, and every rosette and cup she had acquired since her leading-rein days was proudly displayed in a huge, glass-fronted cabinet in the Eastwood's sitting-room.

Philippa, who was tall and thin with long brown hair, and quite pretty, led a very different life. Her parents had divorced and her mother had married again, so she had a stepfather and a younger half-brother and sister. Both her mother and stepfather worked, so in the holidays she looked after Charles and Minty.

Philippa's pony, Chocolate Soldier, Choccy for short, was a dark brown gelding, twelve hands high and brilliant at bending. He had been an eighth birthday present from her grandmother, but now Philippa's long thin legs dangled round his knees and it was nine-year-old Charlie who really fitted him. Her parents were always promising her a new pony, and her grandmother had offered to pay half, but somehow life at Orchard Cottage was always a rush, and there just didn't seem to be time to drive round the countryside trying the ponies that were advertised for sale.

Except for Pony Club gymkhanas, Hayford was the only show that the Scotts went to and it was a great day in their year. Despite the fact that Minty's hamster had been ignored by the judges and that Pip, their spaniel, had been seized by shyness and refused to wag his tail at all, the whole family were enjoying themselves tremendously. Minty and Choccy had come second in the leading-rein class and though Charlie had been hopeless in the egg and spoon, he had won the ten and under bending.

Philippa had decided that she was really too large and heavy to ride Choccy in all the senior gymkhana events, so she had only entered for the bending and when, after three tough heats, Choccy was second by a nose, she tied him up in a shady spot and went to watch Fiona jumping. Lately, Cobweb hadn't been doing as well as usual, and the Eastwood parents' confidence in their daughter's ability to win had been shaken, so when Philippa joined them, just as Fiona cantered through the start, they both seemed very tense and anxious.

"She's *still* off form," said Mrs Eastwood, giving agonised gasps as Cobweb cleared the fences by only millimetres. "She's not the pony she used to be; the sparkle has quite gone out of her."

"I don't know what's the matter with the animal. We've tried everything," added Mr Eastwood angrily. "We've changed the bit, the bridle, the saddle. We've given her more oats, less oats, six different brands of pony nuts. We've given her a rest, we've exercised her hard and we've bought Fiona spurs, but there she is heaving herself over the jumps like any old crock at the Pony Club instead of a JA jumper."

As Fiona cantered out the public address system announced a clear round.

"Talk about stale, the pony looks half asleep," complained Mrs Eastwood. "Do for goodness sake go and tell Fi to wake her up before the jump-off," she told her husband. "She'd better give her a gallop and then put her over a really big practice fence just before she comes in." Mr Eastwood strode away muttering angrily.

The clear rounds were announced, there were only six. As the stewards raised the course, Philippa watched Fiona's efforts to wake Cobweb up. Several sharp whacks and a gallop round the field did no good at all, you could see that it was only obedience to her rider that made Cobweb heave herself over the practice fence, all her spirit and energy had gone and she, who had won so often for Fiona in the past, no longer had any pleasure in jumping.

The jump-off course looked enormous and Philippa felt very sad for Cobweb; whatever was wrong it hardly seemed fair to force her round these fences.

The first four riders each had one down and Mr Eastwood began to look more cheerful. Mrs Eastwood was signalling to Fiona to keep the pony on her toes as she waited in the collecting ring.

"If *only* she can go clear," Mrs Eastwood murmured through gritted teeth as her daughter cantered in.

"Come *on,* you lazy lump," growled Mr Eastwood, as Cobweb heaved herself dutifully over the brush, the gate and the wall. "For heaven's sake give her a whack, Fi, you haven't the speed for the combination."

Fiona was riding as hard as she could, but Cobweb had no impulsion at all. Mr Eastwood groaned, Mrs Eastwood covered her eyes with a hand as the pony refused.

The combination was a huge treble. All three fences were wide as well as high, and built solidly of countless heavy poles. Fiona had turned and was trying to get up the speed she knew she needed, but Cobweb didn't respond. She cantered up slowly and stopped.

Fiona took her back for a third try but the same

thing happened. Then the bell rang.

"Oh, Cobweb, how *could* you?" said Mrs Eastwood with a choke in her voice. "To be eliminated *and* at a local show."

Mr Eastwood swore and Philippa followed them as they hurried through the collecting ring.

Fiona was scarlet in the face and struggling with tears.

"Beastly pony," she said as she flung herself off. "I'm never, ever going to jump her again. She just made up her mind she wouldn't jump; I whacked her as hard as I could and I spurred her like mad, but she didn't take any notice."

"You did everything you could; we could see that, pet," Mrs Eastwood told her soothingly. "The pony's just packed up on us, goodness knows why, but we'll just have to cut our losses and buy a new one."

"Yes," agreed Mr Eastwood, "we ought to have done it before. We've hung about all summer waiting for her to come back on form and now she does this to us."

"It's simply not fair on Fi," Mrs Eastwood went on. "It's not good enough, after all you're only young once; the pony will have to go."

"Can we start looking for a new one tomorrow?" asked Fiona, perking up.

Philippa had been stroking Cobweb's neck. She was such a lovely pony, so gentle and good and obliging, but now all the energy seemed to have gone out of her.

"Do you think she could be ill?" Philippa asked the Eastwoods.

"We had the vet to her a couple of months ago, when she started to go wrong," Mr Eastwood answered.

"He couldn't find anything wrong. And you can see for yourself, look at her eyes and her coat; that's not a sick pony."

"She's never been the same since last summer. She was turned out for three weeks when we went to the Costa Brava," Mrs Eastwood explained to Philippa. "We sent her to that very pricey stable near Foxley, where they're supposed to take great care of them, but it wouldn't surprise me if she had picked up something there, a virus or something."

"It might be her legs," said Philippa, crouching down. She looked for swellings, for bowed tendons, over-reaches and speedy cuts. Cobweb blew in her hair, the pony seemed to understand that she was trying to help.

"Who cares what's wrong with her; we've been going over and over it all summer," said Fiona in an exasperated voice. "She won't jump and that's all that matters. Let's get rid of her quickly, before she gets worse. And she'll have to go to a sale; it's no use people coming to try her when she won't jump."

"Yes, Fi's right. It looks like we've come to the end of the road," agreed Mr Eastwood.

"I wonder if my parents could afford to buy her," said Philippa diffidently. "She'd be lovely to hack with Charlie and Minty and I could gymkhana her." The Eastwoods' faces brightened and their voices changed.

"What a brill idea." Fiona sounded enthusiastic. "She'd be just the pony for you."

"Perfect," agreed Mrs Eastwood. "She's absolutely safe with small children; I've never seen her kick or bite. And it would be nice to know she'd gone to a good home."

"I'd better have a chat with your parents, hadn't I?" suggested Mr Eastwood, looking round. "Are they still here?"

"Yes, they're looking after the stall in aid of the church tower," Philippa explained. "They promised to take it over for an hour so that the Baxters could have tea." She watched Mr Eastwood vanish into the crowd. Her heart seemed to be missing beats and her stomach was behaving oddly too. Oh, please let them say yes, she thought. She had always loved Cobweb but it had never entered her head that one day she might possibly be her owner.

"I'm hot, I want an ice cream, Mummy," said Fiona.

"All right, pet, you shall have one. Would you like to ride the pony round, Philippa dear?"

"No, I don't think I will. It may be just the heat that's affecting her, but she seems so tired," answered Philippa. "But I'll look after her, if you want to go for ice creams."

Left alone with Cobweb, Philippa led her across to where Choccy was tied in the deep shade of a chestnut tree and, sitting on a log, she held the pony who, with head hanging and tail swishing lazily, drifted off into sleep.

Presently Mrs Eastwood and Fiona returned, bringing Philippa an ice cream. "I really do think she would be the perfect pony for you Scotts," said Mrs Eastwood between bites. "I mean, you really don't jump at all and Cobby's one hundred per cent in traffic and never any trouble to catch or shoe."

"Yes," agreed Philippa, freezing her mouth as she bolted the rest of her ice cream, for she could see her mother and Mr Eastwood coming.

Mrs Eastwood immediately began to recite a catalogue of Cobweb's virtues.

"Yes, well of course, living so near we feel that we've known her for years," interrupted Mrs Scott, "but I just wanted to make sure that Philippa has thought this through and really doesn't mind having a pony that won't jump. I mean if Fiona can't get Cobweb jumping there isn't the smallest hope that we will." She looked hard at Philippa.

"I *would* like a jumping pony," Philippa admitted, "but they're terribly expensive; you're never going to afford one. Cobweb's perfect in every other way and it'll be lovely to go out for proper rides with Charlie."

"Well, if you're certain, Richard's agreed to us buying her provided she passes the vet. We'll ring Mr Smythe first thing on Monday," she told the Eastwoods, "and ask him to come over as soon as he can."

"Great," said Mr Eastwood, shaking Mrs Scott's hand. "And I'm sure Philippa can't wait to have her new pony, so we'll turn her out in your orchard when we get home."

"And would you like to borrow our tack, just for a couple of days till you get your own?" suggested Mrs Eastwood, obviously delighted to have disposed of Cobweb so easily.

Philippa couldn't believe it. Cobweb is mine, Cobweb is mine, she told herself as she ran across the showground looking for Charlie and Minty. They were overjoyed too.

"She's the second nicest pony in the world," said Minty.

"She's the nicest *mare* in the world, and we'll be able to go for decent rides at last," added Charlie.

So long as she passes the vet, Philippa reminded herself.

The thought of Cobweb waiting in their orchard, and of Choccy's surprise when he found she had come to live with him, made Charlie and Minty quite willing to go home the moment the open jumping was over; there were no arguments about whether they should stay for the scurry and consolation classes.

The orchard was large with high, overgrown hedges, a few very old apple trees and a hollow where Choccy liked to shelter from winter winds. Cobweb was grazing,

she seemed very content with her new surroundings.

They stayed with the ponies while they ate their feeds and then they left them grazing side by side. Philippa decided to take Fiona's tack up to her bedroom; it was very new-looking, not a mend anywhere, and she didn't want anything awful to happen to it.

Her stepfather came home later. "Well, I've given

the Eastwoods their cheque," he told her, "but don't get too starry-eyed, love. I had a beer with one of the judges and he thought there might possibly be something wrong with Cobweb's heart, or that she could be starting ring-bone, both of which would make her a useless buy, even for us."

"It's all right, I won't count on it," lied Philippa.

"Oh, I do hope she *is* okay," said Charlie anxiously, "because Choccy's looking over the moon now he's got a girlfriend at last."

"We must keep our fingers crossed and hope," said Mrs Scott. "She really is the sweetest pony and I don't know how the Eastwoods could part with her so easily."

On Sunday morning Philippa woke early and with a great feeling of happiness. Then, suddenly, she remembered; Cobweb was hers. She jumped out of bed, dressed quickly, and ran down the garden to the orchard gate. Choccy was standing alone on the hump by the hollow. He looked strangely alert, with his head high and his ears pricked, as though he was on guard. He whinnied to Philippa, but he didn't move; there was no sign of Cobweb.

Suddenly afraid, Philippa ran towards him, "What's the matter, what's happened, Choccy?" she asked. Then they both looked down into the hollow where Cobweb, with a proud face and shining eyes, was nuzzling a small, dark-coated foal.

The Trek

Josephine Pullein-Thompson

We hated each other at first sight. Mrs Cale, the District Commissioner, introduced us with woolly kindness.

"Fiona Ross, June Harper, both new members, almost the same age, both riding greys. You *must* get on together," she said. And then, as we stood in silence hating each other, her voice trailed away and she scurried on to the next pair. It was too late to change now; the trek was about to start.

I was relieved to see my mother deep in conversation. What on earth would she say when she saw June's jeans, her loud red-and-black checked shirt, the huge antique-looking ring on her right hand, her lavish eye make-up? I could tell that June was hating my appearance; my correct riding-kit, including a white shirt and Pony Club tie.

Mr Cale was handing round exercise books, one for each pair. "Trek diary. Your instructions are on the first page. Read them over and make sure you understand them," he told us in a schoolmasterly manner.

We dismounted and read them together. The greys nibbled at the hedge.

Our first objective was the summit of Cat's Tor, right out in the moor. We were to report in the trek diary on what we found there and spend the night in Shepherd's Cottage. *Key with Mrs Copplestone at Cat's Tor Farm (the only other building in sight)*, said the instructions. The second day we were to visit Dowberry Pool, Black Moor Cross and the church at Trewester. And we were to spend that night in the Henderson's barn at Colnworthy, returning to the starting-point by twelve-thirty next morning. *Horsemastership will be taken into account*, said a note below the instructions. *Spot checks may be made to see that horses, saddlery, etc., are being cared for. Marks will be given for the Trek Diary, which should be written up each evening, and for enterprise in introducing objects of interest and for visiting and finding out about landmarks, antiquities, etc., near but not included in the official route.*

"Do you know any landmarks, etc., etc.?" I asked June.

"No. I live on the coast. I don't know these parts at all except that I was with my brother in his MG on the A30 once when the radiator burst or something. We had a hideous time and got home at two in the morning."

Clueless, I thought angrily. Well, at least I was good at horsemanship. I dragged my map out of the saddlebag and tried to find our route. I could hear Mrs Cale talking to Mum.

"I do hope they'll be all right," Mrs Cale was saying. She sounded anxious. "It's rather hard on the two new ones to put them together, but you know how it is – friends don't want to split up. We tried threes last year, but it wasn't a success."

"Oh, Fiona will be all right," my mother told her confidently. "We've brought her up to be self-reliant. She'll manage."

Would I? I wondered, suddenly appalled at the thought of vast, uninhabited moors, bogs and deserted cottages. So far I hadn't even managed to find Cat's Tor on the map.

"Can *you* see this tor?" I asked June.

"Oh, it's no good expecting me to understand maps," she answered firmly. "My brother Chris says I'm the most hopeless navigator in existence; worse than any of his girl-friends."

"Well, since you've come on a trek you might *try*," I told her disagreeably.

We started, all thought lost in the clatter of sixty-four hoofs and the difficulty of controlling excited horses. Mercury was showing off to June's Valentine, a calmer, stouter sort. Pairs of riders began to leave the

main body. They wheeled away at crossroads, calling, "Don't get lost!" and "Beware of bogs!" The rest of the party shouted remarks like "Don't quarrel!" and "Remember what happened last year!"

Presently June and I found ourselves alone. It was very quiet; we slowed to a walk. I said, "When we get to this Moor Gate place we'd better stop and look at the map again."

"And have lunch; I'm starving," said June.

I felt very irritable. There was I, worried to death about the route and all the rest of it and she just thought about food. I decided that I was going to make her share my forebodings; after all, she was my partner.

"I suppose you realise how risky it is to get lost on the moor," I said. "Mists come down suddenly and there are bogs everywhere. I've got a compass and a first-aid kit and a whistle to blow if we have an accident; not that that'll be much use if the whole place is uninhabited, though I suppose it might lead a search party to you if you were lying with a broken leg. It might save one from dying of exposure, as that man did in the Lake District the other day."

"Oh, cheer up! It can't be that bad. They wouldn't have turned a hopless nit like me loose if it was."

"Mrs Cale was worried about it," I pointed out. "Didn't you hear her talking to my mother?"

"Oh, some music will cheer us up," said June. "Look, don't you think Chris was brilliant to make this little case for my radio? I always take it riding with me; Val loves music." She tuned in to Radio One, and the sound of pop music filled the narrow, bank-sheltered lane.

We came to a cattle grid and went through the gate

beside it on to the moor. The road lay ahead, a narrow, unfenced black ribbon stretching out into the desolate waste of green. I knew that presently it ended and only faint tracks would indicate the way. We crossed a stream. Mercury and Val edged towards a convenient watering place, so we let them go down and drink the tumbling water.

"Now let's have lunch," shouted June above the stream and Radio One.

We took off the horse's nosebandless bridles and held them by their headcollars, which they were wearing underneath, with the ropes knotted round their necks in true trekking style. Mum had made my lunch, a neat packet of sandwiches and an apple. June was gnawing a chicken leg, eating crisps. I looked at the moor; green, bluish green, yellowish green, greyish green and bracken green, it filled our view. On the lower land groups of ponies and cattle grazed industriously. Beyond them, hills rose through heathered heights to cut the skyline with craggy outcrops of rock. I shared my apple with Mercury and then got out the map. Cat's Tor was there, the third highest tor on the moor; but to reach it was the problem.

"Do turn that radio down and take an interest," I screamed at June. "It's not fair to leave everything to me."

"You take it all so seriously," complained June. "It's supposed to be fun."

It took us three hours to reach the tor, and by then the sky was overcast and stormclouds hid the view.

"I wanted to show you where we live, but we can't even see the sea," complained June.

We explored the summit, looking for an object to describe in the trek diary.

"A mouldy old heap of stones, not even in the shape of a cat, that's how I should describe it," said June.

"Perhaps we're on the wrong tor," I wailed as the thought struck me. June would only giggle.

We rode down to the only farm in sight. It stood among tiny fields fenced by banks, small and grey among its matching farm buildings. I hate knocking on doors and talking to strangers. June didn't seem to mind. She was soon in the kitchen, talking to Mrs Copplestone about the difficulties of running a hotel, while I held the horses on the doorstep. Presently she emerged carrying a huge key and a Cornish pasty. "It's up there," she said, pointing. "There's a pump for water and if you want a bath you bathe in the stream – ugh!" She shuddered.

Mercury was very pleased to see Shepherd's Cottage, with its small stone barn and little paddock; he'd been wondering for some time where his next meal was coming from. We found the pump and the store of oats and bran and nuts we'd been told would be provided at each stopping-place, and we left the horses tied up in the barn eating their feeds while we went to explore the cottage. It was quite plain: two rooms up and two down, a cupboard with a few cups and plates, a frying-pan, a saucepan and a kettle. The furniture consisted of two camp-beds, two canvas chairs and a wooden table.

June was looking for the loo. "There must be one," she said, "and if I don't find it soon I'll burst."

I decided to light the fire. There was a great pile of

logs and sticks in the porch and newspapers in the cupboard. I had a box of matches. It lit all right, but the chimney was damp or something and smoke filled the room, making my eyes smart and water. It was just beginning to settle down when June crashed in, creating a sudden draught which sent smoke everywhere.

"It's right down the end of the garden," she shrieked. "*Hideous* if anyone has to go in the night. The garden's full of nettles."

"Shut the door," I shouted disagreeably.

June shut it and stood looking at me. I didn't care if I had offended her. I was tired of being the sensible, practical one, of doing everything.

"The horses have both finished," she said. "Shall I turn Mercury out for you?"

"No, I must come and groom him," I answered. "He can't go out with a saddle mark."

"Why not?" asked June. "He'll roll."

"You didn't read the trek instructions very carefully," I told her. "Horsemastership counts."

"Oh, all right, then, but I *do* wish you didn't take it all so seriously," complained June.

Later we ate a very peculiar meal of Cornish pasty, my tinned stew, June's fish-fingers, baked beans and Crunchie bars and my apple-pie. Afterwards we quarrelled over whether we should clean our tack. June said that no one in their senses would come all this way just to look at our tack, that hers wasn't dirty – she'd cleaned it the night before – and that, anyway, she hadn't brought her saddle soap. We quarrelled again over the trek diary. I wanted to write a serious account of our journey. June seemed determined to send the whole thing up. Finally she said, "Okay, you write it, then," and, turning up the radio, she removed her eye-shadow and got into bed. We'd brought the beds into the living-room so that we could sleep by the fire.

I wakened full of bitter memories, hating June. She seemed quite cheerful. She showed me the insides of her knees. "Look, rubbed raw," she said.

"If you'd had the sense to wear jodhpurs it wouldn't have happened," I told her.

"Too late now," she laughed. "I expect they'll harden off. Anyway, I must just put up with it."

"Didn't you bring any plasters?" I asked.

"No, I couldn't find any at home. Besides, poor old Val was already groaning under the weight of me and my luggage."

"You are *incompetent.* I don't know what you *have* brought besides make-up," I said. "Here, I suppose you'd better have some of mine."

"No, thanks; I'll be all right," June answered.

We didn't talk much after that until we'd fed the horses and had our own breakfasts; then we had to discuss our plans.

"Trewester is quite a big village," I said, looking at the map. "We can buy tonight's supper there." We were only supposed to carry one day's food with us. "But we ought to collect some of these extra points for enterprise. There are some barrows marked here on the hills above Black Moor Cross, and a hill fort near Three Lanes."

"Toss up," suggested June. "Or there's a place called the Devil's Kitchen, which might be a bit more interesting."

"If you turned off that radio," I said, "I might be able to think."

We left Shepherd's Cottage under a dark and lowering sky, returned the key to Mrs Copplestone who gloomily forecast a downpour, but helpfully pointed out the track leading over the shoulder of High Tor, which we must take to Dowberry Pool.

We were on High Tor and had left the track for a sheep path which meandered among rocks and boulders, when the first rain fell. The clouds were gathered now, black and menacing. We stopped and put on our mackintoshes. A few moments later the rain was lashing us, stinging our hands and faces. The horses went crabwise, trying to protect their heads. We were on the exposed

side of the Tor and there was no shelter anywhere. As we slipped and slithered, with water oozing down our necks, I comforted myself with a fantasy. June and I – the newcomers – would astonish everyone by our conquest of the wild and inhospitable moor, while our stable management and map-reading would both prove far superior to that of the local members. I was just imagining a little scene, with Mr Cale saying, "Their trek diary really is a model – no, a remarkable document. I must read you all an extract," when a horrible thought panicked me. I turned in my saddle and fumbled frantically with the sodden strap and buckle of a saddlebag. Washing things, first-aid kit, matches, raisins, knife, socks – no, there was no exercise book! I tried the other saddlebag, though I knew it contained only Mercury's luggage, dandy-brush, hoof pick, saddle soap and lunchtime feed. I felt my pockets and then gave a sort of moan.

June, who was ahead, turned in her saddle.

"What's wrong?" she asked.

"The trek diary," I answered. "You didn't pack it, did you?"

"No; I thought you were looking after it."

I couldn't blame June. I'd made it clear that I considered myself the keeper of the diary. "We must go back," I said.

"Oh, *no,* not in this," protested June. "We've been riding for well over an hour."

"We must," I insisted. "They'll think we're hopelessly incompetent if we turn up without it. We'll be the worst pair of the lot.

"Who cares what they think?" asked June.

I knew that I did. "You wait here or ride on slowly and I'll go back. It's my fault," I added unwillingly.

June wouldn't hear of this. She said we'd been told all along that we must stick together and that Chris, who climbed with a youth club, had said that this was absolutely right.

"I don't *mind* going down in history as the most hopeless pair on record – really, I don't," she assured me.

I did. I could see Mum and Dad's disappointed faces, hear their faintly reproachful tones.

"We must go back," I said. "For one thing, I can't remember tomorrow's instructions."

"We could telephone Mrs Cale from Colnworthy and ask her what they were," suggested June.

"No, we couldn't," I answered.

June groaned. "Oh, well, but let's make sure that you haven't got it first. What about your sleeping bag? You may have rolled it up in there."

We unpacked everything. Fortunately, the rain had slackened to a drizzle; but we found no diary.

We turned back. June gave me half a Crunchie – she seemed to have an inexhaustible supply – and switched on the radio. Mercury had sensed my incompetence; he no longer went with pricked ears, but became irritable and stumbled at intervals.

We had ridden for about twenty minutes when, having looked in vain for landmarks, I voiced my growing fears. "June, this isn't the path we came up, is it? We ought to be able to see the farm by now."

"I was just thinking that too," agreed June.

I tried to get out the map, but Mercury wouldn't

stand still, so I had to dismount. The map would blow about and I couldn't make out where north was any more; I'd lost my sense of direction. I became more and more flustered and shouted at the fidgeting Mercury as I searched feverishly for my compass.

June took the map from me. "Look," she said, "we must have gone too far round to the left. If we go on down and then keep on going round to the right we shall find the farm again."

"But if there's no track in the right direction we may get into a bog," I pointed out.

"Well, we've got eyes and I'd rather risk a bog than make poor old Val carry me up that hill *again,*" answered June.

I felt hopeless and I knew that I had no sensible suggestion to offer, so we rode on down the narrow path between the scattered boulders which looked like the debris left by a giants' battle. Below us the grey waste of the moor stretched roadless and houseless for as far as we could see. It began to rain hard again; squalls lashed at us from every direction. My hands turned blue and would hardly hold the wet, slippery reins. I felt deeply dispirited, downcast by my inefficiency, I who had complained of June. And the fact that she hadn't reproached me filled me with a strange mixture of relief and shame.

Suddenly Mercury swung round, cannoning into Valentine. "Sorry," I said as my knee cracked against June's and we shot past her up the path.

When I had Mercury under control again I turned back. June had dismounted. "There's a pony lying here and there's something wrong with it," she called.

I hurried the snorting Mercury back. A small bay

mare lay flat on her side, just off the path. Her nostrils were wide and her breathing laboured; her eyes were filmed and all around her was a trodden muddy patch as though she'd been pawing in pain or struggling to get up for a very long time.

June had let go of Val and was feeling the pony's legs. "They don't *seem* broken," she said, "but she's sweating; it's not just rain," she added as she felt the dark, wet coat.

"We must keep her warm," I said, "and if it's colic she ought to be walked about. Do you think we could get her up?"

June tried to raise the pony's head and neck, but she was too sick to care who pulled her about; she just flopped back again without any expression in her dull, filmed eyes.

"We'll have to fetch help," June said.

We unzipped our sleeping bags and laid them over the pony and then, with a quick look round to memorise the spot, we hurried down the path. June jumped off several times and made lipstick crosses on convenient rocks. "I can just see a hideous situation with us unable to find her," she said breathlessly as she climbed back on Val for the fourth time.

The path brought us at last to a grassy cart-track. It looked recently used and purposefully straight.

"Which way?" asked June.

"Downhill, I should think," I answered.

I was looking back at the path. Landmarkless, it was already fading into the moor; I ripped off my Pony Club tie and fastened it to a stout thistle; then I pursued June down the track. It was wonderful to be able to express feelings of urgency, to be able to gallop flat out. Signs of civilisation, banks, stone walls, gates, materialised beside us. Ahead, concealed in this little hollow, was a small grey farmhouse – not the Copplestones', but another very like it. We came to a gate and clattered through into a farmyard. I looked in the farm buildings while June hammered on the farmhouse door.

"There's a pony very ill up on the hillside," I heard her say.

"Oh dear, and I've got the baby poorly and my husband's had to go into town . . . "

I joined June. "It's a small bay mare with two white socks and a star," I said.

The farmer's wife looked at us helplessly.

"Couldn't you telephone for a vet?" suggested June.

"We don't have no telephone here. Nearest one's about two miles away, up on the moor road."

"We can go. We'll phone him," June and I both offered at once. "Just tell us how to get there," I added.

The farmer's wife was not to be hurried. "It'll be one of our ponies, I expect," she said. "A little bay? That'll be the new Welsh one; she had colic a week or two ago. Just a minute now while I call Johnnie."

We waited. I was expecting Johnnie to be a strong young man, a typical farmer's son, who'd take charge. When he came he looked about eight. His mother told him what had happened.

"I'll gallop to the phone on Taffy," he lisped rather than spoke, for both his front teeth were missing. "What's Mr Hobbes's number, Mum?" He ran to a sheep-pen, plonked a felt pad and a nosebandless bridle on a tiny brown pony, scrambled up, and then, with his elbows and gumbooted legs waving, was off, galloping up the track.

"If you think it's colic, do you have a drench?" I asked the farmer's wife. "I know how to give one."

That was a long, long afternoon. June and I rode back up the hillside and drenched the pony. We spilled a lot. It was awkward getting the pony's head high enough, especially as I had to keep Mercury's reins looped round my arm, but we comforted ourselves with the fact that she was a very small pony and couldn't possibly need a whole bottle. We wrapped her up in the sleeping bags again, gave our horses their lunch-time feeds and settled down to wait in the rain. Johnnie visited us at

intervals, first to tell us that the vet was out on a farm somewhere but would be sent as soon as he could be found, then with a Thermos of tea. Val and Mercury became increasingly restless and the radio batteries gave out and the rain turned to sleet. But we were cheered because the pony seemed a little better; she raised her head to look at our horses and when she lay back again her eyes seemed brighter, less filmed. June felt under the sleeping bags and announced that she was warm and quite reasonably dry. Then Johnnie reappeared to say that the vet had left his Land-Rover on the track and was walking up.

Mr Hobbes was a small, quiet man. He examined the pony and said that it was definitely colic and that he would give her a shot of morphine to deaden the pain and then it might be possible to walk her down to the farm.

"Lucky you found her," he told us as he filled his hypodermic syringe. "She'd have been dead by morning."

Then, as we waited for the injection to work, Johnnie reappeared on a now rather weary-looking Taffy to announce that his father was just coming and bringing a halter and rug.

June and I decided that it was time to be on our way and we asked for the quickest route to the Hendersons' at Colnworthy; all the places of interest had had it as far as we were concerned, but it seemed that there was no shorter way. We rolled up our sodden sleeping bags and set out across the grey, rain-soaked moor as the men heaved the little pony to her feet and started on their long, slow journey down to the farm.

We saw a watery sunset over Dowberry Pool, we

clattered past Black Moor Cross without stopping to read the legend of its Celtic saint; Trewester's grocer had long since closed, and the church spire was dark and sharp against the twilight sky. I began to wonder what sort of reception we would get from the Hendersons, arriving hours late without food or trek diary, pictures of bedraggled incompetence.

"They've probably been searching the moor for us for hours; they're probably furious. We ought to have telephoned," I fussed.

June giggled. "Some hope," she said, "seeing that these are the first houses we've seen for hours."

"My parents practically have nervous breakdowns if I'm half an hour late," I said gloomily. "I hope they haven't been told we're missing."

"Ours never know where we are," said June. "They're far too busy with the hotel. They just about count heads at bedtime."

Our clopping hoofs sounded very loud in the dusk-shrouded street of Colnworthy and then at last we came to the Hendersons' white gates. Mercury and Val were delighted to turn in and to see the stables and hear their tentative whinnies answered by a loud chorus of neighs. June and I dismounted stiffly and began to apologise to the dark figures which gathered round us.

"We know, we know," said the Hendersons. "Jack Hobbes telephoned us as soon as he was off the moor. He said two of our girls would be a bit late clocking in, but that you'd been doing a grand job."

There was no sleeping in barns that night. We were chivvied into hot baths, fed splendidly in a dining-room and then given the best spare room beds. June was delighted. I was filled with guilt; this wasn't trekking at all.

In the morning it was just as bad. We wakened late, and I panicked as I imagined us arriving at the finishing point hours late with muddy horses, filthy tack and, of course, no diary, but when we got downstairs they told us that our horses were fed, our breakfasts ready. Later everyone helped us to get off.

It was a wonderful morning. The sky was cloudless blue, the sun hot, and North Moor stretched before us green and benign like a vast pleasure ground. The sky was full of larks singing and soaring.

"I wouldn't mind doing yesterday's trek again in fine weather," said June suddenly. "I feel I've missed something. I mean, we had to hurry by the pool, and the cross looked quite interesting, and it was too dark to see the church. Let's do it again, Fiona. If I came and stayed with you we could do that part of it in a day if we made an early start. And later on you could come and stay with me and ride on the sands; it'll be fantastic in the autumn when the holiday-makers have gone."

Suddenly I wanted to know the moor better, to ride up all the tors in turn and know the farms and streams. June would make a good companion: she didn't fuss when things went wrong. But if she stayed with us, what on earth would Mum say about her make-up or Dad about her giggling? He only likes serious conversation. But then, I told myself, she's my friend, not theirs, and who wants all their friends to think and look and behave exactly like themselves?

"Yes," I said to June. "Let's do that – soon – next week. I'll speak to Mum about it as soon as I see her."

A Real Live Ghost

Christine Pullein-Thompson

"Mandy, Mandy, where are you?" shrieked my brother Michael, taking the stairs two at a time.

I put down the book I was reading.

"You know the ponies in the park? They're ill, they aren't well. You must come and look straight away," he said, his dark hair awry.

"But they're nothing to do with us," I said, slowly getting off my bed. "They belong to Mrs Horncastle."

"Mrs Horncastle is dead," answered Michael. "Now are you coming to investigate? I thought you cared about horses."

"Of course I do," I said, searching for my shoes. "But how was I to know that Mrs Horncastle was dead? No one's told me until now. How did you find out, anyway?"

"I stopped at the shop. They knew. Anyway the house is shut up. It's ghastly. I went for a bike ride. I was fed up and bored so I went down the drive and there they were. Two ponies, one lying stretched out as if it were dead; and the other as big as a mountain."

"It was probably sleeping," I suggested, following

my brother downstairs. "After all, the sun is shining."

We haven't any ponies. We ride at the local riding-school as often as we can afford it which is about twice a month. I don't want to win prizes. I don't even want to be an expert. But I would like a pony I could call my own, or rather two because a pony shouldn't live alone. I would like them there all the time, something to love and fuss over. A mane or two to cry into when I'm upset, that's all I really want.

I fetched my bike from the garage. Mum was out working for the local solicitors. Dad was abroad selling electrical goods. The sun was burning down, turning our small lawn the colour of old hay.

The drive to the Hall was stony and patchy with weeds. I had filled my pocket with lumps of sugar. Michael was streaming ahead, standing on his pedals with excitement, while I was still sceptical, not quite believing him because he's younger and less horsey than I am.

We had all heard of Mrs Horncastle living alone in the Hall with her animals. Now she was dead and it was like the end of something, of a dream or a mystery or a cross between the two. We had never met her, but she was like a legend in the village. We weren't quite the village, being just outside it in a house in a row. We were known as the newcomers and there were several hundred of us. We had been told we would remain newcomers for at least twenty-five years, so we had ceased attempting to be anything else.

The park was fenced by old railings mended with wire where they had broken. There were rabbits everywhere and, beyond, the great house stood shuttered. I leaned my bike against the railings. The ponies were grey and chestnut and the grey was still lying down with a stomach like a football and his eyes besieged by flies. I knelt down beside him and offered him sugar, but he was beyond wanting anything.

"Don't start blubbering, Mandy, because it won't help. Let's go and find someone – fast," said Michael, wiping his own eyes with the back of his hand.

We mounted our bikes and I *was* blubbering now, the tears streaming down my face like rain.

The front door to the great house was bolted and barred, but we found a back door and an old man sitting in a lovely old-fashioned kitchen drinking beer out of a mug. "And what do you want?" he asked. "I'm in charge here."

"It's about the ponies. They're ill. They need a vet," I said.

"And if you're in charge, you can help," suggested my brother.

"There's nothing wrong with the ponies. They've got the whole park to roam in and a tank full of water. What more do they want?" asked the old man, glaring at us with eyes which seemed to be saying "And you dare contradict me!"

"It's too much. They've got too much," I answered.

"I'm caretaker here and they'll stay where they are until the future of this place is decided. And that will take a few weeks yet, so you just get on your bikes and skedaddle." The old man turned away from us to throw the dregs of his beer into an ancient stone sink.

"They'll die and what will the old lady think then?" I asked.

"She's dead, ain't she? So she can't think. And she always trusted me. Gave me a key to the place when she went away and I never let her down, never."

"Hasn't she any relations?" asked my brother.

"Four children. They came to the funeral; then shoved off saying to me, 'You look after everything, Harry, we trust you.' As soon as probate's done they'll be putting this place on the market. Most of them live abroad anyway; only one of them lives in London, and he's only after the money."

"But didn't they say anything about the ponies?" I asked.

"Not a lot. But they *are* all right with me. They won't come to no harm."

We left Harry sitting on the stool in the kitchen.

"We had better call in the RSPCA, because there's nothing else we can do," I said.

"Silly old fool, that's what he is, an old fool," shouted Michael.

We were by the stable now. "Let's just look inside, just for a second. It's sure to be converted into a house as soon as the place is sold," I said.

"Houses, more likely," my brother answered.

The stable was ancient and cobwebby; loose boxes and stalls with Staffordshire brick floors which seemed to reek of history. The two smallest loose boxes had been used quite recently.

"I expect she shut them in there," I said.

"Shut what in?"

"The ponies, of course, to stop them eating too much, you idiot," I answered.

"I wonder how she died?" my brother said.

We were in what must once have been the harness-room. Stairs led out of it to a loft. There were two head-collars hanging on a hook and grooming tools in a bag.

"It's so sad isn't it? Like the end of a world. But we can't stay, we must do something about the grey," I said. "Come on, we've spent too long here already. Hurry, Michael."

But Michael seemed spellbound and stood staring at the stairs which led to the loft overhead. I looked up and saw a lady coming down them, dressed in trousers and a sweater, neither young nor old. She stood and looked at us, and I felt suddenly very cold, so cold that I started to shiver, while my brother kept muttering, "Yes,

yes, it's all right, don't worry," as though he was talking to a nervous horse.

"I'm Gladys Horncastle. The ponies are mine. Please bring them in before they die. Please," she said in an educated and timeless voice, which seemed to whisper yet was quite audible. It was a voice one automatically obeyed, so that my brother said:

"Yes, Mrs Horncastle, what should we do with them?"

"You can have them. You must have them. You will love them, and they need love. Ask Farmer Wells. He'll take them. Tell him I ask him to do that for me. And keep them in or Soda will die."

"She isn't real, is she?" asked my brother, and now he sounded frightened.

"She's a ghost," I said, picking up the headcollars. "A real live ghost."

"That's impossible," whispered Michael. "You can't be alive and a ghost."

The voice seemed to follow us outside though there was no sign of anything now, just this voice saying, "They're called Whiskey and Soda. Keep them in. Don't let them eat too much. You are only just in time. I willed it. I willed you to come here. Don't let me down."

"I feel funny, sort of unreal," Michael said, following me to the park.

"I feel sort of scared. And what will horrible Harry say?" I asked. "He won't believe us. No one will. Have you thought of that?"

"It doesn't matter," Michael said.

We dragged the grey, which we decided was Soda, to his feet. We had to push him and shout to get him to walk at all, but Whiskey was all right and hurried along, dragging us after him. We put them in the two used boxes and they went straight to the mangers, even Soda, hobbling like an old man. "You can't have anything to eat, you're far too fat already," I told them.

The boxes were already bedded in shavings. We found buckets and filled them up with water. I looked at my watch. It was nearly one o'clock. "Mum will be home, let's go home and tell her about it," I said.

"What about Harry? Shouldn't we tell him what we've done?" asked Michael.

But at that moment Harry appeared. He looked old and bent, and very angry. "And what do you think you're doing? I'm in charge here," he shouted.

"Not any more," I said. "Gladys Horncastle told us to put Whiskey and Soda in the stable. She begged us to look after them."

"How do you know her first name? And their names, come to that?" shouted Harry.

"She told us, that's how," I answered, mounting my bike.

"But she's dead. She died last week," shouted Harry.

"Well, she came back to tell us. She knew Soda was dying of laminitis from overeating," shouted Michael. "So leave the ponies where they are. We'll be back later to see them."

"They're to go to Farmer Wells, that's what she said," I told him.

"But I'm in charge here."

"Not any more. We're obeying her orders, not yours," I shouted back, pedalling faster and faster down the drive in pursuit of my brother.

Mum didn't believe our story at first. Then she said, "I think I had better ring my boss. He's got the Horncastle Will in the safe. And we need to contact that child of hers in London as soon as possible. We just can't take the ponies away. But whether there's a ghost or not, it's obvious we must do something about them, even unhorsey me can see that. Poor old lady, fancy having to come back from the dead to tell you that they needed looking after. What awful children she must have," Mum finished.

"So you do believe us then?" Michael asked.

"I'm trying not to, but it's a pretty convincing story whichever way you look at it. And I know you're not liars," Mum said.

The solicitors gave Mum the name of Mrs Horncastle's son. She telephoned him straight away at his office in London. Afterwards she told us that he seemed upset. He kept saying, "Oh dear. Oh dear. We just didn't think. Yes, please take the ponies to the farmer my mother suggested." He said that it was just like his mother to come back from the dead as she loved the ponies more than anything else in the end. She wouldn't move, not into sheltered housing, nor a home.

"Apparently she died in the harness-room," Mum told us. "She fell dead by the stairs with a bag of grooming tools in her hand. Her son in London said that it was the way she would have wanted to go but that it was very sudden and unexpected. He sounded awfully posh, but nice with it. He says he's coming down this weekend to sort things out," Mum finished, collapsing into a chair. "And he's writing to Harry straight away, you'll be glad to hear."

We went back that evening to look at the ponies. We gave them a few handfuls of hay from the loft, more water, then we brushed them. Gladys Horncastle didn't appear again that day though we waited hopefully for some time by the stairs. But her face haunted me and it was weeks later, when the ponies had become ours and lived at the farm, that I knew why, for leafing through an old annual I had bought at a jumble sale, I found her featured as "The well-known rider Gladys Horncastle on her champion hunter King's Realm". In the photograph she looked just the same, or almost. Not older, nor younger than her ghost, just a little more worldly! And she's given us all I've ever wanted – two ponies to love. I just wish we could have saved the stable as well because it is going to be converted, which means we will never see Gladys Horncastle again. But whenever I ride Soda or Whiskey I am so grateful to her. And though few of our friends believe our story, Michael and I know it's true, and that's all which really matters.

Miserable Wreck

Christine Pullein-Thompson

"Why did you buy him for heaven's sake, he's so ugly," cried Maureen.

"And thin," said David.

"And he's got sickle hocks and a goose rump," added Maureen.

"And a ewe neck and a fiddle face," added David.

I looked at my new horse. He was dun with dark points and as thin as a razor. He had a dorsal stripe down his back and was just fifteen hands.

"I was sorry for him and I fell for his eye. It's so big and kind," I replied.

I recalled him standing in the market, his head hanging. I remembered him raising it to look at me, our eyes meeting. "I fell in love with him," I confessed.

"He must be riddled with red worm. Have you had the vet yet?" asked Maureen, large in stretch jeans, her eyes made up, wearing a shirt with SAVE THE HORSES written across the front.

"Not yet, but I've wormed him."

"Are you calling him Thin Man or Toast Rack?" asked David, laughing.

"I'm calling him Mariner, and why don't you leave with your nasty remarks?" I said. "Just come back in a month and see how he is then."

"He won't be here in a month, he'll be dead," replied David.

"Oh, I'm sorry, we don't mean to be nasty, but really, Carol, he is a sight. I mean, didn't you look at him properly before you bought him?" asked Maureen.

"He's just thin," I answered stubbornly, though

inside I was devastated by their remarks. "He'll pick up when the new grass starts growing. You wait and see."

They mounted their bikes and rode away. I put my arms around Mariner's neck and my mouth was salty with swallowed tears.

I fed Mariner hard food three times a day; also carrots, apples and the best hay.

Mum said, "You're going mad. Can't you think of anything else, darling?"

Dad wasn't there – he had left us for someone else.

I started to lunge Mariner. Then I rode him quietly alone in the field. He was too thin and weak to take to horse shows, so that at times I almost hated him, wondering why I had bought him instead of waiting until I had found something which could jump and gallop. But at least he was still alive! At other times I knew I had done the right thing, saving a horse from the abattoir, a horse with the kindest nature I had ever met, with large eyes which looked at me from under a dark forelock with such honesty and affection.

David and Maureen rode their horses with the drag hunt. I stayed at home and, hearing the horn in the distance, wept.

I was grooming Mariner several weeks later when Mum called, "Darling, there's someone to see you. It's about Mariner."

And I thought, It's The Royal Society for the Prevention of Cruelty to Animals and they've come to prosecute me!

Then I saw a lady wearing brown cords and a thick jumper running towards me. "Thank heavens I've found you," she cried before throwing her arms round Mariner and muttering, "oh, my poor poppet, my poor little horse."

She'll take him away I thought. Obviously he was stolen. And my heart seemed to fall into my boots.

"You bought him from a horse-dealer, didn't you?" she asked next. "I've been looking for him ever since I returned from abroad. He was the best horse I ever owned."

"He was skin and bone and he still looks terrible. I'm sorry," I replied guiltily.

"But I'm so grateful," replied the lady, who was called Angela Gray. "You see, I've discovered that all last year he was kept on a tether. I was so afraid he was dead. I thought I had sold him to a perfect home, but he was sold on and on. But I can see he's all right with you. I'm so happy!" she finished.

I imagined my ugly duckling turning into a swan. I imagined us competing all over England. I imagined David and Maureen watching.

"If you ever want to sell him, I'll buy him back," promised Angela Gray later, getting into her car, "and here's my address." She handed me a piece of paper. "I just thank God you rescued him," she said, driving away.

I put the piece of paper in my pocket, went back to Mariner and looked at him again. Now his hocks seemed straighter and his neck thicker and his quarters much rounder. And everywhere the grass was growing, and the winter mud drying, and the whole summer lay ahead. And I knew now that I had been right. I had rescued a miserable wreck who had once been a winner. I had bought him out of pity and he was soon to pay me back tenfold, but that's another story!

Too Scared to Ride

Christine Pullein-Thompson

"Time to mount," announced Christina Edwards. "Remember to tighten your girths."

Ponies were untied and led out of stables.

"Come on, Louise, get going," said Christina, who was tall and slim, with hair tied back in a knot and long legs in black boots. "What's the matter?"

"I can't. I'm sorry but I can't." Louise had flaxen hair and a smile which creased her face and a nose which turned up at the end. Her eyes were blue.

"What do you mean, you can't?"

All the other riders were staring now.

"Don't you want to trek? Why did you come if you don't want to ride?"

"My parents sent me, didn't they? I used to ride and then I got scared," Louise said.

"Firefly's marvellous. He is, I promise. He never puts a foot wrong. Don't be silly, please," said Christina. "Your father's paid for you to ride, Louise. I can't say you wouldn't, can I?"

"No, definitely not."

Someone was holding Firefly. He was a solidly built,

liver-chestnut with a small star. He stood resting a leg while Christina said, "We only walk. Nothing will happen."

But Louise's legs felt like jelly now; she was hot all over and there was a peculiar feeling at the bottom of her spine. She could not describe her fear. It was beyond description. As she looked at Firefly it grew until it was the largest thing in the yard, it took over, it made her hands tremble and brought tears to her eyes. It became reality; everything else was a dream.

"For goodness sake," cried Christina. "You look like a zombie. Time is passing, Louise. We're going out for four hours. You'll love it, I know you will."

But Louise could only remember Pedro, his elegant pulled mane, his shining neck, his thudding hoofs. The faces of startled pedestrians as she galloped by, the cars hooting, the truck which missed her by a centimetre. She could only remember pulling and nothing happening; the hill which went down and down and never seemed to end . . . the sheer terror of it. "I can't. I'm sorry but I can't," she said, and ran for the house, into a warm old-fashioned kitchen with a flagstone floor.

"Come back," yelled Christina. "Where are you going? We'll go without you then – goodbye."

Then Louise heard a boy ask scornfully, "Whatever's the matter with her. I've only ridden once before and *I'm* not scared."

She slammed the door after her and bolted it as though fear could be locked out, then sat on a chair, panting as though she had run a mile instead of a mere thirty metres. After the runaway her father had said she should get straight up again. He had told her to be brave and that he had fallen off in a steeplechase and cracked his skull and that life was full of knocks. Louise had not been able to explain that it was simply the terror of being out of control which had shaken her, not the toss at the end. She had never wanted Pedro. He had cost thousands. She had wanted to keep her round, sensible, dun pony, Honey; she hadn't wanted to win rosettes.

An old lady sitting in a chair by the window turned to look at her. Her face was like pale brown leather.

"Haven't you gone then?" she inquired. Her eyes were small amid the lines in her face, like birds' eyes.

"No, I'm staying here."

"What are you going to do then, alone all day?" asked the old lady.

"Sweep up the yard, clean out the stables, give Christina a lovely surprise."

"But you're not paid to do that."

"I don't want to be paid. I like doing it. I always did it until Daddy became famous. I used to sweep our yard every evening."

"Christina told me you were coming here. I've seen your father on television, haven't I? He's a very good-looking man. You must be proud of him," said the old lady.

"I am, but I can't live up to his expectations. I'm just not brave enough."

"You've given up riding then, you've had an accident?" asked the old lady. To Louise she now seemed a very wise old lady.

"That's right. I'm scared, yellow."

"It will pass. Everything passes with time."

"I'm just not good enough to be his daughter. I liked it when we were ordinary, like everyone else. Now everyone says, 'Are you really *his* daughter? You don't act like him, you don't look like him either.' And I don't . . . I've got spots and blackheads, and my hair is always in a mess, and I can't act. I don't even want to," wailed Louise.

"What about your mother?"

"She's beautiful. They're in New York at this minute discussing some marvellous film. We have a groom cum-everything because they're never at home now, and I go to boarding-school, which I hate."

"Don't be so upset. Life goes on. Don't lose courage," said the old lady. "Try, try again, that's my motto."

Louise was going out into the yard again.

"Come and have dinner with me, or do you call it lunch? It's only a casserole. Do you eat casserole?" The old lady was out of her chair now and leaning on the table. She was tiny. "Your packed lunch won't be enough," she called.

"Yes, I eat casserole, thank you," shouted Louise.

She could see the trekkers in the distance, riding along a ridge in single file. Firefly whinnied anxiously from his loose box when she crossed the yard which was covered with wisps of straw. Louise found a broom and started to sweep. A cat sat on a bucket watching her. Bantams scratched on the muckheap. Sweeping slowly, Louise hated herself. She hated herself for not being up there on the ridge with the others. She dreaded their return, and imagined the scathing remarks they would make. They must be wondering why I'm here and why I didn't say no to my father, she thought, sweeping, and, as she swept, her tears watered the yard.

She started to tidy the muckheap, throwing the spillings up, and the sun came out and warmed her back. She thought, How am I going to bear a whole week here? And how am I going to pretend I rode every day when I get home again? And what if my parents ring up and say, "How is Louise doing?" And Christina tells the truth?

When she had finished tidying the muckheap she filled up the water buckets, while the cat followed her, purring round her legs. She thought, My father will have to face up to the truth one day. He must know sooner or later that I will never ride again. He must have noticed that I am too frightened now to put a foot in a stirrup and mount and that the very sight of a pony turns my legs to jelly and my hands to pulp. Surely he knows that I never wanted Pedro and I just wanted to keep Honey.

Louise couldn't see the riders any more now; they had vanished among the sombre hills, among the sheep and the grey walls. Her father had said, "It will do you good. You'll learn history too, look out for Hadrian's Wall; you might even find some remains if you dig. I expect you to be brown and disgustingly healthy and on a horse when we return. All right, poppet?"

And her mother had said, "Look after yourself, darling, don't worry, we'll be all right." And they had both looked wonderful, smart and scented, rich and brave.

It's no use. I'm no good, Louise thought, putting away the broom. I'm not like them. She looked at the yard before she went indoors and everything seemed in its place and the wisps of straw all gone. She knocked on the door, lifted the latch and went in.

"Am I too early? I haven't got a watch," she said.

The table was laid for two. A casserole bubbled on an ancient Raeburn cooker. There was a bottle of cider on the table and two glasses. A clock by the Raeburn said ten minutes to one.

She stood and looked around and it was then that she saw the old lady lying in a heap by the door which led upstairs. Her heart seemed to rush into her mouth and she wanted to run outside and fetch someone, but there was no one to fetch, so she went forward gingerly and knelt beside the old lady and said, "What's happened? Are you all right?"

A ridiculous question, she thought afterwards.

The old lady's mouth looked twisted, but she managed to say, "Get a doctor. I need a doctor."

Louise put her coat over her, which smelt of horse. "Don't worry," she said and looked for a telephone.

"There's no telephone here," whispered the old lady, following Louise with her eyes. "You'll have to go to the kiosk. The doctor's number is 3362. Tell him I've had a stroke. Take some money out of my purse."

"I've got some money, where's the kiosk?" Louise couldn't bring herself to look at the old lady again.

"A mile down the road, turn left outside the gate."

"Can't you move?"

"No, dear, not at all, not any more. Please hurry."

And Louise suddenly knew what she had to do; it was as though it had all been planned, because if she was to be quick there was no other way. She was no longer afraid, because suddenly the old lady mattered much more than her fear – her condition completely overshadowed it and made it nothing. She ran to the tack room and found Firefly's tack. Another minute and he was ready. Louise put her foot in the stirrup as she had so many times before, automatically. She swung Firefly round without thought, turned left outside the gate and pushed him into a gallop, and all the time in her mind she was imagining the old lady dying alone in the kitchen because she had taken too long to fetch the doctor. The first kiosk had the receiver ripped out, so she galloped on, and the wind was soft on her face and straight from the hills and the air was as pure as mountain air.

She found another kiosk, dialled the number and pushed in a coin and said, "Is that a doctor? The old lady at the trekking centre has had a stroke. Please come at once. I think she's dying."

The voice at the other end said, "I'll be there as soon as I can."

And Louise said, "There isn't much time. She's lying on the floor and I'm afraid to move her."

And he repeated, "I'll be there as soon as I can."

How soon is that? Louise wondered.

Standing outside the kiosk afterwards she waited for the fear to come back, and it was like waiting for the return of a pain which isn't there any more. Then she patted Firefly and mounted and saw that the trekkers were coming home along the road.

"Good heavens, what are you doing here?" cried Christina. "I thought you were too scared to ride."

"The old lady has had a stroke. I've just phoned for the doctor. You go on ahead, I'll be all right. I'll look after the others," she said.

"Oh no, not another stroke. Is she very bad?" cried Christina.

"I don't know. I don't know anything about strokes. She's in the kitchen on the floor. She can't move but she *is* talking. I didn't know what to do."

The riders watched Christina gallop away along the grass verge, and a boy said, "I thought you were too scared to ride. Were you pretending?"

And Louise didn't know how to answer. "No, I *was* scared, but I'm not any more," she said eventually, pushing Firefly with her legs.

"Can we trot?" asked a girl on a piebald.

"No, not the last mile home, never the last mile home," replied Louise.

In a way it was the end of a nightmare, for now Louise could see her runaway in perspective. And she knew now that it was an isolated incident; and if she improved her riding it would never happen again. She decided that her fear had been like an illness and that with luck it would never return.

"Christina Edwards is cantering," insisted the girl on the piebald.

"It's an emergency for her. You can even canter on roads in an emergency," Louise said.

"I wish it was an emergency then," the girl answered, and Louise could recall being just like that, when a canter was better than a birthday cake or being given a whole lot of money, when a canter was suddenly paradise.

When they reached the trekking centre, an ambulance was parked in the yard and the old lady was being carried out on a stretcher. She had a striped blanket over her, and when she saw that Louise was riding she gave a thumbs-up sign.

"I'm better," she croaked, "and you are riding. Isn't that lovely?"

"Yes. Get well soon," called Louise. "I want us to have our lunch together before I go."

Untacking Firefly she said to Christina, "The old lady is never afraid, is she? She lives alone and she's not afraid. I hope I'm like that one day."

"We are all afraid some time in our lives," answered Christina. "People who are not afraid are not really brave because they have nothing to be brave about. Most likely your father has been afraid hundreds of times. But because he's an actor he can disguise it better

than the rest of us, that's the difference."

"So I'm quite normal?" asked Louise.

"Very much so. If a horse ran away with me I would be scared stiff. Losing control of anything is terrifying. Did you sweep the yard and tidy the muckheap? It's marvellous."

"Yes, it was me. You don't despise me then?" asked Louise.

"For goodness sake; you're brave. You've just saved an old lady. You ought to have a medal. Your father would be proud of you. Okay? *And* I mean it," cried Christina. "I'm not sucking up. It's true – and I'm going to tell your parents all about it. And if you want to, you can work for me next year, because you're marvellous with a broom too. And you are going to be beautiful," continued Christina. "And you ride very nicely."

Louise felt as though she was being given too much to eat. She could not swallow so many compliments, but suddenly she was happy.

"Just be yourself, Louise," said Christina, beginning to laugh. "And don't forget your famous parents. You are a chip off the old block. Don't worry. It sticks out a mile!"